I0778858

A Multitude
of Worlds

A Multitude of Worlds

THIRTEEN SCIENCE FICTION STORIES

Robert Silverberg

star traveler press

ISBN: 979-8-9930162-5-2

Editor and Publisher, Justin T. O'Conor Sloane
Cover art: *A Multitude of Worlds* © 2025 by Bob Eggleton
Book design by F. J. Bergmann

star traveler press
an imprint of Starship Sloane Publishing Company, Inc.
Austin–Round Rock, Texas
starshipsloane.com

Table of Contents

FOREWORD

I don't even know how to begin.

Maybe I should start when I was thirteen and I was buying Ace Double Novels, as fast as they came out.

The editor was Donald A. Wollheim. He started out publishing reprints of novels by well-established authors in the field, like Isaac Asimov, Jack Williamson, A. E. Van Vogt, Poul Anderson, Gordon R. Dickson, Andrew Norton, Leigh Brackett, Eric Frank Russell, Philip K. Dick, H. Beam Piper, Cyril Kornbluth and Judith Merrill writing as Cyril Judd, and my personal favorite, Murray Leinster.

(And a decade later, Harlan Ellison!)

My first introduction to Asimov was *The 1,000 Year Plan*. I met Philip K. Dick through *The World Jones Made* and Andre Norton through *Daybreak—2250 AD*. I confess, I liked Leinster's *The Other Side Of Here* more.

The Ace Doubles cost 35 cents, but they were cost-effective because you got two novels—and most of them were written by some of the biggest names in science fiction. I was one of the hundreds of thousands of teenage nerds who bought every double novel, and probably paid the bills for a lot of writers.

And then, there was *The 13th Immortal* by Robert Silverberg.

I had never heard of Robert Silverberg before, but I trusted Ace Doubles. So I read it. I have never reread it. And six decades later, I remember nothing at all about the novel except that I didn't like it very much. To be fair, Robert Silverberg has occasionally acknowledged that it was his first novel and even he didn't regard it as noteworthy.

But it must have been good enough, because unlike a couple of other authors who I eventually learned to avoid, even in my years of arrogant nerdiness, I could recognize that this Silverberg guy was okay.

In the fifties, science fiction was not considered a respectable genre. It was <snicker-snicker> "little green men" fiction. But to boys like I once was— smart, unathletic, socially awkward, and often just plain weird—science fiction was something special. It wasn't just a vision of the future, it was a vision of possibility—spaceships, time machines, robots, aliens, other worlds, and even other ways of being.

We found our heroes there. And for those of us who paid attention, not all of our heroes were fictional. Our real heroes were the names on the covers and the spines. We learned to recognize very quickly which names were a promise of an afternoon or two lost in wonder. Very quickly, Robert Silverberg became a recognized member of this nerd's pantheon.

I attended my first science fiction convention in 1968. It was held in Los Angeles, over July 4th weekend. I had one or two minor credentials of my own—I'd sold a script and a rewrite to a science fiction television show, one that was well-regarded at the time, but I was mostly there as a fan.

There were quite a few notables in attendance: Fred Pohl, Lester Del Rey, Poul and Karen Anderson, Robert Bloch, Harry Harrison, Terry Carr, Norman Spinrad, Jerry Pournelle, Larry Niven—oh, and Harlan Ellison.

But this essay is about Robert Silverberg, so I will leave out the stories of incidents that are probably better left unmentioned. I will say only this—yes, I probably met Robert Silverberg at that convention, but it must have been forgettable because neither of us remembers it. I probably looked like just another wide-eyed fanboy astonished to be in the same room with the people who had populated my imagination for so many years.

A few weeks later, I rode my motorcycle up to Berkeley to attend the 1968 World Science Fiction Convention. (That TV script I wrote had been nominated for a Hugo. My name was on the same ballot with Norman Spinrad, Theodore Sturgeon, Jerome Bixby, and Harlan Ellison. In case you're wondering, I came in second. By three votes.)

But the real honor was sitting in the bar with even more of the authors whose works had informed my adolescence. Frank Herbert, Gordon R. Dickson, James Gunn, Poul Anderson, Anne McCaffrey—who, as Secretary-Treasurer of the Science Fiction Writers of America, promptly signed me up as a member. It was $5. I probably spent some more time hanging out with Robert Silverberg and Terry Carr, but Silverberg doesn't remember that either, and Terry Carr is no longer with us, dammit. I do remember that Silverberg was the toastmaster for the award ceremony, though.

(I'm working my way up to the good stuff; be patient.)

I went to the 1969 World Science Fiction Convention in St. Louis, held at the Hotel of Usher, site of the infamous Movie Screen Incident which has been retold in fannish history more times and more ways than the incident reported in Kurosawa's *Rashomon*. Once again, Silverberg was there—Robert Silverberg had never missed a Worldcon. (It wasn't until Forry Ackerman died that Silverberg finally broke Forry's record for most Worldcons attended.)

I will share this one though, because I witnessed it. Harlan, upset about his interpretation of the aftermath of the Great Movie Screen Incident, went storming out of the hall, muttering loudly that he'd never attend another Worldcon. As he passed Silverberg, Bob said, "See you next year, Harlan." It was then that I realized that Silverberg had a wit so dry that camels would die of thirst in his presence.

But I also remember that Worldcon because it was there that Harry Harrison introduced me to Gail Wendroff, then editor at Dell who was apparently impressed enough with me that she bought two novels and an anthology from me before the end of the year, and that made me a *real* science-fiction writer, not just a TV-scribe.

This is also a good place to mention that by now, Bob Silverberg had developed a reputation that he could turn out a new novel every week. Apparently he wrote his novels in his spare time after writing his short stories, novelettes, and novellas. (I really liked *Nightwings* and *The Book of Changes*, and his incredible short story "Passengers.")

I moved to Manhattan for a while in 1970 and I wrote. I wrote a lot. I sat in my tiny room and typed. (It was work therapy; I was escaping some of the local horrors in L.A.) I sold stories to *Galaxy* and *If* and *Worlds Of Tomorrow*, three of the best magazines on the stands.

And somehow after that, I began selling books to Betty Ballantine. Ballantine Books was the only other paperback house publishing two or more science fiction novels every month. In the Ballantine stable were Arthur C. Clarke, Theodore Sturgeon, Robert Silverberg, Larry Niven, and eventually me. Betty Ballantine was special to authors. She made the genre respectable.

I think it was Ballantine Books that hosted a small gathering at the Algonquin Hotel in 1971. Perhaps it was to honor Arthur C. Clarke who was in town for some event. Also in attendance were Alfred Bester, Lester Del Rey, Fred Pohl, Ian Ballantine, Isaac Asimov, Anne McCaffrey, and Robert Silverberg (of course, because this essay is supposed to be about him), and probably a few others, whose names I will not remember until after this hits print.

What I remember is a remark made by Clarke. He looked around the room, pointed at the ceiling, and said, "If an engine were to fall off one of those new 747 airplanes and hit this hotel room, all of science fiction would be wiped out.

And Bob Silverberg quietly replied, "I'm not worried. I've got twelve novels in the safe."

After we all had an appreciative laugh, Clarke said, "He's not joking."

Fortunately, an engine did not fall off a 747 and we all survived. And I assume those twelve novels eventually made it to the bookstores.

But the point was made: Robert Silverberg was a threat to forests everywhere. The man published stories faster than most people could read. His output probably rivaled all of the rest of the field combined. In that regard, he was amazing—but more amazing was the fact that everything he published was pretty damn good, except when it was great.

Let me skip forward to 1973. I was on the Hugo Ballot for my first novel, *When HARLIE Was One*. My book was up against one by Asimov and two by

Silverberg. There are times when "It's an honor just to be nominated" is an understatement. This was one of them. Silverberg was on the ballot twice! He'd been nominated for *The Book Of Skulls* and *Dying Inside*.

Both were memorable. I was reading every new book that Silverberg published and I could see that he was stretching himself now, tackling themes and ideas that were far beyond the usual tropes of the genre. He had elevated himself from excellent to ambitious—and I was always ready to see what he would attempt next.

But it was at a reception a couple nights before the award ceremony where something else happened that left me stunned. Bob Silverberg came up to me and said, "David, would you do me a favor please? The next time you write a book that good, please tell me in advance so I don't have to compete on the same ballot with you."

When one of the giants of the field gives you a compliment like that … I'm not sure how to finish that sentence. I am still gobsmacked all these years later.

To get that kind of a compliment, that kind of encouragement, that measure of respect—that was the moment I had to stop being the nerdy little weird kid and accept that I might be a respected colleague. And I began to realize that Robert Silverberg and I weren't just casual colleagues in the genre anymore. I dunno, what do you call a friend you only see every few years? In the SF world, you call them friend, because that's how the SF world works. You keep in touch with your friends by reading their books.

In the SF world, some books feel like they were written just for you. Silverberg managed that regularly.

At some event after that, I wandered into the bar next to Silverberg, he turned to me and said, "David, in all the years we've known each other, you've never bought me a drink." Well, okay—I was quick to remedy that omission.

I might have a couple more stories to share about this man. I could share about how, at the 2015 Hugo Ceremony, he led an auditorium full of fans in a Buddhist chant. Or I could share about the Harlan Ellison memorial panel, where he had all the best lines. At the end of the panel, Nat Segaloff concluded, "There'll never be another one like Harlan," to which Bob Silverberg quietly replied, "That's true. And one was more than enough."

Did I mention that the man has a very dry wit? (Yes, I did, but I'm not going to overwork that metaphor.)

I will leave it to others to list Silverberg's incredible output, his travels, his ability to do research, his intelligence, and his amazing skill at weaving a compelling narrative. His Majipoor books are epics of imagination. His other novels are equally ambitious. But don't overlook his shorter works—so many of them are vivid. If there's room, the publishers of this book will include a list.

And if you hand Robert Silverberg a microphone, you're going to see him at his charming best—authoritative and memorable and with a wit so dry that—never mind, I promised I wouldn't.

I'll just say it this way.

I admire and respect the man. He's intelligent. He's credible. He's learned. He's well-traveled. I love being in Robert Silverberg's company. He always has something interesting to relate.

I have known this man for decades.

He is one of the best.

And I'm glad I got the chance to say that here.

—David Gerrold

Introduction

When I was thirteen years old, which was during the presidency of Harry S. Truman, an era which must seem as remote in time to most of you as the presidencies of McKinley and Benjamin Harrison do, I acquired an anthology of science fiction called *Adventures in Time and Space*, edited by Raymond Healy and J. Francis McComas, which in its 39 stories encompassed the state of the art in science fiction as it was known in the 1940s. It is still one of the best anthologies of s-f ever compiled, and it has remained constantly in print for nearly seventy years, a testimony to the fact that it still rewards reading today.

I learned about alien life from that anthology.

I had, by then, read H. G. Wells's *The War of the Worlds*, and knew about Orson Welles's famous radio broadcast derived from that novel, so I was aware that such a concept as life on other worlds existed. But Mars is very close by; and it was *Adventures in Time and Space* that first left me thinking about the possibility that the whole vast universe is full of alien life-forms, that the multitude of stars that brighten our nights and that are just a fraction of the totality of stars in the universe are, in all likelihood, populated by beings—not human beings, of course, but intelligent beings of some sort.

There was John W. Campbell's frightening "Who Goes There?", in which an apparently invincible alien creature comes to Earth, and A. E. van Vogt's "Black Destroyer," which showed an equally terrifying alien on its home grounds, and, to provide an alternative view of aliens, Eric Frank Russell's "Symbiotica," with a spaceship crewed by intelligent beings of various species. And much, much more of that ilk, which led me for the first time to think seriously about a universe full of amazing life-forms.

Once we believed that Earth was the center of the universe, that God had created mankind in His own image, etc., etc. By now such thinking is obsolete, and we know for a certainty that the Earth revolves around the sun rather than vice versa, and that the sun is just one of many in the immense universe. It is less certain that there are other inhabited worlds, but the probability that there are is quite high, considering how many stars there are out there and how many of them, as we have come to discover in recent years, have solar systems of their own and planets not too different from our own. I lean toward that view myself: I think the heavens are well stocked with life—not precisely the kind of life I read about long ago in the Healy-McComas book, of course, but life of some sort, vigorous and astonishing and intelligent. In an essay long ago I calculated just how many inhabited worlds were likely to be out there. I figured there were twelve billion stars in our local galaxy alone that are neither too big nor too small to provide the energy that life-forms of our sort require. "If half of these have planets," I wrote, "and half of those planets lie at the correct distance to maintain water in its liquid state, and half of those are large enough to retain an atmosphere, that leaves us with a billion and a half potentially habitable worlds in our immediate galactic vicinity. Say that a billion of these must be rejected because they're so large that gravity would be a problem, or because they have no water, or because they're in some other way unsuitable. That still leaves 500 million possible Earths in the Milky Way galaxy. And there are millions of galaxies." By way of supporting the idea of an inhabited cosmos, I offered a thought that was put forth about 300 BC by the Greek philosopher Metrodoros the Epicurean:

> To consider the Earth the only populated world in infinite space is as absurd as to assert that in an entire field sown with millet only one grain will grow.

I am neither an astronomer nor a philosopher, but these arguments seem incontrovertible to me. The alternative is the medieval Christian one, put forth most vigorously in the thirteenth century by Thomas Aquinas, who based his ideas to some extent on the teachings of Plato, seventeen hundred years before him. St. Thomas argued that the Earth was the unique and special creation of God, the center of the universe and the only place in the cosmos where life existed. This became the established dogma of the Roman Catholic Church, which means it was the only permissible way of thinking about these things in Western Europe for hundreds of years. But, since the existence of God Himself gradually became a matter for dispute rather than automatic acceptance, it was more and more difficult for serious thinkers to rely purely on the faith that the Church fathers had a perfect understanding of His intentions. Gradually, under the assaults of such men as Copernicus and Galileo, the idea of the Earth as the center of the universe was weakened, and by 1686 it was possible for the French poet and philosopher Bernard de Fontenelle to publish a clever little book called *A Plurality of Worlds* that portrayed the Earth as one of many inhabited planets in the universe. I think that's true. But I also think that there is no chance whatever that we will encounter any of those intelligent alien life-forms.

Back in far-off 2004 I wrote an essay for one of the science-fiction magazines titled "*Neque Illorum Ad Nos Pervenire Potest,*" which is Latin for "None of us can go to them, and none of them come to us." The phrase was that of the twelfth-century philosopher Guillaume de Conches, writing about the supposed inhabitants of the Antipodes, the lands that lay beyond the fiery sea that was thought to cut Europe off from the as yet unexplored Southern

Hemisphere. I used it to express my belief that we are never going to have any close encounters with the inhabitants of other solar systems. They're just too far away. The speed of light is going to remain the limiting velocity not just for us, but for all those lively and interesting people out there in the adjacent galaxies, and that puts the kibosh on the whole concept of alien contact.

Nevertheless, it's fun to write about it. The boy who stayed up half the night to read about alien beings in the Healy-McComas book *Adventures in Time and Space* grew up to write quite a lot of science fiction about alien beings himself, just as he wrote stories about time travel and resuscitating the dead and a lot of other things that he doesn't really believe in except for the sake of telling a good story. I've collected a group of them here. They cover about sixty years of my writing career, ranging in style from a couple of the colorful, action-based stories I wrote for the pulp magazines of the 1950s to such quiet, reflective ones as "We Are For the Dark" and "Defenders of the Frontier" written many decades later. I don't think that any of them reflects a real scientific possibility. But I think they're good lively science-fiction stories, and I hope you will, too.

—Robert Silverberg

Collecting Team

From *Super-Science Fiction*, December 1956

From fifty thousand miles up, the situation looked promising. It was a middle-sized, brown-and-green, inviting-looking planet, with no sign of cities or any other such complications. Just a pleasant sort of place, the very sort we were looking for to redeem what had been a pretty futile expedition.

I turned to Clyde Holdreth, who was staring reflectively at the thermocouple.

"Well? What do you think?"

"Looks fine to me. Temperature's about seventy down there—nice and warm, and plenty of air. I think it's worth a try."

Lee Davison came strolling out from the storage hold, smelling of animals, as usual. He was holding one of the blue monkeys we picked up on Alpheraz, and the little beast was crawling up his arm. "Have we found something, gentlemen?"

"We've found a planet," I said. "How's the storage space in the hold?"

"Don't worry about that. We've got room for a whole zoo-full more, before we get filled up. It hasn't been a very fruitful trip."

"No," I agreed. "It hasn't. Well? Shall we go down and see what's to be seen?"

"Might as well," Holdreth said. "We can't go back to Earth with just a couple of blue monkeys and some anteaters, you know."

"I'm in favor of a landing too," said Davison. "You?"

I nodded. "I'll set up the charts, and you get your animals comfortable for deceleration."

Davison disappeared back into the storage hold, while Holdreth scribbled furiously in the logbook, writing down the coordinates of the planet below, its general description, and so forth. Aside from being a collecting team for the zoological department of the Bureau of Interstellar Affairs, we also double as a survey ship, and the planet down below was listed as unexplored on our charts.

I glanced out at the mottled brown-and-green ball spinning slowly in the viewport, and felt the warning twinge of gloom that came to me every time we made a landing on a new and strange world. Repressing it, I started to figure out a landing orbit. From behind me came the furious chatter of the blue monkeys as Davison strapped them into their acceleration cradles, and under that the deep, unmusical honking of the Rigelian anteaters noisily bleating their displeasure.

The planet was inhabited, all right. We hadn't had the ship on the ground more than a minute before the local fauna began to congregate. We stood at the viewport and looked out in wonder.

"This is one of those things you dream about," Davison said, stroking his little beard nervously. "Look at them! There must be a thousand different species out there."

"I've never seen anything like it," said Holdreth.

I computed how much storage space we had left and how many of the thronging creatures outside we would be able to bring back with us. "How are we going to decide what to take and what to leave behind?"

"Does it matter?" Holdreth said gaily. "This is what you call an embarrassment of riches, I guess. We just grab the dozen most bizarre creatures and blast off and save the rest for another trip. It's too bad we wasted all that time wandering around near Rigel."

"We *did* get the anteaters," Davison pointed out. They were his finds, and he was proud of them.

I smiled sourly. "Yeah. We got the anteaters there." The anteaters honked at that moment, loud and clear. "You know, that's one set of beasts I think I could do without."

"Bad attitude," Holdreth said. "Unprofessional."

"Whoever said I was a zoologist, anyway? I'm just a spaceship pilot, remember. And if I don't like the way those anteaters talk—and smell—I see no reason why I—"

"Say, look at that one," Davison said suddenly.

I glanced out the viewport and saw a new beast emerging from the thick-packed vegetation in the background. I've seen some fairly strange creatures since I was assigned to the zoological department, but this one took the grand prize.

It was about the size of a giraffe, moving on long, wobbly legs and with a tiny head up at the end of a preposterous neck. Only it had six legs and a bunch of writhing snakelike tentacles as well, and its eyes, great violet globes, stood out nakedly on the ends of two thick stalks. It must have been twenty feet high. It moved with exaggerated grace through the swarm of beasts surrounding our ship, pushed its way smoothly towards the vessel, and peered gravely in at the viewport. One purple eye stared directly at me, the other at Davison. Oddly, it seemed to me as if it were trying to tell us something.

"Big one, isn't it?" Davison said finally.

"I'll bet you'd like to bring one back, too."

"Maybe we can fit a young one aboard," Davison said. "If we can find a young one." He turned to Holdreth. "How's that air analysis coming? I'd like to get out there and start collecting. God, that's a crazy-looking beast!"

The animal outside had apparently finished its inspection of us, for it pulled its head away and, gathering its legs under itself, squatted near the ship. A small doglike creature with stiff spines running along its back began to bark at the big creature, which took no notice. The other animals, which came in all shapes and sizes, continued to mill around the ship, evidently very curious about the newcomer to their world. I could see Davison's eyes thirsty with the desire to take the whole kit and caboodle back to Earth with him. I knew what was running through his mind. He was dreaming of the umpteen thousand species of extraterrestrial wildlife roaming around out there, and to each one he was attaching a neat little tag: *Something-or-other davisoni.*

"The air's fine," Holdreth announced abruptly, looking up from his test-tubes. "Get your butterfly nets and let's see what we can catch."

There was something I didn't like about the place. It was just too good to be true, and I learned long ago that nothing ever is. There's always a catch someplace.

Only this seemed to be on the level. The planet was a bonanza for zoologists, and Davison and Holdreth were having the time of their lives, hip deep in obliging specimens.

"I've never seen anything like it," Davison said for at least the fiftieth time, as he scooped up a small purplish squirrel-like creature and examined it curiously. The squirrel stared back, examining Davison just as curiously.

"Let's take some of these," Davison said. "I like them."

"Carry 'em on in, then," I said, shrugging. I didn't care which specimens they chose, so long as they filled up the storage hold quickly and let me blast off on schedule. I watched as Davison grabbed a pair of the squirrels and brought them into the ship.

Holdreth came over to me. He was carrying a sort of a dog with insect-faceted eyes and gleaming furless skin. "How's this one, Gus?"

"Fine," I said bleakly. "Wonderful."

He put the animal down—it didn't scamper away, just sat there smiling at us—and looked at me. He ran a hand through his fast-vanishing hair. "Listen, Gus, you've been gloomy all day. What's eating you?"

"I don't like this place," I said.

"Why? Just on general principles?"

"It's too *easy*, Clyde. Much too easy. These animals just flock around here waiting to be picked up."

Holdreth chuckled. "And you're used to a struggle, aren't you? You're just angry at us because we have it so simple here!"

"When I think of the trouble we went through just to get a pair of miserable vile-smelling anteaters, and—"

"Come off it, Gus. We'll load up in a hurry, if you like. But this place is a zoological gold mine!"

I shook my head. "I don't like it, Clyde. Not at all."

Holdreth laughed again and picked up his faceted-eyed dog. "Say, know where I can find another of these, Gus?"

"Right over there." I said, pointing. "By that tree. With its tongue hanging out. It's just waiting to be carried away."

Holdreth looked and smiled. "What do you know about that!" He snared his specimen and carried both of them inside.

I walked away to survey the grounds. The planet was too flatly incredible for me to accept on face value, without at least a look-see, despite the blithe way my two companions were snapping up specimens.

For one thing, animals just don't exist this way—in big miscellaneous quantities, living all together happily. I hadn't noticed more than a few of each kind, and there must have been five hundred different species, each one stranger-looking than the next. Nature doesn't work that way.

For another, they all seemed to be on friendly terms with one another, though they acknowledged the unofficial leadership of the giraffe-like creature. Nature doesn't work that way, either. I hadn't seen one quarrel between the animals yet. That argued that they were all herbivores, which didn't make sense ecologically.

I shrugged my shoulders and walked on.

Half an hour later, I knew a little more about the geography of our bonanza. We were on either an immense island or a peninsula of some sort, because I could see a huge body of water bordering the land some ten miles off. Our vicinity was fairly flat, except for a good-sized hill from which I could see the terrain.

There was a thick, heavily-wooded jungle not too far from the ship. The forest spread out all the way towards the water in one direction, but ended abruptly in the other. We had brought the ship down right at the edge of the clearing. Apparently most of the animals we saw lived in the jungle.

On the other side of our clearing was a low, broad plain that seemed to trail away into a desert in the distance; I could see an uninviting stretch of barren sand that contrasted strangely with the fertile jungle to my left. There was a small lake to the side. It was, I saw, the sort of country likely to attract a varied fauna, since there seemed to be every sort of habitat within a small area.

And the fauna! Although I'm a zoologist only by osmosis, picking up both my interest and my knowledge second-hand from Holdreth and Davison, I couldn't help but be astonished by the wealth of strange animals. They came in all different shapes and sizes, colors and odors, and the only thing they all had in common was their friendliness. During the course of my afternoon's wanderings a hundred animals must have come marching boldly right up to me, given me the once-over, and walked away. This included half a dozen kinds that I hadn't seen before, plus one of the eye-stalked, intelligent-looking giraffes and a furless dog. Again, I had the feeling that the giraffe seemed to be trying to communicate.

I didn't like it, I didn't like it at all.

I returned to our clearing, and saw Holdreth and Davison still buzzing madly around, trying to cram as many animals as they could into our hold.

"How's it going?" I asked.

"Hold's all full," Davison said. "We're busy making our alternate selections now." I saw him carrying out Holdreth's two furless dogs and picking up instead a pair of eight-legged penguinish things that uncomplainingly allowed themselves to be carried in. Holdreth was frowning unhappily.

"What do you want *those* for, Lee? Those dog-like ones seem much more interesting, don't you think?"

"No," Davison said. "I'd rather bring along these two. They're curious beasts, aren't they? Look at the muscular network that connects the—"

"Hold it, fellows," I said. I peered at the animal in Davison's hands and glanced up. "This is a curious beast," I said. "It's got eight legs."

"You becoming a zoologist?" Holdreth asked, amused.

"No—but I am getting puzzled. Why should this one have eight legs, some of the others here six, and some of the others only four?"

They looked at me blankly, with the scorn of professionals.

"I mean, there ought to be some sort of logic to evolution here, shouldn't there? On Earth we've developed a four-legged pattern of animal life; on Venus, they usually run to six legs. But have you ever seen an evolutionary hodgepodge like this place before?"

"There are stranger setups," Holdreth said. "The symbiotes on Sirius Three, the burrowers of Mizar—but you're right, Gus. This *is* a peculiar evolutionary dispersal. I think we ought to stay and investigate it fully."

Instantly I knew from the bright expression on Davison's face that I had blundered, had made things worse than ever. I decided to take a new tack.

"I don't agree," I said. "I think we ought to leave with what we've got, and come back with a larger expedition later."

Davison chuckled. "Come on, Gus, don't be silly! This is a chance of a lifetime for us—why should we call in the whole zoological department on it?"

I didn't want to tell them I was afraid of staying longer. I crossed my arms. "Lee, I'm the pilot of this ship, and you'll have to listen to me. The schedule calls for a brief stopover here, and we have to leave. Don't tell me I'm being silly."

"But you are, man! You're standing blindly in the path of scientific investigation, of—"

"Listen to me, Lee. Our food is calculated on a pretty narrow margin, to allow you fellows more room for storage. And this is strictly a collecting team. There's no provision for extended stays on any one planet. Unless you want to wind up eating your own specimens, I suggest you allow us to get out of here."

They were silent for a moment. Then Holdreth said, "I guess we can't argue with that, Lee. Let's listen to Gus and go back now. There's plenty of time to investigate this place later when we can take longer."

"But—oh, all right," Davison said reluctantly. He picked up the eight-legged penguins. "Let me stash these things in the hold, and we can leave." He looked strangely at me, as if I had done something criminal.

As he started into the ship, I called to him.

"What is it, Gus?"

"Look here, Lee. I don't *want* to pull you away from here. It's simply a matter of food," I lied, masking my nebulous suspicions.

"I know how it is, Gus." He turned and entered the ship.

I stood there thinking about nothing at all for a moment, then went inside myself to begin setting up the blastoff orbit.

I got as far as calculating the fuel expenditure when I noticed something. Feedwires were dangling crazily down from the control cabinet. Somebody had wrecked our drive mechanism but thoroughly.

For a long moment, I stared stiffly at the sabotaged drive. Then I turned and headed into the storage hold.

"Davison?"

"What is it, Gus?"

"Come out here a second, will you?"

I waited, and a few minutes later he appeared, frowning impatiently. "What do you want, Gus? I'm busy and I—" His mouth dropped open. "*Look at the drive!*"

"You look at it," I snapped. "I'm sick. Go get Holdreth, on the double."

While he was gone I tinkered with the shattered mechanism. Once I had the cabinet panel off and could see the inside, I felt a little better; the drive wasn't damaged beyond repair, though it had been pretty well scrambled. Three or four days of hard work with a screwdriver and solderbeam might get the ship back into functioning order.

But that didn't make me any less angry. I heard Holdreth and Davison entering behind me, and I whirled to face them.

"All right, you idiots. Which one of you did this?"

They opened their mouths in protesting squawks at the same instant. I listened to them for a while, then said, "One at a time!"

"If you're implying that one of us deliberately sabotaged the ship," Holdreth said, "I want you to know—"

"I'm not implying anything. But the way it looks to me, you two decided you'd like to stay here a while longer to continue your investigations, and figured the easiest way of getting me to agree was to wreck the drive." I glared hotly at them. "Well, I've got news for you. I can fix this, and I can fix it in a couple of days. So go on—get about your business! Get all the zoologizing you can in, while you still have time. I—"

Davison laid a hand gently on my arm. "Gus," he said quietly, "*we didn't do it.* Neither of us."

Suddenly all the anger drained out of me and was replaced by raw fear. I could see that Davison meant it.

"If you didn't do it, and Holdreth didn't do it, and I didn't do it—then who did?"

Davison shrugged.

"Maybe it's one of us who doesn't know he's doing it," I suggested. "Maybe—" I stopped. "Oh, that's nonsense. Hand me that toolkit, will you, Lee?"

They left to tend to the animals, and I set to work on the repair job, dismissing all further speculations and suspicions from my mind, concentrating solely on joining Lead A to Input A and Transistor F to Potentiometer K, as indicated. It was slow, nerve-harrowing work, and by mealtime I had accomplished only the barest preliminaries. My fingers were starting to quiver from the strain of small-scale work, and I decided to give up the job for the day and get back to it tomorrow.

I slept uneasily, my nightmares punctuated by the moaning of the accursed anteaters and the occasional squeals, chuckles, bleats, and hisses of the various other creatures in the hold. It must have been four in the morning before I dropped off into a really sound sleep, and what was left of the night passed swiftly. The next thing I knew, hands were shaking me, and I was looking up into the pale, tense faces of Holdreth and Davison.

I pushed my sleep-stuck eyes open and blinked. "Huh? What's going on?"

Holdreth leaned down and shook me savagely. "Get up, Gus!"

I struggled to my feet slowly. "Hell of a thing to do, wake a fellow up in the middle of the—"

I found myself being propelled from my cabin and led down the corridor to the control room. Blearily, I followed where Holdreth pointed, and then I woke up in a hurry.

The drive was battered again. Someone—or *something*—had completely undone my repair job of the night before.

If there had been bickering among us, it stopped. This was past the category of a joke now; it couldn't be laughed off, and we found ourselves working together as a tight unit again, trying desperately to solve the puzzle before it was too late.

"Let's review the situation," Holdreth said, pacing nervously up and down the control cabin. "The drive has been sabotaged twice. None of us knows who did it, and on a conscious level each of us is convinced *he* didn't do it."

He paused. "That leaves us with two possibilities. Either, as Gus suggested, one of us is doing it unaware of it even himself, or someone else is doing it while we're not looking. Neither possibility is a very cheerful one."

"We can stay on guard, though," I said. "Here's what I propose: first, have one of us awake at all times—sleep in shifts, that is, with somebody guarding the drive until I get it fixed. Two—jettison all the animals aboard ship."

"What?"

"He's right," Davison said. "We don't know what we may have brought aboard. They don't seem to be intelligent, but we can't be sure. That purple-eyed baby giraffe, for instance—suppose he's been hypnotizing us into damaging the drive ourselves? How can we tell?"

"Oh, but—" Holdreth started to protest, then stopped and frowned soberly. "I suppose we'll have to admit the possibility," he said, obviously unhappy about the prospect of freeing our captives. "We'll empty out the hold, and you see if you can get the drive fixed. Maybe later we'll recapture them all, if nothing further develops."

We agreed to that, and Holdreth and Davison cleared the ship of its animal cargo while I set to work determinedly at the drive mechanism. By nightfall, I had managed to accomplish as much as I had the day before.

I sat up as watch the first shift, aboard the strangely quiet ship. I paced around the drive cabin, fighting the great temptation to doze off, and managed to last through until the time Holdreth arrived to relieve me.

Only—when he showed up, he gasped and pointed at the drive. It had been ripped apart a third time.

Now we had no excuse, no explanation. The expedition had turned into a nightmare.

I could only protest that I had remained awake my entire spell on duty, and that I had seen no one and no thing approach the drive panel. But that was hardly a satisfactory explanation, since it either cast guilt on me as the saboteur or implied that some unseen external power was repeatedly wrecking the drive. Neither hypothesis made sense, at least to me.

By now we had spent four days on the planet, and food was getting to be a major problem. My carefully budgeted flight schedule called for us to be two days out on our return journey to Earth by now. But we still were no closer to departure than we had been four days ago.

The animals continued to wander around outside, nosing up against the ship, examining it, almost fondling it, with those damned pseudo-giraffes staring soulfully at us always. The beasts were as friendly as ever, little knowing how the tension was growing within the hull. The three of us walked around like zombies, eyes bright and lips clamped. We were scared—all of us.

Something was keeping us from fixing the drive.

Something didn't want us to leave this planet.

I looked at the bland face of the purple-eyed giraffe staring through the viewport, and it stared mildly back at me. Around it was grouped the rest of the local fauna, the same incredible hodgepodge of improbable genera and species.

That night, the three of us stood guard in the control room together. The drive was smashed anyway. The wires were soldered in so many places by now that the control panel was a mass of shining alloy, and I knew that a few more such sabotagings and it would be impossible to patch it together anymore—if it wasn't so already.

The next night, I just didn't knock off. I continued soldering right on after dinner (and a pretty skimpy dinner it was, now that we were on close rations) and far on into the night.

By morning, it was as if I hadn't done a thing.

"I give up," I announced, surveying the damage. "I don't see any sense in ruining my nerves trying to fix a thing that won't stay fixed."

Holdreth nodded. He looked terribly pale. "We'll have to find some new approach."

"Yeah. Some new approach."

I yanked open the food closet and examined our stock. Even figuring in the synthetics we would have fed to the animals if we hadn't released them, we were low on food. We had overstayed even the safety margin. It would be a hungry trip back—if we ever did get back.

I clambered through the hatch and sprawled down on a big rock near the ship. One of the furless dogs came over and nuzzled in my shirt. Davison stepped to the hatch and called down to me.

"What are you doing out there, Gus?"

"Just getting a little fresh air. I'm sick of living aboard that ship." I scratched the dog behind his pointed ears, and looked around.

The animals had lost most of their curiosity about us, and didn't congregate the way they used to. They were meandering all over the plain, nibbling at little deposits of a white doughy substance. It precipitated every night. "Manna," we called it. All the animals seemed to live on it.

I folded my arms and leaned back.

We were getting to look awfully lean by the eighth day. I wasn't even trying to fix the ship anymore; the hunger was starting to get me. But I saw Davison puttering around with my solderbeam.

"What are you doing?"

"I'm going to repair the drive," he said. "You don't want to, but we can't just sit around, you know." His nose was deep in my repair guide, and he was fumbling with the release on the solderbeam.

I shrugged. "Go ahead, if you want to." I didn't care what he did. All I cared about was the gaping emptiness in my stomach, and about the dimly grasped fact that somehow we were stuck here for good.

"Gus?"

"Yeah?"

"I think it's time I told you something. I've been eating the manna for four days. It's good. It's nourishing stuff."

"You've been eating—the manna? Something that grows on an alien world? You crazy?"

"What else can we do? Starve?"

I smiled feebly, admitting that he was right. From somewhere in the back of the ship came the sounds of Holdreth moving around. Holdreth had taken this thing worse than any of us. He had a family back on Earth, and he was beginning to realize that he wasn't ever going to see them again.

"Why don't you get Holdreth?" Davison suggested. "Go out there and stuff yourselves with the manna. You've got to eat something."

"Yeah. What can I lose?" Moving like a mechanical man, I headed towards Holdreth's cabin. We would go out and eat the manna and cease being hungry, one way or another.

"Clyde?" I called. "Clyde?"

I entered his cabin. He was sitting at his desk, shaking convulsively, staring at the two streams of blood that trickled in red spurts from his slashed wrists.

"*Clyde!*"

He made no protest as I dragged him towards the infirmary cabin and got tourniquets around his arms, cutting off the bleeding. He just stared dully ahead, sobbing.

I slapped him and he came around. He shook his head dizzily, as if he didn't know where he was.

"Easy, Clyde. Everything's all right."

"It's *not* all right," he said hollowly. "I'm still alive. Why didn't you let me die? Why didn't you—"

Davison entered the cabin. "What's been happening, Gus?"

"It's Clyde. The pressure's getting him. He tried to kill himself, but I think he's all right now. Get him something to eat, will you?"

We had Holdreth straightened around by evening. Davison gathered as much of the manna as he could find, and we held a feast.

"I wish we had nerve enough to kill some of the local fauna," Davison said. "Then we'd have a feast—steaks and everything!"

"The bacteria," Holdreth pointed out quietly. "We don't dare."

"I know. But it's a thought."

"No more thoughts," I said sharply. "Tomorrow morning we start work on the drive panel again. Maybe with some food in our bellies we'll be able to keep awake and see what's happening here."

Holdreth smiled. "Good. I can't wait to get out of this ship and back to a normal existence. God, I just can't wait!"

"Let's get some sleep," I said. "Tomorrow we'll give it another try. We'll get back," I said with a confidence I didn't feel.

The following morning I rose early and got my toolkit. My head was clear, and I was trying to put the pieces together without much luck. I started towards the control cabin.

And stopped.

And looked out the viewport.

I went back and awoke Holdreth and Davison. "Take a look out the port," I said hoarsely.

They looked. They gaped.

"It looks just like my house," Holdreth said. "My house on Earth."

"With all the comforts of home inside, I'll bet." I walked forward uneasily and lowered myself through the hatch. "Let's go look at it."

We approached it, while the animals frolicked around us. The big giraffe came near and shook its head gravely. The house stood in the middle of the clearing, small and neat and freshly painted.

I saw it now. During the night, invisible hands had put it there. Had assembled and built a cosy little Earth-type house and dropped it next to our ship for us to live in.

"Just like my house," Holdreth repeated in wonderment.

"It should be," I said. "They grabbed the model from your mind, as soon as they found out we couldn't live on the ship indefinitely."

Holdreth and Davison asked as one, "What do you mean?"

"You mean you haven't figured this place out yet?" I licked my lips, getting myself used to the fact that I was going to spend the rest of my life here. "You mean you don't realize what this house is intended to be?"

They shook their heads, baffled. I glanced around, from the house to the useless ship to the jungle to the plain to the little pond. It all made sense now.

"They want to keep us happy," I said. "They know we weren't thriving aboard the ship, so they—they built us something a little more like home."

"*They?* The giraffes?"

"Forget the giraffes. They tried to warn us, but it's too late. They're intelligent beings, but they're prisoners just like us. I'm talking about the ones who run this place. The super-aliens who make us sabotage our own ship and not even know we're doing it, who stand someplace up there and gape at us. The ones who dredged together this motley assortment of beasts from all over the galaxy. Now we've been collected too. This whole damned place is just a zoo—a zoo for aliens so far ahead of us we don't dare dream what they're like."

I looked up at the shimmering blue-green sky, where invisible bars seemed to restrain us, and sank down dismally on the porch of our new home. I was resigned. There wasn't any sense in struggling against *them*.

I could see the neat little placard now:

EARTHMEN. Native Habitat, Sol III.

World of a Thousand Colors

From *Super-Science Fiction*, June 1957

When Jolvar Hollinrede discovered that the slim, pale young man opposite him was journeying to the World of a Thousand Colors to undergo the Test, he spied a glittering opportunity for himself. And in that moment was the slim, pale young man's fate set.

Hollinrede's lean fingers closed on the spun-fibre drinkflask. He peered across the burnished tabletop. "The *Test*, you say?"

The young man smiled diffidently. "Yes. I think I'm ready. I've waited years—and now's my big chance." He had had a little too much of the cloying liqueur he had been drinking; his eyes shone glassily, and his tongue was looser than it had any right to be.

"Few are called and fewer are chosen," Hollinrede mused. "Let me buy you another drink."

"No, I—"

"It will be an honor. Really. It's not every day I have a chance to buy a Testee a drink."

Hollinrede waved a jeweled hand and the servomech brought them two more drinkflasks. Lightly Hollinrede punctured one, slid it along the tabletop, kept the other in his hand unopened. "I don't believe I know your name," he said.

"Derveran Marti. I'm from Earth. You?"

"Jolvar Hollinrede. Likewise. I travel from world to world on business, which is what brings me to Niprion this day."

"What sort of business?"

"I trade in jewels," Hollinrede said, displaying the bright collection studding his fingers. They were all morphosims, not the originals, but only careful chemical analysis would reveal that. Hollinrede did not believe in exposing millions of credits' worth of merchandise to anyone who cared to lop off his hand.

"I was a clerk," Marti said. "But that's all far behind me. I'm on to the World of a Thousand Colors to take the Test! The Test!"

"The Test!" Hollinrede echoed. He lifted his unpunctured drinkflask in a gesture of salute, raised it to his lips, pretended to drain it. Across the table Derveran Marti coughed as the liqueur coursed down his throat. He looked up, smiling dizzily, and smacked his lips.

"When does your ship leave?" Hollinrede asked.

"Tomorrow midday. It's the *Star Climber*. I can't wait. This stopover at Niprion is making me fume with impatience."

"No doubt," Hollinrede agreed. "What say you to an afternoon of whist, to while away the time?"

An hour later Derveran Marti lay slumped over the inlaid cardtable in Hollinrede's hotel suite, still clutching a handful of waxy cards. Arms folded, Hollinrede surveyed the body.

They were about of a height, he and the dead man, and a chemotherm mask would alter Hollinrede's face sufficiently to allow him to pass as Marti. He switched on the playback of the room's recorder to pick up the final fragments of their conversation.

"… care for another drink, Marti?"

"I guess I'd better not, old fellow. I'm getting kind of muzzy, you know. No, please don't pour it for me. I said I didn't want it, and—well, all right. Just a little one. There, that's enough. Thanks."

The tape was silent for a moment, then recorded the soft thump of Marti's body falling to the table as the quick-action poison unlatched his synapses. Smiling, Hollinrede switched the recorder to record and said, mimicking Marti, "*I guess I'd better not, old fellow. I'm getting kind of muzzy, you know.*"

He activated the playback, listened critically to the sound of his voice, then listened to Marti's again for comparison. He was approaching the light, flexible quality of the dead man's voice. Several more attempts and he had it almost perfect. Producing a vocal homologizer, he ran off first Marti's voice, then his own pronouncing the same words.

The voices were alike to three decimal places. That would be good enough to fool the most sensitive detector; three places was the normal range of variation in any man's voice from day to day.

In terms of mass there was a trifling matter of some few grams which could easily be sweated off in the gymnasium the following morning. As for the dead man's gesture-complex, Hollinrede thought he could manage a fairly accurate imitation of Marti's manner of moving; he had studied the young clerk carefully for nearly four hours, and Hollinrede was a clever man.

When the preparations were finished, he stepped away and glanced at the mirror, taking a last look at his own face—the face he would not see again until he had taken the Test. He donned the mask. Jolvar Hollinrede became Derveran Marti.

Hollinrede extracted a length of cotton bulking from a drawer and wrapped it around Marti's body. He weighed the corpse, and added four milligrams more of cotton so that Marti would have precisely the mass Jolvar Hollinrede had had. He donned Marti's clothes finally, dressed the body in his own, and, smiling sadly at the convincing but worthless morphosim jewels on his fingers, transferred the rings to Marti's already-stiffening hands.

"Up with you," he grunted, and bundled the body across the room to the disposall.

"Farewell, old friend," he exclaimed feelingly, and hoisted Marti feet-first to the lip of the chute. He shoved, and the dead man vanished, slowly, gracefully, heading downward towards the omnivorous maw of the atomic converter buried in the deep levels of Stopover Planet Niprion.

Reflectively Hollinrede turned away from the disposall unit. He gathered up the cards, put away the liqueur, poured the remnant of the poisoned drink in the disposall chute.

An atomic converter was a wonderful thing, he thought pleasantly. By now the body of Marti had been efficiently reduced to its component molecules, and those were due for separation into atoms shortly after, and from atoms into subatomic particles. Within an hour the prime evidence to the crime would be nothing but so many protons, electrons, and neutrons—and there would be no way of telling which of the two men in the room had entered the chute, and which had remained alive.

Hollinrede activated the tape once more, rehearsed for the final time his version of Marti's voice, and checked it with the homologizer. Still three decimal places; that was good enough. He erased the tape.

Then, depressing the communicator stud, he said, "I wish to report a death."

A cold robot face appeared on the screen. "Yes?"

"Several minutes ago my host, Jolvar Hollinrede, passed on of an acute embolism. He requested immediate dissolution upon death and I wish to report that this has been carried out."

"Your name?"

"Derveran Marti. Testee."

"A Testee? You were the last to see the late Hollinrede alive?"

"That's right."

"Do you swear that all information you might give will be accurate and fully honest?"

"I so swear," Hollinrede said.

The inquest was brief and smooth. The word of a Testee goes without question; Hollinrede had reported the details of the meeting exactly as if he had been Marti, and after a check of the converter records revealed that a mass exactly equal to the late Hollinrede's had indeed been disposed of at precisely the instant the witness claimed, the inquest was at its end. The verdict was natural death. Hollinrede told the officials that he had not known the late jewel trader before that day, and had no interest in his property, whereupon they permitted him to depart.

Having died intestate, Hollinrede knew his property became that of the Galactic Government. But, as he pressed his hand, clad in its skintight chemotherm, against the doorplate of Derveran Marti's room, he told himself that it did not matter. Now he was Derveran Marti, Testee. And once he had taken and passed the Test, what would the loss of a few million credits in baubles matter to him?

Therefore it was with a light heart that the pseudo-Derveran Marti quitted his lodgings the next day and prepared to board the *Star Climber* for the voyage to the World of a Thousand Colors.

The clerk at the desk peered at him sympathetically as he pressed his fingers into the checkout plate, thereby erasing the impress from the doorplate upstairs.

"It was too bad about that old fellow dying on you yesterday, wasn't it, sir? I do hope it won't affect your Test result."

Hollinrede smiled blankly. "It was quite a shock to me when he died so suddenly. But my system has already recovered; I'm ready for the Test."

"Good luck to you, sir," the clerk said as Hollinrede left the hotel and stepped out on the flaring skyramp that led to the waiting ship.

The steward at the passenger hatch was collecting identiplates. Hollinrede handed his over casually. The steward inserted it tip-first in the computer near the door, and motioned for Hollinrede to step within the beam while his specifications were being automatically compared with those on the identiplate.

He waited, tensely. Finally the chattering of the machine stopped and a dry voice said, "Your identity is in order, Testee Derveran Marti. Proceed within."

"That means you're okay," the steward told him. "Yours is Compartment Eleven. It's a luxury job, you know. But you Testees deserve it. Best of luck, sir."

"Thanks," Hollinrede grinned. "I don't doubt I'll need it."

He moved up the ramp and into the ship. Compartment Eleven *was* a luxury job; Hollinrede, who had been a frugal man, whistled in amazement when he saw it. It was nearly eight feet high and almost twelve broad, totally private with an opaquer attached to the doorscope. Clinging curtains of ebony synthoid foam from Ravensmusk VIII had been draped lovingly over the walls, and the acceleration couch was trimmed in golden bryozone. The rank of Testee carried with it privileges that the late Derveran Marti certainly would never have mustered in private life—nor Jolvar Hollinrede either.

At 1143 the doorscope chimed; Hollinrede leaped from the soft couch a little too nervously and transluced the door. A crewman stood outside.

"Everything all right, sir? We blast in seventeen minutes."

"I'm fine," Hollinrede said. "Can't wait to get there. How long do you think it'll take?"

"Sorry sir. Not at liberty to reveal. But I wish you a pleasant trip, and should you lack for aught hesitate not to call on me."

Hollinrede smiled at the curiously archaic way the man had of expressing himself. "Never fear; I'll not hesitate. Many thanks." He opaqued the doorscope and resumed his seat.

At precisely 1200 the drive-engines of the *Star Climber* throbbed heavily; the pale green light over the door of Hollinrede's compartment glowed brightly for an instant, signaling the approaching blastoff. He sank down on the acceleration couch to wait.

A moment later came the push of acceleration, and then, as the gravshields took effect, the 7g escape force dwindled until Hollinrede felt comfortable again. He increased the angle of the couch in order to peer out the port.

The world of Niprion was vanishing rapidly in the background: already it was nothing but a mottled grey-and-gold ball swimming hazily in a puff of atmosphere. The sprawling metal structure that was the stopover hotel was invisible.

Somewhere back on Niprion, Hollinrede thought, the atoms that once had been Testee Derveran Marti were now feeding the plasma intake of a turbine or heating the inner shell of a reactor.

He let his mind dwell on the forthcoming Test. He knew little about it, really, considering he had been willing to take a man's life for a chance to compete. He knew the Test was administered once every five years to candidates chosen by Galaxywide search. The world where the Test was given was known only as the World of a Thousand Colors, and precisely where this world was no member of the general public was permitted to know.

As for the Test itself, by its very nature it was unknown to the Galaxy. For no winning Testee had ever returned from the World of a Thousand Colors. Some losers returned, their minds carefully wiped clean of any memories of the planet—but the winners never came back.

The Test's nature was unknown; the prize, inconceivable. All anyone knew was that the winners were granted the soul's utmost dream. Upon winning, one neither returned to his home world nor desired to return.

Naturally many men ignored the Test—it was something for "other people" to take part in. But millions, billions throughout the Galaxy competed in the preliminaries. And every five years, six or seven were chosen.

Jolvar Hollinrede was convinced he would succeed in the Test—but he had failed three times running in the preliminaries, and was thus permanently disqualified. The preliminaries were simple; they consisted merely of an intensive mental scanning. A flipflop circuit would flash YES or NO after that.

If YES, there were further scannings, until word was beamed through the Galaxy that the competitors for the year had been chosen.

Hollinrede stared moodily at the blackness of space. He had been eliminated unfairly, he felt; he coveted the unknown prize the Test offered, and felt bitter at having it denied him. When chance had thrown Testee Derveran Marti in his path, Hollinrede had leaped to take advantage of the opportunity.

And now he was on his way.

Surely, he thought, they would allow him to take the Test, even if he were discovered to be an impostor. And once he took it, he knew he would succeed. He had always succeeded in his endeavors. There was no reason for failure now.

Beneath the false mask of Derveran Marti, Hollinrede's face was tensely set. He dreamed of the Test and its winning—and of the end to the long years of wandering and toil.

The voice at the door said, "We're here, Testee Derveran. Please open up."

Hollinrede grunted, pulled himself up from the couch, threw open the door. Three dark-faced spacemen waited there for him.

"Where are we?" he asked nervously. "Is the trip over?"

"We have come to pilot you to the Test planet, sir," one of the spacemen told him. "The *Star Climber* is in orbit around it, but will not make a landing itself. Will you follow us?"

"Very well," Hollinrede said.

They entered a lifeship, a slim grey tube barely thirty meters long, and fastened acceleration cradles. There were no ports. Hollinrede felt enclosed, hemmed in.

The lifeship began to slide noiselessly along the ejection channel, glided the entire length of the *Star Climber*, and burst out into space. A preset orbit was operating. Hollinrede clung to the acceleration cradle as the lifeship spun tightly inward towards a powerful gravitational field not far away.

The ship came to rest. Hollinrede lay motionless, flesh cold with nervousness, teeth chattering.

"Easy does it, sir. Up and out."

They lifted him and gently nudged him through a manifold compression lock. He moved forward on numb feet.

"Best of luck, sir!" an envious voice called behind him.

Then the lock clanged shut, and Hollinrede was on his own.

A riotous blaze of color swept down at him from every point of the compass.

He stood in the midst of what looked like a lunar crater; far in the distance on all sides was the massive upraised fissured surface of a ringwall, and the ground beneath him was barren red-brown rock, crumbling to pumice here and there but bare of vegetation.

In the sky was a solitary sun, a blazing Type A blue-white star. That sun alone was incapable of accounting for this flood of color.

Streamers of every hue seemed to sprout from the rocks, staining the ringwall olive-grey and brilliant cerise and dark, lustrous green. Pigments of every sort bathed the air; now it seemed to glow with currents of luminous pink, now a flaming red, now a pulsing pure white.

His eyes adjusted slowly to the torrent of color. World of a Thousand Colors, they called this place? That was an underestimate. *Hundred thousand. Million. Billion.* Shades and near-shades mingled to form new colors.

"Are you Derveran Marti?" a voice asked.

Startled, Hollinrede looked around. It seemed as if a band of color had spoken: a swirling band of rich brown that spun tirelessly before him.

"Are you Derveran Marti?" the voice repeated, and Hollinrede saw that it had indeed come from the band of brown.

It seemed a desecration to utter the lie here on this world of awesome beauty, and he felt the temptation to claim his true identity. But the time for that was later.

"Yes," he said loudly. "I am Derveran Marti."

"Welcome, Derveran Marti. The Test will soon begin."

"Where?"

"Here."

"Right out here? Just like this?"

"Yes," the band of color replied. "Your fellow competitors are gathering."

Hollinrede narrowed his eyes and peered towards the far reaches of the ringwall. Yes; he saw tiny figures located at great distances from each other along the edge of the crater. One, two, three ... there were seven all told, including himself. Seven, out of the whole Galaxy!

Each of the other six was attended by a dipping, bobbing blotch of color. Hollinrede noticed a squareshouldered giant from one of the Inner Worlds surrounded by a circlet of violent orange; to his immediate left was a sylphlike female, probably from one of the worlds of Dubhe, wearing only the revealing token garment of her people but shielded from inquisitive eyes by a robe of purest blue light. There were others; Hollinrede wished them well. He knew it was possible for all competitors to win, and now that he was about to attain his long-sought goal he held no malice for anyone. His mind was suffused with pity for the dead Derveran Marti, sacrificed that Jolvar Hollinrede might be in this place at this time.

"Derveran Marti," the voice said, "you have been chosen from among your fellow men to take part in the Test. This is an honor that comes to few; we of this world hope you appreciate the grace that has fallen upon you."

"I do," Hollinrede said humbly.

"We ourselves are winners of the prize you seek," the voice went on. "Some of us are members of the first expedition that found this world, eleven hundred years ago. As you see, life has unlimited duration in our present state of matter. Others of us have come more recently. The bank of pale purple moving above you to the left was a winner in the previous competition to this.

"We of the World of a Thousand Colors have a rare gift to offer: total harmony of mind. We exist divorced of body, as a stream of photons only. We live in perfect freedom and eternal delight. Once every five years we find it possible to increase our numbers by adding to our midst such throughout the Galaxy as we feel would desire to share our way of life—and whom we would feel happy to welcome to us."

"You mean," Hollinrede said shakily, "that all these beams of light— were once *people?*"

"They were that—until welcomed into us. Now they are men no more. This is the prize you have come to win."

"I see."

"You are not required to compete. Those who, after reaching our world, decide to remain in the material state, are returned to their home worlds with their memories cleared of what they have been told here and their minds free and happy to the end of their lives. Is this what you wish?"

Hollinrede was silent, letting his dazzled eyes take in the flamboyant sweep of color that illuminated the harsh, rocky world. Finally he said: "I will stay."

"Good. The Test will shortly begin."

Hollinrede saw the band of brown swoop away from him upward to rejoin its never-still comrades in the sky. He waited, standing stiffly, for something to happen.

Then this is what I killed a man for, he thought. His mind dwelled on the words of the band of brown.

Evidently many hundreds of years ago an exploratory expedition had come upon some unique natural phenomenon here at a far end of the universe. Perhaps it had been an accident, a stumbling into a pool of light perhaps, that had dematerialized them, turned them into bobbing immortal streaks of color. But that had been the beginning.

The entire Test system had been developed to allow others to enter this unique society, to leave the flesh behind and live on as pure energy. Hollinrede's fingers trembled; this was, he saw, something worth killing for!

He could see why some people might turn down the offer—those would be the few who cautiously would prefer to remain corporeal and so returned to their home worlds to live out their span.

But not me!

He faced upward and waited for the Test to begin. His shrewd mind was at the peak of its agility; he was prepared for anything they might throw at him. He wondered if anyone yet had come to the World of a Thousand Colors so determined to succeed.

Probably not. For most, the accolade was the result of luck—a mental scanning that turned up whatever mysterious qualities were acceptable to the people of this world. They did not have to work for their nomination. They did not have to kill for it.

But Hollinrede had clawed his way here—and he was determined to succeed.

He waited.

Finally the brown band descended from the mass of lambent color overhead and curled into a tight bowknot before him.

"The Test is about to begin, Jolvar Hollinrede."

Use of his own name startled him. In the past week he had so thoroughly associated his identity with that of Derveran Marti that he had scarcely let his actual name drift through his mind.

"So you know," he said.

"We have known since the moment you came. It is unfortunate; we would have wanted Derveran Marti among us. But now that you are here, we will test you on your own merits, Jolvar Hollinrede."

It was just as well that way, he thought. The pretense had to end sooner or later, and he was willing to stand or fall as himself rather than under an assumed identity.

"Advance to the center of the crater, Jolvar Hollinrede," came the command from the brown band.

Leadenly Hollinrede walked forward. Squinting through the mist of color that hazed the view, he saw the other six competitors were doing the same. They would meet at the center.

"The Test is now under way," a new and deeper voice said.

Seven of them. Hollinrede looked around. There was the giant from the Inner World—Fondelfor, he saw now. Next to him, the near-nude sylph of Dubhe, and standing by her side, one diamond-faceted eye glittering in his forehead, a man of Alpheraz VII.

The selectors had cast their nets wide. Hollinrede saw another Terran, dark of skin and bright of eye; a being of Deneb IX, squat and muscular. The sixth Testee was a squirming globule from Spica's tenth world; the seventh was Jolvar Hollinrede, itinerant; home world, Terra.

Overhead hung a circular diadem of violet light. It explained the terms of the Test.

"Each of you will be awarded a characteristic color. It will project before you into the area you ring. Your object will be to blend your seven colors into one; when you have achieved this, you will be admitted into us."

"May I ask what the purpose of this is?" Hollinrede said coldly.

"The essence of our society is harmony—total harmony among us all, and inner harmony within those groups which were admitted at the same temporal juncture. Naturally if you seven are incapable even of this inner harmony, you will be incapable of the greater harmony of us all—and will be rejected."

Despite the impatient frowns of a few of his fellow contestants, Hollinrede said, "Therefore we're to be judged as a unit? An entity?"

"Yes and no," the voice replied. "And now the Test."

Hollinrede saw to his astonishment a color spurt from his arm and hang hovering before him—a pool of inky blackness deeper in hue than the dark of space. His first reaction was one of shock; then he realized that he could control the color, make it move.

He glanced around. Each of his companions similarly faced a hovering mass of color. The giant of Fondelfor controlled red; the girl of Dubhe, orange. The Alpherazian stared into a whirling bowl of deep yellow, the Terran green, the Spican radiant violet, the Denebian pearly grey.

Hollinrede stared at his globe of black. A voice above him seemed to whisper, *"Marti's color would have been blue. The spectrum has been violated."*

He shrugged away the words and sent his globe of black spinning into the area between the seven contestants ringed in a circle. At the same time each of the others directed his particular color inward.

The colors met. They clashed, pinwheeled, seemed to throw off sparks. They began to swirl in a hovering arc of radiance.

Hollinrede waited breathlessly, watching the others. His color of black seemed to stand in opposition to the other six. Red, orange, yellow, green, violet. The pearl-grey of the Denebian seemed to enfold the other colors warmly—all but Hollinrede's. The black hung apart.

To his surprise he saw the Dubhian girl's orange beginning to change hue. The girl herself stood stiffly, eyes closed, her body now bare. Sweat poured down her skin. And her orange hue began to shift towards the grey of the Denebian.

The others were following. One by one, as they achieved control over their Test color. First to follow was the Spican, then the Alpherazian.

Why can't I do that? Hollinrede thought wildly.

He strained to alter the color of his black, but it remained unchanged. The others were blending, now, swirling around; there was a predominantly grey cast, but it was not the grey of the Denebian but a different grey tending towards white. Impatiently he redoubled his efforts; it was necessary for the success of the group that he get his obstinate black to blend with the rest.

"The black remains aloof," someone said near him.

"We will fail if the black does not join us."

His streak of color now stood out boldly against the increasing milkiness of the others. None of the original colors were left now but his. Perspiration streamed down him; he realized that his was the only obstacle preventing the seven from passing the Test.

"The black still will not join us," a tense voice said.

Another said, "The black is a color of evil."

A third said, "Black is not a color at all. Black is the absence of color; white is the totality of color."

A fourth said, "Black is holding us from the white."

Hollinrede looked from one to the other in mute appeal. Veins stood out on his forehead from the effort, but the black remained unchanging. He could not blend it with the others.

From above came the voice of their examiner, suddenly accusing: "Black is the color of murder."

The girl from Dubhe, lilting the ugly words lightly, repeated it. "Black is the color of *murder*."

"Can we permit a murderer among us?" asked the Denebian.

"The answer is self-evident," said the Spican, indicating the recalcitrant spear of black that marred the otherwise flawless globe of near-white in their midst.

"The murderer must be cast out ere the Test be passed," muttered the giant of Fondelfor. He broke from his position and moved menacingly towards Hollinrede.

"Look!" Hollinrede yelled desperately. "Look at the red!"

The giant's color had split from the grey and now darted wildly towards Hollinrede's black.

"This is the wrong way, then," the giant said, halting. "We must all join in it or we all fail."

"Keep away from me," Hollinrede said. "It's not my fault if—"

Then they were on him—four pairs of hands, two rough claws, two slick tentacles. Hollinrede felt himself being lifted aloft. He squirmed, tried to break from their grasp, but they held him up—

And dashed him down against the harsh rock floor.

He lay there, feeling his life seep out, knowing he had failed—and watched as they returned to form their circle once again. The black winked out of being.

As his eyes started to close, Hollinrede saw the six colors again blend into one. Now that the murderer had been cast from their midst, nothing barred the path of their harmony. Pearly grey shifted to purest white— the totality of color—and as the six merged into one, Hollinrede, with his dying glance, bitterly saw them take leave forever of their bodies and slip upward to join their brothers hovering brightly above.

Death's Planet

From *Super-Science Fiction*, October 1957

I found out about World Seven of Star System A quick, and the hard way. I pulled short straw and came down out of the Exploration Team's ship first. There was just about time for me to take three or four hesitant steps on the purplish grass when something came bounding out of the thick jungle and knocked me end over nose.

I got to my feet dizzy and started to grope for my blaster. This time I got a good view of the whatever-it-was. It was the size of a man, roughly, except that about a third of it was head, one-sixth stomach, and half a pair of huge, coiled kangaroo-like legs. I caught the flash of white teeth the length of my fingers, of staring red eyes and scaly yellow skin. Then the kangaroo legs tensed, released, and the thing bashed into my chest and knocked me sprawling a second time.

I didn't have a suit on, so I couldn't radio for help. They were probably watching me, up in the ship, waiting for a clear chance to fire. I found myself facing a headful of spike-like teeth. Some getaway, I thought. Escape from a murder rap on Velliran only to be gobbled up alive in this unexplored system.

But just as those teeth seemed ready to bury themselves in my neck, the weight began to lift. Some other friendly beast had come forth from the Jungle. I was being granted a reprieve.

This new one was a lulu. It was tall and thin, maybe fifteen feet high and a foot wide. It looked like a walking telescope, green all over, with two tremendously long dangling arms, a pair of tiny legs tucked away underneath it, and a petal-like arrangement at the very top. One of the dangling arms had grabbed the thing that was sitting on me, and was now hoisting it in the air.

I got to my feet again and stepped back into the shadow of the ship, and watched. The beast with the teeth was kicking and squirming, but the telescope thing had a good grip on it and wasn't letting go. I saw the animal rise higher and higher, until the spindly arm held it over the petal arrangement on top. Then the arm let go.

The petals spread wide to receive the animal.

There was a lump, live and kicking, in the telescope thing's throat. Then, slowly, horribly, that lump started to sink stomachward. I shuddered.

The telescope creature folded its long arms around its middle, hugged itself in a little dance of contentment and joy, and waddled back into the jungle. A second later, I was surrounded by my shipmates.

"We've been welcomed," I said.

Death came quick and fast and ugly on World Seven of Star System A. But it came just as fast on the allegedly civilized world of Velliran, and when it came you had to look out or it would sweep you in along with the intended victim.

That's what happened to me.

I'm from Earth, originally; I wasn't born on any of the outworlds, but right on Homeworld herself. Not that that meant anything. With umpty-ump billion people scrabbling for a living on Earth, I made like everybody else and took off for the outworlds, where, I thought, I could live comfortably and well and breathe fresh air.

I went to Velliran. Velliran's a world in the Pollux system; it's big but not too dense, and so the all-important grav ratio is 1:1 with Earth. I settled on Velliran and I lived there eight years, and I probably would still be there except for the events that led me to World Seven of Star System A.

Velliran is populated chiefly by native life—small, finely-formed blue-skinned humanoids whose ancestry goes back into the dim years of the universe. They speak softly to each other in a strange, liquid language, and they keep pretty much to themselves, not mingling with the Earthmen who have built cities on their world. They have a keen sense of the ethical, and I'm told their religion is one of the galaxy's noblest. I don't know. I never had much to do with them.

I was operating a yangskin syndicate on Velliran, and bringing in a tidy profit. I employed six Terran hunters who ventured into the interior to hunt the strange eight-legged yangs, and I employed three skinners and four curers and two packers. At its best it was a medium-big syndicate, and I was bringing in some 20,000 credits a year profit, with more orders tumbling in day by day as the women of Earth found it more and more fashionable to deck their shoulders with the soft, clinging black-and-white skins.

I was on the way to the bank one morning with the week's loot in my pocket. It was a bright, clear morning, the sky having the fantastic transparent look that makes Velliran so lovely. I remember thinking about how glad I was just to be here. The streets weren't crowded; a couple of slim, soft-eyed little natives were walking up ahead, and a few Terrans.

Exactly what came next I wasn't sure. It felt like I'd been clubbed over the head and struck with lightning simultaneously, except that when it was all over I was still standing right where I was, and the street was just as quiet.

Only now I was holding a jeweled knife tight in my right hand. It was dripping bright red. *Blood red*—but not Earthman red. Oh, no. The only people who had blood as flame-red as that were the native Vellirani.

There was one of them at my feet, looking peaceful even in death. But he hadn't died peacefully at all. His blue body had been ripped open with a knife. With the knife I now was staring stupidly at.

They reeled me into court a little while later—naturally, a Corpsman came strolling along while I gaped at the murder-weapon I held—and the trial took about six minutes. The judge was a stranger to me, which was too bad.

He squinted down from the bench and said, "Defendant Crawford, you have slain a Vellirani in broad daylight. Do you have any explanation for this crime?"

I blinked. "None."

What else could I say? I couldn't argue with the bloody knife in my hand.

The judge said, "The crime lies outside the jurisdiction of Terran court on Velliran. But, of course, this does not mean you will go unpunished."

I stared at him. "I didn't do it. It couldn't have been me."

"The Vellirani have ways of justice of their own. To them do we commend you."

And they turned me loose.

I stood outside the courtroom a few minutes, looking up at the transparent sky and wondering how it was that your life could crumble to hell inside half an hour. The deposit was still in my pocket. Two thousand credits, backed by pretty Terran platinum. They weren't going to get to the bank, now. I was going to need them. And there wasn't much time.

Someone had put the frame to me, but there was no point trying to convince anyone of my innocence. The Vellirani would never understand the concept of falsely blaming another for a crime he hadn't committed. To them, I had killed their countryman, and I had to die. That was the way Vellirani justice worked. And, I knew, their methods of execution were unpleasant.

There was a man I could see, though. His name was Geoffrey Hallan, and he was an Expediter. He made things easy for people.

He was a small, squint-eyed man with a sharp nose and a pale face. He said, "You really didn't kill the alien?"

"Honest. Unless I had a sudden kill-fit and now I can't remember it."

He shrugged. "Well, it doesn't matter whether you killed him or not, does it? As far as the Vellirani are concerned, *someone* has to die for the crime, and it might as well be you as anyone else."

"Exactly." I took out my bank deposit, flicked the bills with my fingers, and slapped them down on my desk. "Here's two thousand, Hallan. Can you get me off Velliran by nightfall?"

He took the bills, riffled through them speculatively, studied the serial numbers, rubbed his thumbs over the portrait in the middle. At length he said, "Maybe."

"Maybe?"

"There's an Exploratory Corps ship in town, due to leave tonight. Their ecologist died in space, and they asked me to find them a new one. I contacted the Corps headquarters and had them ship a replacement out here. His name is Paul Markham, and he's here in the city."

"So?"

"Suppose," he said, "I got you aboard that ship instead of Markham."

"Me? I'm no ecologist! I don't know anything about—"

Hallan smiled bleakly. "You don't have to. All you need to do is get aboard that ship. They're bound for unexplored territory in the Andromeda region, and if you can bluff your way until you're in hyperspace, you've got it made. They won't turn back on your account. If there's any trouble, I'll make up some story or other. When they return, you go to some other planet and change your name. The galaxy's big; the Vellirani won't bother you."

"What about this Markham?"

"Him? He'll just miss the boat, that's all. There are plenty of ways of delaying a man past blastoff time."

The three moons of Velliran were high overhead, casting their orange light, when I arrived at the spaceport. I had spent the day at Kalian's, arranging things. He would hold all my property and my bank account for me, and when I returned from my exploratory jaunt he would forward them to me on my new world. I didn't trust him too much, but under the circumstances I was happy to get away from Velliran alive, let alone with any property.

He drove me down to the spaceport at 19:45, and the ship was there—tall, slim, glittering faintly in the moonlight. He escorted me to the ship's elevator.

"Okay. You should make it clear from here, Crawford—ah, *Markham*. Take it smooth, and I'll watch for the word from you."

"Thanks, Hallan. Thanks."

I stepped into the elevator and rode up into the ship. Eight or nine men were waiting for me.

"I'm Markham," I said. "The new ecologist."

A tall man in blue-and-gold uniform said, "Welcome aboard. I'm Captain Hendrin. These are the men you'll work with."

He introduced me rapidly around: there was a biologist, a medic, an anthropologist, a botanist, a chemist, and so on—all the usual manpower of an exploratory mission. Captain Hendrin said, "We're bound for the Andromeda system, as you may have heard. It's going to be the standard six-month jaunt. We're beginning in Star System A, and the orders are to name and survey as many worlds as we can within our time period."

I grinned, trying to make it look scientific. "Glad to be aboard, Captain."

Gradually I settled into shipboard routine, bluffing mightily as I went. Actually, it wasn't too hard. The Exploratory Corps has been dealt with pretty frequently in adventure fiction, and from the novels I'd read I had a fair knowledge of shipboard routine and the like. Of course, I didn't know a thing about ecology, but from my readings in the ship's tape-library, I slowly acquired a working knowledge of my subject.

All that mattered was that I had gotten off Velliran alive. I didn't know who had framed me or why, nor did I think at the time that I'd ever find out, but all that was behind me. I had been put in a situation where it was get offworld or else, and no time to argue about the rights and wrongs and moral undertones of the thing.

It was a three-week journey—the first two days in standard ion drive, then, when we were clear of the Pollux system, the conversion and wrenching screech into hyperdrive. Three weeks in the nothingness of warp, as the ship gulped up space.

Then we were out of our galaxy altogether, and into the Andromeda cluster. It hung all around, bright strange starry dots against the black field of space. In the first few minutes after we emerged from warp, I peered out the viewplate, looking at the immensity of stars.

I was thinking that the universe was appallingly big. Here we were, exploring a galaxy the size of our own—and, on and on through the endless night, there lay galaxy after galaxy, millions of them, each with its thousand billion stars or so. Man could send out Exploratory Teams from here to the end of time and probably not have a chance to touch down on each world of space as much as once.

The autopilot homed in on the arbitrarily named System A, a group of eleven worlds revolving around a bright young yellow main sequence sun. We'd spend our next six months in System A, and probably not even do that job thoroughly. Near-infinite worlds, near-infinite life forms—

I realized I had been developing a pretty provincial attitude, in my previous life as a prosperous yangskin-exporter on Velliran. The universe was a big place. I was only now getting to appreciate that.

The eleven worlds of Star System A hung outside our viewplate like spinning bright-colored globes. Two of the planets were ringed; one spun so close to the sun that it could not possibly have any form of life; two more, double worlds, revolved about each other in a strange orbit that would require detailed investigation.

But Captain Hendrin selected World Seven of Star System A as our first port of call. We swung into a landing orbit, and as the ship spiraled down, the chemical team studied the atmosphere and reported that it would be breathable.

We landed. The tests were checked and double-checked. It was clear that we could go out without spacesuits. Custom now dictated a lottery; we drew, and I got the short straw.

Captain Hendrin chuckled. "I suppose it's fitting that our ecologist should be the first one out on World Seven. You'll be the first to see the fauna."

I stepped through the lock and out. I was the first to see the fauna, all right. But the fauna saw me, too—and they moved faster than I did.

My nine shipmates were standing around me, looking worried.

"You all right?" Hendrin asked.

"Pretty good. That beast with the teeth took me by surprise. I guess I'd have been down the old alimentary canal by now if the other one hadn't come along."

I flicked some sweat from my forehead and stared at the dark forest. The air was thick, hot, hard to breathe; a sort of sweltering moistness about it made it unpleasant. Far within the thicket of sharp green leaves, I heard a cry: a harsh, croaking, desperate cry.

A death-cry.

"This is a rough, primitive world," said Lazenby. He was the biologist. "It's a young world. Life is cheap here."

Hendrin nodded. "We'd better operate in teams on any explorations," the Captain said. "And go about heavily armed. Wide-beam blasters for everyone. There's no telling what strange beasts are lurking in there."

I was still shaking a little. That sudden encounter with the toothed creature hadn't done my nervous system any good. I said, "Maybe we'd better leave this world, Captain. It's too dangerous for us. We ought to go on to some of the other planets in this system."

Hendrin wheeled around to face me, and I saw all the joviality drain from his face. The *real* Hendrin pocked forth for the first time since I had come aboard. His face was the face of an ascetic; of a man dedicated to his job, ready to perform it no matter what the cost. I felt chilled.

"Markham," he said, "You haven't been with us long, so I can forgive you for that remark. But coming from a member of the Exploratory Corps, and from an ecologist as well, your words shock me. Once an Exploratory Corps ship lands on a planet, it stays there until its job is done. I've operated that way for thirteen years, and I'll keep on operating that way." His voice crackled like a whip. He turned to the other men of the team. "Is there anyone else who feels like leaving now?"

No one spoke.

I nibbled my lip unhappily. Part of me wanted to tell Hendrin that I was no ecologist, no Exploratory Corps man at all, just a fugitive yangskin-exporter who was fleeing a phony murder rap and had used his ship as a handy way out. But I saw that would never do at all. Hendrin was too dedicated to his lofty principles to let me stay at large if he knew the truth. From the expression on his face, I knew he was the sort who would bring me for the duration of the voyage and return me to Velliran when it was all over.

Geoffrey Hallan probably had known that. Well, Hallan was just out for a buck, like the rest of us. I was going to have to keep up the pretense of being an ecologist until Hendrin decided he'd explored World Seven of System A fully enough. It wasn't going to be easy.

Another death-cry sounded in the forest.

"I'm sorry. Captain," I said, making my voice appear humble. "The experience of being suddenly attached—my nerves—"

"Okay Markham," he said. His voice was gruff but sympathetic. "I understand. But no more talking of leaving here until our job is done!"

I forced a grin. "Right, Captain!"

But as I heard the sounds of rending and killing coming from that wild, steaming jungle all around us, I wondered whether I would have been safer back on Velliran.

We began formal full-scale exploration of World Seven an hour later, after a quick briefing aboard ship.

By this time I had soaked up enough of standard exploration procedure to be fairly confident of passing as a genuine Corps man, provided no one studied me too closely. I knew the general routine.

The purpose of the Exploratory Corps was to size up each of the worlds of the universe, of which there were billions, and to file a full report with Central Control back on Earth. Central Control, the vast computer that made existence in a galaxy of a hundred billion people possible, would digest and tape the reports.

We were supposed to bring back, primarily, a yes-no statement on the world's value as a potential Terran colony; a comprehensive report on the planet's natural wealth, its minerals and soil fertility and livestock; a comment on the presence of intelligent life on the world. All this data went into the great hopper of Central Control, and the Exploratory Corps moved ever onward into unexplored regions of space.

My job as ecologist was to study the relationships between animals and their environment on World Seven, and prepare a report indicating how these relationships could be put to use in the event of Earth colonization of the planet: which animals controlled the breeding of which other animals, how the extermination of certain forms of plant life would affect the distribution of life, etc. In a way, it was an easy job; in another way, it was an overpoweringly hard one—because it required me to get out there and explore that jungle.

Which was one thing I had little desire to do. Murray, the cartographer, had it easy: he spent his hours aloft, in the tiny copter the ship carried, mapping out the world. Unless there were monsters of the air, he'd be in no danger.

But me? I was going to have to get a first-hand look at life on World Seven.

I was teamed with Lazenby, the biologist. He was a slim, stoop-shouldered man in his middle forties, mild-mannered, quiet. Just the sort who would spend his life roving from world to world, collecting algae and protozoa. I had been hoping to be matched with Bartlett, the anthropologist—a big, square-built, blocky man who would be of some value in case of trouble. But Bartlett was paired with Dorvin, the chemist, and I drew little Lazenby.

We rode down the ship's elevator together, out of the ship and to the ground. This time, before venturing into the little clearing that surrounded the ship, I looked around in all directions. I wasn't taking chances.

The coast was clear, though. "Come on," I said to Lazenby. "No trouble in sight."

We were armed with stubby blasters, but we were weighted down with note-taking apparatus too, and Lazenby carried a couple dozen collecting bottles slung in a harness around his waist.

The jungle was heavy with moisture: not rain but dew, precipitated straight from the air and beading out on anything and everything, leaves, stones, ground, us. I glanced at my watch. We had arranged to cover as much ground as we could in an hour's time, and then return to the ship.

I kept my ears tuned. I knew this forest was full of strange and probably dangerous creatures, and I wanted to be ready for them.

It didn't take long.

We had been walking for perhaps five minutes when I heard rustling up ahead. I glanced at Lazenby. He was kneeling over a tiny pond, scooping up samples of its water for later bacterial analysis. I said, "Better look sharp. Something's coming."

"Where? I don't hear anything."

"Listen up ahead."

The sound of thrashing vines and splintering saplings came to us—and then, thundering toward us like a runaway express, came an animal. I caught Lazenby's arm and dragged him into the shade of a thick, gnarled tree.

The creature was perhaps twenty feet long, glossy brown in color. It had four legs that terminated in splaying toes, a long, thin neck, an equally long tail at the other end. It weighed perhaps ten tons, and it was moving fast.

It had no head.

At the end of that neck was a jagged slash, and then nothing but welling gouts of blood that pulsed forth with each convulsion of the animal's heart, and squirted out over the trees. The beast was dead, but it was so slow-witted it hadn't realized it.

"We ought to follow it," Lazenby said. "It's bound to drop soon. I'd like to examine it close-up."

I shook my head. "Uh-uh. That boy may be dead, but I'll bet the thing that did it to him will be along any minute now. Let's wait."

I was right.

The animal that appeared moved with almost sickening grace: it slid through the forest as if it were on wheels, gliding along effortlessly. It was ten feet high, standing upright on two tapering legs with two more up beneath its throat. A mouth full of razors yawned at us, and dripped blood. It sped past us and pounced on the headless beast we had seen first, which had stumbled and fallen in the underbrush ahead.

I watched, chilled, as the killer dug its two tiny forepaws deep into the still-quivering flesh of the other, and brought its teeth down for the first bite. I couldn't stand the sight. Before I knew what I was doing, I had the firing stud of my blaster yanked back, and gave the killer full beam.

He sizzled and fried for a second or two before he knew what hit him. Then he reared up from the dead or dying body, came at me, and actually travelled three or four feet before he fell. I finished ashing him and lowered my blaster. I realized I had been shouting incoherently all through it.

Within moments half a thousand tiny creatures had come from nowhere—out of the trees, out from under rocks, up from the pond. They began to feed on the two hulking corpses. The smell of death pervaded the place.

I turned and saw Lazenby staring at me in utter horror. For the first time in minutes, I regained self-control.

"I've never seen anything like that," he said, in a hushed voice.

"The killer? Vicious bastard, wasn't he?"

"No," Lazenby said. He looked pale and uneasy. "I mean *you*. The sadistic joy with which you killed the animal! The cries of hate! Markham, it was horrible!"

"Look here, Lazenby—that animal was a killer. I had to blast him."

"Why?"

That stopped me. I didn't have any answer.

He said, "It had already killed its prey. It hadn't attacked you at all. Your job was to record the feeding process, not to interfere with that damned blaster of yours. But you did."

"I lost my head. Something just broke open inside me and I had to fire. Silly of me," I said.

"Silly? It was downright criminal! For an ecologist to destroy life wantonly when he could've been observing the process of—"

That was when the tree wrapped its arms around Lazenby and lifted him off the ground.

"*Lazenby!*"

He was pinioned by a thick green tendril that had wrapped itself three or four times around his waist. His face was gray ashen; he was ten feet off the ground, and rising. I saw the treetop writhing in anticipation; there was something uncomfortably like a mouth up there.

Carnivorous trees?

"For the love of God, get me out of here!" Lazenby was pleading. I drew my blaster and tried to aim it, but he was kicking and squirming wildly, trying to fight the inexorable lift of that tendril.

"Hold still," I shouted. "I don't want to hit you."

I fired above his head, at the tendril, and missed. I caught a limb of the tree instead. The tree shook convulsively. I fired again, and this time I nailed the tendril squarely.

The tree screamed.

It was a bellowed howl of pain and rage that wrung itself up out of the thick trunk and sounded all over the forest. Lazenby came tumbling down, bouncing from branch to branch. I caught him and broke his fall. The seared-off tendril still clung to his middle, and his face was pale green.

I unwrapped the tendril and flung it to one side. He got up, shakily.

"Thanks," he said hoarsely.

I looked up at the tree, which had resumed its stationery position now. It looked totally innocent. Scowling, I looked at the ground at my feet, as if I expected it to open a fanged mouth and swallow me.

"Let's go back to the ship," I said. "We can explore some other time."

Back in the safety of the ship, I was able to let my tight-strung nerves slacken a little.

Hendrin had been aboard ship, dictating log notes, and he came forward to demand why we had returned so soon. I told him.

"Carnivorous trees?" he repeated. "We'll have to send Grover out for a look at those." Grover was the botanist of the group. "Did you get films of the attack, Markham?"

"I was too busy getting Lazenby out of that tree," I said. "I couldn't think about films."

Hendrin frowned. "Saving Lazenby was important, of course. But you should have taken films. And I hope you don't expect to take the rest of the day off, do you?"

"We're a little shaken up, sir," Lazenby began diffidently. "Some time to rest before we go back out—"

"All right," Hendrin said. "Take half an hour. But don't waste any more time than that. I don't want the schedule chopped up."

We left the Captain, heading for the ship's lounge to have a drink or two before returning to the job outside. "He really means business, doesn't he?" I said.

Lazenby grunted. "It's the right way to run an Exploratory Team. You get the job done, that way."

We had a couple of drinks each, and I saw the color come back into Lazenby's face. He wasn't as ruffled by his narrow escape as I might have expected him to be; he took it more in the line of an occupational hazard, which it was—something that might happen in the course of everyday work.

He turned to me and said, "There was something I was meaning to ask you before that tree got me."

"Shoot."

He paused for a second, then said, squinting up his eyes, "Who are you, Markham? *Really*, I mean."

I put my drink down. "Huh?"

"Don't play innocent." There was a sudden strength behind the watery eyes. "I know damned well you're not Paul Markham of the Exploration Corps. Suppose you tell me just who you *are*."

"Lazenby, has that tree-thing driven you nuts? Of course I'm Markham!"

I'm afraid I wasn't a very good liar. The little biologist smiled wryly. "You're no more of a trained ecologist than I am a circus strongman, *Markham*. You might as well admit it. The real Markham had been in the Corps five years. I don't know him, but I know damned well you aren't any ecologist with five years' field training. The way you blasted down that killer animal before—"

I looked at him coldly. He had me nicely pinpointed. "Suppose I'm not Markham. What of it?"

"Nothing. You saved my life, whoever you are, and I don't intend to turn you in. But it's unusual, to say the least, to have an impostor in an Exploration Team. For my own curiosity, I'd like to know why."

I look a deep breath. "My name is Ree Carpenter. I'm a native of Earth, and I lived on Velliran for eight years. Somebody framed me while your ship was down to pick up the real Markham, and I had to get off planet in a hurry. This was the quickest way."

"And what happened to Markham? The *real* one?"

I shrugged. "A friend of mine was supposed to arrange that he show up late at the spaceport. I don't think they did anything to him."

Lazenby smiled and said, "How much of this am I supposed to believe?"

"As much or as little as you want," I said. "It all happens to be true. I was framed for murder—they accused me of having killed a Vellirani native. It wasn't so. But the evidence made it look that way, and on Velliran, that's enough. So I'm here, on this hellworld."

He was looking at me strangely. "You were accused of killing a Vellirani native?"

"Damned right! I don't know how it was done, but I found myself holding a bloody blade, with a dead Vellirani lying in the street at my toes. I didn't kill him."

Lazenby smiled. "I'm sure you didn't. That reminds me of a very funny story. Remind me to tell it to you some time."

He wouldn't elaborate on that, though I tried to pry it out of him. After a while we decided we had rested enough, and went back outside for another survey of the forest.

Lazenby was very helpful. As we advanced warily, inch by inch, through the sweating jungle, he made occasional comments that were designed to help me in compiling my report, pointed out things that I, as a presumably skilled ecologist, should have noticed, and was generally of assistance. We didn't encounter any other carnivorous trees, or anything else that was really dangerous. But every minute I spent in the jungle of World Seven, I liked the planet less.

There was something *sick* about it—something broodingly rotten. Every manifestation of life shared that characteristic.

"Look here," Lazenby said. He pointed down, at a pool of water perhaps three feet across. There were tiny creatures swimming in it.

"So? A puddle with tadpoles in it."

"Take a look at the tadpoles," he said.

I knelt while he stood guard and peered into that puddle. The "tadpoles" were small dark things about an inch long—with bright little teeth, jagged and sharp. They moved fast, those "tadpoles." And they were busy.

A snakelike creature about twenty inches long lay beneath the muddy water, wriggling slowly—while the tadpoles energetically picked away pieces of its flesh. The snake evidently had taken a shortcut through the puddle, or perhaps he had wanted a bath. But the tadpoles had been lying in wait.

"It's the same everywhere on this planet," I said. "The animals are killers. The plants are killers."

Lazenby nodded. "Life is short and tough, here. You have to be fast to survive, and you need a good pair of teeth."

"It's a vicious world," I said.

"No. Nature isn't vicious, or ugly, or any of the other moralistic tags you're probably getting ready to toss up. That's just life you see down there. And on World Seven life is a tough proposition."

"It's a tough proposition anywhere," I said. "But here it's more obvious."

"Exactly."

I looked down at the hungry little beasts in the puddle and shuddered, "I'm a lousy excuse for a scientist," I said. "I can't be cool and detached in a place like this. Not where even the trees try to eat you. I'd like to get the hell off this planet. There's something filthy about it."

He only smiled. "You don't have the true scientific mind. You aren't detached."

"I won't have to bluff being a scientist for long," I said. "Just till Hendrin decides he's ready to return to civilization. If I'm still alive by then," I said, looking at the quivering fronds of a huge fern nearby. "If this planet doesn't get us all first."

As it happened, not every member of the team seemed to share Lazenby's calm, precise, scientific attitude. That became clear that evening, when we were gathered back aboard the ship to compare notes on the day's work.

Murray, the cartographer, said, "This is the nastiest world I've ever seen."

I snickered. "You see it from a thousand feet up. Go take a walk through the jungle if you want to find out how nasty it can be."

"I did," he said. "I brought the copter down to let Chung, here, study some geological formation. We weren't on the ground ten minutes when a brawl started. Some big blue and red beast the size of a hill came toward us looking mean. But before he got anywhere, three jag-toothed flying creatures came swooping down like dive-bombers on him. Sliced his neck open and had themselves a feast."

"I didn't get to see the formation I was interested in, either," Chung, the geologist who had flown with Murray, said. "We decided not to wait."

"It's the same everywhere," said Grover, the botanist. "I went out to examine that devilish carnivorous tree that nearly swallowed Lazenby."

"Did it perform for you?" Lazenby asked.

"Damned right it did! I had no sooner got there than it lashed out with a tendril and swooped up a hulking deer-like creature. I filmed the whole thing. It wasn't pretty."

Fernandez, the medic, a swarthy heavyset giant, looked up from his brooding silence in the corner and said, "This is no world for a ten-man team. We ought to go on to the next place, and let Earth send a fully armed expedition out here if they're interested. We're risking our lives every time we step outside the ship."

"Yeah," said Bartlett, the brawny antropologist. "We already know this planet isn't suitable for colonization—at least not for another hundred million years or so. Why are we sticking around?"

"Why don't you ask Captain Hendrin that?" Lazenby suggested quietly. He was loyal to Hendrin, I knew. "He seems very interested in giving this world detailed study. And I am too; it's quite a remarkable primitive tropical planet."

Bartlett's eyes blazed. "Remarkable! Remarkable, when every beast in that jungle's waiting to feed on you? I'd like to get moving—to a safe planet."

"What's that, Bartlett?" said a cold voice at the door.

We all turned. It was Captain Hendrin, standing at the entrance, one hand clamping the edge of the bulkhead. "Would you care to repeat that in my presence, Bartlett?"

The husky anthropologist was pale, but he looked squarely at Hendrin and said, "I was expressing the opinion, sir, that possibly we had achieved all we could achieve on this planet and should move on, since it's obviously an unsafe world."

"Oh. I see," Hendrin said in a dead, flat voice. "You didn't hear the little speech I made to Markham when he advanced the same idea, earlier?"

"I heard it. I think it's suicide to stay here. Captain."

"Who else feels this way?" Hendrin demanded. He glared around the cabin. "Chung? Grover? Lazenby?"

"I'm not so happy here," Fernandez admitted quietly. But none of the rest of us spoke up.

At length Hendrin said, "You seem to be in the minority, Bartlett. We'll stay here and do it the way the Corps always does it. This planet will need at least a month's intensive work."

Bartlett smothered down his anger. It required a visible effort.

"Let's have no more talk of leaving," Hendrin said. "Is that understood?"

It was. But it wasn't understood or accepted gracefully, I could see. After Hendrin left, Bartlett and Fernandez had a conversation of low whispers in one corner of the room, and after a while, they called Grover over. I didn't know what was going on, but I could guess they were planning some way of getting Hendrin to change his mind.

In a way, I was a little disillusioned. Only Hendrin and Lazenby, of all these men, was a Corpsman in the sense I was accustomed to from reading the adventure stories. The rest of them were ordinary people like me—scientifically trained, but not particularly anxious to martyr themselves in the name of scientific investigation. This was a bitch of a world; they recognized the fact, and they wanted out, just the same as I did.

That night, the forest howled and hooted at us from sundown to sunup. I spent a good chunk of the night staring out the viewplate at the waiting jungle outside. World Seven had two moons, but they weren't attractive golden spheres like the three of Velliran; they were jagged little rocks that cast a pale white light, old and baleful. In their glimmer, I saw strange wolf-like animals range themselves around the ship and bay their anger, and slinking cat-beasts that slipped among them and fought in the World Seven; the others didn't last long at all.

The next two days saw the pattern spread out and intensify. I learned more about World Seven, and the more I learned the more anxious I was to get offworld fast—and most of my shipmates seemed to feel the same way.

Lazenby and I turned up sights on our rambles through the forest that sickened me—and once even bent the slim biologist's scientific poise. That was the little incident where we came upon a bloated black-and-gray striped mammal lying on its side in a swamp—*her* side, I should say, because the creature was plainly a female.

She looked something like a wart hog, something like a Minervan *brolla*, and something indescribable. She was perhaps eight feet long, and had recently given birth. A little cluster of offspring, small enough to be cute if they weren't so hideous, jostled and pushed at each other in order to suckle.

Seven of the little ones managed to get in on the food supply. Two more were left out in the cold—and, when the seven had fed, mama calmly lifted her massive head and snapped up the two weaklings in a mouthful apiece.

I looked at Lazenby. He hadn't enjoyed that.

"Survival of the fittest," I said acidly. "Mother Nature in action."

He glanced at me for a second, then back at the chop-licking beast in the swamp. "I've never seen a world like this," he said curtly, and began to scribble notes.

That was what World Seven was like. We slogged through the mud and slime and heat, and the more I saw of it the less happy I was about the eventual report I'd be expected to file. The planet was an ecologist's nightmare, an interlocking series of biological dependencies that seemed to have no end. Even with Lazenby's help, I'd never be able to bluff my way through and fool Hendrin.

Somehow we avoided the carnivorous trees and the various toothy killers long enough to make a fairly complete survey of our sector. Work was proceeding on other fronts, too. Murray was preparing his aerial maps, and Chung, flying with him, had given the geology of the planet a thoroughgoing job. Since there was no intelligent life here, anthropologist Bartlett could not function in his specialty, so he teamed with Dorwin the chemist and served as lab assistant. The report was shaping up.

Then Evans, who doubled as radioman and assistant chemist, came back from his hike carrying what was left of botanist Grover.

I didn't get a good look at Grover. I only got half a look, and that was enough. Fernandez, who's a medic and who doesn't get bothered by such sights easily, grabbed up a plastic tarpaulin and wrapped it around the body in a double hurry.

Captain Hendrin appeared, looking grimmer than usual, and glanced around.

"What happened to Grover?"

"He—fell, Captain," Evans said. The radioman licked his lips nervously. "He saw a plant he wanted to examine, and took a couple of steps off the beaten road. Then he yelled and slipped out of sight. It was some sort of trap—it looked like solid ground, but it wasn't. It—I don't know what it was. Whether it was a plant or an animal or what. He screamed a couple of times. I saw something yellow frothing around, and thin little tentacles waving.

He held out his hands. They were red, raw, blistered. "I reached in and yanked him out. Some of the stuff spilled on my hands. It was like acid, sir. Like acid."

Hendrin was silent for a moment. Then he said, "Bartlett, Murray—get a grave dug outside the ship. And make it deep, this planet may have a few ghouls along with its other forms of life."

They shambled off to do the job. We were all pretty stunned at Grover's death—not so much the fact that a man had died, as the *way* he had died. He'd been eaten alive by—what? A pool of protozoa? Who knew?

He was the first human victim of World Seven. The planet's deadly spell was extending to us, now.

Grover's death cast a shadow over the rest of that day. No one went out of the ship after sundown; the moons had risen, and their cold light glittered on the crude grave outside. We spent our time filing reports, transcribing notes, doing anything at all to keep our minds busy.

Later that night, Fernandez came over to where I sat in the ship's study, and tapped me gently on the shoulder. I looked up, startled.

"Markham?"

"What is it?"

"Can you come to my cabin for a minute? I want to talk to you."

I didn't object. I followed the hulking medic up the narrow companionway to his private cabin and we went inside. He clicked the lock closed.

"What's this all about, Fernandez?"

He held up one beefy hand. "Patience, friend. All in good time." Going to his closet, he drew forth a drink flask containing an unmistakably sparkling liquid, and handed it to me, grinning. "Have a drink first."

The stuff was Vellirani whiskey, one of the finest beverages known to the universe. I had missed it. "Where'd you get this?" I asked, as I punctured the drink flask seal and took a sip. "Is it allowed on board?"

"Medicinal purposes," Fernandez said blandly. "A little privilege of my position. Have another drink."

I had another, and two or three more. Then I said, "You didn't invite me here to drink your liquor. What's on your mind, Doc?"

"Hendrin."

"Eh?"

"Grover's death this afternoon could have been avoided—if we'd left this planet yesterday. I don't know how you feel about this, Markham. You're new to the crew. The rest of us have been together a long time, and Grover's death hurt. Hurt hard. You want me to stop talking, or should we go on?"

"Go on," I said.

"Okay. You may or may not know the clause in the Corps charter that refers to replacement of superior officer when he no longer is capable of commanding ship."

"I'm familiar with it." I saw now what Fernandez was driving at. "I'm with you so far," I said. "Keep talking."

"Some of us—Bartlett, Murray, myself, mainly—have come to the conclusion that remaining here is not in the best interest of the group's common safety. We're not equipped for a world like this, and it's suicide to keep wandering around on foot in that jungle. This ought to be a three-ship team, with land-crawlers and heavy artillery. You were the first one of us to be attacked by native wildlife. You know what it's like.

"In my position as medic, I can issue an opinion that Hendrin is temporarily insane. It'll stand up anywhere in the galaxy. We'll remove him from command, put him down below where he can't interfere, and get off World Seven. But I won't issue the opinion unless I have a majority behind me. That's why I have to know where you stand, Markham."

I frowned. "You're proposing mutiny, in other words?"

"No. Legal removal of a temporarily insane commander is not mutiny. And it'll mean the deaths of all of us if we stay here the full period. Well, Markham? Are you with us?"

Grinning, I said, "What do you think? I like to stay alive just as much as the next man."

I had a few more drinks and left Fernandez' cabin, and so far as I knew the mutiny remained in abeyance for the next day or two. Perhaps Fernandez was waiting until he had a unanimous backing behind him; I didn't know. So far as I knew four of the eight crewmen were in favor of deposing Hendrin—Fernandez, Murray, Bartlett, and myself. Only one—Lazenby—seemed to prefer remaining on World Seven to complete the observation. The other three, Chung, Evans, and Dorwin, had made no definite statement, at least not to me, but I was fairly certain where their sympathies lay. None of them was the deep-down dedicated type that would vote to remain on a suicide world like this one.

But nothing happened, during the next day. I saw little of Captain Hendrin, and what little I did see I didn't like: he was dour, grim, and stern, as if he expected what was brewing and was determined to squash it the moment it started.

For some reason, the field pairings were switched around the next day. It seemed that Chung wanted to investigate the geology of our region more closely, and had requested that he be teamed with someone who had been working in the area. I was paired with him; Lazenby was shifted over to work with Bartlett, and Murray did his stint in the copter with Dorwin. With the death of Grover, the balance of the teams was disrupted; we had always had four-two-man teams out and two men guarding the ship, but now the breakdown was three two-man outfits and three men back at ship.

Chung and I set out on a parallel track to fine-comb the area, and Lazenby and Bartlett roamed out somewhere near us. The forest was so thick there was no way of seeing anyone nearby.

Chung devoted most of his time to rocks and ridges, while I, feeling a little lost without Lazenby, bluffed my way through an ecology tour. Luckily, Chung didn't say much, and I wasn't forced to reveal just how ignorant of my specialty I really was.

We were gone about half an hour when I heard a very human yell echo from the left.

Chung was bent over, studying a quartz outcropping. I said, "You hear that?"

"Sorry, no. Some animal?"

"Animal hell! That sounded like Lazenby, and I'll bet he's in trouble!"

As if to punctuate my mark with an exclamation point, another yell came from the adjoining glade.

"Come on," I said. "Let's see what's going on."

We cut our way blindly through the infuriatingly thick overhang of vines, slashing madly in the direction of the noise. I yelled, "Lazenby! Bartlett! Is there any trouble?"

After a moment Bartlett's voice, quite close, said, "No, no trouble at all."

I hesitated—but then I saw Bartlett dimly veiled by close-packed fern fronds, and decided to see what was up anyway. I stepped through the ferns, followed by Chung.

Bartlett stood there, looking down at the ground. At Lazenby.

The little biologist was lying sprawled grotesquely on his stomach, rigid, corpselike. I felt chilled. That Lazenby, who of all of us had the most vivid interest in searching the forest for its secrets, should meet death this way—

"What happened?" I asked.

Bartlett was very pale. The anthropologist said, "I didn't know. Something sprang at him from the tree up there, and he fell over. I couldn't see what it was."

There was a moment of silence. Then I went white as the "corpse" wriggled, painfully flopped over, and stared at us. I could see the knife wound in his chest.

"That's a lie," Lazenby said in a half-whisper. "It wasn't any animal. Bartlett knifed me ... the way he did the Vellirani native... because I was going to tell you ..."

He slumped, caught at his middle, tensed. His face was a mask of agony. I looked up from him to Bartlett, and now I saw the bloody knife clutched in the anthropologist's powerful hand.

"You had to be nearby?" Bartlett asked bitterly. "You had to get here before he died? You had to hear everything?"

I saw Chung backing away, frightened. "What is this, Bartlett?" I asked in a voice I didn't recognize.

"I killed him. Sure, I killed him. Like I killed a blueskin on Velliran."

"*Why?*"

"I didn't mean to. Never meant to. The native wouldn't answer questions; threatened to report me for unethical practices. Lazenby ... gave me a drug. I used it on you. It stepped your time-perception; I killed the native, put the knife in your hand, left you standing there."

My mouth sagged open. I heard the chittering of the million insects on the forest floor. "You—"

"Me. It didn't have to be you. It could have been anyone; it just happened to be you that came along. And then I saw you join the crew as Markham. Why did it have to be *you?*"

So Bartlett had killed the Vellirani, and planted the weapon on a total stranger—me. Only I had followed him to World Seven. That was the "funny story" Lazenby had enigmatically promised to tell me, someday ... and now, never would.

I stared at Bartlett across Lazenby's stiffening body. And then Bartlett leaped.

The knife went high, but my hands were quick. I slapped his wrist, deflecting the aim outward, and clamped my other hand down before he could compensate. I twisted; the knife fell.

"Get help, Chung! He's out of his mind!" I managed to yell. Bartlett, weaponless, pummeled me back against a tree. I caught a freezing glimpse of some forest creature crawling out to feed on Lazenby's body. I blocked Bartlett's fists as well as I could, landed a cross to the chin, followed up my advantage with a heavy smash to his stomach.

He reeled back, stunned. I hit him again. I wanted to knock him out, to bring him back to the ship, and eventually back to Velliran to clear my name. But it wasn't going to be that way.

He staggered, off balance. I landed another blow and he took three awkward wide falling steps backward—

And the ground gave way.

He sank down with a little terrified gasp, and I saw something yellow and slimy in the ground, and fifty shiny transparent tentacles twine up and wrap around him. Within seconds he was below the surface, and out of sight. The yellow liquid swirled satedly, and then the trap began to close over again.

I stood staring at it, feeling sick. The trap was simple: the fluid at the surface congealed, forming a sticky, fragile surface to which leaves would adhere, creating a seemingly innocent patch of ground that gave way when a foot touched it. And then … it fed.

I shuddered and turned away. Chasing a small striped feeder from Lazenby's body, I shouldered the corpse and sadly made my way back to the ship to announce that World Seven had claimed two more human victims.

As I drew near the ship, I heard a strange sound: the high sucking whine of a blaster being fired. I moved faster, despite the burden on my back.

Then I stepped into the clearing, and saw the ship. Chung lay dead some twenty yards from the ship's elevator, a blaster-hole where his chest should be. A little closer to the ship was Dorwin, his face a crust of ash. The sound of shouting, struggles came from the ship.

Somehow my mind found time to tally the score as I ran toward the ship. Five members of the team were dead; I, the sixth, was out here. That left Hendrin, inside, holding off Fernandez, Evans, and Murray. *Damn* this world anyway, I thought.

I looked up. The hatch opened, and someone tumbled down. Murray. A second later Fernandez' head poked out. "Markham! Where's Bartlett?"

"Dead. What's going on?"

"We sprang the mutiny on Hendrin, but he's holed up in the front now with a blaster. Just Evans and me left inside. You have a gun?"

"Yes," I said.

"Come on up here. But be careful."

I heard a blaster-shot, and Evans came staggering out to fall almost at my feet. That made seven corpses for World Seven, I thought. Nice and neat.

I edged my way toward the fore cabin. The sound of struggle reached me: a fistfight, it seemed like. But I wasn't going to risk anything foolishly. I clung to the cold metal skin of the wall, and went forward step by step.

Then I saw them in the cabin—Hendrin and Fernandez, looking like two wild men, slugging it out with bare fists. Hendrin's blaster lay discarded, on the floor; out of charge most likely. Fernandez turned his head a second and yelled, "Markham! He's unarmed! Help me!"

Hendrin's captain's uniform hung in tatters. I crept around behind him, snaked an arm around his throat, and yanked back. I bolstered my blaster and pinioned him with my other arm.

"Hold still, Captain," I said warningly. "I've got a blaster here."

Hendrin held still. But suddenly, before I knew what was happening, Fernandez grabbed the blaster from my hip and felled Hendrin with a single shot. I let the Captain's body drop, jumped forward, and clamped Fernandez' wrist.

But I didn't need to. The gun dropped of its own accord, and Fernandez stood there, a giant of a man, brooding foolishly like a small boy over Hendrin's body.

I picked up the gun. "Why'd you kill him? He was under control. Why'd you kill him, Fernandez?"

He looked into my face, and I saw sheer horror in his eyes. "I don't know," he said quietly. "I ... was out of my head. It's all over now." He was shaking convulsively. He found a seat and took it, head in his hands.

"They're all dead," I said. "Every last one but you and me. Some expedition."

Fernandez was sobbing. It hurts to see a man his size sob. He said, "I'm supposed to be a healer, a curer ... and I killed him. I didn't need to. I just killed him."

"You couldn't help it. There was killing in the air. This World could drive anybody crazy."

We worked for four hours straight, and when we got through seven more graves were ranged alongside Grover's. The jungle trumpeted defiant noises at us as we worked.

When it was done, Fernandez looked up at me, an ironic smile on his heavy face. "Well, it's done with now. We know all we need to know about World Seven of Star System A. We can go back now. I'll pilot the ship. But—"

"But what?"

"We're forgetting one thing … according to regulations, the last thing an Exploration Team's supposed to do before it winds up a tour is to name the planet. We haven't done that."

I looked at the jungle—the pestilent steaming hothouse of a jungle—and down at the eight graves. "That's easy," I said. "We'll call it *Death's Planet.*"

Spacerogue

From *Infinity Science Fiction,* November 1958

They were selling a proteus in the public auctionplace at Borlaam, when the stranger wandered by. The stranger's name was Barr Herndon, and he was a tall man, with a proud, lonely face. It was not the face he had been born with, though his own had been equally proud, equally lonely.

He shouldered his way through the crowd. It was a warm and muggy day and a number of idling passersby had stopped to watch the auction. The auctioneer was an Agozlid, squat and bull-voiced, and he held the squirming proteus at arm's length, squeezing it to make it perform.

"Observe, ladies and gentlemen—observe the shapes, the multitude of strange and exciting forms!"

The proteus now had the shape of an eight-limbed star, blue-green at its core, fiery red in each limb. Under the auctioneer's merciless prodding it began to change, slowly, as its molecules lost their hold on one another and sought a new conformation.

A snake, a tree, a hooded deathworm—

The Agozlid grinned triumphantly at the crowd, baring fifty, inch-long yellow teeth. "What am I bid?" he demanded in the guttural Borlaamese language. "Who wants this creature from another sun's world?"

"Five stellors," said a bright-painted Borlaamese noblewoman down front.

"Five stellors! Ridiculous, milady. Who'll begin with fifty? A hundred?"

Barr Herndon squinted for a better view. He had seen proteus life-forms before, and knew something of them. They were strange, tormented creatures, living in agony from the moment they left their native world. Their flesh flowed endlessly from shape to shape, and each change was like the wrenching-apart of limbs by the rack.

"Fifty stellors," chuckled a member of the court of Seigneur Krellig, absolute ruler of the vast world of Borlaam. "Fifty for the proteus."

"Who'll say seventy-five?" pleaded the Agozlid. "I brought this being here at the cost of three lives, slaves worth more than a hundred between them. Will you make me take a loss? Surely five thousand stellors—"

"Seventy-five," said a voice.

"Eighty," came an immediate response.

"One hundred," said the noblewoman in the front row.

The Agozlid's toothy face became mellow as the bidding rose spontaneously. From his vantage-point in the last row, Barr Herndon watched.

The proteus wriggled, attempted to escape, altered itself wildly and pathetically. Herndon's lips compressed tightly. He knew something himself of what suffering meant.

"Two hundred," he said.

"A new voice!" crowed the auctioneer. "A voice from the back row! Five hundred, did you say?"

"Two hundred," Herndon repeated coldly.

"Two-fifty," said a nearby noble promptly.

"And twenty-five more," a hitherto-silent circus proprietor said.

Herndon scowled. Now that he had entered into the situation, he was—as always—fully committed to it. He would not let the others get the proteus.

"Four hundred," he said.

For an instant there was silence in the auction-ring, silence enough for the mocking cry of a low-swooping sea-bird to be clearly audible. Then a quiet voice from the front said, "Four-fifty."

"Five hundred," Herndon said.

"Five-fifty."

Herndon did not immediately reply, and the Agozlid auctioneer craned his stubby neck, looking around for the next bidder. "I've heard five-fifty," he said crooningly. "That's good, but not good enough."

"Six hundred," Herndon said.

"Six-twenty-five."

Herndon fought down a savage impulse to draw his needler and gun down his bidding opponent. Instead he tightened his jaws and said, "Six-fifty."

The proteus squirmed and became a pain-smitten pseudo-cat on the auction stand. The crowd giggled in delight.

"Six-seventy-five," came the voice.

It had become a two-man contest now, with the others merely hanging on for the sport of it, waiting to see which man would weaken first. Herndon eyed his opponent: it was the courtier, a swarthy red-bearded man with blazing eyes and a double row of jewels round his doublet. He looked immeasurably wealthy. There was no hope of outbidding him.

"Seven hundred stellors," Herndon said. He glanced around hurriedly, found a small boy standing nearby, and bent to whisper to him.

"Seven-twenty-five," said the noble.

Herndon whispered, "You see that man down front—the one who just spoke? Run down there and tell him his lady has sent for him, and wants him at once."

He handed the boy a golden five-stellor piece. The boy stared at it popeyed a moment, grinned, and slid through the onlookers toward the front of the ring.

"Nine hundred," Herndon said.

It was considerably more than a proteus might be expected to bring at auction, and possibly more than even the wealthy noble cared to spend. But Herndon was aware there was no way out for the noble except retreat—and he was giving him that avenue.

"Nine hundred is bid," the auctioneer said. "Lord Moaris, will you bid more?"

"I would," Moaris grunted. "But I am summoned, and must leave." He looked blankly angry, but he did not question the boy's message. Herndon noted that down for possible future use. It had been a lucky guess—but Lord Moaris of the Seigneur's court came running when his lady bid him do so.

"Nine hundred is bid," the auctioneer repeated. "Do I hear more? Nine hundred for this fine proteus—who'll make it an even thousand?"

There was no one. Seconds ticked by, and no voice spoke. Herndon waited tensely at the edge of the crowd as the auctioneer chanted, "At nine hundred once, at nine hundred for two, at nine hundred ultimate—

"Yours for nine hundred, friend. Come forward with your cash. And I urge you all to return in ten minutes, when we'll be offering some wonderful pink-hued maidens from Villidon." His hands described a feminine shape in the air with wonderfully obscene gusto.

Herndon came forward. The crowd had begun to dissipate, and the inner ring was deserted as he approached the auctioneer. The proteus had taken on a frog-like shape and sat huddled in on itself like a statue of gelatin.

Herndon eyed the foul-smelling Agozlid and said, "I'm the one who bought the proteus. Who gets my money?"

"I do," croaked the auctioneer. "Nine hundred stellors gold, plus thirty stellors fee, and the beast's yours."

Herndon touched the money-plate at his belt and a coil of hundred-stellor links came popping forth. He counted off nine of them, broke the link, and laid them on the desk before the Agozlid. Then he drew six five-stellor pieces from his pocket and casually dropped them on the desk.

"Let's have your name for the registry," said the auctioneer after counting out the money and testing it with a soliscope.

"Barr Herndon."

"Home-world?"

Herndon paused a moment. "Borlaam."

The Agozlid looked up. "You don't seem much like a Borlaamese to me. Pure-bred?"

"Does it matter to you? I am. I'm from the River Country of Zonnigog, and my money's good."

Painstakingly the Agozlid inscribed his name in the registry. Then he glanced up insolently and said, "Very well, Barr Herndon of Zonnigog. You now own a proteus. You'll be pleased to know that it's already indoctrinated and enslaved."

"This pleases me very much," said Herndon flatly.

The Agozlid handed Herndon a bright planchet of burnished copper with a nine-digit number inscribed on it. "This is the code key. In case you lose your slave, take this to Borlaam Central and they'll trace it for you." He took from his pocket a tiny projector and slid it across the desk. "And here's your resonator. It's tuned to a mesh network installed in the proteus on the submolecular level—it can't change to affect it. You don't like the way the beast behaves, just twitch the resonator. It's essential for proper discipline of slaves."

Herndon accepted the resonator. He said, "The proteus probably knows enough of pain without this instrument. But I'll take it."

The auctioneer seized the proteus and scooped it down from the auction-stand, dropping it next to Herndon. "Here you are, friend. All yours now."

The marketplace had cleared somewhat; a crowd had gathered at the opposite end, where some sort of jewel auction was going on, but as Herndon looked around he saw he had a clear path over the cobbled square to the quay beyond.

He walked a few steps away from the auctioneer's booth. The auctioneer was getting ready for the next segment of his sale, and Herndon caught a glimpse of three frightened-looking naked Villidon girls behind the curtain being readied for display.

He stared seaward. Two hundred yards away was the quay, rimmed by the low sea-wall, and beyond it was the bright green expanse of the Shining Ocean. For an instant his eyes roved beyond the ocean even, to the far continent of Zonnigog where he had been born. Then he looked at the terrified little proteus, halfway through yet another change of shape.

Nine hundred thirty-five stellors, altogether, for this proteus. Herndon scowled bitterly. It was a tremendous sum of money, far more than he could easily have afforded to throw away in one morning— particularly his first day back on Borlaam after his sojourn on the outplanets.

But there had been no help for it. He had allowed himself to be drawn into a situation, and he refused to back off halfway. Not any more, he said to himself, thinking of the burned and gutted Zonnigog village plundered by the gay looters of Seigneur Krellig's army.

"Walk toward the sea-wall," he ordered the proteus.

A half-formed mouth said blurredly, "M-master?"

"You understand me, don't you? Then walk toward the sea-wall. Keep going and don't turn around."

He waited. The proteus formed feet and moved off in an uncertain shuffle over the well-worn cobbles. Nine hundred thirty-five stellors, he thought bitterly.

He drew his needler.

The proteus continued walking, through the marketplace and toward the sea. Someone yelled, "Hey, that thing's going to fall in! We better stop it!"

"I own it," Herndon called coolly. "Keep away from it, if you value your own lives."

He received several puzzled glances, but no one moved. The proteus had almost reached the edge of the sea-wall now, and paused indecisively. Not even the lowest of life-forms will welcome its own self-destruction, no matter what surcease from pain can be attained thereby.

"Mount the wall," Herndon called to it.

Blindly, the proteus obeyed. Herndon's finger caressed the firing-knob of the needler. He watched the proteus atop the low wall, staring down into the murky harbor water, and counted to three.

On the third count he fired. The slim needle-projectile sped brightly across the marketplace and buried itself in the back of the proteus' body. Death must have been instantaneous; the needle contained a nerve-poison that was effective on all known forms of life.

The creature stood frozen on the wall an instant, caught midway between changes, and toppled forward into the water. Herndon nodded and holstered his weapon. He saw people's heads nodding. He heard a murmured comment: "Just paid almost a thousand for it, and first thing he does is shoot it."

It had been a costly morning. Herndon turned as if to walk on, but he found his way blocked by a small wrinkle-faced man who had come out of the jewelry-auction crowd across the way.

"My name is Bollar Benjin," the little prune of a man said. His voice was a harsh croak. His body seemed withered and skimpy. He wore a tight gray tunic of shabby appearance. "I saw what you just did."

"What of it? It's not illegal to dispose of slaves in public," Herndon said.

"Only a special kind of man would do it, though," said Bollar Benjin. "A cruel man—or a foolhardy one. Which are you?"

"Both," Herndon said. "And now, if you'll let me pass—"

"Just one moment." The croaking voice suddenly acquired the snap of a whip. "Talk to me a moment. If you can spare a thousand stellors to buy a slave you kill the next moment, you can spare me a few words."

"What do you want with me?"

"Your services," Benjin said. "I can use a man like you. Are you free and unbonded?"

Herndon thought of the thousand stellors—almost half his wealth—that he had thrown away just now. He thought of the Seigneur Krellig, whom he hated and whom he had vowed so implacably to kill. And he thought of the wrinkled man before him.

"I am unbonded," he said. "But my price is high. What do you want, and what can you offer?"

Benjin smiled obliquely and dipped into a hidden pocket of his tunic. When he drew forth his hand, it was bright with glittering jewels.

"I deal in these," he said. "I can pay well."

The jewels vanished into the pocket again. "If you're interested," Benjin said, "come with me."

Herndon nodded. "I'm interested."

"Follow me, then."

Herndon had been gone from Borlaam for a year, before this day. A year before—the seventeenth of the reign of the Seigneur Krellig—a band of looters had roared through his home village in Zonnigog, destroying and killing. It had been a high score for the Herndon family—his father and mother killed in the first sally, his young brother stolen as a slave, his sister raped and ultimately put to death.

The village had been burned. And only Barr Herndon had escaped, taking with him twenty thousand stellors of his family's fortune and killing eight of the Seigneur's best men before departing.

He had left the system, gone to the nineteen-world complex of Meld, and on Meld XVII he had bought himself a new face that did not bear the tell-tale features of the Zonnigog aristocracy. Gone were the sharp, almost razorlike cheekbones, the pale skin, the wide-set black eyes, the nose jutting from the forehead.

For eight thousand stellors the surgeons of Meld had taken these things away and given him a new face: broad where the other had been high, tan-skinned, narrow-eyed, with a majestic hook of a nose quite unlike any of Zonnigog. He had come back wearing the guise of a spacerogue, a freebooter, an unemployed mercenary willing to sign on to the highest bidder.

The Meldian surgeons had changed his face, but they had not changed his heart. Herndon nurtured the desire for revenge against Krellig—Krellig the implacable, Krellig the invincible, who cowered behind the great stone walls of his fortress for fear of the people's hatred.

Herndon could be patient. But he swore death to Krellig, someday and somehow.

He stood now in a narrow street in the Avenue of Bronze, high in the winding complex of streets that formed the Ancient Quarter of the City of Borlaam, capital of the world of the same name. He had crossed the city silently, not bothering to speak to his gnomelike companion Benjin, brooding only on his inner thoughts and hatred.

Benjin indicated a black metal doorway to their left. "We go in here," he said. He touched his full hand to the metal of the door and it jerked upward and out of sight. He stepped through.

Herndon followed and it was as if a great hand had appeared and wrapped itself about him. He struggled for a moment against the stasis-field.

"Damn you, Benjin, unwrap me!"

The stasis-field held; calmly, the little man bustled about Herndon, removing his needler and his four-chambered blaster and the ceremonial sword at his side.

"Are you weaponless?" Benjin asked. "Yes; you must be. The field subsides."

Herndon scowled. "You might have warned me. When do I get my weapons back?"

"Later," Benjin said. "Restrain your temper and come within."

He was led to an inner room where three men and a woman sat around a wooden conference table. He eyed the foursome curiously. The men comprised an odd mixture: one had the unmistakable stamp of noble birth on his face, while the other two had the coarseness of clay. As for the woman, she was hardly worth a second-look: slovenly, big-breasted, and raw-faced she was undoubtedly the mistress of one or more of the others.

Herndon stepped toward them.

Benjin said, "This is Barr Herndon, free spacerogue. I met him at the market. He had just bought a proteus at auction for nearly a thousand stellors. I watched him order the creature toward the sea-wall and put a needle in its back."

"If he's that free with his money," remarked the noble-seeming one in a rich bass voice, "What need does he have of our employ?"

"Tell us why you killed your slave," Benjin said.

Herndon smiled grimly. "It pleased me to do so."

One of the leather-jerkined commoners shrugged and said, "These spacerogues don't act like normal men. Benjin, I'm not in favor of hiring him."

"We need him," the withered man retorted. To Herndon he said, "Was your act an advertisement, perhaps? To demonstrate your willingness to kill and your indifference to the moral codes of humanity?"

"Yes," Herndon lied. It would only hurt his own cause to explain that he had bought and then killed the proteus only to save it from a century-long life of endless agony. "It pleased me to kill the creature. And it served to draw your attention to me."

Benjin smiled and said, "Good. Let me explain who we are, then. First, names: this is Heitman Oversk, younger brother of the Lord Moaris."

Herndon stared at the noble. A second son—ah, yes. A familiar pattern. Second sons, propertyless but bearing within themselves the spark of nobility, frequently deviated into shadowy paths. "I had the pleasure of outbidding your brother this morning," he said.

"Outbidding Moaris? Impossible!"

Herndon shrugged. "His lady beckoned him in the middle of the auction, and he left. Otherwise the proteus would have been his, and I'd have nine hundred stellors more in my pocket right now."

"These two," Benjin said, indicating the commoners, "are named Dorgel and Razumod. They have full voice in our organization; we know no social distinctions. And this—" gesturing to the girl—"is Marya. She belongs to Dorgel, who does not object to making short-term loans."

Herndon said, "*I* object. But state your business with me, Benjin."

The dried little man said, "Fetch a sample, Razumod."

The burly commoner rose from his seat and moved into a dark corner of the poorly-lit room; he fumbled at a drawer for a moment, then returned with a gem that sparkled brightly even through his fisted fingers. He tossed it down on the table, where it gleamed coldly. Herndon noticed that neither Heitman Oversk nor Dorgel let their glance linger on the jewel more than a second, and he likewise turned his head aside.

"Pick it up," Benjin said.

The jewel was icy-cold. Herndon held it lightly and waited.

"Go ahead," Benjin urged. "Study it. Examine its depths. It's a lovely piece, believe me."

Hesitantly Herndon opened his cupped palm and stared at the gem. It was broad-faceted, with a luminous inner light, and—he gasped—a face, within the stone. A woman's face, languorous, beckoning, seeming to call to him as from the depths of the sea—

Sweat burst out all over him. With an effort he wrenched his gaze from the stone and cocked his arm; a moment later he had hurled the gem with all his force into the farthest corner of the room. He whirled, glared at Benjin, and leaped for him.

"Cheat! Betrayer!"

His hands sought Benjin's throat, but the little man jumped lithely back, and Dorgel and Razumod interposed themselves hastily between them. Herndon stared at Razumod's sweaty bulk a moment and gave ground, quivering with tension.

"You might have warned me," he said.

Benjin smiled apologetically. "It would have ruined the test. We must have strong men in our organization. Oversk, what do you think?"

"He threw down the stone," Heitman Oversk said heavily. "It's a good sign. I think I like him."

"Razumod?"

The commoner gave an assenting grunt, as did Dorgel. Herndon tapped the table and said, "So you're dealing in starstones? And you gave me one without warning? What if I'd succumbed?"

"We would have sold you the stone and let you leave," Benjin said.

"What sort of work would you have me do?"

Heitman Oversk said, "Our trade is to bring starstones in from the Rim worlds where they are mined, and sell them to those who can afford our price. The price, incidentally, is fifty thousand stellors. We pay eight thousand for them, and are responsible for shipping them ourselves. We need a supervisor to control the flow of starstones from our source-world to Borlaam. We can handle the rest at this end."

"It pays well," Benjin added. "Your wage would be five thousand stellors per month, plus a full voice in the organization."

Herndon considered. The starstone trade was the most vicious in the galaxy; the hypnotic gems rapidly became compulsive, and within a year after being exposed to one constantly a man lost his mind and became a drooling idiot, able only to contemplate the kaleidoscopic wonders locked within his stone.

The way to addiction was easy. Only a strong man could voluntarily rip his eyes from a starstone, once he had glimpsed it. Herndon had proven himself strong. The sort of man who could slay a newly-purchased slave could look up from a starstone.

He said, "What are the terms?"

"Full bonding," Benjin said. "Including surgical implantation of a safety device."

"I don't like that."

"We all wear them," Oversk said. "Even myself."

"If all of you wear them," Herndon said, "To whom are you responsible?"

"There is joint control. I handle the outworld contacts; Oversk, here, locates prospective patrons. Dorgel and Razumod are expediters who deal in collection problems and protection. We control each other."

"But there must be somebody who has the master-control for the safety devices," Herndon protested. "Who is that?"

"It rotates from month to month. I hold them this month," Benjin said. "Next month it is Oversk's turn."

Herndon paced agitatedly up and down in the darkened room. It was a tempting offer; five thousand a month could allow him to live on high scales. And Oversk was the brother of Lord Moaris, who was known to be the Seigneur's confidante.

And Lord Moaris' lady controlled Lord Moaris. Herndon saw a pattern taking shape, a pattern that ultimately would put the Seigneur Krellig within his reach.

But he did not care to have his body invaded by safety devices. He knew how those worked; if he were to cheat against the organization, betray it, attempt to leave it without due cause, whoever operated the master-control could reduce him to a groveling pain-racked slave instantly. The safety-device could only be removed by the surgeon who had installed it.

It meant accepting the yoke of this group of starstone smugglers. But there was a higher purpose in mind for Herndon.

"I conditionally accept," he said. "Tell me specifically what my duties will be."

Benjin said, "A consignment of starstones has been mined for us on our source-world, and is soon to be shipped. We want you to travel to that world and accompany the shipment through space to Borlaam. We lose much by way of thievery on each shipment—and there is no way of insuring starstones against loss."

"We know who our thief is," Oversk said. "You would be responsible for finding him in the act and killing him."

"I'm not a murderer," Herndon said quietly.

"You wear the garb of a spacerogue. That doesn't speak of a very high moral caliber," Oversk said.

"Besides, no one mentions murder," said Benjin. "Merely execution. Yes: execution."

Herndon locked his hands together before him and said, "I want two months' salary in advance. I want to see evidence that all of you are wearing neuronic mesh under your skins before I let the surgeon touch me."

"Agreed," Benjin said after a questioning glance around the room.

"Furthermore, I want as an outright gift the sum of nine hundred thirty golden stellors, which I spent this morning to attract the attention of a potential employer."

It was a lie, but there was cause for it. It made sense to establish a dominating relationship with these people as soon as possible. Then later concessions on their part would come easier.

"Agreed," Benjin said again, more reluctantly.

"In that case," Herndon said. "I consider myself in your employ. I'm ready to leave tonight. As soon as the conditions I state have been fulfilled to my complete satisfaction, I will submit my body to the hands of your surgeon."

He bound himself over to the surgeon later that afternoon, after money to the amount of ten thousand, nine hundred thirty golden stellors had been deposited to his name in the Royal Borlaam Bank in Galaxy Square, and after he had seen the neuronic mesh that was embedded in the bodies of Benjin, Oversk, Dorgel, and Razumod. Greater assurance of good faith than this he could not demand; he would have to risk the rest.

The surgeon's quarters were farther along the Avenue of Bronze, in a dilapidated old house that had no doubt been built in Third Empire days. The surgeon himself was a wiry fellow with a puckered ray-slash across one cheek and a foreshortened left leg. A retired pirate-vessel medic, Herndon realized. No one else would perform such an operation unquestioningly. He hoped the man had skill.

The operation itself took an hour, during which time Herndon was under total anesthesia. He woke to find the copper operating-dome lifting off him. He felt no different, even though he knew a network of metal had been blasted into his body on the submolecular level.

"Well? Is it finished?"

"It is," the surgeon said.

Herndon glanced at Benjin. The little man held a glinting metal object on his palm. "This is the control, Herndon. Let me demonstrate."

His hand closed, and instantaneously Herndon felt a bright bolt of pain shiver through the calf of his leg. A twitch of Benjin's finger and an arrow of red heat lanced Herndon's shoulder. Another twitch and a clammy hand seemed to squeeze his heart.

"Enough!" Herndon shouted. He realized he had signed away his liberty forever, if Benjin chose to exert control. But it did not matter to him. He had actually signed away his liberty the day he had vowed to watch the death of the Seigneur Krellig.

Benjin reached into his tunic-pocket and drew forth a little leather portfolio. "Your passport and other travelling necessities," he explained.

"I have my own passport," Herndon said.

Benjin shook his head. "This is a better one. It comes with a visa to Vyapore." To the surgeon he said, "How soon can he travel?"

"Tonight, if necessary."

"Good. Herndon, you'll leave tonight."

The ship was the *Lord Nathiir*, a magnificent super-liner bound on a thousand light-year cruise to the Rim stars. Benjin had arranged for Herndon to travel outward on a luxury liner without cost, as part of the entourage of Lord and Lady Moaris. Oversk had obtained the job for him—second steward to the noble couple, who were vacationing on the Rim pleasure-planet of Molleccogg. Herndon had not objected when he learned that he was to travel in the company of Lord—and especially Lady—Moaris.

The ship was the greatest of the Borlaam luxury fleet. Even on Deck C, in his steward's quarters, Herndon rated a full-grav room with synthik drapery and built-in chromichron; he had never lived so well even at his parents' home, and they had been among the first people of Zonnigog at one time.

His duties called for him to pay court upon the nobles each evening, so that they might seem more resplendent in comparison with the other aristocrats travelling aboard. The Moarises had brought the largest entourage with them, over a hundred people including valets, stewards, cooks, and paid sycophants.

Alone in his room during the hour of blastoff, Herndon studied his papers. A visa to Vyapore. So *that* was where the starstones came from—! Vyapore, the jungle planet of the Rim, where civilization barely had a toehold. No wonder the starstone trade was so difficult to control.

When the ship was safely aloft and the stasis generators had caused the translation into nullspace, Herndon dressed in the formal black-and-red court garments of Lord Moaris' entourage. Then, making his way up the broad companionway, he headed for the Grand Ballroom, where Lord Moaris and his lady were holding court for the first night of the voyage outward.

The ballroom was festooned with ropes of living light. A dancing bear from Albireo XII cavorted clumsily near the entrance as Herndon entered. Borlaamese in uniforms identical to his own stood watch at the door, and nodded to him when he identified himself as Second Steward.

He stood for a moment alone at the threshold of the ballroom, watching the glittering display. The *Lord Nathiir* was the playground of the wealthy, and a goodly number of Borlaam's wealthiest were here, vying with the ranking nobles, the Moarises, for splendor.

Herndon felt a twinge of bitterness. His people were from beyond the sea, but by rank and preference he belonged in the bright lights of the ballroom, not standing here in the garment of a steward. He moved forward.

The noble couple sat on raised thrones at the far end, presiding over a dancing-area in which the grav had been turned down; the couples drifted gracefully, like figures out of fable, feet touching the ground only at intervals.

Herndon recognized Lord Moaris from the auction. A dour, short, thick-bodied individual he was, resplendent in his court robes, with a fierce little beard stained bright red after the current fashion. He sat stiffly upright on his throne, gripping the armrests of the carven chair as if he were afraid of floating off toward the ceiling. In the air before him shimmered the barely perceptible haze of a neutralizer field designed to protect him from the shots of a possible assassin.

By his side sat his Lady, supremely self-possessed and lovely. Herndon was astonished by her youth. No doubt the nobles had means of restoring lost freshness to a woman's face, but there was no way of recreating the youthful bloom so convincingly. The Lady Moaris could not have been more than twenty-three or twenty-five. Her husband was several decades older. It was small wonder that he guarded her so jealously.

She smiled in sweet content at the scene before her. Herndon, too, smiled—at her beauty, and at the use to which he hoped to put it. Her skin was soft pink; a wench of the bath Herndon had met belowdecks had told him she bathed in the cream of the ying-apple twice daily. Her eyes were wide-set and clear, her nose finely made, her lips two red arching curves. She wore a dress studded with emeralds; it flowed from her like light. It was open at the throat, revealing a firm bosom and strong shoulders. She clutched a diamond-crusted scepter in one small hand.

Herndon looked around, found a lady of the court who was unoccupied at the moment, and asked her to dance. They danced silently, gliding in and out of the grav field; Herndon might have found it a pleasant experience, but he was not primarily in search of pleasant experiences now. He was concerned only with attracting the attention of the Lady Moaris.

He was successful. It took time; but he was by far biggest and most conspicuous man of the court assembled there, and it was customary for Lord and Lady to leave their thrones, mingle with their courtiers, even dance with them. Herndon danced with lady after lady, until finally he found himself face to face with the Lady Moaris.

"Will you dance with me?" she asked. Her voice was like liquid gossamer.

Herndon lowered himself in a courtly bow. "I would consider it the greatest of honors, good Lady."

They danced. She was easy to hold; he sensed her warmness near him, and he saw something in her eyes—a distant pinched look of pain, perhaps—that told him all was not well between Lord and Lady.

She said, "I don't recognize you. What's your name?"

"Barr Herndon, milady. Of Zonnigog."

"Zonnigog, indeed! And why have you crossed ten thousand miles of ocean to our city?"

Herndon smiled and gracefully dipped her through a whirling series of pirouettes. "To seek fame and fortune, milady. Zonnigog is well and good to live in, but the place to become known is the City of Borlaam. For this reason I petitioned the Heitman Oversk to have me added to the retinue of the Lord Moaris."

"You know Oversk, then? Well?"

"Not at all well. I served him a while; then I asked to move on."

"And so you go, climbing up and over your former masters, until you scramble up the shoulders of the Lord Moaris to the feet of the Seigneur. Is that the plan?"

She smiled disarmingly, drawing any possible malice from the words she had uttered. Herndon nodded, saying in all sincerity, "I confess this is my aim. Forgive me, though, for saying that there are reasons that might cause me to remain in the service of the Lord Moaris longer than I had originally intended."

A flush crossed her face. She understood. In a half-whisper she said. "You are impertinent. I suppose it comes with good looks and a strong body."

"Thank you, milady."

"I wasn't complimenting you," she said as the dance came to an end and the musicians subsided. "I was criticizing. But what does it matter? Thank you for the dance."

"May I have the pleasure of milady's company once again soon?" Herndon asked.

"You may—but not too soon." She chuckled. "The Lord Moaris is highly possessive. He resents it when I dance twice the same evening with one member of the court."

Sadness darkened Herndon's face a moment. "Very well, then. But I will go to Viewplate A and stare at the stars a while. If the Lady seeks a companion, she will find one there."

She stared at him and flurried away without replying. But Herndon felt a glow of inner satisfaction. The pieces were dropping into place.

The ladder was being constructed. Soon it would bring him to the throneroom of the Seigneur Krellig. Beyond that he would need no plans.

Viewplate A, on the uppermost deck of the vast liner, was reserved for the first-class passengers and the members of their retinues. It was an enormous room, shrouded at all times in darkness, at one end of which a viewscreen opened out onto the glory of the heavens. In nullspace, a hyperbolic section of space was visible at all times, the stars in weird out-of-focus colors forming a breathtaking display. Geometry went awry. A blazing panorama illuminated the room.

The first-class viewing-room was also known to be a trysting-place. There, under cover of darkness, ladies might meet and make love to cooks, lords to scullery-maids. An enterprising rogue with a nolight camera might make a fortune taking a quick shot of such a room and black-mailing his noble victims. But scanners at the door prevented such devices from entering.

Herndon stood staring at the fiery gold and green of the closest stars a while, his back to the door, until he heard a feminine voice whisper to him.

"Barr Herndon?"

He turned. In the darkness it was difficult to tell who spoke; he saw a girl about the height of the Lady Moaris, but in the dimness of the illumination of the plate he could see it was not the Lady. This girl's hair was dull red; the Lady's was golden. And he could see the pale whiteness of this girl's breasts; the Lady's garment, while revealing, had been somewhat more modest.

This was a lady of the court, then, perhaps enamoured of Herndon, perhaps sent by the Lady Moaris as a test or as a messenger.

Herndon said, "I am he. What do you want?"

"I bring a message from—a noble lady," came the answering whisper.

Smiling in the darkness Herndon said, "What does your mistress have to say to me?"

"It cannot be spoken. Hold me in a close embrace as if we were lovers, and I will give you what you need."

Shrugging, Herndon clasped the go-between in his arms with feigned passion. Their lips met; their bodies pressed tight. Herndon felt the girl's hand searching for his, and slipping something cool, metallic into it. Her lips left his, travelled to his ear, and murmured:

"This is her key. Be there in half an hour."

They broke apart. Herndon nodded farewell to her and returned his attention to the glories of the viewplate. He did not glance at the object in his hand, but merely stored it in his pocket.

He counted out fifteen minutes in his mind, then left the viewing-room and emerged on the main deck. The ball was still in progress, but he learned from a guard on duty that the Lord and Lady Moaris had already left for sleep, and that the festivities were soon to end.

Herndon slipped into a washroom and examined the key—for key it was. It was a radionic opener, and imprinted on it were the numbers 1160.

His throat felt suddenly dry. The Lady Moaris was inviting him to her room for the night—or was this a trap, and would Moaris and his court be waiting for him, to gun him down and provide themselves with some amusement? It was not beyond these nobles to arrange such a thing.

But still—he remembered the clearness of her eyes, and the beauty of her face. He could not believe she would be party to such a scheme.

He waited out the remaining fifteen minutes. Then, moving cautiously along the plush corridors, he found his way to Room 1160.

He listened a moment. Silence from within. His heart pounded frantically, irking him; this was his first major test, possibly the gateway to all his hopes, and it irritated him that he felt anxiety.

He touched the tip of the radionic opener to the door. The substance of the door blurred as the energy barricade that composed it was temporarily dissolved. Herndon stepped through quickly. Behind him, the door returned to a state of solidity.

The light of the room was dim. The Lady Moaris awaited him, wearing a gauzy dressing-gown. She smiled tensely at him; she seemed ill-at-ease.

"Would I do otherwise?"

"I—wasn't sure. I'm not in the habit of doing things like this."

Herndon repressed a cynical smile. Such innocence was touching, but highly improbable. He said nothing, and she went on: "I was caught by your face—something harsh and terrible about it struck me. I had to send for you, to know you better."

Ironically Herndon said, "I feel honored. I hadn't expected such an invitation."

"You won't—think it's cheap of me, will you?" she said plaintively. It was hardly the thing Herndon expected from the lips of the noble Lady Moaris. But, as he stared at her slim body revealed beneath the filmy robe, he understood that she might not be so noble after all once the gaudy pretense was stripped away. He saw her as perhaps she truly was: a young girl of great loveliness, married to a domineering nobleman who valued her only for her use in public display. It might explain this bedchamber summons to a Second Steward.

He took her hand. "This is the height of my ambitions, milady. Beyond this room, where can I go?"

But it was empty flattery he spoke. He darkened the room illumination exultantly. *With your conquest, Lady Moaris,* he thought, *do I begin the conquest of the Seigneur Krellig!*

The voyage to Molleccogg lasted a week, absolute time aboard ship. After their night together, Herndon had occasion to see the Lady Moaris only twice more, and on both occasions she averted her eyes from him, regarding him as if he were not there.

It was understandable. But Herndon held a promise from her that she would see him again in three months' time, when she returned to Borlaam; and she had further promised that she would use her influence with her husband to have Herndon invited to the court of the Seigneur.

The *Lord Nathiir* emerged from nullspace without difficulty and was snared by the landing-field of Molleccogg Spacefield. Through the viewing-screen on his own deck, Herndon saw the colorful splendor of the pleasure-planet on which they were about to land, growing larger now that they were in the final spiral.

But he did not intend to remain long on the world of Molleccogg.

He found the Chief Steward and applied for a leave of absence from Lord Moaris' service, without pay.

"But you've just joined us," the Steward protested. "And now you want to leave?"

"Only for a while," Herndon said. "I'll be back on Borlaam before any of you are. I have business to attend to on another world in the Rim area, and then I promise to return to Borlaam at my own expense to rejoin the retinue of the Lord Moaris."

The Chief Steward grumbled and complained, but he could not find anything particularly objectionable in Herndon's intentions, and so finally he reluctantly granted the spacerogue permission to leave Lord Moaris' service temporarily. Herndon packed his court costume and clad himself in his old spacerogue garb; when the great liner ultimately put down in Danzibool Harbor on Molleccogg, Herndon was packed and ready, and he slipped off ship and into the thronged confusion of the terminal.

Bollar Benjin and Heitman Oversk had instructed him most carefully on what he was to do now. He pushed his way past a file of vile-smelling lily-faced green Nnobonn and searched for a ticket-seller's window. He found one, eventually, and produced the pre-paid travel vouchers Benjin had given him.

"I want a one-way passage to Vyapore," he said to the flat-featured, triple-eyed Guzmanno clerk who stared out from back of the wicker screen.

"You need a visa to get to Vyapore," the clerk said. "These visas are issued at infrequent intervals to certified personages. I don't see how you—"

"I have a visa," Herndon snapped, and produced it. The clerk blinked—one-two-three, in sequence—and his pale rose face flushed deep cerise.

"So you do," he remarked at length. "It seems to be in order. Passage will cost you eleven hundred sixty-five stellors of the realm."

"I'll take a third-class ship," Herndon said. "I have a paid voucher for such a voyage."

He handed it across. The clerk studied it for a long moment, then said: "You have planned this very well. I accept the voucher. Here."

Herndon found himself holding one paid passage to Vyapore aboard the freight-ship *Zalasar*.

The *Zalasar* turned out to be very little like the *Lord Nathiir*. It was an old-fashioned unitube ship that rattled when it blasted off, shivered when it translated to nullspace, and quivered all the week-long journey from Molleccogg to Vyapore. It was indeed a third-class ship. Its cargo was hardware: seventy-five thousand dry-strainers, eighty thousand pressors, sixty thousand multiple fuse-screens, guarded by a supercargo team of eight taciturn Ludvuri. Herndon was the only human aboard. Humans did not often get visas to Vyapore.

They reached Vyapore seven days and a half after setting out from Molleccogg. Ground temperature as they disembarked was well over a hundred. Humidity was overpowering. Herndon knew about Vyapore: it held perhaps five hundred humans, one spaceport, infinite varieties of deadly local life, and several thousand non-humans of all descriptions, some of them hiding, some of them doing business, some of them searching for starstones.

Herndon had been well briefed. He knew who his contact was, and he set about meeting him.

There was only one settled city on Vyapore, and because it was the only one it was nameless. Herndon found a room in a cheap boarding-house run by a swine-eared Dombruun, and washed the sweat from his face with the unpleasantly acrid water of the tap.

Then he went downstairs into the bright noonday heat. The stench of rotting vegetation drifted in from the surrounding jungle on a faint breeze. Herndon said at the desk, "I'm looking for a Vonnimooro named Mardlin. Is he around?"

"Over there," said the proprietor, pointing.

Mardlin the Vonnimooro was a small, weaselly-looking creature with the protuberant snout, untrustworthy yellow eyes, and pebbly brown-purple fur of his people. He looked up when Herndon approached. When he spoke, it was in lingua spacia with a whistling, almost obscene inflection.

"You looking for me?"

"It depends," Herndon said. "Are you Mardlin?"

The jackal-creature nodded. Herndon lowered himself to a nearby seat and said in a quiet voice, "Bollar Benjin sent me to meet you. Here are my credentials."

He tossed a milky-white clouded cube on the table between them. Mardlin snatched it up hastily in his leathery claws and nudged the activator. An image of Bollar Benjin appeared in the cloudy depths, and a soft voice said, "Benjin speaking. The bearer of this cube is known to me, and I trust him fully in all matters. You are to do the same. He will accompany you to Borlaam with the consignment of goods."

The voice died away and the image of Benjin vanished. The jackal scowled. He muttered, "If Benjin sent a man to convey his goods, why must I go?"

Herndon shrugged. "He wants both of us to make the trip, it seems. What do you care? You're getting paid, aren't you?"

"And so are you," snapped Mardlin. "It isn't like Benjin to pay two men to do the same job. And I don't like you, Rogue."

"Mutual," Herndon responded heartily. He stood up. "My orders say I'm to take the freighter *Dawnlight* back to Borlaam tomorrow evening. I'll meet you here one hour before to examine the merchandise."

He made one other stop that day. It was a visit with Brennt, a jewelmonger of Vyapore who served as the funnel between the native starstone-miners and Benjin's courier, Mardlin.

Herndon gave his identifying cube to Brennt and said, once he had satisfactorily proven himself, "I'd like to check your books on the last consignment."

Brennt glanced up sharply. "We keep no books on starstones, idiot. What do you want to know?"

Herndon frowned. "We suspect our courier of diverting some of our stones to his own pocket. We have no way of checking up on him, since we can't ask for vouchers of any kind in starstone traffic."

The Vyaporan shrugged. "All couriers steal."

"Starstones cost us eight thousand stellors apiece," Herndon said. "We can't afford to lose any of them, at that price. Tell me how many are being sent in the current shipment."

"I don't remember," Brennt said.

Scowling, Herndon said, "You and Mardlin are probably in league. We have to take his word for what he brings us—but always, three or four of the stones are defective. We believe he buys, say, forty stones from you, pays the three hundred twenty thousand stellors over to you from the account we provide, and then takes three or four from the batch and replaces them with identical but defective stones worth a hundred stellors or so apiece. The profit to him is better than twenty thousand stellors a voyage.

"Or else," Herndon went on, "You deliberately sell him defective stones at eight thousand stellors. But Mardlin's no fool, and neither are we."

"What do you want to know?" the Vyaporan asked.

"How many functional starstones are included in the current consignment?"

Sweat poured down Brennt's face. "Thirty-nine," he said after a long pause.

"And did you also supply Mardlin with some blanks to substitute for any of these thirty-nine?"

"N-no," Brennt said.

"Very good," said Herndon. He smiled. "I'm sorry to have seemed so overbearing, but we had to find out this information. Will you accept my apologies and shake?"

He held out his hand. Brennt eyed it uncertainly, then took it. With a quick inward twitch Herndon jabbed a needle into the base of the other's thumb. The quick-acting truth-drug took only seconds to operate.

"Now," Herndon said, "the preliminaries are over. You understand the details of our earlier conversation. Tell me, now: how many starstones is Mardlin paying you for?"

Brennt's fleshless lips curled angrily, but he was defenseless against the drug. "Thirty-nine," he said.

"At what total cost?"

"Three hundred twelve thousand stellors."

Herndon nodded. "How many of those thirty-nine are actually functional starstones?"

"Thirty-five," Brennt said reluctantly.

"The other four are duds?"

"Yes."

"A sweet little racket. Did you supply Mardlin with the duds?"

"Yes. At two hundred stellors each."

"And what happens to the genuine stones that we pay for but that never arrive on Borlaam?"

Brennt's eyes rolled despairingly. "Mardlin—Mardlin sells them to someone else and pockets the money. I get five hundred stellors per stone for keeping quiet."

"You've kept very quiet today," Herndon said. "Thanks very much for the information, Brennt. I really should kill you—but you're much too valuable to us for that. We'll let you live, but we're changing the terms of our agreement. From now on we pay you only for actual functioning starstones, not for an entire consignment. Do you like that setup?"

"No," Brennt said.

"At least you speak truthfully now. But you're stuck with it. Mardlin is no longer courier, by the way. We can't afford a man of his tastes in our organization. I don't advise you try to make any deals with his successor, whoever he is."

He turned and walked out of the shop.

Herndon knew that Brennt would probably notify Mardlin that the game was up immediately, so the Vonnimooro could attempt to get away. Herndon was not particularly worried about Mardlin escaping, since he had a weapon that would work on the jackal-creature at any distance whatever.

But he had sworn an oath to safeguard the combine's interests, and Herndon was a man of his oath. Mardlin was in possession of thirty-nine starstones for which the combine had paid. He did not want the Vonnimooro to take those with him.

He legged it across town hurriedly to the house where the courier lived while at the Vyapore end of his route. It took him fifteen minutes from Brennt's to Mardlin's—more than enough time for a warning.

Mardlin's room was on the second story. Herndon drew his weapon from his pocket and knocked.

"Mardlin?"

There was no answer. Herndon said, "I know you're in there, jackal. The game's all over. You might as well open the door and let me in."

A needle came whistling through the door, embedded itself against the opposite wall after missing Herndon's head by inches. Herndon stepped out of range and glanced down at the object in his hand.

It was the master-control for the neuronic network installed in Mardlin's body. It was quite carefully gradated; shifting the main switch to six would leave the Vonnimooro in no condition to fire a gun. Thoughtfully Herndon nudged the indicator up through the degrees of pain to six and left it there.

He heard a thud within.

Putting his shoulder to the door, he cracked it open with one quick heave. He stepped inside. Mardlin lay sprawled in the middle of the floor, writhing in pain. Near him, but beyond his reach, lay the needler he had dropped.

A suitcase sat open and half-filled on the bed. He had evidently intended an immediate getaway.

"*Shut ... that ... thing ... off ...*" Mardlin muttered through pain-twisted lips.

"First some information," Herndon said cheerfully. "I just had a talk with Brennt. He says you've been doing some highly improper things with our starstones. Is this true?"

Mardlin quivered on the floor but said nothing. Herndon raised the control a quarter of a notch, intensifying the pain but not yet bringing it to the killing range.

"Is this true?" he repeated.

"Yes—yes! Damn you, shut it off."

"At the time you had the network installed in your body, it was with the understanding that you'd be loyal to the combine and so it would never need to be used. But you took advantage of circumstances and cheated us. Where's the current consignment of stones?"

"... suitcase lining," Mardlin muttered.

"Good," Herndon said. He scooped up the needler, pocketed it, and shut off the master-control switch. The pain subsided in the Vonnimooro's body, and he lay slumped, exhausted, too battered to rise.

Efficiently Herndon ripped away the suitcase lining and found the packet of starstones. He opened it. They were wrapped in shielding tissue that protected any accidental viewer. He counted through them; there were thirty-nine, as Brennt had said.

"Are any of these defective?" he asked.

Mardlin looked up from the floor with eyes yellow with pain and hatred. "Look through them and see."

Instead of answering, Herndon shifted the control switch past six again. Mardlin doubled up, clutching his head with clawlike hands. "Yes! Yes! Six defectives!"

"Which means you sold six good ones for forty-eight thousand stellors, less the three thousand you kicked back to Brennt to keep quiet. So there should be forty-five thousand stellors here that you owe us. Where are they?"

"Dresser drawer … top …"

Herndon found the money, neatly stacked. A second time he shut off the control device, and Mardlin relaxed.

"Okay," Herndon said. "I have the cash and I have the stones. But there must be thousands of stellors that you've previously stolen from us."

"You can have that too! Only don't turn that thing on again, please!"

Shrugging, Herndon said, "There isn't time for me to hunt down the other money you stole from us. But we can ensure against your doing it again."

He fulfilled the final part of Benjin's instructions by turning the control switch to ten, the limit of sentient endurance. Every molecule of Mardlin's wiry body felt unbearable pain; he screamed and danced on the floor, but only for a moment. Nerve cells unable to handle the overload of pain stimuli short-circuited. In seconds, his brain was paralyzed. In less than a minute he was dead, though his tortured limbs still quivered with convulsive post-mortuary jerks.

Herndon shut the device off. He had done his job. He felt neither revulsion nor glee. All this was merely the preamble to what he regarded as his ultimate destiny.

He gathered up jewels and money and walked out.

A month later, he arrived on Borlaam via the freighter *Dawnlight*, as scheduled, and passed through customs without difficulty despite the fact that he was concealing more than three hundred thousand stellors' worth of proscribed starstones on his person.

His first stop was the Avenue of Bronze, where he sought out Benjin and the Heitman Oversk.

He explained crisply and briefly his activities since leaving Borlaam, neglecting to mention the matter of the shipboard romance with the Lady Moaris. While he spoke, both Benjin and Oversk stared eagerly at him, and when he told of intimidating Brennt and killing the treacherous Mardlin they beamed.

Herndon drew the packet of starstones from his cloak and laid them on the wooden table. "There," he said. "The starstones. There were some defectives, as you know, and I've brought back cash for them." He added forty-five thousand stellors to the pile.

Benjin quickly caught up the money and the stones and said, "You've done well, Herndon. Better than we expected. It was a lucky day when you killed that proteus."

"Will you have more work for me?"

Oversk said, "Of course. You'll take Mardlin's place as the courier. Didn't you realize that?"

Herndon had realized it, but it did not please him. He wanted to remain on Borlaam, now that he had made himself known to the Lady Moaris. He wanted to begin his climb toward Krellig. And if he were to shuttle between Vyapore and Borlaam, the all-important advantage he had attained would be lost.

But the Lady Moaris would not be back on Borlaam for nearly two months. He could make one more round-trip for the combine without seriously endangering his position. After that, he would have to find some means of leaving their service. Of course, if they preferred to keep him on they could compel him, but—

"When do I make the next trip?" he asked.

Benjin shrugged lazily. "Tomorrow, next week, next month—who knows? We have plenty of stones on hand. There is no hurry for the next trip. You can take a vacation now, while we sell these."

"No," Herndon said. "I want to leave immediately."

Oversk frowned at him. "Is there some reason for the urgency?"

"I don't want to stay on Borlaam just now," Herndon said. "There's no need for me to explain further. It pleases me to make another trip to Vyapore."

"He's eager," Benjin said. "It's a good sign."

"Mardlin was eager at first too," Oversk remarked balefully.

Herndon was out of his seat and at the nobleman's throat in an instant. His needler grazed the skin of Oversk's adam's-apple.

"If you intend by that comparison to imply—"

Benjin tugged at Herndon's arm, "Sit down, rogue, and relax. The Heitman is tired tonight, and the words slipped out. We trust you. Put the needler away."

Reluctantly Herndon lowered the weapon. Oversk, white-faced despite his tan, fingered his throat where Herndon's weapon had touched it, but said nothing. Herndon regretted his hasty action, and decided not to demand an apology. Oversk still could be useful to him.

"A spacerogue's word is his bond," Herndon said. "I don't intend to cheat you. When can I leave?"

"Tomorrow, if you wish," Benjin said. "We'll cable Brennt to have another shipment ready for you."

This time he travelled to Vyapore aboard a transport freighter, since there were no free tours with noblemen to be had at this season. He reached the jungle world a little less than a month later. Brennt had thirty-two jewels waiting for him. Thirty-two glittering little starstones, each in its protective sheath, each longing to rob some man's mind away with its beckoning dreams.

Herndon gathered them up and arranged a transfer of funds to the amount of two hundred fifty-six thousand stellors. Brennt eyed him bitterly throughout the whole transaction, but it was obvious that the Vyaporan was in fear for his life, and would not dare attempt duplicity. No word was said of Mardlin or his fate.

Bearing his precious burden, Herndon returned to Borlaam aboard a second-class liner out of Diirhav, a neighboring world of some considerable population. It was expensive, but he could not wait for the next freight ship. By the time he returned to Borlaam the Lady Moaris would have been back several weeks. He had promised the Steward he would rejoin Moaris' service, and it was a promise he intended to keep.

It had become winter when he reached Borlaam again with his jewels. The daily sleet-rains sliced across the cities and the plains, showering them with billions of icy knife-like particles. People huddled together, waiting for the wintry cold to end.

Herndon made his way through streets clogged with snow that glistened blue-white in the light of the glinting winter moon, and delivered his gems to Oversk in the Avenue of Bronze. Benjin, he learned, would be back shortly; he was engaged in an important transaction.

Herndon warmed himself by the heat-wall and accepted cup after cup of Oversk's costly Thrucian blue wine to ease his inner chill. The commoner Dorgel entered after a while, followed by Marya and Razumod, and together they examined the new shipment of starstones Herndon had brought back, storing them with the rest of their stock.

At length Benjin entered. The little man was almost numb with cold, but his voice was warm as he said, "The deal is settled, Oversk! Oh—Herndon—you're back, I see. Was it a good trip?"

"Excellent," Herndon said.

Oversk remarked, "You saw the Secretary of State, I suppose. Not Krellig himself."

"Naturally. Would Krellig let someone like me into his presence?"

Herndon's ears rose at the mention of his enemy's name. He said, "What's this about the Seigneur?"

"A little deal," Benjin chortled. "I've been doing some very delicate negotiating while you were away. And I signed the contract today."

"*What* contract?" Herndon demanded.

"We have a royal patron now, it seems. The Seigneur Krellig has gone into the starstone business himself. Not in competition with us, though. He's bought a controlling interest in us."

Herndon felt as if his vital organs had been transmuted to lead. In a congealed voice he said, "And what are the terms of this agreement?"

"Simple. Krellig realized the starstone trade, though illegal, was unstoppable. Rather than alter the legislation and legalize the trade, which would be morally undesirable and which would also tend to lower the price of the gems, he asked the Lord Moaris to place him in contact with some group of smugglers who would work for the Crown. Moaris, naturally, suggested his brother. Oversk preferred to let me handle the negotiations, and for the past month I've been meeting secretly with Krellig's Secretary of State to work out a deal."

"The terms of which are?"

"Krellig guarantees us immunity from prosecution, and at the same time promises to crack down heavily on our competition. He pledges us a starstone monopoly, in other words, and so we'll be able to lower our price to Brennt and jack up the selling price to whatever the traffic will bear. In return for this we turn over eight per cent of our gross profits to the Seigneur, and agree to supply him with six starstones annually, at cost, for the Seigneur to use as gifts to his enemies. Naturally we also transfer our fealties from the combine to the Seigneur himself. He holds our controls to assure loyal service."

Herndon sat as if stunned. His hands felt chilled; coldness rippled through his body. Loyalty to Krellig? His enemy, the person he had sworn to destroy?

The conflict seared through his mind and body. How could he fulfill his earlier vow, now that this diametrically opposed one was in effect? Transfer of fealty was a common thing. By the terms of Benjin's agreement, Herndon now was a sworn vassal of the Seigneur.

If he killed Krellig, that would violate his bond. If he served the Seigneur in all faith, he would break trust with himself and leave home and parents unavenged. It was an impossible dilemma. He quivered with the strain of resolving it.

"The spacerogue doesn't look happy about the deal," Oversk commented. "Or are you sick, Herndon?"

"I'm all right," Herndon said stonily. "It's the cold outside, that's all. Chills a man."

Fealty to Krellig! Behind his back they had sold themselves and him to the man he hated most. Herndon's ethical code was based entirely on the concept of loyalty and unswerving obedience, of the sacred nature of an oath. But now he found himself bound to two mutually exclusive oaths. He was caught between them, racked and drawn apart; the only escape from the torment was death.

He stood up. "Excuse me," he said. "I have an appointment elsewhere in the city. You can reach me at my usual address if you need me for anything."

It took him the better part of a day to get to see the Chief Steward of Moaris Keep and explain to him that he had been unavoidably detained in the far worlds, and that he fully intended to re-enter the Moaris' service and perform his duties loyally and faithfully. After quite some wrangling he was reinstated as one of the Second Stewards, and given functions to carry out in the daily life of the sprawling residence that was Moaris Keep.

Several days passed before he caught as much as a glimpse of the Lady Moaris. That did not surprise him; the Keep covered fifteen acres of Borlaam City, and Lord and Lady occupied private quarters on the uppermost level, the rest of the huge place being devoted to libraries, ballrooms, art galleries, and other housings, for the Moaris treasures, all of these rooms requiring a daily cleaning by the household staff.

He saw her finally as he was passing through the fifth-level hallway in search of the ramp that would take him to his next task, cataloguing the paintings of the sixth-level gallery. He heard a rustle of crinoline first, and then she proceeded down the hall, flanked on each side by copper-colored Toppidan giants and in front and back by glistening-gowned ladies-in-waiting.

The Lady Moaris herself wore sheer garments that limned the shapely lines of her body. Her face was sad; it seemed to Herndon, as he saw her from afar, that she was under some considerable strain.

He stepped to one side to let the procession go past; but she saw him, and glanced quickly to the side at which he stood. Her eyes widened in surprise as she recognized him. He did not dare a smile. He waited until she had moved on, but inwardly he gloated. It was not difficult to read the expression in her eyes.

Later that day, a blind Agozlid servant came up to him and silently handed him a sealed note. Herndon pocketed it, waiting until he was alone in a corridor that was safe from the Lord Moaris' spy-rays. He knew it was safe; the spy-ray in that corridor had been defective, and he himself had removed it that morning, meaning to replace it later in the day.

He broke the seal. The note said simply: *I have waited a month for you. Come to me tonight; M. is to spend the night at the Seigneur's palace. Karla will admit you.*

The photonically-sensitized ink faded from sight in a moment; the paper was blank. He thrust it in a disposal hatch, smiling.

He quietly made his way toward the eleventh-level chamber of the Lady Moaris when the Keep had darkened for the night. Her lady-in-waiting Karla was on duty, the bronze-haired one who had served as go-between aboard the *Lord Nathiir*. Now she wore night robes of translucent silk; a test of his fidelity, no doubt. Herndon carefully kept his eyes from her body and said, "I am expected."

"Yes. Come with me."

It seemed to him that the look in her eyes was a strange one: desire, jealousy, hatred perhaps? But she turned and led him within, down corridors lit only with a faint nightglow. She nudged an opener; a door before him flickered and was momentarily nullified. He stepped through and it returned to the solid state behind him.

The Lady Moaris was waiting.

She wore only the filmiest of gowns, and the longing was evident in her eyes. Herndon said, "Is this safe?"

"It is. Moaris is away at Krellig's." Her lip curled in a bitter scowl. "He spends half his nights there, toying with the Seigneur's cast-off women. The room is sealed against spy-rays. There's no way he can find out you've been here."

"And the girl—Karla? You trust her?"

"As much as I can trust anyone." Her arms sought his shoulders. "My rogue," she murmured. "Why did you leave us at Molleccogg?"

"Business of my own, milady."

"I missed you. Molleccogg was a bore without you."

Herndon smiled gravely. "Believe me, I didn't leave you because I chose to. But I had sworn to carry out duty elsewhere."

She pulled him urgently to her. Herndon felt pity for this lonely noblewoman, first in rank among the ladies of the court, condemned to seek lovers among the stewards and grooms.

"Anything I have is yours," she promised him. "Ask for anything! Anything!"

"There is one prize you might secure for me," Herndon said grimly.

"Name it. The cost doesn't matter."

"There is no cost," Herndon said. "I simply seek an invitation to the court of the Seigneur. You can secure this through your husband. Will you do it for me?"

"Of course," she whispered. She clung to him hungrily. "I'll speak to Moaris—tomorrow."

At the end of the week, Herndon visited the Avenue of Bronze and learned from Bollar Benjin that sales of the starstones proceeded well, that the arrangement under royal patronage was a happy one, and that they would soon be relieved of most of their stock. It would, therefore, be necessary for him to make another trip to Vyapore during the next several weeks. He agreed, but requested an advance of two months' salary.

"I don't see why not," Benjin agreed. "You're a valuable man, and we have the money to spare."

He handed over a draft for ten thousand stellors. Herndon thanked him gravely, promised to contact him when it was time for him to make the journey to Vyapore and left.

That night he departed for Meld XVII, where he sought out the surgeon who had altered his features after his flight from sacked Zonnigog. He requested certain internal modifications. The surgeon was reluctant, saying the operation was a risky one, very difficult, and entailed a fifty per cent chance of total failure, but Herndon was stubborn.

It cost him twenty-five thousand stellors, nearly all the money he had, but he considered the investment a worthy one. He returned to Borlaam the next day. A week had elapsed since his departure.

He presented himself at Moaris Keep, resumed his duties, and once again spent the night with the Lady Moaris. She told him that she had wangled a promise from her husband, and that he was soon to be invited to court. Moaris had not questioned her motives, and she said the invitation was a certainty.

Some days later a message was delivered to him, addressed to Barr Herndon of Zonnigog. It was in the hand of the private secretary to Moaris, and it said that the Lord Moaris had chosen to exert his patronage in favor of Barr Herndon, and that Herndon would be expected to pay his respects to the Seigneur Krellig.

The invitation from the Seigneur came later in the day, borne by a resplendent Toppidan footman, commanding him to present himself at the court reception the following evening, on pain of displeasing the Seigneur. Herndon exulted. He had attained the pinnacle of Borlaamese success, now; he was to be allowed into the presence of the sovereign. This was the culmination of all his planning.

He dressed in the court robes that he had purchased weeks before for just such an event—robes that had cost him more than a thousand stellors, sumptuous with inlaid precious gems and rare metals. He visited a tonsorial parlor and had an artificial beard affixed, in the fashion of many courtiers who disliked growing beards but who desired to wear them at ceremonial state functions. He was bathed and combed, perfumed, and otherwise prepared for his debut at court. He also made certain that the surgical modifications performed on him by the Meldian doctor would be effective when the time came.

The shadows of evening dropped. The moons of Borlaam rose, dancing brightly across the sky. The evening fireworks display cast brilliant light through the winter sky, signifying that this was the birthmonth of Borlaam's Seigneur.

Herndon sent for the carriage he had hired. It arrived, a magnificent four-tube model bright with gilt paint, and he left his shabby dwelling-place. The carriage soared into the night sky; twelve minutes later, it descended in the courtyard of the Grand Palace of Borlaam, that monstrous heap of masonry that glowered down at the capital city from the impregnable vantage-point of the Hill of Fire.

Floodlights illuminated the Grand Palace. Another man might have been stirred by the imposing sight; Herndon merely felt an upwelling of anger. Once his family had lived in a palace too: not of this size, to be sure, for the people of Zonnigog were modest and unpretentious in their desires. But it had been a palace all the same, until the armies of Krellig razed it.

He dismounted from his carriage and presented his invitation to the haughty Seigneurial guards on duty. They admitted him, after checking to see that he carried no concealed weapons, and he was conducted to an antechamber in which he found the Lord Moaris.

"So you're Herndon," Moaris said speculatively. He squinted and tugged at his beard.

Herndon compelled himself to kneel. "I thank you for the honor your Grace bestows upon me this night."

"You needn't thank me," Moaris grunted. "My wife asked for your name to be put on my invitation list. But I suppose you know all that. You look familiar, Herndon. Where have I seen you before?"

Presumably Moaris knew that Herndon had been employed in his own service. But he merely said, "I once had the honor of bidding against you for a captive proteus in the slave market, milord."

A flicker of recognition crossed Moaris' seamed face, and he smiled coldly. "I seem to remember," he said.

A gong sounded.

"We mustn't keep the Seigneur waiting," said Moaris. "Come."

Together, they went forward to the Grand Chamber of the Seigneur of Borlaam.

Moaris entered first, as befitted his rank, and took his place to the left of the monarch, who sat on a raised throne decked with violet and gold. Herndon knew protocol; he knelt immediately.

"Rise," the Seigneur commanded. His voice was a dry whisper, feathery-sounding, barely audible and yet commanding all the same. Herndon rose and stared levelly at Krellig.

The monarch was a tiny man, dried and fleshless; he seemed almost to be a humpback. Two beady, terrifying eyes glittered from a wrinkled, world-weary face. Krellig's lips were thin and bloodless, his nose a savage slash, his chin wedge-shaped.

Herndon let his eyes rove. The hall was huge, as he had expected; vast pillars supported the ceiling, and rows of courtiers flanked the walls. There were women, dozens of them: the Seigneur's mistresses, no doubt.

In the middle of the hall hung suspended something that looked to be a giant cage, completely cloaked in thick draperies of red velvet. Some pet of the Seigneur's probably lurked within: a vicious pet, Herndon theorized, possibly a Villidoni gyrfalcon with honed talons.

"Welcome to the court," the Seigneur murmured. "You are the guest of my friend Moaris, eh?"

"I am, Sire," Herndon said. In the quietness of the hall his voice echoed cracklingly.

"Moaris is to provide us all with some amusement this evening," remarked the monarch. The little man chuckled in anticipatory glee. "We are very grateful to your sponsor, the Lord Moaris, for the pleasure he is to bring us this night."

Herndon frowned. He wondered obscurely whether he was to be the source of amusement. He stood his ground unafraid; before the evening had ended, he himself would be amused at the expense of the others.

"Raise the curtain," Krellig commanded.

Instantly two Toppidan slaves emerged from the corners of the throneroom and jerked simultaneously on heavy cords that controlled the curtain over the cage. Slowly the thick folds of velvet lifted, revealing, as Herndon had suspected, a cage.

There was a girl in the cage.

She hung suspended by her wrists from a bar mounted at the roof of the cage. She was naked; the bar revolved, turning her like an animal trussed to a spit. Herndon froze, not daring to move, staring in sudden astonishment at the slim bare body dangling there.

It was a body he knew well.

The girl in the cage was the Lady Moaris.

Seigneur Krellig smiled benignly; he murmured in a gentle voice, "Moaris, the show is yours and the audience awaits. Don't keep us waiting."

Moaris slowly moved toward the center of the ballroom floor. The marble under his feet was brightly polished and reflected him; his boots thundered as he walked.

He turned, facing Krellig, and said in a calm, controlled tone, "Ladies and gentlemen of the Seigneur's court, I beg leave to transact a little of my domestic business before your eyes. The lady in the cage, as most of you, I believe, are aware, is my wife."

A ripple of hastily-hushed comment was emitted by the men and women of the court. Moaris gestured and a spotlight flashed upward, illuminating the woman in the cage.

Herndon saw that her wrists were cruelly pinioned and that the blue veins stood out in sharp relief against her pale arms. She swung in a small circle as the bar above her turned in its endless rotation. Beads of sweat trickled down her back and down her stomach, and the harsh sobbing intake of her breath was audible in the silence.

Moaris said casually, "My wife has been unfaithful to me. A trusted servant informed me of this not long ago: she has cheated me several times with no less a personage than an obscure member of our household, a groom or a lackey or some other person. When I questioned her, she did not deny this accusation. The Seigneur"—Moaris bowed in a throneward direction—"has granted me permission to chastise her here, to provide me with greater satisfaction and you with a moment of amusement."

Herndon did not move. He watched as Moaris drew from his sash a glittering little heat-gun. Calmly the nobleman adjusted the aperture to minimum. He gestured; a side of the cage slid upward, giving him free target.

He lifted the heat-gun.

Flick!

A bright tongue of flame licked out—and the girl in the cage uttered a little moan as a pencil-thin line was seared across her flanks.

Flick!

Again the beam played across her body. *Flick!* Again. Lines of pain were traced across her breasts, her throat, her knees, her back. She revolved helplessly as Moaris amused himself, carving line after line along her body with the heat-ray. It was only with an effort that Herndon held still. The members of the court chuckled as the Lady Moaris writhed and danced in an effort to escape the inexorable lash of the beam.

Moaris was an expert. He sketched patterns on her body, always taking care that the heat never penetrated below the upper surface of the flesh. It was a form of torture that might endure for hours, until the blood bubbled in her veins and she died.

Herndon realized the Seigneur was peering at him. "Do you find this courtly amusement to your taste, Herndon?" Krellig asked.

"Not quite, Sire." A hum of surprise rose that such a newcomer to the court should dare to contradict the Seigneur. "I would prefer a quicker death for the lady."

"And rob us of our sport?" Krellig asked.

"I would indeed do that," said Herndon. Suddenly he thrust open his jewelled cloak; the Seigneur cowered back as if he expected a weapon to come forth, but Herndon merely touched a plate in his chest, activating the device that the Meldian had implanted in his body. The neuronic mesh functioned in reverse; gathering a charge of deadly force, it sent the bolt surging along Herndon's hand. A bright arc of fire leaped from Herndon's pointing finger and surrounded the girl in the cage.

"Barr!" she screamed, breaking her silence at last, and died.

Again Herndon discharged the neuronic force, and Moaris, his hands singed, dropped his heat-gun.

"Allow me to introduce myself," Herndon said, as Krellig stared white-faced at him and the nobles of the court huddled together in fright. "I am Barr Herndon, son of the First Earl of Zonnigog. Somewhat over a year ago a courtier's jest roused you to lay waste to your fief of Zonnigog and put my family to the sword. I have not forgotten that day."

"Seize him!" Krellig shrieked.

"Anyone who touches me will be blasted with the fire," Herndon said. "Any weapon directed at me will recoil upon its owner. Hold your peace and let me finish.

"I am also Barr Herndon, Second Steward to Lord Moaris, and the lover of the woman who died before you. It must comfort you, Moaris, to know that the man who cuckolded you was no mere groom, but a noble of Zonnigog.

"I am also," Herndon went on, in the dead silence, "Barr Herndon the spacerogue, driven to take up a mercenary's trade by the destruction of my household. In that capacity I became a smuggler of starstones, and"—he bowed—"through an ironic twist, found myself owing a debt of fealty to none other than you, Seigneur.

"I hereby revoke that oath of fealty, Krellig—and for the crime of breaking an oath to my monarch, I sentence myself to death. But also, Krellig, I order a sentence of death upon your head for the wanton attack upon my homeland. And you, Moaris—for your cruel and barbaric treatment of this woman whom you never loved, you must die too.

"And all of you—you onlookers and sycophants, you courtiers and parasites, you too must die. And you, the court clowns, the dancing bears and captive life-forms of far worlds, I will kill you too, as once I killed a slave proteus—not out of hatred, but simply to spare you from further torment."

He paused. The hall was terribly silent; then someone to the right of the throne shouted, "He's crazy! Let's get out of here!"

He dashed for the great doors, which had been closed. Herndon let him get within ten feet of safety, then blasted him down with a discharge of life-force. The mechanism within his body recharged itself, drawing its power from the hatred within him and discharging through his fingertips.

Herndon smiled at Lord Moaris, pale now. He said, "I'll be more generous to you than you to your Lady. A quick death for you."

He hurled a bolt of force at the nobleman. Moaris recoiled, but there was no hiding possible; he stood bathed in light for a moment, and then the charred husk dropped to the ground.

A second bolt raked the crowd of courtiers. A third Herndon aimed at the throne; the costly hangings of the throne-area caught first, and Krellig half-rose before the bolt of force caught him and hurled him back dead.

Herndon stood alone in the middle of the floor. His quest was at its end; he had achieved his vengeance. All but the last: on himself, for having broken the oath he had involuntarily sworn to the Seigneur.

Life held no further meaning for him. It was odious to consider returning to a spacerogue's career, and only death offered absolution from his oaths.

He directed a blazing beam of force at one of the great pillars that supported the throneroom's ceiling. It blackened, then buckled. He blasted apart another of the pillars, and the third.

The roof groaned; the tons of masonry were suddenly without support, after hundreds of years. Herndon waited, and smiled in triumph as the ceiling hurtled down at him.

The Sixth Palace

From *Galaxy*, February 1965

There was the treasure, and there was the guardian of the treasure. And there were the whitening bones of those who had tried in vain to make the treasure their own. Even the bones had taken on a kind of beauty, lying out there by the gate of the treasure vault, under the blazing arch of heavens. The treasure itself lent beauty to everything near it—even the scattered bones, even the grim guardian.

The home of the treasure was a small world that belonged to red Valzar. Hardly more than moonsized, really, with no atmosphere to speak of, a silent, dead little world that spun through darkness a billion miles from its cooling primary. A wayfarer had stopped there once. Where from, where bound? No one knew. He had established a cache there, and there it lay, changeless and eternal, treasure beyond belief, presided over by the faceless metal man who waited with metal patience for his master's return.

There were those who would have the treasure. They came, and were challenged by the guardian, and died.

On another world of the Valzar system, men undiscouraged by the fate of their predecessors dreamed of the hoard, and schemed to possess it. Lipescu was one: a tower of a man, golden beard, fists like hammers, gullet of brass, back as broad as a tree of a thousand years. Bolzano was another: awl-shaped, bright of eye, fast of finger, twig thick, razor sharp. They had no wish to die.

Lipescu's voice was like the rumble of island galaxies in collision. He wrapped himself around a tankard of good black ale and said, "I go tomorrow, Bolzano."

"Is the computer ready?"

"Programmed with everything the beast could ask me," the big man boomed. "There won't be a slip."

"And if there is?" Bolzano asked, peering idly into the blue, oddly pale, strangely meek eyes of the giant. "And if the robot kills you?"

"I've dealt with robots before."

Bolzano laughed. "That plain is littered with bones, friend. Yours will join the rest. Great bulky bones, Lipescu. I can see them now."

"You're a cheerful one, friend."

"I'm realistic."

Lipescu shook his head heavily. "If you were realistic, you wouldn't be in this with me," he said slowly. "Only a dreamer would do such a thing as this." One meaty paw hovered in the air, pounced, caught Bolzano's forearm. The little man winced as bones ground together. Lipescu said, "You won't back out? If I die, you'll make the attempt?"

"Of course I will, you idiot."

"Will you? You're a coward, like all little men. You'll watch me die, and then you'll turn tail and head for another part of the universe as fast as you know how. Won't you?"

"I intend to profit by your mistakes," Bolzano said in a clear, testy voice. "Let go of my arm."

Lipescu released his grip. The little man sank back in his chair, rubbing his arm. He gulped ale. He grinned at his partner and raised his glass.

"To success," Bolzano said.

"Yes. To the treasure."

'And to long life afterward."

"For both of us," the big man boomed.

"Perhaps," said Bolzano. "Perhaps."

He had his doubts. The big man was sly, Ferd Bolzano knew, and that was a good combination, not often found: slyness and size. Yet the risks were great. Bolzano wondered which he preferred—that Lipescu should gain the treasure on his attempt, thus assuring Bolzano of a share without risk, or that Lipescu should die, forcing Bolzano to venture his own life. Which was better, a third of the treasure without hazard, or the whole thing for the highest stake?

Bolzano was a good enough gambler to know the answer to that. Yet there was more than yellowness to the man; in his own way, he longed for the chance to risk his life on the airless treasure world.

Lipescu would go first. That was the agreement. Bolzano had stolen the computer, had turned it over to the big man, and Lipescu would make the initial attempt. If he gained the prize, his was the greater share. If he perished, it was Bolzano's moment next. An odd partnership, odd terms, but Lipescu would have it no other way, and Ferd Bolzano did not argue the point with his beefy compatriot. Lipescu would return with the treasure, or he would not return at all. There would be no middle way, they both were certain.

Bolzano spent an uneasy night. His apartment, in an airy shaft of a building overlooking glittering Lake His, was a comfortable place, and he had little longing to leave it. Lipescu, by preference, lived in the stinking slums beyond the southern shore of the lake, and when the two men parted for the night they went in opposite ways. Bolzano considered bringing a woman home for the night but did not. Instead, he sat moody and wakeful before the televector screen, watching the procession of worlds, peering at the green and gold and ochre planets as they sailed through the emptiness.

Toward dawn, he ran the tape of the treasure. Octave Merlin had made that tape, a hundred years before, as he orbited sixty miles above the surface of the airless little world. Now Merlin's bones bleached on the plain, but the tape had come home and bootlegged copies commanded a high price in hidden markets. His camera's sharp eye had seen much.

There was the gate; there was the guardian. Gleaming, ageless, splendid. The robot stood ten feet high, a square, blocky, black shape topped by the tiny anthropomorphic head dome, featureless and sleek. Behind him the gate, wide open but impassable all the same. And behind him, the treasure, culled from the craftsmanship of a thousand worlds, left here who knew why, untold years ago.

No more mere jewels. No dreary slabs of so-called precious metal. The wealth here was not intrinsic; no vandal would think of melting the treasure into dead ingots. Here were statuettes of spun iron that seemed to move and breathe. Plaques of purest lead, engraved with lathework that dazzled the mind and made the heart hesitate. Cunning intaglios in granite, from the workshops of a frosty world half a parsec from nowhere. A scatter of opals, burning with an inner light, fashioned into artful loops of brightness.

A helix of rainbow-colored wood. A series of interlocking strips of some beast's bone, bent and splayed so that the pattern blurred and perhaps abutted some other dimensional continuum. Cleverly carved shells, one within the other, descending to infinity. Burnished leaves of nameless trees. Polished pebbles from unknown beaches. A dizzying spew of wonders, covering some fifty square yards, sprawled out behind the gate in stunning profusion.

Rough men unschooled in the tenets of esthetics had given their lives to possess the treasure. It took no fancy knowledge to realize the wealth of it, to know that collectors strung from galaxy to galaxy would fight with bared fangs to claim their share. Gold bars did not a treasure make. But these things? Beyond duplication, almost beyond price?

Bolzano was wet with a fever of yearning before the tape had run its course. When it was over, he slumped in his chair, drained, depleted.

Dawn came. The silvery moons fell from the sky. The red sun splashed across the heavens. Bolzano allowed himself the luxury of an hour's sleep.

And then it was time to begin . . .

As a precautionary measure, they left the ship in a parking orbit three miles above the airless world. Past reports were unreliable, and there was no telling how far the robot guardian's power extended. If Lipescu were successful, Bolzano could descend and get him—and the treasure. If Lipescu failed, Bolzano would land and make his own attempt.

The big man looked even bigger, encased in his suit and in the outer casement of a dropshaft. Against his massive chest he wore the computer, an extra brain as lovingly crafted as any object in the treasure hoard. The guardian would ask him questions; the computer would help him answer. And Bolzano would listen. If Lipescu erred, possibly his partner could benefit by knowledge of the error and succeed.

"Can you hear me?" Lipescu asked.

"Perfectly. Go on, get going!"

"What's the hurry? Eager to see me die?"

"Are you that lacking in confidence?"' Bolzano asked. "Do you want me to go first?"

"Fool," Lipescu muttered. "Listen carefully. If I die, I don't want it to be in vain."

"What would it matter to you?"

The bulky figure wheeled around. Bolzano could not see his partner's face, but he knew Lipescu must be scowling. The giant rumbled, "Is life that valuable? Can't I take a risk?"

"For *my* benefit?"

"For mine," Lipescu said. "I'll be coming back."

"Go, then. The robot is waiting."

Lipescu walked to the lock. A moment later he was through and gliding downward, a one-man spaceship, jets flaring beneath his feet. Bolzano settled by the scanner to watch. A televector pickup homed in on Lipescu just as he made his landing, coming down in a blaze of fire. The treasure and its guardian lay about a mile away. Lipescu rid himself of the dropshaft, stepping with giant bounds toward the waiting guardian.

Bolzano watched.

Bolzano listened.

The televector pickup provided full fidelity. It was useful for Bolzano's purposes, and useful, too, for Lipescu's vanity, for the big man wanted his every moment taped for posterity. It was interesting to see Lipescu dwarfed by the guardian. The black faceless robot, squat and motionless, topped the big man by better than three feet.

Lipescu said, "Step aside."

The robot's reply came in surprisingly human tones, though void of any distinguishing accent. "What I guard is not to be plundered."

"I claim them by right," Lipescu said.

"So have many others. But their right did not exist. Nor does yours. I cannot step aside for you."

"Test me," Lipescu said. "See if I have the right or not!"

"Only my master may pass."

"Who is your master? I am your master!"

"My master is he who can command me. And no one can command me who shows ignorance before me."

"Test me, then," Lipescu demanded.

"Death is the penalty for failure."

"Test me."

"The treasure does not belong to you."

"Test me and step aside."

"Your bones will join the rest here."

"Test me," Lipescu said.

Watching from aloft, Bolzano went tense. His thin body drew together like that of a chilled spider. Anything might happen now. The robot might propound riddles, like the Sphinx confronting Oedipus.

It might demand the proofs of mathematical theorems. It might ask the translation of strange words. So they gathered, from their knowledge of what had befallen other men here. And, so it seemed, to give a wrong answer was to earn instant death.

He and Lipescu had ransacked the libraries of the world. They had packed all knowledge, so they hoped, into their computer. It had taken months, even with multi-stage programming. The tiny shining globe of metal on Lipescu's chest contained an infinity of answers to an infinity of questions.

Below, there was long silence as man and robot studied one another. Then the guardian said, "Define latitude."

"Do you mean geographical latitude?" Lipescu asked.

Bolzano congealed with fear. The idiot, asking for a clarification! He would die before he began!

The robot said, "Define latitude."

Lipescu's voice was calm. "The angular distance of a point on a planet's surface north or south of the equator, as measured from the center of the planet."

"Which is more consonant," the robot asked, "the minor third or the major sixth?''

There was a pause. Lipescu was no musician. But the computer would feed him the answer.

"The minor third," Lipescu said.

Without a pause, the robot fired another question. "Name the prime numbers between 5,237 and 7,641."

Bolzano smiled as Lipescu handled the question with ease. So far, so good. The robot had stuck to strictly factual questions, schoolbook stuff, posing no real problems to Lipescu. And after the initial hesitation and quibble over latitude, Lipescu had seemed to grow in confidence from moment to moment. Bolzano squinted at the scanner, looking beyond the robot, through the open gate, to the helter-skelter pile of treasures. He wondered which would fall to his lot when he and Lipescu divided them, two-thirds for Lipescu, the rest for him.

"Name the seven tragic poets of Elifora," the robot said.

"Domiphar, Halionis, Slegg, Hork-Sekan—"

"The fourteen signs of the zodiac as seen from Morneez," the robot demanded.

"The Teeth, the Serpents, the Leaves, the Waterfall, the Blot—"

"What is a pedicel?"

"The stalk of an individual flower of an inflorescence."

"How many years did the Siege of Lamina last?"

"Eight."

"What did the flower cry in the third canto of Somner's *Vehicles*?"

"'I ache, I sob, I whimper, I die,'" Lipescu boomed.

"Distinguish between the stamen and the pistil."

"The stamen is the pollen-producing organ of the flower; the pistil—"

And so it went. Question after question. The robot was not content with the legendary three questions of mythology; it asked a dozen, and then asked more. Lipescu answered perfectly, prompted by the murmuring of the peerless compendium of knowledge strapped to his chest. Bolzano kept careful count: the big man had dealt magnificently with seventeen questions. When would the robot concede defeat? When would it end its grim quiz and step aside?

It asked an eighteenth question, pathetically easy. All it wanted was an exposition of the Pythagorean Theorem. Lipescu did not even need the computer for that. He answered, briefly, concisely, correctly. Bolzano was proud of his burly partner.

Then the robot struck Lipescu dead.

It happened in the flickering of an eyelid. Lipescu's voice had ceased, and he stood there, ready for the next question, but the next question did not come. Rather, a panel in the robot's vaulted belly slid open, and something bright and sinuous lashed out, uncoiling over the ten feet or so that separated guardian from challenger, and sliced Lipescu in half. The bright something slid back out of sight. Lipescu's trunk toppled to one side. His massive legs remained absurdly planted for a moment; then they crumpled, and a spacesuited leg kicked once, and all was still.

Stunned, Bolzano trembled in the loneliness of the cabin, and his lymph turned to water. What had gone wrong? Lipescu had given the proper answer to every question, and yet the robot had slain him. Why? Could the big man possibly have misphrased Pythagoras? No: Bolzano had listened. The answer had been flawless, as had the seventeen that preceded it. Seemingly the robot had lost patience with the game, then. The robot had cheated. Arbitrarily, maliciously, it had lashed out at Lipescu, punishing him for the correct answer.

Did robots cheat, Bolzano wondered? Could they act in malicious spite? No robot he knew was capable of such actions; but this robot was unlike all others.

For a long while, Bolzano remained huddled in the cabin. The temptation was strong to blast free of orbit and head home, treasureless but alive. Yet the treasure called to him. Some suicidal impulse drove him on. Sirenlike, the robot drew him downward.

There had to be a way to make the robot yield, Bolzano thought, as he guided his small ship down the broad barren plain. Using the computer had been a good idea, whose only defect was that it hadn't worked. The records were uncertain, but it appeared that in the past men had died when they finally gave a wrong answer after a series of right ones. Lipescu had given no wrong answers. Yet he too had died. It was inconceivable that the robot understood some relationship of the squares on the hypotenuse and on the other two sides that was different from the relationship Lipescu had expressed

Bolzano wondered what method would work.

He plodded leadenly across the plain toward the gate and its guardian. The germ of an idea formed in him as he walked doggedly on.

He was, he knew, condemned to death by his own greed. Only extreme agility of mind would save him from sharing Lipescu's fate. Ordinary intelligence would not work. Odyssean cleverness was the only salvation.

Bolzano approached the robot. Bones lay everywhere. Lipescu weltered in his own blood. Against that vast dead chest lay the computer, Bolzano knew. But he shrank from reaching for it. He would do without it. He looked away, unwilling to let the sight of Lipescu's severed body interfere with the coolness of his thoughts.

He collected his courage. The robot showed no interest in him.

"Give ground," Bolzano said. "I am here. I come for the treasure."

"Win your right to it."

"What must I do?"

"Demonstrate truth," the robot said. "Reveal inwardness. Display understanding."

"I am ready," said Bolzano.

The robot offered a question. "What is the excretory unit of the vertebrate kidney called?"

Bolzano contemplated. He had no idea. The computer could tell him, but the computer lay strapped to fallen Lipescu. No matter. The robot wanted truth, inwardness, understanding. Lipescu had offered information. Lipescu had perished.

"The frog in the pond," Bolzano said, "utters an azure cry."

There was silence. Bolzano watched the robot's front, waiting for the panel to slide open, the sinuous something to chop him in half.

The robot said, "During the War of Dogs on Vanderveer IX, the embattled colonists drew up thirty-eight dogmas of defiance. Quote the third, the ninth, the twenty-second, and the thirty-fifth."

Bolzano pondered. This was an alien robot, product of unknown hand. How did its maker's mind work? Did it respect knowledge? Did it treasure facts for their own sake? Or did it recognize that information is meaningless, insight a nonlogical process?

Lipescu had been logical. He lay in pieces.

"The mereness of pain," Bolzano responded, "is ineffable and refreshing."

The robot said, "The monastery of Kwaisen was besieged by the soldiers of Oda Nobunaga on the third of April 1582. What words of wisdom did the abbot utter?"

Bolzano spoke quickly and buoyantly. "Eleven, forty-one, elephant, voluminous."

The last word slipped from his lips despite an effort to retrieve it. Elephants were voluminous, he thought. A fatal slip? The robot did not appear to notice.

Sonorously, ponderously, the great machine delivered the next question.

"What is the percentage of oxygen in the atmosphere of Muldonar VII?"

"False witness bears a swift sword," Bolzano replied.

The robot made an odd humming sound. Abruptly it rolled on massive treads, moving some six feet to its left. The gate of the treasure trove stood wide, beckoning.

"You may enter," the robot said.

Bolzano's heart leaped. He had won! He had gained the high prize!

Others had failed, most recently less than an hour before, and their bones glistened on the plain. They had tried to answer the robot, sometimes giving right answers, sometimes giving wrong ones, and they had died. Bolzano lived.

It was a miracle, he thought. Luck? Shrewdness? Some of each, he told himself. He had watched a man give eighteen right answers and die. So the accuracy of the responses did not matter to the robot. What did? Inwardness. Understanding. Truth.

There could be inwardness and understanding and truth in random answers, Bolzano realized. Where earnest striving had failed, mockery had succeeded. He had staked his life on nonsense, and the prize was his.

He staggered forward, into the treasure trove. Even in the light gravity, his feet were like leaden weights. Tension ebbed in him. He knelt among the treasures.

The tapes, the sharp-eyed televector scanners, had not begun to indicate the splendor of what lay here. Bolzano stared in awe and rapture at a tiny disk, no greater in diameter than a man's eye, on which myriad coiling lines writhed and twisted in patterns of rare beauty. He caught his breath, sobbing with the pain of perception as a gleaming marble spire, angled in mysterious swerves, came into view. Here, a bright beetle of some fragile waxy substance rested on a pedestal of yellow jade. There, a tangle of metallic cloth spurted dizzying patterns of luminescence. And over there—and beyond—and there—

The ransom of a universe, Bolzano thought.

It would take many trips to carry all this to his ship. Perhaps it would be better to bring the ship to the hoard, eh? He wondered, though, if he would lose his advantage if he stepped back through the gate. Was it possible that he would have to win entrance all over again? And would the robot accept his answers as willingly the second time?

It was something he would have to chance, Bolzano decided. His nimble mind worked out a plan. He would select a dozen, two dozen of the finest treasures, as much as he could comfortably carry, and take them back to the ship. Then he would lift the ship and set it down next to the gate. If the robot raised objections about his entering, Bolzano would simply depart, taking what he had already secured. There was no point in running undue risks. When he had sold this cargo, and felt pinched for money, he could always return and try to win admission once again. Certainly, no one else would steal the hoard if he abandoned it.

Selection, that was the key now.

Crouching, Bolzano picked through the treasure, choosing for portability and easy marketability. The marble spire? Too big. But the coiling disk, yes, certainly, and the beetle, of course, and this small statuette of dull hue, and the cameos showing scenes no human eye had ever beheld, and this, and this, and this—

His pulse raced. His heart thundered. He saw himself traveling from world to world, vending his wares. Collectors, museums, governments would vie with one another to have these prizes. He would let them bid each object up into the millions before he sold. And, of course, he would keep one or two for himself—or perhaps three or four—souvenirs of this great adventure.

And someday when wealth bored him he would return and face the challenge again. And he would dare the robot to question him, and he would reply with random absurdities, demonstrating his grasp of the fundamental insight that in knowledge there is only hollow merit, and the robot would admit him once more to the treasure trove.

Bolzano rose. He cradled his lovelies in his arms. Carefully, carefully, he thought. Turning, he made his way through the gate.

The robot had not moved. It had shown no interest as Bolzano plundered the hoard. The small man walked calmly past it.

The robot said, "Why have you taken those? What do you want with them?"

Bolzano smiled. Nonchalantly he replied, "I've taken them because they're beautiful. Because I want them. Is there a better reason?"

"No," the robot said, and the panel slid open in its ponderous black chest.

Too late, Bolzano realized that the test had not yet ended, that the robot's question had arisen out of no idle curiosity. And this time he had replied in earnest, speaking in rational terms.

Bolzano shrieked. He saw the brightness coming toward him.

Death followed instantly.

Thesme and the Ghayrog

From *Majipoor Chronicles*, February 1982

For six months now Thesme had lived alone in a hut that she had built with her own hands, in the dense tropical jungle half a dozen miles or so east of Narabal, in a place where the sea breezes did not reach and the heavy humid air clung to everything like a furry shroud. She had never lived by herself before, and at first she wondered how good she was going to be at it; but she had never built a hut before either, and she had done well enough at that, cutting down slender sijaneel saplings, trimming away the golden bark, pushing their slippery sharpened ends into the soft moist ground, lashing them together with vines, finally tying on five enormous blue vramma leaves to make a roof. It was no masterpiece of architecture, but it kept out the rain, and she had no need to worry about cold. Within a month her sijaneel timbers, trimmed though they were, had all taken root and were sprouting leathery new leaves along their upper ends, just below the roof; and the vines that held them were still alive too, sending down fleshy red tendrils that searched for and found the rich fertile soil. So now the house was a living thing, daily becoming more snug and secure as the vines tightened and the sijaneels put on girth, and Thesme loved it. In Narabal nothing stayed dead for long; the air was too warm, the sunlight too bright, the rainfall too copious, and everything quickly transformed itself into something else with the riotous buoyant ease of the tropics.

Solitude was turning out to be easy too. She had needed very much to get away from Narabal, where her life had somehow gone awry: too much confusion, too much inner noise, friends who became strangers, lovers who turned into foes. She was twenty-five years old and needed to stop, to take a long look at everything, to change the rhythm of her days before it shook her to pieces. The jungle was the ideal place for that. She rose early, bathed in a pond that she shared with a sluggish old gromwark and a school of tiny crystalline chichibors, plucked her breakfast from a thokka vine, hiked, read, sang, wrote poems, checked her traps for captured animals, climbed trees and sunbathed in a hammock of vines high overhead, dozed, swam, talked to herself, and went to sleep when the sun went down. In the beginning she thought there would not be enough to do, that she would soon grow bored, but that did not seem to be the case; her days were full and there were always a few projects to save for tomorrow.

At first she expected that she would go into Narabal once a week or so, to buy staple goods, to pick up new books and cubes, to attend an occasional concert or a play, even to visit her family or those of her friends that she still felt like seeing. For a while she actually did go to town fairly often. But it was a sweaty, sticky trek that took half a day, nearly, and as she grew accustomed to her reclusive life she found Narabal ever more jangling, ever more unsettling, with few rewards to compensate for the drawbacks. People there stared at her. She knew they thought she was eccentric, even crazy, always a wild girl and now a peculiar one, living out there by herself and swinging through the treetops. So her visits became more widely spaced. She went only when it was unavoidable. On the day she found the injured Ghayrog she had not been to Narabal for at least five weeks.

She had been roving that morning through a swampy region a few miles northeast of her hut, gathering the sweet yellow fungi known as calimbots. Her sack was almost full and she was thinking of turning back when she spied something strange a few hundred yards away: a creature of some sort with gleaming, metallic-looking gray skin and thick tubular limbs, sprawled awkwardly on the ground below a great sijaneel tree. It reminded her of a predatory reptile her father and brother once had killed in Narabal Channel, a sleek, elongated, slow-moving thing with curved claws and a vast toothy mouth. But as she drew closer she saw that this life-form was vaguely human in construction, with a massive, rounded head, long arms, powerful legs. She thought it might be dead, but it stirred faintly when she approached and said, "I am damaged. I have been stupid and now I am paying for it."

"Can you move your arms and legs?" Thesme asked.

"The arms, yes. One leg is broken, and possibly my back. Will you help me?"

She crouched and studied it closely. It did look reptilian, yes, with shining scales and a smooth, hard body. Its eyes were green and chilly and did not blink at all; its hair was a weird mass of thick black coils that moved of their own accord in a slow writhing; its tongue was a serpent-tongue, bright scarlet, forked, flickering constantly back and forth between the narrow fleshless lips.

"What are you?" she asked.

"A Ghayrog. Do you know of my kind?"

"Of course," she said, though she knew very little, really. All sorts of non-human species had been settling on Majipoor in the past hundred years, a whole menagerie of aliens invited here by the Coronal Lord Melikand because there were not enough humans to fill the planet's immensities. Thesme had heard that there were four-armed ones and two-headed ones and tiny ones with tentacles and these scaly snake-tongued snake-haired ones, but none of the alien beings had yet come as far as Narabal, a town on the edge of nowhere, as distant from civilization as one could get. So this was a Ghayrog, then? A strange creature, she thought, almost human in the shape of its body and yet not at all human in any of its details, a monstrosity, really, a nightmare being, though not especially frightening. She pitied the poor Ghayrog, in fact—a wanderer, doubly lost, far from its home world and far from anything that mattered on Majipoor. And badly hurt, too. What was she going to do with it? Wish it well and abandon it to its fate? Hardly. Go all the way into Narabal and organize a rescue mission? That would take at least two days, assuming anyone cared to help. Bring it back to her hut and nurse it to good health? That seemed the most likely thing to do, but what would happen to her solitude, then, her privacy, and how did one take care of a Ghayrog, anyway, and did she really want the responsibility? And the risk, for that matter: this was an alien being and she had no idea what to expect from it.

It said, "I am Vismaan."

Was that its name, its title, or merely a description of its condition? She did not ask. She said, "I am called Thesme. I live in the jungle an hour's walk from here. How can I help you?"

"Let me brace myself on you while I try to get up. Do you think you are strong enough?"

"Probably."

"You are female, am I right?"

She was wearing only sandals. She smiled and touched her hand lightly to her breasts and loins and said, "Female, yes."

"So I thought. I am male and perhaps too heavy for you."

Male? Between his legs he was as smooth and sexless as a machine. She supposed that Ghayrogs carried their sex somewhere else. And if they were reptiles, her breasts would indicate nothing to him about her sex. Strange, all the same, that he should need to ask.

She knelt beside him, wondering how he was going to rise and walk with a broken back. He put his arm over her shoulders. The touch of his skin against hers startled her: it felt cool, dry, rigid, smooth, as though he wore armor. Yet it was not an unpleasant texture, only odd. A strong odor came from him, swampy and bitter with an undertaste of honey. That she had not noticed it before was hard to understand, for it was pervasive and insistent; she decided she must have been distracted by the unexpectedness of coming upon him. There was no ignoring the odor now that she was aware of it, and at first she found it intensely disagreeable, though within moments it ceased to bother her.

He said, "Try to hold steady. I will push myself up."

Thesme crouched, digging her knees and hands into the soil, and to her amazement he succeeded in drawing himself upward with a peculiar coiling motion, pressing down on her, driving his entire weight for a moment between her shoulder blades in a way that made her gasp. Then he was standing, tottering, clinging to a dangling vine. She made ready to catch him if he fell, but he stayed upright.

"This leg is cracked," he told her. "The back is damaged but not, I think, broken."

"Is the pain very bad?"

"Pain? No, we feel little pain. The problem is functional. The leg will not support me. Can you find me a strong stick?"

She scouted about for something he might use as a crutch and spied, after a moment, the stiff aerial root of a vine dangling out of the forest canopy. The glossy black root was thick but brittle, and she bent it backward and forward until she succeeded in snapping off some two yards of it. Vismaan grasped it firmly, draped his other arm around Thesme, and cautiously put his weight on his uninjured leg. With difficulty he took a step, another, another, dragging the broken leg along. It seemed to Thesme that his body odor had changed: sharper, now, more vinegar, less honey. The strain of walking, no doubt. The pain was probably less trivial than he wanted her to think. But he was managing to keep moving, at any rate.

"How did you hurt yourself?" she asked.

"I climbed this tree to survey the territory just ahead. It did not bear my weight."

He nodded toward the slim shining trunk of the tall sijaneel. The lowest branch, which was at least forty feet above her, was broken and hung down by nothing more than shreds of bark. It amazed her that he had survived a fall from such a height; after a moment she found herself wondering how he had been able to get so high on the slick smooth trunk in the first place.

He said, "My plan is to settle in this area and raise crops. Do you have a farm?"

"In the jungle? No, I just live here."

"With a mate?"

"Alone. I grew up in Narabal, but I needed to get away by myself for a while." They reached the sack of calimbots she had dropped when she first noticed him lying on the ground, and she slung it over her shoulder. "You can stay with me until your leg has healed. But it's going to take all afternoon to get back to my hut this way. Are you sure you're able to walk?"

"I am walking now," he pointed out.

"Tell me when you want to rest."

"In time. Not yet."

Indeed it was nearly half an hour of slow and surely painful hobbling before he asked to halt, and even then he remained standing, leaning against a tree, explaining that he thought it unwise to go through the whole difficult process of lifting himself from the ground a second time. He seemed altogether calm and in relatively little discomfort, although it was impossible to read expression into his unchanging face and unblinking eyes: the constant flickering of his forked tongue was the only indicator of apparent emotion she could see, and she had no idea how to interpret those ceaseless darting movements. After a few minutes they resumed the walk. The slow pace was a burden to her, as was his weight against her shoulder, and she felt her own muscles cramping and protesting as they edged through the jungle. They said little. He seemed preoccupied with the need to exert control over his crippled body, and she concentrated on the route, searching for shortcuts, thinking ahead to avoid streams and dense undergrowth and other obstacles he would not be able to cope with. When they were halfway back to her hut a warm rain began to fall, and after that they were enveloped in hot clammy fog the rest of the way. She was nearly exhausted by the time her little cabin came into view.

"Not quite a palace," she said, "but it's all I need. I built it myself. You can lie down here." She helped him to her zanja-down bed. He sank onto it with a soft hissing sound that was surely relief. "Would you like something to eat?" she asked.

"Not now."

"Or to drink? No? I imagine you just want to get some rest. I'll go outside so you can sleep undisturbed."

"This is not my season of sleep," Vismaan said.

"I don't understand."

"We sleep only one part of the year. Usually in winter."

"And you stay awake all the rest of the time?"

"Yes," he said. "I am finished with this year's sleep. I understand it is different with humans."

"Extremely different," she told him. "I'll leave you to rest by yourself, anyway. You must be terribly tired."

"I would not drive you from your home."

"It's all right," Thesme said, and stepped outside. The rain was beginning again, the familiar, almost comforting rain that fell every few hours all day long. She sprawled out on a bank of dark yielding rubbermoss and let the warm droplets of rain wash the fatigue from her aching back and shoulders.

A houseguest, she thought. And an alien one, no less. Well, why not? The Ghayrog seemed undemanding: cool, aloof, tranquil even in calamity. He was obviously more seriously hurt than he was willing to admit, and even this relatively short journey through the forest had been a struggle for him. There was no way he could walk all the way into Narabal in this condition. Thesme supposed that she could go into town and arrange for someone to come out in a floater to get him, but the idea displeased her. No one knew where she was living and she did not care to lead anyone here, for one thing. And she realized in some confusion that she did not want to give the Ghayrog up, that she wanted to keep him here and nurse him until he had regained his strength. She doubted that anyone else in Narabal would have given shelter to an alien, and that made her feel pleasantly perverse, set apart in still another way from the citizens of her native town. In the past year or two she had heard plenty of muttering about the offworlders who were coming to settle on Majipoor. People feared and disliked the reptilian Ghayrogs and the giant hulking hairy Skandars and the little tricky ones with the many tentacles—Vroons, were they?—and the rest of that bizarre crew, and even though aliens were still unknown in remote Narabal the hostility toward them was already there. Wild and eccentric Thesme, she thought, was just the kind who *would* take in a Ghayrog and pat his fevered brow and give him medicine and soup, or whatever you gave a Ghayrog with a broken leg. She had no real idea of how to care for him, but she did not intend to let that stop her. It occurred to her that she had never taken care of anyone in her life, for somehow there had been neither opportunity nor occasion; she was the youngest in her family and no one had ever allowed her any sort of responsibility, and she had not married or borne children or even kept pets, and during the stormy period of her innumerable turbulent love affairs she had never seen fit to visit any of her lovers while he was ill. Quite likely, she told herself, that was why she was suddenly so determined to keep this Ghayrog at her hut. One of the reasons she had quitted Narabal for the jungle was to live her life in a new way, to break with the uglier traits of the former Thesme.

She decided that in the morning she would go into town, find out if she could what kind of care the Ghayrog needed, and buy such medicines or provisions as seemed appropriate.

After a long while she returned to the hut. Vismaan lay as she had left him, flat on his back with arms stiff against his sides, and he did not seem to be moving at all, except for the perpetual serpentine writhing of his hair. Asleep? After all his talk of needing none? She went to him and peered down at the strange massive figure on her bed. His eyes were open, and she saw them tracking her.

"How do you feel?" she asked.

"Not well. Walking through the forest was more difficult than I realized."

She put her hand to his forehead. His hard scaly skin felt cool. But the absurdity of her gesture made her smile. What was a Ghayrog's normal body temperature? Were they susceptible to fever at all, and if so, how could she tell? They were reptiles, weren't they? Did reptiles run high temperatures when they were sick? Suddenly it all seemed preposterous, this notion of nursing a creature of another world.

He said, "Why do you touch my head?"

"It's what we do when a human is sick. To see if you have a fever. I have no medical instruments here. Do you know what I mean by running a fever?"

"Abnormal body temperature. Yes. Mine is high now."

"Are you in pain?"

"Very little. But my systems are disarranged. Can you bring me some water?"

"Of course. And are you hungry? What sort of things do you normally eat?"

"Meat. Cooked. And fruits and vegetables. And a great deal of water."

She fetched a drink for him. He sat up with difficulty—he seemed much weaker than when he had been hobbling through the jungle; most likely he was suffering a delayed reaction to his injuries—and drained the bowl in three greedy gulps. She watched the furious movements of his forked tongue, fascinated. "More," he said, and she poured a second bowl. Her water jug was nearly empty, and she went outside to fill it at the spring. She plucked a few thokkas from the vine, too, and brought them to him. He held one of the juicy blue-white berries at arm's length, as though that was the only way he could focus his vision properly on it, and rolled it experimentally between two of his fingers. His hands were almost human, Thesme observed, though there were two extra fingers and he had no fingernails, only lateral scaly ridges running along the first two joints.

"What is this fruit called?" he asked.

"Thokka. They grow on a vine all over Narabal. If you like them, I'll bring you as many as you want."

He tasted it cautiously. Then his tongue flickered more rapidly, and he devoured the rest of the berry and held out his hand for another. Now Thesme remembered the reputation of thokkas as aphrodisiacs, but she looked away to hide her grin, and chose not to say anything to him about that. He described himself as male, so the Ghayrogs evidently had sexes, but did they have sex? She had a sudden fanciful image of male Ghayrogs squirting milt from some concealed orifice into tubs into which female Ghayrogs climbed to fertilize themselves. Efficient but not very romantic, she thought, wondering if that was actually how they did it—fertilization at a distant remove, like fishes, like snakes.

She prepared a meal for him of thokkas and fried calimbots and the little many-legged delicate-flavored hiktigans that she netted in the stream. All her wine was gone, but she had lately made a kind of fermented juice from a fat red fruit whose name she did not know, and she gave him some of that. His appetite seemed healthy. Afterward she asked him if she could examine his leg, and he told her she could.

The break was more than midway up, in the widest part of his thigh. Thick though his scaly skin was, it showed some signs of swelling there. Very lightly she put her fingertips to the place and probed. He made a barely audible hiss but otherwise gave no sign that she might be increasing his discomfort. It seemed to her that something was moving inside his thigh. The broken ends of the bone, was it? Did Ghayrogs *have* bones? She knew so little, she thought dismally—about Ghayrogs, about the healing arts, about anything.

"If you were human," she said, "we would use our machines to see the fracture, and we would bring the broken place together and bind it until it knitted. Is it anything like that with your people?"

"The bone will knit of its own," he replied. "I will draw the break together through muscular contraction and hold it until it heals. But I must remain lying down for a few days, so that the leg's own weight does not pull the break apart when I stand. Do you mind if I stay here that long?"

"Stay as long as you like. As long as you need to stay."

"You are very kind."

"I'm going into town tomorrow to pick up supplies. Is there anything you particularly want?"

"Do you have entertainment cubes? Music, books?"

"I have just a few here. I can get more tomorrow."

"Please. The nights will be very long for me as I lie here without sleeping. My people are great consumers of amusement, you know."

"I'll bring whatever I can find," she promised.

She gave him three cubes—a play, a symphony, a color composition—and went about her after-dinner cleaning. Night had fallen, early as always, this close to the equator. She heard a light rainfall beginning again outside. Ordinarily she would read for a while, until it grew too dark, and then lie down to sleep. But tonight everything was different. A mysterious reptilian creature occupied her bed; she would have to put together a new sleeping-place for herself on the floor; and all this conversation, the first she had had in so many weeks, had left her mind buzzing with unaccustomed alertness. Vismaan seemed content with his cubes. She went outside and collected bubblebush leaves, a double armful of them and then another, and strewed them on the floor near the door of her hut. Then, going to the Ghayrog, she asked if she could do anything for him; he answered by a tiny shake of his head, without taking his attention from the cube. She wished him a good night and lay down on her improvised bed. It was comfortable enough, more so than she had expected. But sleep was impossible. She turned this way and that, feeling cramped and stiff, and the presence of the other a few yards away seemed to announce itself by a tangible pulsation in her soul. And there was the Ghayrog's odor, too, pungent and inescapable. Somehow she had ceased noticing it while they ate, but now, with all her nerve-endings tuned to maximum sensitivity as she lay in the dark, she perceived it almost as she would a trumpet-blast unendingly repeated. From time to time she sat up and stared through the darkness at Vismaan, who lay motionless and silent. Then at some point slumber overtook her, for when the sounds of the new morning came to her, the many familiar piping and screeching melodies, and the early light made its way through the door-opening, she awakened into the kind of disorientation that comes often when one has been sleeping soundly in a place that is not one's usual bed. It took her a few moments to collect herself, to remember where she was and why.

He was watching her. "You spent a restless night. My being here disturbs you."

"I'll get used to it. How do you feel?"

"Stiff. Sore. But I am already beginning to mend, I think. I sense the work going on within."

She brought him water and a bowl of fruit. Then she went out into the mild misty dawn and slipped quickly into the pond to bathe. When she returned to the hut the odor hit her with new impact. The contrast between the fresh air of morning and the acrid Ghayrog-flavored atmosphere indoors was severe; yet soon it passed from her awareness once again.

As she dressed she said, "I won't be back from Narabal until nightfall. Will you be all right here by yourself?"

"If you leave food and water within my reach. And something to read."

"There isn't much. I'll bring more back for you. It'll be a quiet day for you, I'm afraid."

"Perhaps there will be a visitor."

"A visitor?" Thesme cried, dismayed. "Who? What sort of visitor? No one comes here! Or do you mean some Ghayrog who was traveling with you and who'll be out looking for you?"

"Oh, no, no. No one was with me. I thought, possibly friends of yours—"

"I have no friends," said Thesme solemnly.

It sounded foolish to her the instant she said it—self-pitying, melodramatic. But the Ghayrog offered no comment, leaving her without a way of retracting it, and to hide her embarrassment she busied herself elaborately in the job of strapping on her pack.

He was silent until she was ready to leave. Then he said, "Is Narabal very beautiful?"

"You haven't seen it?"

"I came down the inland route from Til-omon. In Til-omon they told me how beautiful Narabal is."

"Narabal is nothing," Thesme said. "Shacks. Muddy streets. Vines growing over everything, pulling the buildings apart before they're a year old. They told you that in Til-omon? They were joking with you. The Til-omon people despise Narabal. The towns are rivals, you know—the two main tropical ports. If anyone in Til-omon told you how wonderful Narabal is, he was lying, he was playing games with you."

"But why do that?"

Thesme shrugged. "How would I know? Maybe to get you out of Til-omon faster. Anyway, don't look forward to Narabal. In a thousand years it'll be something, I suppose, but right now it's just a dirty frontier town."

"All the same, I hope to visit it. When my leg is stronger, will you show me Narabal?"

"Of course," she said. "Why not? But you'll be disappointed, I promise you. And now I have to leave. I want to get the walk to town behind me before the hottest part of the day."

As she made her way briskly toward Narabal she envisioned herself turning up in town one of these days with a Ghayrog by her side. How they'd love that, in Narabal! Would she and Vismaan be pelted with rocks and clots of mud? Would people point and snicker, and snub her when she tried to greet them? Probably. There's that crazy Thesme, they would say to each other, bringing aliens to town, running around with snaky Ghayrogs, probably doing all sorts of unnatural things with them out in the jungle. Yes. Yes. Thesme smiled. It might be fun to promenade about Narabal with Vismaan. She would try it as soon as he was capable of making the long trek through the jungle.

The path was no more than a crudely slashed track, blaze-marks on the trees and an occasional cairn, and it was overgrown in many places. But she had grown skilled at jungle travel and she rarely lost her way for long; by late morning she reached the outlying plantations, and soon Narabal itself was in view, straggling up one hillside and down another in a wobbly arc along the seashore.

Thesme had no idea why anyone had wanted to put a city here— halfway around the world from anywhere, the extreme southwest point of Zimroel. It was some idea of Lord Melikand's, the same Coronal who had invited all the aliens to settle on Majipoor, to encourage development on the western continent. In Lord Melikand's time Zimroel had only two cities, both of them terribly isolated, virtual geographic accidents founded in the earliest days of human settlement on Majipoor, before it became apparent that the other continent was going to be the center of Majipoori life. There was Pidruid up in the northwest, with its wondrous climate and its spectacular natural harbor, and there was Piliplok all the way across on the eastern coast, where the hunters of the migratory sea-dragons had their base. But now also there was a little outpost called Ni-moya on one of the big inland rivers, and Til-omon had sprung up on the western coast at the edge of the tropical belt, and evidently some settlement was being founded in the central mountains, and supposedly the Ghayrogs were building a town a thousand miles or so east of Pidruid, and there was Narabal down here in the steaming rainy south, at the tip of the continent with sea all around. If one stood by the shore of Narabal Channel and looked toward the water one felt the terrible weight of the knowledge that at one's back lay thousands of miles of wilderness, and then thousands of miles of ocean, separating one from the continent of Alhanroel where the real cities were. When she was young Thesme had found it frightening to think that she lived in a place so far from the centers of civilized life that it might as well be on some other planet; and other times Aihanroel and its thriving cities seemed merely mythical to her, and Narabal the true center of the universe. She had never been anywhere else, and had no hope of it. Distances were too great. The only town within reasonable reach was Til-omon, but even that was far away, and those who had been there said it was much like Narabal, anyway, only with less rain and the sun standing constantly in the sky like a great boring inquisitive green eye.

In Narabal she felt inquisitive eyes on her wherever she turned: everyone staring, as though she had come to town naked. They all knew who she was—wild Thesme who had run off to the jungle—and they smiled at her and waved and asked her how everything was going, and behind those trivial pleasantries were the eyes, intent and penetrating and hostile, drilling into her, plumbing her for the hidden truths of her life. *Why do you despise us? Why have you withdrawn from us? Why are you sharing your house with a disgusting snake-man?* And she smiled and waved back, and said, "Nice to see you again," and "Everything's just fine," and replied silently to the probing eyes, *I don't hate anybody, I just needed to get away from myself, I'm helping the Ghayrog because it's time I helped someone and he happened to come along.* But they would never understand.

No one was at home at her mother's house. She went to her old room and stuffed her pack with books and cubes, and ransacked the medicine cabinet for drugs that she thought might do Vismaan some good, one to reduce inflammation, one to promote healing, a specific for high fever, and some others—probably all useless to an alien, but worth trying, she supposed. She wandered through the house, which was becoming strange to her even though she had lived in it nearly all her life. Wooden floors instead of strewn leaves—real transparent windows—doors on hinges—a cleanser, an actual mechanical cleanser with knobs and handles!—all those civilized things, the million and one humble little things that humanity had invented so many thousands of years ago on another world, and from which she had blithely walked away to live in her humid little hut with live branches sprouting from its walls—

"Thesme?"

She looked up, taken by surprise. Her sister Mirifaine had come in: her twin, in a manner of speaking, same face, same long thin arms and legs, same straight brown hair, but ten years older, ten years more reconciled to the patterns of her life, a married woman, a mother, a hard worker. Thesme had always found it distressing to look at Mirifaine. It was like looking in a mirror and seeing herself old.

Thesme said, "I needed a few things."

"I was hoping you'd decided to move back home."

"What for?"

Mirifaine began to reply—most likely some standard homily, about resuming normal life, fitting into society and being useful, et cetera, et cetera—but Thesme saw her shift direction while all that was still unspoken, and Mirifaine said finally, "We miss you, love."

"I'm doing what I need to do. It's been good to see you, Mirifaine."

"Won't you at least stay the night? Mother will be back soon—she'd be delighted if you were here for dinner—"

"It's a long walk. I can't spend more time here."

"You look good, you know. Tanned, healthy. I suppose being a hermit agrees with you, Thesme."

"Yes. Very much."

"You don't mind living alone?"

"I adore it," Thesme said. She began to adjust her pack. "How are you, anyway?"

A shrug. "The same. I may go to Til-omon for a while."

"Lucky you."

"I think so. I wouldn't mind getting out of the mildew zone for a little holiday. Holthus has been working up there all month, on some big scheme to build new towns in the mountains—housing for all these aliens that are starting to move in. He wants me to bring the children up, and I think I will."

"Aliens?" Thesme said.

"You don't know about them?"

"Tell me."

"The offworlders that have been living up north are starting to filter this way, now. There's one kind that looks like lizards with human arms and legs that's interested in starting farms in the jungles."

"Ghayrogs."

"Oh, you've heard of them, then? And another kind, all puffy and warty, frog-faced ones with dark gray skins—they do practically all the government jobs now in Pidruid, Holthus says, the customs-inspectors and market clerks and things like that—well, they're being hired down here too, and Holthus and some syndicate of Til-omon people are planning housing for them inland—"

"So that they won't smell up the coastal cities?"

"What? Oh, I suppose that's part of it—nobody knows how they'll fit in here, after all—but really I think it's just that we don't have accommodations for a lot of immigrants in Narabal, and I gather it's the same in Til-omon, and so—"

"Yes, I see," said Thesme. "Well, give everyone my love. I have to begin heading back. I hope you enjoy your holiday in Til-omon."

"Thesme, please—"

"Please what?"

Mirifaine said sadly, "You're so brusque, so distant, so chilly! It's been months since I've seen you, and you barely tolerate my questions, you look at me with such anger—anger for what, Thesme? Have I ever hurt you? Was I ever anything other than loving? Were any of us? You're such a mystery, Thesme."

Thesme knew it was futile to try once more to explain herself. No one understood her, no one ever would, least of all those who said they loved her. Trying to keep her voice gentle, she said, "Call it an overdue adolescent rebellion, Miri. You were all very kind to me. But nothing was working right and I had to run away." She touched her fingertips lightly to her sister's arm. "Maybe I'll be back one of these days."

"I hope so."

"Just don't expect it to happen soon. Say hello to everybody for me," said Thesme, and went out.

She hurried through town, uneasy and tense, afraid of running into her mother or any of her old friends and especially any of her former lovers; and as she carried out her errands she looked about furtively, like a thief, more than once ducking into an alleyway to avoid someone she needed to avoid. The encounter with Mirifaine had been disturbing enough. She had not realized, until Mirifaine had said it, that she had been showing anger; but Miri was right, yes, Thesme could still feel the dull throbbing residue of fury within her. These people, these dreary little people with their little ambitions and their little fears and their little prejudices, going through the little rounds of their meaningless days— they infuriated her. Spilling out over Majipoor like a plague, nibbling at the unmapped forests, staring at the enormous uncrossable ocean, founding ugly muddy towns in the midst of astounding beauty, and never once questioning the purpose of anything—that was the worst of it, their bland unquestioning natures. Did they never once look up at the stars and ask what it all meant, this outward surge of humanity from Old Earth, this replication of the mother world on a thousand conquered planets? Did they care? This could be Old Earth for all it mattered, except that that was a tired drab plundered forgotten husk of a world and this, even after centuries and centuries of human occupation, was still beautiful; but long ago Old Earth had no doubt been as beautiful as Majipoor was now; and in five thousand more years Majipoor would be the same way, with hideous cities stretching for hundreds of miles wherever you looked, and traffic everywhere, and filth in the rivers, and the animals wiped out and the poor cheated Shapeshifters penned up in reservations somewhere, all the old mistakes carried out once again on a virgin world. Thesme boiled with an indignation so fierce it amazed her. She had never known that her quarrel with the world was so cosmic. She had thought it was merely a matter of failed love affairs and raw nerves and muddled personal goals, not this irate dissatisfaction with the entire human universe that had so suddenly overwhelmed her. But the rage held its power in her. She wanted to seize Narabal and push it into the ocean. But she could not do that, she could not change a thing, she could not halt the spread of what they called civilization here; all she could do was flee, back to her jungle, back to the interlacing vines and the steamy foggy air and the shy creatures of the marshes, back to her hut, back to her lame Ghayrog, who was himself part of the tide that was overwhelming the planet but for whom she would care, whom she would even cherish, because the others of her kind disliked or even hated him and so she could use him as one of her ways of distinguishing herself from them, and because also he needed her just now and no one had ever needed her before.

Her head was aching and the muscles of her face had gone rigid, and she realized she was walking with her shoulders hunched, as if to relax them would be to surrender to the way of life that she had repudiated. As swiftly as she could, she escaped once again from Narabal; but it was not until she had been on the jungle trail for two hours, and the last outskirts of the town were well behind her, that she began to feel the tensions ebbing. She paused at a little lake she knew and stripped and soaked herself in its cool depths to rid herself of the last taint of town, and then, with her going-to-town clothes slung casually over her shoulder, she marched naked through the jungle to her hut.

Vismaan lay in bed and did not seem to have moved at all while she was gone. "Are you feeling better?" she asked. "Were you able to manage by yourself?"

"It was a very quiet day. There is somewhat more of a swelling in my leg."

"Let me see."

She probed it cautiously. It *did* seem puffier, and he pulled away slightly as she touched him, which probably meant that there was real trouble in there, if the Ghayrog sense of pain was as weak as he claimed. She debated the merit of getting him into Narabal for treatment. But he seemed unworried, and she doubted that the Narabal doctors knew much about Ghayrog physiology anyway. Besides, she wanted him here. She unpacked the medicines she had brought from town and gave him the ones for fever and inflammation, and then prepared fruits and vegetables for his dinner. Before it grew too dark she checked the traps at the edge of the clearing and found a few small animals in them, a young sigimoin and a couple of mintuns. She wrung their necks with a practiced hand— it had been terribly hard at first, but meat was important to her and no one else was likely to do her killing for her, out here—and dressed them for roasting. Once she had the fire started she went back inside. Vismaan was playing one of the new cubes she had brought him, but he put it aside when she entered.

"You said nothing about your visit to Narabal," he remarked.

"I wasn't there long. Got what I needed, had a little chat with one of my sisters, came away edgy and depressed, felt better as soon as I was in the jungle."

"You have great hatred for that place."

"It's worth hating. Those dismal boring people, those ugly squat little buildings—" She shook her head. "Oh: my sister told me that they're going to found some new towns inland for offworlders, because so many are moving south. Ghayrogs, mainly, but also some other kind with warts and gray skins—"

"Hjorts," said Vismaan.

"Whatever. They like to work as customs-inspectors, she told me. They're going to be settled inland because no one wants them in Tilomon or Narabal, is my guess."

"I have never felt unwanted among humans," the Ghayrog said.

"Really? Maybe you haven't noticed. I think there's a great deal of prejudice on Majipoor."

"It has not been evident to me. Of course, I have never been in Narabal, and perhaps it is stronger there than elsewhere. Certainly in the north there is no difficulty. You have never been in the north?"

"No.

"We find ourselves welcome among humans in Pidruid."

"Is that true? I hear that the Ghayrogs are building a city for themselves somewhere east of Pidruid, quite a way east, on the Great Rift. If everything's so wonderful for you in Pidruid, why settle somewhere else?"

Vismaan said calmly, "It is we who are not altogether comfortable living with humans. The rhythms of our lives are so different from yours—our habits of sleep, for instance. We find it difficult living in a city that goes dormant eight hours every night, when we ourselves remain awake. And there are other differences. So we are building Dulorn. I hope you see it someday. It is quite marvelously beautiful, constructed entirely from a white stone that shines with an inner light. We are very proud of it."

"Why don't you live there, then?"

"Is your meat not burning?" he asked.

She reddened and ran outside, barely in time to snatch dinner from the spits. A little sullenly she sliced it and served it, along with some thokkas and a flask of wine she had bought that afternoon in Narabal. Vismaan sat up, with some awkwardness, to eat.

He said after a while, "I lived in Dulorn for several years. But that is very dry country, and I come from a place on my planet that is warm and wet, like Narabal. So I journeyed down here to find fertile lands. My distant ancestors were farmers, and I thought to return to their ways. When I heard that in the tropics of Majipoor one could raise six harvests a year, and that there was land everywhere for the claiming, I set out to explore the territory."

"Alone?"

"Alone, yes. I have no mate, though I intend to obtain one as soon as I am settled."

"And you'll raise crops and market them in Narabal?"

"So I intend. On my home world there is scarcely any wild land anywhere, and hardly enough remaining for agriculture. We import most of our food, do you know that? And so Majipoor has a powerful appeal for us, this gigantic planet with its sparse population and its great wilderness awaiting development. I am very happy to be here. And I think that you are not right, about our being unwelcome among your fellow citizens. You Majipoori are kind and gentle folk, civil, law-abiding, orderly."

"Even so; if anyone knew I was living with a Ghayrog, they'd be shocked."

"Shocked? Why?"

"Because you're an alien. Because you're a reptile."

Vismaan made an odd snorting sound. Laughter? "We are not reptiles! We are warm-blooded, we nurse our young—"

"Reptilian, then. *Like* reptiles."

"Externally, perhaps. But we are nearly as mammalian as you, I insist."

"Nearly?"

"Only that we are egg-layers. But there are some mammals of that sort, too. You much mistake us if you think—"

"It doesn't really matter. Humans perceive you as reptiles, and we aren't comfortable with reptiles, and there's always going to be awkwardness between humans and Ghayrogs because of that. It's a tradition that goes back into prehistoric times on Old Earth. Besides—" She caught herself just as she was about to make a reference to the Ghayrog odor. "Besides," she said clumsily, "you look scary."

"More so than a huge shaggy Skandar? More so than a Su-Suheris with two heads?" Vismaan turned toward her and fixed his unsettling lidless eyes on her. "I think you are telling me that *you* are uncomfortable with Ghayrogs yourself, Thesme."

"No."

"The prejudices of which you speak have never been visible to me. This is the first time I have heard of them. Am I troubling to you, Thesme? Shall I go?"

"No. No. You're completely misunderstanding me. I want you to stay here. I want to help you. I feel no fear of you at all, no dislike, nothing negative whatever. I was only trying to tell you—trying to explain about the people in Narabal, how they feel, or how I think they feel, and—" She took a long gulp of her wine. "I don't know how we got into all of this. I'm sorry. I'd like to talk about something else."

"Of course."

But she suspected that she had wounded him, or at least aroused some discomfort in him. In his cool alien way he seemed to have considerable insight, and maybe he was right, maybe it was her own prejudice that was showing, her own uneasiness. She had bungled all of her relationships with humans; quite conceivably she was incapable of getting along with anyone, she thought, human or alien, and had shown Vismaan in a thousand unconscious ways that her hospitality was merely a willed act, artificial and half reluctant, intended to cover an underlying dislike for his presence here. Was that so? She understood less and less of her own motivations, it appeared, as she grew older. But wherever the truth might lie, she did not want him to feel like an intruder here. In the days ahead, she resolved, she would find ways of showing him that her taking him in and caring for him were genuinely founded.

She slept more soundly that night than the one before, although she was still not accustomed to sleeping on the floor in a pile of bubblebush leaves or having someone with her in the hut, and every few hours she awakened. Each time she did, she looked across at the Ghayrog, and saw him busy with the entertainment cubes. He took no notice of her. She tried to imagine what it was like to do all of one's sleeping in a single three-month stretch, and to spend the rest of one's time constantly awake; it was, she thought, the most alien thing about him. And to lie there hour after hour, unable to stand, unable to sleep, unable to hide from the discomfort of the injury, making use of whatever diversion was available to consume the time—few torments could be worse. And yet his mood never changed: serene, unruffled, placid, impassive. Were all Ghayrogs like that? Did they never get drunk, lose their tempers, brawl in the streets, bewail their destinies, quarrel with their mates? If Vismaan was a fair sample, they had no human frailties. But, then, she reminded herself, they were not human.

In the morning she gave the Ghayrog a bath, sponging him until his scales glistened, and changed his bedding. After she had fed him she went off for the day, in her usual fashion; but she felt guilty wandering the jungle by herself while he remained marooned in the hut, and wondered if she should have stayed with him, telling him stories or drawing him into a conversation to ease his boredom. But she was aware that if she were constantly at his side they would quickly run out of things to talk about, and very likely get on each other's nerves; and he had dozens of entertainment cubes to help him ward off boredom, anyway. Perhaps he preferred to be alone most of the time. In any case she needed solitude herself, more than ever now that she was sharing her hut with him, and she made a long reconnaissance that morning, gathering an assortment of berries and roots for dinner. At midday it rained, and she squatted under a vramma tree whose broad leaves sheltered her nicely. She let her eyes go out of focus and emptied her mind of everything, guilts, doubts, fears memories, the Ghayrog, her family, her former lovers, her unhappiness, her loneliness. The peace that settled over her lasted well into the afternoon.

She grew used to having Vismaan living with her. He continued to be easy and undemanding, amusing himself with his cubes, showing great patience with his immobility. He rarely asked her questions or initiated any sort of talk, but he was friendly enough when she spoke with him, and told her about his home world—shabby and horribly overpopulated, from the sound of things—and about his life there, his dream of settling on Majipoor, his excitement when he first saw the beauty of his adopted planet. Thesme tried to visualize him showing excitement. His snaky hair jumping around, perhaps, instead of just coiling slowly. Or maybe he registered emotion by changes of body odor.

On the fourth day he left the bed for the first time. With her help he hauled himself upward, balancing on his crutch and his good leg and tentatively touching the other one to the ground. She sensed a sudden sharpness of his aroma—a kind of olfactory wince—and decided that her theory must be right, that Ghayrogs did show emotion that way.

"How does it feel?" she asked. "Tender?"

"It will not bear my weight. But the healing is proceeding well. Another few days and I think I will be able to stand. Come, help lift-walk a little. My body is rusting from so little activity."

He leaned on her and they went outside, to the pond and back at a slow, wary hobble. He seemed refreshed by the little journey. To her surprise she realized that she was saddened by this first show of progress, because it meant that soon—a week, two weeks?—he would be strong enough to leave, and she did not want him to leave. *She did not want him to leave.* That was so odd a perception that it astonished her. She longed for her old reclusive life, the privilege of sleeping in her own bed and going about her forest pleasures without worrying about whether her guest was being sufficiently well amused, and all of that; in some ways she was finding it more and more irritating to have the Ghayrog around. And yet, and yet, and yet, she felt downcast and disturbed at the thought that he would shortly leave her. How strange, she thought, how peculiar, how very Thesme-like.

Now she took him walking several times a day. He still could not use the broken leg, but he grew more agile without it, and he said that the swelling was abating and the bone appeared to be knitting properly. He began to talk of the farm he would establish, the crops, the ways of clearing the jungle.

One afternoon at the end of the first week Thesme, as she returned from a calimbot-gathering expedition in the meadow where she had first found the Ghayrog, stopped to check her traps. Most were empty or contained the usual small animals; but there was a strange violent thrashing in the underbrush beyond the pond, and when she approached the trap she had placed there she discovered she had caught a bilantoon. It was the biggest creature she had ever snared. Bilantoons were found all over western Zimroel—elegant fast-moving little beasts with sharp hooves, fragile legs, a tiny upturned tufted tail—but the Narabal form was a giant, twice the size of the dainty northern one. It stood as high as a man's waist, and was much prized for its tender and fragrant meat. Thesme's first impulse was to let the pretty thing go: it seemed much too beautiful to kill, and much too big, also. She had taught herself to slaughter little things that she could seize in one hand, but this was another matter entirely, a major animal, intelligent-looking and noble, with a life that it surely valued, hopes and needs and yearnings, a mate probably waiting somewhere nearby. Thesme told herself that she was being foolish. Droles and mintuns and sigimoins also very likely were eager to go on living, certainly as eager as this bilantoon was, and she killed them without hesitation. It was a mistake to romanticize animals, she knew—especially when in her more civilized days she had been willing to eat their flesh quite gladly, if slain by other hands. The bilantoon's bereaved mate had not mattered to her then.

As she drew nearer she saw that the bilantoon in its panic had broken one of its delicate legs, and for an instant she thought of splinting it and keeping the creature as a pet. But that was even more absurd. She could not adopt every cripple the jungle brought her. The bilantoon would never calm down long enough for her to examine its leg; and if by some miracle she did manage to repair it, the animal would probably run away the first chance that it got. Taking a deep breath, she came around behind the struggling creature, caught it by its soft muzzle, and snapped its long, graceful neck.

The job of butchering it was bloodier and more difficult than Thesme expected. She hacked away grimly for what seemed like hours, until Vismaan called from within the hut to find out what she was doing.

"Getting dinner ready," she answered. "A surprise. A great treat: roast bilantoon!"

She chuckled quietly. She sounded so wifely, she thought, as she crouched here with blood all over her naked body, sawing away at haunches and ribs, while a reptilian alien creature lay in her bed waiting for his dinner.

But eventually the ugly work was done and she had the meat smouldering over a smoky fire, as one was supposed to do, and she cleansed herself in the pond and set about collecting thokkas and boiling some ghumba-root and opening the remaining flasks of her new Narabal wine. Dinner was ready as darkness came, and Thesme felt immense pride in what she had achieved.

She expected Vismaan to gobble it without comment, in his usual phlegmatic way, but no: for the first time she thought she detected a look of animation on his face—a new sparkle in the eyes, maybe, a different pattern of tongue-flicker. She decided she might be getting better at reading his expressions. He gnawed the roast bilantoon enthusiastically, praised its flavor and texture, and asked again and again for more. For each serving she gave him she took one for herself, forcing the meat down until she was glutted and going onward anyway well past satiation, telling herself that whatever was not consumed now would spoil before morning. "The meat goes so well with the thokkas," she said, popping another of the blue-white berries into her mouth.

"Yes. More, please."

He calmly devoured whatever she set before him. Finally she could eat no more, nor could she even watch him. She put what remained within his reach, took a last gulp of the wine, shuddered a little, laughed as a few drops trickled down her chin and over her breasts. She sprawled out on the bubblebush leaves. Her head was spinning. She lay face down, clutching the floor, listening to the sounds of biting and chewing going on and on and on not far away. Then even the Ghayrog was done feasting, and all was still. Thesme waited for sleep, but sleep would not come. She grew dizzier, until she feared being flung in some terrible centrifugal arc through the side of the hut. Her skin was blazing, her nipples felt hard and sore. I have had much too much to drink, she thought, and I have eaten too many thokkas. Seeds and all, the most potent way, a dozen berries at least, their fiery juice now coursing wildly through her brain.

She did not want to sleep alone, huddled this way on the floor.

With exaggerated care Thesme rose to her knees, steadied herself, and crawled slowly toward the bed. She peered at the Ghayrog, but her eyes were blurred and she could make out only a rough outline of him.

"Are you asleep?" she whispered.

"You know that I would not be sleeping."

"Of course. Of course. Stupid of me."

"Is something wrong, Thesme?"

"Wrong? No, not really. Nothing wrong. Except—it's just that—" She hesitated. "I'm drunk, do you know? Do you understand what being drunk means?"

"Yes."

"I don't like being on the floor. Can I lie beside you?"

"If you wish."

"I have to be very careful. I don't want to bump into your bad leg. Show me which one it is."

"It's almost healed, Thesme. Don't worry. Here: lie down." She felt his hand closing around her wrist and drawing her upward. She let herself float, and drifted easily to his side. She could feel the strange hard shell-like skin of him against her from breast to hip, so cool, so scaly, so smooth. Timidly she rubbed her hand across his body. Like a fine piece of luggage, she thought, digging her fingertips in a little, probing the powerful muscles beneath the rigid surface. His odor changed, becoming spicy, piercing.

"I like the way you smell," she murmured.

She buried her forehead against his chest and held tight to him. She had not been in bed with anyone for months and months, almost a year, and it was good to feel him so close. Even a Ghayrog, she thought. Even a Ghayrog. Just to have the contact, the closeness. It feels so good.

He touched her.

She had not expected that. The entire nature of their relationship was that she cared for him and he passively accepted her services. But suddenly his hand—cool, ridged, scaly, smooth—was passing over her body. Brushing lightly across her breasts, trailing down her belly, pausing at her thighs. What was this? Was Vismaan making *love* to her? She thought of his sexless body, like a machine. He went on stroking her. This is very weird, she thought. Even for Thesme, she told herself, this is an extremely weird thing. He is not human. And I—And I am very lonely—

And I am very drunk—

"Yes, please," she said softly. "Please."

She hoped only that he would continue stroking her. But then he slipped one arm about her shoulders and lifted her easily, gently, rolling her over on top of him and lowering her, and she felt the unmistakable jutting rigidity of maleness against her thigh. What? Did he carry a concealed penis somewhere beneath his scales, that he let slide out when it was needed for use? And was he going to—

Yes.

He seemed to know what to do. Alien he might be, uncertain at their first meeting even whether she was male or female, and nevertheless he plainly understood the theory of human lovemaking. For an instant, as she felt him entering her, she was engulfed by terror and shock and revulsion, wondering if he would hurt her, if he would be painful to receive, and thinking also that this was grotesque and monstrous, this coupling of human and Ghayrog, something that quite likely had never happened before in the history of the universe. She wanted to pull herself free and run out into the night. But she was too dizzy, too drunk, too confused to move; and then she realized that he was not hurting her at all, that he was sliding in and out like some calm clockwork device, and that waves of pleasure were spreading outward from her loins, making her tremble and sob and gasp and press herself against that smooth leathery carapace of his—

She let it happen, and cried out sharply at the best moment, and afterward lay curled up against his chest, shivering, whimpering a little, gradually growing calm. She was sober now. She knew what she had done, and it amazed her, but more than that it amused her. Take that, Narabal! The Ghayrog is my lover! And the pleasure had been so intense, so extreme. Had there been any pleasure in it for him? She did not dare ask. How did one tell if a Ghayrog had an orgasm? Did they have them at all? Would the concept mean anything to him? She wondered if he had made love to human women before. She did not dare ask that, either. He had been so capable—not exactly skilled, but definitely very certain about what needed to be done, and he had done it rather more competently than many men she had known, though whether it was because he had had experience with humans or simply because his clear, cool mind could readily calculate the anatomical necessities she did not know, and she doubted that she would ever know.

He said nothing. She clung to him and drifted into the soundest sleep she had had in weeks.

In the morning she felt strange but not repentant. They did not talk about what had passed between them that night. He played his cubes; she went out at dawn for a swim to clear her throbbing head, and tidied some of the debris left from their bilantoon feast, and made breakfast for them, and afterward she took a long walk toward the north, to a little mossy cave, where she sat most of the morning, replaying in her mind the texture of his body against her and the touch of his hand on her thighs and the wild shudder of ecstasy that had run through her body. She could not say that she found him in any way attractive. Forked tongue, hair like live snakes, scales all over his body—no, no, what had happened last night had not had anything whatever to do with physical attraction, she decided. Then why had it happened? The wine and the thokkas, she told herself, and her loneliness, and her readiness to rebel against the conventional values of the citizens of Narabal. Giving herself to a Ghayrog was the finest way she knew of showing her defiance for all that those people believed. But of course such an act of defiance was meaningless unless they found out about it. She resolved to take Vismaan to Narabal with her as soon as he was able to make the trip.

After that they shared her bed every night. It seemed absurd to do otherwise. But they did not make love the second night, or the third, or the fourth; they lay side by side without touching, without speaking. Thesme would have been willing to yield herself if he had reached out for her, but he did not. Nor did she choose to approach him. The silence between them became an embarrassment to her, but she was afraid to break it for fear of hearing things that she did not want to hear—that he had disliked their lovemaking, or that he regarded such acts as obscene and unnatural and had done it that once only because she seemed so insistent, or that he was aware that she felt no true desire for him but was merely using him to make a point in her ongoing warfare against convention. At the end of the week, troubled by the accumulated tensions of so many unspoken uncertainties, Thesme risked rolling against him when she got into the bed, taking trouble to make it seem accidental, and he embraced her easily and willingly, gathering her into his arms without hesitation. After that they made love on some nights and did not on others, and it was always a random and unpremeditated thing, casual, almost trivial, something they occasionally did before she went to sleep, with no more mystery or magic about it than that. It brought her great pleasure every time. The alienness of his body soon became invisible to her.

He was walking unaided now and each day he spent more time taking exercise. First with her, then by himself, he explored the jungle trails, moving cautiously at the beginning but soon striding along with only a slight limp. Swimming seemed to further the healing process, and for hours at a time he paddled around Thesme's little pond, annoying the gromwark that lived in a muddy burrow at its edge; the slow-moving old creature crept from its hiding-place and sprawled out at the pond's rim like some bedraggled bristly sack that had been discarded there. It eyed the Ghayrog glumly and would not return to the water until he was done with his swim. Thesme consoled it with tender green shoots that she plucked upstream, far beyond the reach of the gromwark's little sucker-feet.

"When will you take me to Narabal?" Vismaan asked her one rainy evening.

"Why not tomorrow?" she replied.

That night she felt unusual excitement, and pressed herself insistently against him.

They set out at dawn in light rainshowers that soon gave way to brilliant sunshine. Thesme adopted a careful pace, but soon it was apparent that the Ghayrog was fully healed, and before long she was walking swiftly. Vismaan had no difficulty keeping up. She found herself chattering—telling him the names of every plant or animal they encountered, giving him bits of Narabal's history, talking about her brothers and sisters and people she knew in town. She was desperately eager to be seen by them with him—*look, this is my alien lover, this is the Ghayrog I've been sleeping with*—and when they came to the outskirts she began looking around intently, hoping to find someone familiar; but scarcely anyone seemed to be visible on the outer farms, and she did not recognize those who were. "Do you see how they're staring at us?" she whispered to Vismaan, as they passed into a more thickly inhabited district. "They're afraid of you. They think you're the vanguard of some sort of alien invasion. And they're wondering what I'm doing with you, why I'm being so civil to you."

"I see none of that," said Vismaan. "They appear curious about me, yes. But I detect no fear, no hostility. Is it because I am unfamiliar with human facial expressions? I thought I had learned to interpret them quite well."

"Wait and see," Thesme told him. But she had to admit to herself that she might be exaggerating things a little, or even more than a little. They were nearly in the heart of Narabal, now, and some people had glanced at the Ghayrog in surprise and curiosity, yes, but they had quickly softened their stares, while others had merely nodded and smiled as though it were the most ordinary thing in the world to have some kind of offworld creature walking through the streets. Of actual hostility she could find none. That angered her. These mild sweet people, these bland amiable people, were not at all reacting as she had expected. Even when she finally met familiar people—Khanidor, her oldest brother's best friend, and Hennimont Sibroy who ran the little inn near the waterfront, and the woman from the flower shop—they were nothing other than cordial as Thesme said, "This is Vismaan, who has been living with me lately." Khanidor smiled as though he had always known Thesme to be the sort of person who would set up housekeeping with an alien, and spoke of the new towns for Ghayrogs and Hjorts that Mirifaine's husband was planning to build. The innkeeper reached out jovially to shake Vismaan's hand and invited him down for some wine on the house, and the flower shop woman said over and over, "How interesting, how interesting! We hope you like our little town!" Thesme felt patronized by their cheerfulness. It was as if they were going out of their way not to let her shock them—as if they had already taken all the wildness from Thesme that they were going to take, and now would accept anything, anything at all from her, without caring, without surprise, without comment. Perhaps they misunderstood the nature of her relationship with the Ghayrog and thought he was merely boarding with her. Would they give her the reaction she wanted if she came right out and said they were lovers, that his body had been inside hers, that they had done that which was unthinkable between human and alien? Probably not. Probably even if she and the Ghayrog lay down and coupled in Pontifex Square it would cause no stir in this town, she thought, scowling.

And did Vismaan like their little town? It was, as always, difficult to detect emotional response in him. They walked up one street and down another, past the haphazardly planned plazas and the flat-faced scruffy shops and the little lopsided houses with their overgrown gardens, and he said very little. She sensed disappointment and disapproval in his silence, and for all her own dislike of Narabal she began to feel defensive about the place. It was, after all, a young settlement, an isolated outpost in an obscure corner of a second-class continent, just a few generations old. "What do you think?" she asked finally. "You aren't very impressed by Narabal, are you?"

"You warned me not to expect much."

"But it's even more dismal than I led you to expect, isn't it?"

"I do find it small and crude," he said. "After one has seen Pidruid, or even—"

"Pidruid's thousands of years old."

"—Dulorn," he went on. "Dulorn is extraordinarily beautiful even now, when it is just being built. But of course the white stone they use there is—"

"Yes," she said. "Narabal ought to be built out of stone too, because this climate is so damp that wooden buildings fall apart, but there hasn't been time yet. Once the population's big enough, we can quarry in the mountains and put together something marvelous here. Fifty years from now, a hundred, when we have a proper labor force. Maybe if we got some of those giant four-armed aliens to work here—"

"Skandars," said Vismaan.

"Skandars, yes. Why doesn't the Coronal send us ten thousand Skandars?"

"Their bodies are covered with thick hair. They will find this climate difficult. But doubtless Skandars will settle here, and Vroons, and Su-Suheris, and many, many wet-country Ghayrogs like me. It is a very bold thing your government is doing, encouraging offworld settlers in such numbers. Other planets are not so generous with their land."

"Other planets are not so large," Thesme said. "I think I've heard that even with all the huge oceans we have, Majipoor's land mass is still three or four times the size of any other settled planet. Or something like that. We're very lucky, being such a big world, and yet having such gentle gravity, so that humans and humanoids can live comfortably here. Of course, we pay a high price for that, not having anything much in the way of heavy elements, but still—oh. Hello." The tone of her voice changed abruptly, dropping off to a startled blurt. A slim young man, very tall, with pale wavy hair, had nearly collided with her as he emerged from the bank on the corner, and now he stood gaping at her, and she at him. He was Ruskelorn Yulvan, Thesme's lover for the four months just prior to her withdrawal into the jungle, and the person in Narabal she was least eager to see. But if there had to be a confrontation with him, she intended to make the most of it; and, seizing the initiative after her first moment of confusion, she said, "You look well, Ruskelorn."

"And you. Jungle life must agree with you."

"Very much. It's been the happiest seven months of my life. Ruskelorn, this is my friend Vismaan, who's been living with me the past few weeks. He had an accident while scouting for farmland near my place—broke his leg falling out of a tree—and I've been looking after him."

"Very capably, I imagine," Ruskelorn Yulvan said evenly. "He seems to be in excellent condition." To the Ghayrog he said, "Pleased to meet you," in a way that made it seem as though he might actually mean it.

Thesme said, "He comes from a part of his planet where the climate is a lot like Narabal's. He tells me that there'll be plenty of his countrypeople settling down here in the tropics in the next few years."

"So I've heard." Ruskelorn Yulvan grinned and said, "You'll find it amazingly fertile territory. Eat a berry at breakfast time and toss the seed away, you'll have a vine as tall as a house by nightfall. That's what everyone says, so it must be true."

The light and casual manner of his speaking infuriated her. Did he not realize that this scaly alien creature, this offworlder, this Ghayrog, was his replacement in her bed? Was he immune to jealousy, or did he simply not understand the real situation? With a ferocious silent intensity she attempted to convey the truth of things to Ruskelorn Yulvan in the most graphic possible way, thinking fierce images of herself in Vismaan's arms, showing Ruskelorn Yulvan the alien hands of Vismaan caressing her breasts and thighs and flicking his little scarlet two-pronged tongue lightly over her closed eyelids, her nipples, her loins. But it was useless. Ruskelorn was no more of a mind-reader than she. *He is my lover,* she thought, *he enters me, he makes me come again and again, I can't wait to get back to the jungle and tumble into bed with him,* and all the while Ruskelorn Yulvan stood there smiling, chatting politely with the Ghayrog, discussing the potential for raising niyk and glein and stajja in these parts, or perhaps lusavender-seed in the swampier districts, and only after a good deal of that did he turn his glance back toward Thesme and ask, as placidly as though he were asking the day of the week, whether she intended to live in the jungle indefinitely.

She glared. "So far I prefer it to life in town. Why?"

"I wondered if you missed the comforts of our splendid metropolis, that's all."

"Not yet, not for a moment. I've never been happier."

"Good. I'm so pleased for you, Thesme." Another serene smile. "How nice to have run into you. How good to have met you," he said to the Ghayrog, and then he was gone.

Thesme smouldered with rage. He had not cared, he had not cared in the slightest, she could be coupling with Ghayrogs or Skandars or the gromwark in the pond for all it mattered to him! She had wanted him to be wounded or at least shocked, and instead he had simply been polite. Polite! It must be that he, like all the others, failed to comprehend the real state of affairs between her and Vismaan—that it was simply inconceivable to them that a woman of human stock would offer her body to a reptilian offworlder, and so they did not consider—they did not even suspect—

"Have you seen enough of Narabal now?" she asked the Ghayrog.

"Enough to realize that there is little to see."

"How does your leg feel? Are you ready to begin the journey back?"

"Have you no errands to perform in town?"

"Nothing important," she said. "I'd like to go."

"Then let us go," he answered.

His leg did seem to be giving him some trouble—the muscles stiffening, probably; that was a taxing hike even for someone in prime condition, and he had traveled only much shorter distances since his recovery—but in his usual uncomplaining way he followed her toward the jungle road. This was the worst time of day to be making the trip, with the sun almost straight overhead and the air moist and heavy from the first gatherings of what would be this afternoon's rainfall. They walked slowly, pausing often, though never once did he say he was tired; it was Thesme herself who was tiring, and she pretended that she wanted to show him some geological formation here, some unusual plant there, in order to manufacture occasions to rest. She did not want to admit fatigue. She had suffered enough mortification today.

The venture into Narabal had been a disaster for her. Proud, defiant, rebellious, scornful of Narabal's conventional ways, she had hauled her Ghayrog lover to town to flaunt him before the tame city-dwellers, and they had not cared. Were they such puddings that they could not guess at the truth? Or had they seen instantly through her pretensions, and were determined to give her no satisfaction? Either way she felt outraged, humiliated, defeated—and very foolish. And what about the bigotry she imagined she had found earlier among the Narabal folk? Were they not threatened by the influx of these aliens? They had all been so charming to Vismaan, so friendly. Perhaps, Thesme thought gloomily, the prejudice was in her mind alone and she had misinterpreted the remarks of others, and in that case it had been stupid to give herself to the Ghayrog, it had accomplished nothing, flouted no Narabal decorum, served no purpose at all in the private war she had been fighting against those people. It had only been a strange and willful and grotesque event.

Neither she nor the Ghayrog spoke during the long slow uncomfortable return to the jungle. When they reached her hut he went inside and she bustled about ineffectually in the clearing, checking traps, pulling berries from vines, setting things down and forgetting what she had done with them.

After a while she entered the hut and said to Vismaan, "I think you may as well leave."

"Very well. It *is* time for me to be on my way."

"You can stay here tonight, of course. But in the morning—"

"Why not leave now?"

"It'll be dark soon. You've already walked so many miles today—"

"I have no wish to trouble you. I will go now, I think."

Even now she found it impossible to read his feelings. Was he surprised? Hurt? Angry? He showed her nothing. He offered no gestures of farewell, either, but simply turned and began walking at a steady pace toward the interior of the jungle. Thesme watched him, throat dry, heart pounding, until he disappeared beyond the low-hanging vines. It was all she could do to keep herself from running after him. But then he was gone, and soon the tropical night descended.

She rummaged together a sort of dinner for herself, but she ate very little, thinking, He is out there sitting in the darkness, waiting for the morning to come. They had not even said goodbye. She could have made some little joke, warning him to stay out of sijaneel trees, or he could have thanked her for all she had done on his behalf, but instead there had been nothing, just her dismissal of him and his calm uncomplaining departure. An alien, she thought, and his ways were alien. And yet, when they had been together in bed, and he had touched her and held her and drawn her body down on top of his—

It was a long bleak night for her. She lay huddled in the crudely sewn zanja-down bed that they had so lately shared, listening to the night rain hammering on the vast blue leaves that were her roof, and for the first time since she had entered the jungle she felt the pain of loneliness. Until this moment she had not realized how much she had valued the bizarre parody of domesticity that she and the Ghayrog had enacted here; but now that was over, and she was alone again, somehow more alone than she had been before, and far more cut off from her old life in Narabal than before, also, and he was out there, unsleeping in the darkness, unsheltered from the rain. I am in love with an alien, she told herself in wonderment, I am in love with a scaly *thing* that speaks no words of endearment and asks hardly any questions and leaves without saying thank you or goodbye. She lay awake for hours, crying now and then. Her body felt tense and clenched from the long walk and the day's frustrations; she drew her knees to her breasts and stayed that way a long while, and then put her hands between her legs and stroked herself, and finally there came a moment of release, a gasp and a little soft moan, and sleep after that.

In the morning she bathed and checked her traps and assembled a breakfast and wandered over all the familiar trails near her hut. There was no sign of the Ghayrog. By midday her mood seemed to be lifting, and the afternoon was almost cheerful for her; only as nightfall approached, the time of solitary dinner, did she begin to feel the bleakness descending again. But she endured it. She played the cubes she had brought from home for him, and eventually dropped into sleep, and the next day was a better day, and the next, and the one after that.

Gradually Thesme's life returned to normal. She saw nothing of the Ghayrog and he started to slip from her mind. As the solitary weeks went by she rediscovered the joy of solitude, or so it seemed to her, but then at odd moments she speared herself on some sharp and painful memory of him—the sight of a bilantoon in a thicket or the sijaneel tree with the broken branch or the gromwark sitting sullenly at the edge of the pond—and she realized that she still missed him. She roved the jungle in wider and wider circles, not quite knowing why, until at last she admitted to herself that she was looking for him.

It took her three more months to find him. She began seeing indications of settlement off to the southeast—an apparent clearing, visible two or three hilltops away, with what looked like traces of new trails radiating from it—and in time she made her way in that direction and across a considerable river previously unknown to her, to a zone of felled trees, beyond which was a newly established farm. She skulked along its perimeter and caught sight of a Ghayrog—it was Vismaan, she was certain of that—tilling a field of rich black soil. Fear swept her spirit and left her weak and trembling. Could it be some other Ghayrog? No, no, no, she was sure it was he, she even imagined she detected a little limp. She ducked down out of sight, afraid to approach him. What could she say to him? How could she justify having come this far to seek him out, after having so coolly dismissed him from her life? She drew back into the underbrush and came close to turning away altogether. But then she found her courage and called his name.

He stopped short and looked around.

"Vismaan? Over here! It's Thesme!"

Her cheeks were blazing, her heart pounded terrifyingly. For one dismal instant she was convinced that this was a strange Ghayrog, and apologies for her intrusion were already springing to her lips. But as he came toward her she knew that she had not been mistaken.

"I saw the clearing and thought it might be your farm," she said, stepping out of the tangled brush. "How have you been, Vismaan?"

"Quite excellent. And yourself?"

She shrugged. "I get along. You've done wonders here, Vismaan. It's only been a few months, and look at all this!"

"Yes," he said. "We have worked hard."

"We?"

"I have a mate now. Come: let me introduce you to her, and show you what we have accomplished here."

His tranquil words withered her. Perhaps they were meant to do that—instead of showing any sort of resentment or pique over the way she had sent him out of her life, he was taking his revenge in a more diabolical fashion, through utter dispassionate restraint. But more likely, she thought, he felt no resentment and saw no need for revenge. His view of all that had passed between them was probably entirely unlike hers. Never forget that he is an alien, she told herself.

She followed him up a gentle slope and across a drainage ditch and around a small field that was obviously newly planted. At the top of the hill, half hidden by a lush kitchen-garden, was a cottage of sijaneel timbers not very different from her own, but larger and somewhat more angular in design. From up here the whole farm could be seen, occupying three faces of the little hill. Thesme was astounded at how much he had managed to do—it seemed impossible to have cleared all this, to have built a dwelling, to have made ready the soil for planting, even to have begun planting, in just these few months. She remembered that Ghayrogs did not sleep; but had they no need of rest?

"Turnome!" he called. "We have a visitor, Turnome!"

Thesme forced herself to be calm. She understood now that she had come looking for the Ghayrog because she no longer wanted to be alone, and that she had had some half-conscious fantasy of helping him establish his farm, of sharing his life as well as his bed, of building a true relationship with him; she had even, for one flickering instant, seen herself on a holiday in the north with him, visiting wonderful Dulorn, meeting his countrymen. All that was foolish, she knew, but it had had a certain crazy plausibility until the moment when he told her he had a mate. Now she struggled to compose herself, to be cordial and warm, to keep all absurd hints of rivalry from surfacing—

Out of the cottage came a Ghayrog nearly as tall as Vismaan, with the same gleaming pearly armor of scales, the same slowly writhing serpentine hair; there was only one outward difference between them, but it was a strange one indeed, for the Ghayrog woman's chest was festooned with dangling tubular breasts, a dozen or more of them, each tipped with a dark green nipple. Thesme shivered. Vismaan had said Ghayrogs were mammals, and the evidence was impossible to refute, but the reptilian look of the woman was if anything heightened by those eerie breasts, which made her seem not mammalian but weirdly hybrid and incomprehensible. Thesme looked from one to the other of these creatures in deep discomfort.

Vismaan said, "This is the woman I told you about, who found me when I hurt my leg, and nursed me back to health. Thesme: my mate Turnome."

"You are welcome here," said the Ghayrog woman solemnly.

Thesme stammered some further appreciation of the work they had done on the farm. She wanted only to escape, now, but there was no getting away; she had come to call on her jungle neighbors, and they insisted on observing the niceties. Vismaan invited her in. What was next? A cup of tea, a bowl of wine, some thokkas and grilled mintun? There was scarcely anything inside the cottage except a table and a few cushions and, in the far corner, a curious high-walled woven container of large size, standing on a three-legged stool. Thesme glanced toward it and quickly away, thinking without knowing why that it was wrong to display curiosity about it; but Vismaan took her by the elbow and said, "Let us show you. Come: look." She peered in.

It was an incubator. On a nest of moss were eleven or twelve leathery round eggs, bright green with large red speckles.

"Our firstborn will hatch in less than a month," Vismaan said.

Thesme was swept by a wave of dizziness. Somehow this revelation of the true alienness of these beings stunned her as nothing else had, not the chilly stare of Vismaan's unblinking eyes nor the writhing of his hair nor the touch of his skin against her naked body nor the sudden amazing sensation of him moving inside her. Eggs! A litter! And Turnome already puffing up with milk to nurture them! Thesme had a vision of a dozen tiny lizards clinging to the woman's many breasts, and horror transfixed her: she stood motionless, not even breathing, for an endless moment, and then she turned and bolted, running down the hillside, over the drainage ditch, right across, she realized too late, the newly planted field, and off into the steaming humid jungle.

She did not know how long it was before Vismaan appeared at her door. Time had gone by in a blurred flow of eating and sleeping and weeping and trembling, and perhaps it was a day, perhaps two, perhaps a week, and then there he was, poking his head and shoulders into the hut and calling her name.

"What do you want?" she asked, not getting up.

"To talk. There were things I had to tell you. Why did you leave so suddenly?"

"Does it matter?"

He crouched beside her. His hand rested lightly on her shoulder.

"Thesme, I owe you apologies."

"For what?"

"When I left here, I failed to thank you for all you had done for me. My mate and I were discussing why you had run away, and she said you were angry with me, and I could not understand why. So she and I explored all the possible reasons, and when I described how you and I had come to part, Turnome asked me if I had told you that I was grateful for your help, and I said no, I had not, I was unaware that such things were done. So I have come to you. Forgive me for my rudeness, Thesme. For my ignorance."

"I forgive you," she said in a muffled voice. "Will you go away, now?"

"Look at me, Thesme."

"I'd rather not."

"Please. Will you?" He tugged at her shoulder.

Sullenly she turned to him.

"Your eyes are swollen," he said.

"Something I ate must have disagreed with me."

"You are still angry. Why? I have asked you to understand that I meant no discourtesy. Ghayrogs do not express gratitude in quite the same way humans do. But let me do it now. You saved my life, I believe. You were very kind. I will always remember what you did for me when I was injured. It was wrong of me not to have told you that before."

"And it was wrong of me to throw you out like that," she said in a low voice. "Don't ask me to explain why I did, though. It's very complicated. I'll forgive you for not thanking me if you'll forgive me for making you leave like that."

"No forgiveness was required. My leg had healed; it was time for me to go, as you pointed out. I went on my way and found the land I needed for my farm."

"It was that simple, then?"

"Yes. Of course."

She got to her feet and stood facing him. "Vismaan, why did you have sex with me?"

"Because you seemed to want it."

"That's all?"

"You were unhappy and did not seem to wish to sleep alone. I hoped it would comfort you. I was trying to do the friendly thing, the compassionate thing."

"Oh. I see."

"I believe it gave you pleasure," he said.

"Yes. Yes. It did give me pleasure. But you didn't desire me, then?"

His tongue flickered in what she thought might be the equivalent of a puzzled frown.

"No," he said. "You are human. How can I feel desire for a human? You are so different from me, Thesme. On Majipoor my kind are called aliens, but to me *you* are the alien, is that not so?"

"I suppose. Yes."

"But I was very fond of you. I wished your happiness. In that sense I had desire for you. Do you understand? And I will always be your friend. I hope you will come to visit us, and share in the bounty of our farm. Will you do that, Thesme?"

"I—yes, yes, I will."

"Good. I will go now. But first—"

Gravely, with immense dignity, he drew her to him and enfolded her in his powerful arms. Once again she felt the strange smooth rigidity of his alien skin; once again the little scarlet tongue fluttered across her eyelids in a forked kiss. He embraced her for a long moment.

When he released her he said, "I am extremely fond of you, Thesme I can never forget you."

"Nor I you."

She stood in the doorway, watching until he disappeared from sight beyond the pond. A sense of ease and peace and warmth had come over her spirit. She doubted that she ever would visit Vismaan and Turnome and their litter of little lizards, hut that was all right: Vismaan would understand. Everything was all right. Thesme began to gather her possessions and stuff them into her pack. It was still only mid-morning, time enough to make the journey to Narabal.

She reached the city just after the afternoon showers. It was over a year since she had left it, and a good many months since her last visit; and she was surprised by the changes she saw now. There was a boomtown bustle to the place, new buildings going up everywhere, ships in the Channel, the streets full of traffic. And the town seemed to have been invaded by aliens—hundreds of Ghayrogs, and other kinds too, the warty ones that she supposed were Hjorts, and enormous double-shouldered Skandars, a whole circus of strange beings going about their business and taken absolutely for granted by the human citizens. Thesme found her way with some difficulty to her mother's house. Two of her sisters were there, and her brother Dalkhan. They stared at her in amazement and what seemed like fear.

"I'm back," she said. "I know I look like a wild animal, but I just need my hair trimmed and a new tunic and I'll be human again."

She went to live with Ruskelorn Yulvan a few weeks later, and at the end of the year they were married. For a time she thought of confessing to him that she and her Ghayrog guest had been lovers, but she was afraid to do it, and eventually it seemed unimportant to bring it up at all. She did, finally, ten or twelve years later, when they had dined on roast bilantoon at one of the fine new restaurants in the Ghayrog quarter of town, and she had had much too much of the strong golden wine of the north, and the pressure of old associations was too powerful to resist. When she had finished telling him the story she said, "Did you suspect any of that?" And he said, "I knew it right away, when I saw you with him in the street. But why should it have mattered?"

Symbiont

From *Playboy*, June 1985

Ten years later, when I was long out of the Service and working the turnaround wheel at Betelgeuse Station, Fazio still haunted me. Not that he was dead. Other people get haunted by dead men; I was haunted by a live one. It would have been a lot better for both of us if he had been dead, but as far as I knew Fazio was still alive.

He'd been haunting me a long while. Three or four times a year his little dry thin voice would come out of nowhere and I'd hear him telling me again, "Before we go into that jungle, we got to come to an understanding. If a synsym nails me, Chollie, you kill me right away, hear? None of this shit of calling in the paramedics to clean me out. You just kill me right away. And I'll do the same for you. Is that a deal?"

This was on a planet called Weinstein in the Servadac system, late in the Second Ovoid War. We were twenty years old and we were volunteers: two dumb kids playing hero. "You bet your ass," is what I told him, not hesitating a second. "Deal. Absolutely." Then I gave him a big grin and a handclasp and we headed off together on spore-spreading duty.

At the time, I really thought I meant it. Sometimes I still believe that I did.

Ten years. I could still see the two of us back there on Weinstein, going out to distribute latchenango spores in the enemy-held zone. The planet had been grabbed by the Ovoids early in the war, but we were starting to drive them back from that whole system. Fazio and I were the entire patrol: you get spread pretty thin in galactic warfare. But there was plenty of support force behind us in the hills.

Weinstein was strategically important, God only knows why. Two small continents—both tropical, mostly thick jungle, air like green soup—surrounded by an enormous turbulent ocean: never colonized by Earth, and of no use that anyone had ever successfully explained to me. But the place had once been ours and they had taken it away, and we wanted it back.

The way you got a planet back was to catch a dozen or so Ovoids, fill them full of latchenango spores, and let them return to their base. There is no life-form a latchenango likes better as its host than an Ovoid. The Ovoids, being Ovoids, would usually conceal what had happened to them from their pals, who would kill them instantly if they knew they were carrying deadly parasites. Of course, the carriers were going to die anyway—latchenango infestation is invariably fatal to Ovoids—but by the time they did, in about six standard weeks, the latchenangos had gone through three or four reproductive cycles and the whole army would be infested. All we needed to do was wait until all the Ovoids were dead and then come in, clean the place up, and raise the flag again. The latchenangos were generally dead too by then, since they rarely could find other suitable hosts. But even if they weren't, we didn't worry about it. Latchenangos don't cause any serious problems for humans. About the worst of it is that you usually inhale some spores while you're handling them, and it irritates your lungs for a couple of weeks so you do some pretty ugly coughing until you're desporified.

In return for our latchenangos the Ovoids gave us synsyms.

Synsyms were the first things you heard about when you arrived in the war zone, and what you heard was horrendous. You didn't know how much of it was myth and how much was mere bullshit and how much was truth, but even if you discounted seventy-five percent of it the rest was scary enough. "If you get hit by one," the old hands advised us, "kill yourself fast, while you have the chance." Roving synsym vectors cruised the perimeter of every Ovoid camp, sniffing for humans. They were not parasites but synthetic symbionts: when they got into you, they stayed there, sharing your body with you indefinitely.

In school they teach you that symbiosis is a mutually beneficial state. Maybe so. But the word that passed through the ranks in the war zone was that it definitely did not improve the quality of your life to take a synsym into your body. And though the Service medics would spare no effort to see that you survived a synsym attack—they aren't allowed to perform mercy killings, and wouldn't anyway—everything we heard indicated that you didn't really want to survive one.

The day Fazio and I entered the jungle was like all the others on Weinstein: dank, humid, rainy. We strapped on our spore-tanks and started out, using hand-held heat-piles to burn our way through the curtains of tangled vines. The wet spongy soil had a purplish tinge and the lakes were iridescent green from lightning-algae.

"Here's where we'll put the hotel landing strip," Fazio said lightly. "Over here, the pool and cabanas. The gravity-tennis courts here, and on the far side of that—"

"Watch it," I said, and skewered a low-flying wingfinger with a beam of hot purple light. It fell in ashes at our feet. Another one came by, the mate, traveling at eye-level with its razor-sharp beak aimed at my throat, but Fazio took it out just as neatly. We thanked each other. Wingfingers are elegant things, all trajectory and hardly any body mass, with scaly silvery skins that shine like the finest grade of moonlight, and it is their habit to go straight for the jugular in the most literal sense. We killed twelve that day and I hope it is my quota for this lifetime. As we advanced into the heart of the jungle we dealt just as efficiently with assorted hostile coilworms, eyeflies, dingleberries, leper bats, and other disagreeable local specialties. We were a great team: quick, smart, good at protecting each other.

We were admiring a giant carnivorous fungus a klick and a half deep in the woods when we came upon our first Ovoid. The fungus was a fleshy phallic red tower three meters high with orange gills, equipped with a dozen dangling whiplike arms that had green adhesive knobs at the tips. At the ends of most of the arms hung small forest creatures in various stages of digestion. As we watched, an unoccupied arm rose and shot forth, extended itself to three times its resting length, and by some neat homing tropism slapped its adhesive knob against a passing many-legger about the size of a cat. The beast had no chance to struggle; a network of wiry structures sprouted at once from the killer arm and slipped into the victim's flesh, and that was that. We almost applauded.

"Let's plant three of them in the hotel garden," I said, "and post a schedule of feeding times. It'll be a great show for the guests."

"Shh," Fazio said. He pointed.

Maybe fifty meters away a solitary Ovoid was gliding serenely along a forest path, obviously unaware of us. I caught my breath. Everyone knows what Ovoids look like, but this was the first time I had seen a live one. I was surprised at how beautiful it was, a tapering cone of firm jelly, pale blue streaked with red and gold. Triple rows of short-stalked eyes along its sides like brass buttons. Clusters of delicate tendrils sprouting like epaulets around the eating-orifice at the top of its head. Turquoise ribbons of neural conduit winding round and round its equator, surrounding the dark heart-shaped brain faintly visible within the cloudy depths. The enemy. I was conditioned to hate it, and I did; yet I couldn't deny its strange beauty.

Fazio smiled and took aim and put a numb-needle through the Ovoid's middle. It froze instantly in mid-glide; its color deepened to a dusky flush; the tiny mouth-tendrils fluttered wildly but there was no other motion. We jogged up to it and I slipped the tip of my spore-distributor about five centimeters into its meaty middle. "Let him have it!" Fazio yelled. I pumped a couple of c.c.'s of latchenango spores into the paralyzed alien. Its soft quivering flesh turned blue-black with fear and rage and God knows what other emotions that were strictly Ovoid. We nodded to each other and moved along. Already the latchenangos were spawning within their host; in half an hour the Ovoid, able once more to move, would limp off toward its camp to start infecting its comrades. It is a funny way to wage war.

The second Ovoid, an hour later, was trickier. It knew we had spotted it and took evasive action, zigzagging through a zone of streams and slender trees in a weird, dignified way like someone trying to move very fast without having his hat blow off. Ovoids are not designed for quick movements, but this one was agile and determined, ducking behind this rock and that. More than once we lost sight of it altogether and were afraid it might double back and come down on us while we stood gaping and blinking.

Eventually we bottled it up between two swift little streams and closed in on it from both sides. I raised my needler and Fazio got ready with his spore-distributor and just then something gray and slipper-shaped and about fifteen centimeters long came leaping up out of the left-hand stream and plastered itself over Fazio's mouth and throat.

Down he went, snuffling and gurgling, trying desperately to peel it away. I thought it was some kind of killer fish. Pausing only long enough to shoot a needle through the Ovoid, I dropped my gear and jumped down beside him.

Fazio was rolling around, eyes wild, kicking at the ground in terror and agony. I put my elbow on my chest to hold him still and pried with both hands at the thing on his face. Getting it loose was like pulling a second skin off him, but somehow I managed to lift it away from his lips far enough for him to gasp, "Synsym—I think it's synsym—"

"No, man, it's just some nasty fish," I told him. "Hang in there and I'll rip the rest of it loose in half a minute—

Fazio shook his head in anguish.

Then I saw the two thin strands of transparent stuff snaking up out of it and disappearing into his nostrils, and I knew he was right.

I didn't hear anything from him or about him after the end of the war, and didn't want to, but I assumed all along that Fazio was still alive. I don't know why: my faith in the general perversity of the universe, I guess.

The last I had seen of him was our final day on Weinstein. We both were being invalided out. They were shipping me to the big hospital on Daemmerung for routine desporification treatment, but he was going to the quarantine station on Quixote; and as we lay side by side in the depot, me on an ordinary stretcher and Fazio inside an isolation bubble, he raised his head with what must have been a terrible effort and glared at me out of eyes that already were ringed with the red concentric synsym circles, and he whispered something to me. I wasn't able to understand the words through the wall of his bubble, but I could feel them, the way you feel the light of a blue-white sun from half a parsec out. His skin was glowing. The dreadful vitality of the symbiont within him was already apparent. I had a good notion of what he was trying to tell me. You bastard, he was most likely trying to say. Now I'm stuck with this thing for a thousand years. And I'm going to hate you every minute of the time, Chollie.

Then they took him away. They sent him floating up the ramp into that Quixote-bound ship. When he was out of view I felt released, as though I was coming out from under a pull of six or seven gravs. It occurred to me that I wasn't ever going to have to see Fazio again. I wouldn't have to face those reddened eyes, that taut shining skin, that glare of infinite reproach. Or so I believed for the next ten years, until he turned up on Betelgeuse Station.

A bolt out of the blue: there he was, suddenly, standing next to me in the recreation room on North Spoke. It was just after my shift and I was balancing on the rim of the swimmer web, getting ready to dive. "Chollie?" he said calmly. The voice was Fazio's voice: that was clear, when I stopped to think about it a little later. But I never for a moment considered that this weird gnomish man might be Fazio. I stared at him and didn't even come close to recognizing him. He seemed about seven million years old, shrunken, fleshless, weightless, with thick coarse hair like white straw and strange soft gleaming translucent skin that looked like parchment worn thin by time. In the bright light of the rec room he kept his eyes hooded nearly shut; but then he turned away from the glowglobes and opened them wide enough to show me the fine red rings around his pupils. The hair began to rise along the back of my neck.

"Come on," he said. "You know me. Yeah. Yeah."

The voice, the cheekbones, the lips, the eyes—the eyes, the eyes, the eyes. Yes, I knew him. But it wasn't possible. Fazio? Here? How? So long a time, so many light-years away! And yet—yet—

He nodded. "You got it, Chollie. Come on. Who am I?"

My first attempt at saying something was a sputtering failure. But I managed to get his name out on the second try.

"Yeah," he said. "Fazio. What a surprise."

He didn't look even slightly surprised. I think he must have been watching me for a few days before he approached me—casing me, checking me out, making certain it was really me, getting used to the idea that he had actually found me. Otherwise the amazement would surely have been showing on him now. Finding me—finding anybody along the starways—wasn't remotely probable. This was a coincidence almost too big to swallow. I knew he couldn't have deliberately come after me, because the galaxy is so damned big a place that the idea of setting out to search for someone in it is too silly even to think about. But somehow he had caught up with me anyway. If the universe is truly infinite, I suppose, then even the most wildly improbable things must occur in it a billion times a day.

I said shakily, "I can't believe—"

"You can't? Hey, you better! What a surprise, kid, hey? Hey?" He clapped his hand against my arm. "And you're looking good, kid. Nice and healthy. You keep in shape, huh? How old are you now, thirty-two?"

"Thirty." I was numb with shock and fear.

"Thirty. Mmm. So am I. Nice age, ain't it? Prime of life."

"Fazio—"

His control was terrifying. "Come on, Chollie. You look like you're about to crap in your pants. Aren't you glad to see your old buddy? We had some good times together, didn't we? Didn't we?"

"What was the name of that fuckin' planet? Weinberg? Weinfeld? Hey, hey, don't stare at me like that!"

I had to work hard to make any sound at all. Finally I said, "What the hell do you want me to do, Fazio? I feel like I'm looking at a ghost."

He leaned close and his eyes opened wider. I could practically count the concentric red rings, ten or fifteen of them, very fine lines. "I wish to Christ you were," he said quietly. Such unfathomable depths of pain, such searing intensity of hatred. I wanted to squirm away from him. But there was no way. He gave me a long slow crucifying inspection. Then he eased back and some of the menacing intensity seemed to go out of him. Almost jauntily he said, "We got a lot to talk about, Chollie. You know some quiet place around here we can go?"

"There's the gravity lounge—"

"Sure. The gravity lounge."

We floated face to face, at half pull. "You promised you'd kill me if I got nailed," Fazio murmured. "That was our deal. Why didn't you do it, Chollie? Why the fuck didn't you do it?"

I could hardly bear to look into his red-ringed eyes.

"Things happened too fast, man. How was I to know paramedics would be on the scene in five minutes?"

"Five minutes is plenty of time to put a heat-bolt through a guy's chest."

"Less than five minutes. Three. Two. The paramedic floater was right overhead, man! It was covering us the whole while. They came down on us like a bunch of fucking angels, Fazio!"

"You had time."

"I thought they were going to be able to save you," I said lamely. "They got there so quickly."

Fazio laughed harshly. "They did try to save me," he said. "I'll give them credit for trying. Five minutes and I was on that floater and they were sending tracers all over me to clean the synsym goop out of my lungs and my heart and my liver."

"Sure. That was just what I figured they'd do."

"You promised to finish me off, Chollie, if I got nailed."

"But the paramedics were right there!"

"They worked on me like sonsabitches," he said. "They did everything. They can clean up the vital tissues, they can yank out your organs, synsym and all, and stick in transplants. But they can't get the stuff out of your brain, did you know that? The synsym goes straight up your nose into your brain and it slips its tendrils into your meninges and your neural glia and right into your fucking corpus callosum. And from there it goes everywhere. The cerebellum, the medulla, you name it. They can't send tracers into the brain that will clean out synsym and not damage brain tissue. And they can't pull out your brain and give you a new one, either. Thirty seconds after the synsym gets into your nose it reaches your brain and it's all over for you, no matter what kind of treatment you get. Didn't you hear them tell you that when we first got to the war zone? Didn't you hear all the horror stories?"

"I thought they were just horror stories," I said faintly.

He rocked back and forth gently in his gravity cradle. He didn't say anything.

"Do you want to tell me what it's like?" I asked after a while.

Fazio shrugged. As though from a great distance he said, "What it's like? Ah, it's not all that goddamned bad, Chollie. It's like having a roommate. Living with you in your head, forever, and you can't break the lease. That's all. Or like having an itch you can't scratch. Having it there is like finding yourself trapped in a space that's exactly one centimeter bigger than you are all around, and knowing that you're going to stay walled up in it for a million years." He looked off toward the great clear wall of the lounge, toward giant red Betelgeuse blazing outside far away. "Your synsym talks to you, sometimes. So you're never lonely, you know? Doesn't speak any language you understand, just sits there and spouts gibberish. But at least it's company. Sometimes it makes you spout gibberish, especially when you badly need to make sense. It grabs control of the upper brain centers now and then, you know. And as for the autonomous centers, it does any damned thing it likes with them. Keys into the pain zones and runs little simulations for you—an amputation without anesthetic, say. Just for fun. Its fun. Or you're in bed with a woman and it disconnects your erection mechanism. Or it gives you an erection that won't go down for six weeks. For fun. It can get playful with your toilet training, too. I wear a diaper, Chollie, isn't that sweet? I have to. I get drunk sometimes without drinking. Or I drink myself sick without feeling a thing. And all the time I feel it there, tickling me. Like an ant crawling around within my skull. Like a worm up my nose. It's just like the other guys told us, when we came out to the war zone. Remember? 'Kill yourself fast, while you have the chance.' I never had the chance. I had you, Chollie, and we had a deal, but you didn't take our deal seriously. Why not, Chollie?"

I felt his eyes burning me. I looked away, halfway across the lounge, and caught sight of Elisandra's long golden hair drifting in free float. She saw me at the same moment, and waved. We usually got together in here this time of night. I shook my head, trying to warn her off, but it was too late. She was already heading our way.

"Who's that?" Fazio asked. "Your girlfriend?"

"A friend."

"Nice," he said. He was staring at her as though he had never seen a woman before. "I noticed her last night too. You live together?"

"We work the same shift on the wheel."

"Yeah. I saw you leave with her last night. And the night before."

"How long have you been at the Station, Fazio?"

"Week. Ten days, maybe."

"Came here looking for me?"

"Just wandering around," he said. "Fat disability pension, plenty of time. I go to a lot of places. That's a really nice woman, Chollie. You're a lucky guy." A tic was popping on his cheek and another was getting started on his lower lip. He said, "Why the fuck didn't you kill me when that thing first jumped me?"

"I told you. I couldn't. The paramedics were on the scene too fast."

"Right. You needed to say some Hail Marys first, and they just didn't give you enough time."

He was implacable. I had to strike back at him somehow or the guilt and shame would drive me crazy. Angrily I said, "What the hell do you want me to tell you, Fazio? That I'm sorry I didn't kill you ten years ago? Okay, I'm sorry. Does that do any good? Listen, if the synsym's as bad as you say, how come you haven't killed yourself? Why go on dragging yourself around with that thing inside your head?"

He shook his head and made a little muffled grunting sound. His face abruptly became gray, his lips were sagging. His eyeballs seemed to be spinning slowly in opposite directions. Just an illusion, I knew, but a scary one.

"Fazio?"

He said, "*Chollallula lillalolla loolicholla. Billillolla.*"

I stared. He looked frightening. He looked hideous.

"Jesus, Fazio!"

Spittle dribbled down his chin. Muscles jumped and writhed crazily all over his face. "You see? You see?" he managed to blurt. There was warfare inside him. I watched him trying to regain command. It was like a man wrestling himself to a fall. I thought he was going to have a stroke. But then, suddenly, he seemed to grow calm. His breath was ragged, his skin was mottled with fiery blotches. He collapsed down into himself, head drooping, arms dangling. He looked altogether spent. Another minute or two passed before he could speak. I didn't know what to do for him. I floated there, watching. Finally a little life seemed to return to him.

"Did you see? That's what happens," he gasped. "It takes control. How could I ever kill myself? It wouldn't let me do it."

"Wouldn't let you?"

He looked up at me and sighed wearily. "Think, Chollie, think! It's in symbiosis with me. We aren't independent organisms." Then the tremors began again, worse than before. Fazio made a desperate furious attempt to fight them off—arms and legs flung rigidly out, jaws working—but it was useless. "*Illallomba!*" he yelled. "*Nullagribba!*" He tossed his head from side to side as if trying to shake off something sticky that was clinging to it. "If I—then it—*gillagilla! Holligoolla!* I can't—I can't— oh—Jesus—Christ—!

His voice died away into harsh sputters and clankings. He moaned and covered his face with his hands.

But now I understood.

For Fazio there could never be any escape. That was the most monstrous part of the whole thing, the ultimate horrifying twist. The symbiont knew that its destiny was linked to Fazio's. If he died, the symbiont would also; and so it could not allow its host to damage himself. From its seat in Fazio's brain it had ultimate control over his body. Whatever he tried—jump off a bridge, reach for a flask of poison, pick up a gun—the watchful thing in his mind would be a step ahead of him, always protecting him against harm.

A flood of compassion welled up in me and I started to put my hand comfortingly on Fazio's shoulder. But then I yanked it back as though I were afraid the symbiont could jump from his mind into mine at the slightest touch. And then I scowled and forced myself to touch him after all. He pulled away. He looked burned out.

"Chollie?" Elisandra said, coming up beside us. She floated alongside, long-limbed, beautiful, frowning. "Is this private, or can I join you?"

I hesitated, fumbling. I desperately wanted to keep Fazio and Elisandra in separate compartments of my life, but I saw that I had no way of doing that. "We were—well—just that—"

"Come on, Chollie," Fazio said in a bleak hollow voice. "Introduce your old war buddy to the nice woman."

Elisandra gave him an inquiring glance. She could not have failed to detect the strangeness in his tone.

I took a deep breath. "This is Fazio," I said. "We were in the Servadac campaign together during the Second Ovoid War. Fazio—Elisandra. Elisandra's a traffic-polarity engineer on the turnaround wheel—you ought to see her at work, the coolest cookie you can imagine—"

"An honor to meet you," said Fazio grandly. "A woman who combines such beauty and such technical skills—I have to say—I—I—" Suddenly he was faltering. His face turned blotchy. Fury blazed in his eyes. "No! Damn it, no! No more!" He clutched handfuls of air in some wild attempt at steadying himself. "*Mullagalloola!*" he cried, helpless. "*Jillabongbong! Sampazozozo!*" And he burst into wild choking sobs, while Elisandra stared at him in amazement and sorrow.

"Well, are you going to kill him?" she asked.

It was two hours later. We had put Fazio to bed in his little cubicle over at Transient House, and she and I were in her room. I had told her everything.

I looked at her as though she had begun to babble the way Fazio had. Elisandra and I had been together almost a year, but there were times I felt I didn't know her at all.

"Well?" she said.

"Are you serious?"

"You owe it to him. You owe him a death, Chollie. He can't come right out and say it, because the symbiont won't allow him to. But that's what he wants from you."

I couldn't deny any of that. I'd been thinking the same thing for at least the past hour. The reality of it was inescapable: I had muffed things on Weinstein and sent Fazio to hell for ten years. Now I had to set him free.

"If there was only some way to get the symbiont out of his brain—"

"But there isn't."

"No," I said. "There isn't."

"You'll do it for him, won't you?"

"Quit it," I said.

"I hate the way he's suffering, Chollie."

"You think I don't?"

"And what about you? Suppose you fail him a second time. How will you live with that? Tell me how."

"I was never much for killing, Ellie. Not even Ovoids."

"We know that," she said. "But you don't have any choice this time."

I went to the little fireglobe she had mounted above the sleeping platform, and hit the button and sent sparks through the thick coiling mists. A rustle of angry colors swept the mist, a wild aurora, green, purple, yellow. After a moment I said quietly, "You're absolutely right."

"Good. I was afraid for a moment you were going to crap out on him again."

There was no malice in it, the way she said it. All the same, it hit me like a fist. I stood there nodding, letting the impact go rippling through me and away.

At last the reverberations seemed to die down within me. But then a great new uneasiness took hold of me and I said, "You know, it's totally idiotic of us to be discussing this. I'm involving you in something that's none of your business. What we're doing is making you an accomplice before the fact."

Elisandra ignored me. Something was in motion in her mind, and there was no swerving her now. "How would you go about it?" she asked. "You can't just cut someone's throat and dump him down a disposer chute."

"Look," I said, "do you understand that the penalty could be anything up to—"

She went on, "Any sort of direct physical assault is out. There'd be some sort of struggle for sure—the symbiont's bound to defend the host body against attack—you'd come away with scratches, bruises, worse. Somebody would notice. Suppose you got so badly hurt you had to go to the medics. What would you tell them? A barroom brawl? And then nobody can find your old friend Fazio who you were seen with a few days before? No, much too risky." Her tone was strangely businesslike, matter-of-fact. "And then, getting rid of the body—that's even tougher, Chollie, getting fifty kilos of body mass off the Station without some kind of papers. No destination visa, no transshipment entry. Even a sack of potatoes would have an out-invoice. But if someone just vanishes and there's a fifty-kilo short balance in the mass totals that day—"

"Quit it," I said. "Okay?"

"You owe him a death. You agreed about that."

"Maybe I do. But whatever I decide, I don't want to drag you into it. It isn't your mess, Ellie."

"You don't think so?" she shot right back at me.

Anger and love were all jumbled together in Elisandra's tone. I didn't feel like dealing with that just now. My head was pounding. I activated the pharmo arm by the sink and hastily ran a load of relaxants into myself with a subcue shot. Then I took her by the hand. Gently, trying hard to disengage, I said, "Can we just go to bed now? I'd rather not talk about this anymore."

Elisandra smiled and nodded. "Sure," she replied, and her voice was much softer.

She started to pull off her clothes. But after a moment she turned to me, troubled. "I can't drop it just like that, Chollie. It's still buzzing inside me. That poor bastard." She shuddered.

"Never to be alone in his own head. Never to be sure he has control over his own body. Waking up in a puddle of piss, he said. Speaking in tongues. All that other crazy stuff. What did he say? Like feeling an ant wandering around inside his skull? An itch you can't possibly scratch?"

"I didn't know it would be that bad," I said. "I think I would have killed him back then, if I had known."

"Why didn't you anyway?"

"He was Fazio. A human being. My friend. My buddy. I didn't much want to kill Ovoids, even. How the hell was I going to kill him?"

"But you promised to, Chollie."

"Let me be," I said. "I didn't do it, that's all. Now I have to live with that."

"So does he," said Elisandra.

I climbed into her sleeptube and lay there without moving, waiting for her.

"So do I," she added after a little while.

She wandered around the room for a time before joining me. Finally she lay down beside me, but at a slight distance. I didn't move toward her. But eventually the distance lessened, and I put my hand lightly on her shoulder, and she turned to me.

An hour or so before dawn she said, "I think I see a way we can do it."

We spent a week and a half working out the details. I was completely committed to it now, no hesitations, no reservations. As Elisandra said, I had no choice. This was what I owed Fazio; this was the only way I could settle accounts between us.

She was completely committed to it too: even more so than I was, it sometimes seemed. I warned her that she was needlessly letting herself in for major trouble in case the Station authorities ever managed to reconstruct what had happened. It didn't seem needless to her, she said.

I didn't have a lot of contact with him while we were arranging things. It was important, I figured, not to give the symbiont any hints.

I saw Fazio practically every day, of course—Betelgeuse Station isn't all that big—off at a distance, staring, glaring, sometimes having one of his weird fits, climbing a wall or shouting incoherently or arguing with himself out loud; but generally I pretended not to see him. At times I couldn't avoid him, and then we met for dinner or drinks or a workout in the rec room. But there wasn't much of that.

"Okay," Elisandra said finally. "I've done my part. Now you do yours, Chollie."

Among the little services we run here is a sightseeing operation for tourists who feel like taking a close look at a red giant star. After the big stellar-envelope research project shut down a few years ago we inherited a dozen or so solar sleds that had been used for skimming through the fringes of Betelgeuse's mantle, and we began renting them out for three-day excursions. The sleds are two-passenger jobs without much in the way of luxury and nothing at all in the way of propulsion systems. The trip is strictly ballistic: we calculate your orbit and shoot you out of here on the big repellers, sending you on a dazzling swing across Betelgeuse's outer fringes that gives you the complete lightshow and maybe a view of ten or twelve of the big star's family of planets. When the sled reaches the end of its string, we catch you on the turnaround wheel and reel you in. It sounds spectacular, and it is; it sounds dangerous, and it isn't. Not usually, anyhow.

I tracked Fazio down in the gravity lounge and said, "We've arranged a treat for you, man."

The sled I had rented for him was called the *Corona Queen*. Elisandra routinely handled the dispatching job for these tours, and now and then I worked as wheelman for them, although ordinarily I wheeled the big interstellar liners that used Betelgeuse Station as their jumping-off point for deeper space. We were both going to work Fazio's sled. Unfortunately, this time there was going to be a disaster, because a regrettable little error had been made in calculating orbital polarity, and then there would be a one-in-a-million failure of the redundancy circuits. Fazio's sled wasn't going to go on a tour of Betelgeuse's far-flung corona at all. It was going to plunge right into the heart of the giant red star.

I would have liked to tell him that, as we headed down the winding corridors to the dropdock. But I couldn't, because telling Fazio meant telling Fazio's symbiont also; and what was good news for Fazio was bad news for the symbiont. To catch the filthy thing by surprise: that was essential.

How much did Fazio suspect? God knows. In his place, I think I might have had an inkling. But maybe he was striving with all his strength to turn his mind away from any kind of speculation about the voyage he was about to take.

"You can't possibly imagine what it's like," I said. "It's unique. There's just no way to simulate it. And the view of Betelgeuse that you get from the Station isn't even remotely comparable."

"The sled glides through the corona on a film of vaporized carbon," said Elizandra. "The heat just rolls right off its surface." We were chattering compulsively, trying to fill every moment with talk. "You're completely shielded so that you can actually pass through the atmosphere of the star—"

"Of course," I said, "Betelgeuse is so big and so violent that you're more or less inside its atmosphere no matter where you are in its system—"

"And then there are the planets," Elisandra said. "The way things are lined up this week, you may be able to see as many as a dozen of them—"

"—Otello, Falstaff, Siegfried, maybe Wotan—"

"—You'll find a map on the ceiling of your cabin—"

"—Five gas giants twice the mass of Jupiter—keep your eye out for Wotan, that's the one with rings—"

"—and Isolde, you can't miss Isolde, she's even redder than Betelgeuse, the damndest bloodshot planet imaginable—"

"—with eleven red moons, too, but you won't be able to see them without filters—"

"—Otello and Falstaff for sure, and I think this week's chart shows Aida out of occultation now too—"

"—and then there's the band of comets—"

"—the asteroids, that's where we think a couple of the planets collided after gravitational perturbation of—"

"—and the Einsteinian curvature, it's unmistakable—"

"—the big solar flares—"

"Here we are," Elisandra said.

We had reached the dropdock. Before us rose a gleaming metal wall. Elisandra activated the hatch and it swung back to reveal the little sled, a sleek tapering frog-nosed thing with a low hump in the middle. It sat on tracks; above it arched the coils of the repeller-launcher, radiating at the moment the blue-green glow that indicated a neutral charge. Everything was automatic. We had only to put Fazio on board and give the Station the signal for launch; the rest would be taken care of by the orbital-polarity program Elisandra had previously keyed in.

"It's going to be the trip of your life, man!" I said.

Fazio nodded. His eyes looked a little glazed, and his nostrils were flaring.

Elisandra hit the pre-launch control. The sled's roof opened and a recorded voice out of a speaker in the dropdock ceiling began to explain to Fazio how to get inside and make himself secure for launching. My hands were cold, my throat was dry. Yet I was very calm, all things considered. This was murder, wasn't it? Maybe so, technically speaking. But I was finding other names for it. A mercy killing; a balancing of the karmic accounts; a way of atoning for an ancient sin of omission. For him, release from hell after ten years; for me, release from a lesser but still acute kind of pain.

Fazio approached the sled's narrow entry slot.

"Wait a second," I said. I caught him by the arm. The account wasn't quite in balance yet.

"Chollie—" Elisandra said.

I shook her off. To Fazio I said, "There's one thing I need to tell you before you go."

He gave me a peculiar look, but didn't say anything.

I went on, "I've been claiming all along that I didn't shoot you when the synsym got you because there wasn't time, the medics landed too fast. That's sort of true, but mainly it's bullshit. I had time. What I didn't have was the guts."

"Chollie—" Elisandra said again. There was an edge on her voice.

"Just one more second," I told her. I turned to Fazio again. "I looked at you, I looked at the heat-gun, I thought about the synsym. But I just couldn't do it. I stood there with the gun in my hand and I didn't do a thing. And then the medics landed and it was too late—I felt like such a shit, Fazio, such a cowardly shit—"

Fazio's face was turning blotchy. The red synsym lines blazed weirdly in his eyes.

"Get him into the sled!" Elisandra yelled. "It's taking control of him, Chollie!"

"*Oligabongaboo!*" Fazio said. "*Ungabahoo! Flizz! Thrapp!*"

And he came at me like a wild man.

I had him by thirty kilos, at least, but he damned near knocked me over. Somehow I managed to stay upright. He bounced off me and went reeling around, and Elisandra grabbed his arm. He kicked her hard and sent her flying, but then I wrapped my forearm around the throat from behind, and Elisandra, crawling across the floor, got him around his legs so we could lift him and stuff him into the sled. Even then we had trouble holding him. Two of us against one skinny burned-out ruined man, and he writhed and twisted and wriggled about like something diabolical. He scratched, he kicked, he elbowed, he spat. His eyes were fiery. Every time we forced him close to the entryway of the sled he dragged us back away from it. Elisandra and I were grunting and winded, and I didn't think we could hang on much longer. This wasn't Fazio we were doing battle with, it was a synthetic symbiont out of the Ovoid labs, furiously trying to save itself from a fiery death. God knows what alien hormones it was pumping into Fazio's bloodstream. God knows how it had rebuilt his bones and heart and lungs for greater efficiency. If he ever managed to break free of my grip, I wondered which of us would get out of the dropdock alive.

But all the same Fazio still needed to breathe. I tightened my hold on his throat and felt cartilage yielding. I didn't care. I just wanted to get him on that sled, dead or alive, give him some peace at all. Him and me both. Tighter—tighter—

Fazio made rough sputtering noises, and then a thick nasty gargling sound.

"You've got him," Elisandra said.

"Yeah. Yeah."

I clamped down one notch tighter yet, and Fazio began to go limp, though his muscles still spasmed and jerked frantically. The creature within him was still full of fight; but there wasn't much air getting into Fazio's lungs now and his brain was starving for oxygen. Slowly Elisandra and I shoved him the last five meters toward the sled—lifted him, pushed him up to the edge of the slot, started to jam him into it—

A convulsion wilder than anything that had gone before ripped through Fazio's body. He twisted half around in my grasp until he was face to face with Elisandra, and a bubble of something gray and shiny appeared on his lips. For an instant everything seemed frozen. It was like a slice across time, for just that instant. Then things began to move again. The bubble burst; some fragment of tissue leaped the short gap from Fazio's lips to Elisandra's. The symbiont, facing death, had cast forth a piece of its own lifestuff to find another host. "Chollie!" Elisandra wailed, and let go of Fazio and went reeling away as if someone had thrown acid in her eyes. She was clawing at her face. At the little flat gray slippery thing that had plastered itself over her mouth and was rapidly poking a couple of glistening pseudopods up into her nostrils. I hadn't known it was possible for a symbiont to send out offshoots like that. I guess no one did, or people like Fazio wouldn't be allowed to walk around loose.

I wanted to yell and scream and break things. I wanted to cry. But I didn't do any of those things.

When I was four years old, growing up on Backgammon, my father bought me a shiny little vortex-boat from a peddler on Maelstrom Bridge. It was just a toy, a bathtub boat, though it had all the stabilizer struts and outriggers in miniature. We were standing on the bridge and I wanted to see how well the boat worked, so I flipped it over the rail into the vortex. Of course it was swept out of sight at once. Bewildered and upset because it didn't come back to me, I looked toward my father for help. But he thought I had flung his gift into the whirlpool for the sheer hell of it, and he gave me a shriveling look of black anger and downright hatred that I will never forget. I cried half a day, but that didn't bring back my vortex-boat. I wanted to cry now. Sure. Something grotesquely unfair had happened, and I felt four years old all over again, and there was nobody to turn to for help. I was on my own.

I went to Elisandra and held her for a moment. She was sobbing and trying to speak, but the thing covered her lips. Her face was white with terror and her whole body was trembling and jerking crazily.

"Don't worry," I whispered. "This time I know what to do."

How fast we act, when finally we move. I got Fazio out of the way first, tossing him or the husk of him into the entry slot of the *Corona Queen* as easily as though he had been an armload of straw. Then I picked up Elisandra and carried her to the sled. She didn't really struggle, just twisted about a little. The symbiont didn't have that much control yet.

At the last moment I looked into her eyes, hoping I wasn't going to see the red circles in them. No, not yet, not so soon. Her eyes were the eyes I remembered, the eyes I loved. They were steady, cold, clear. She knew what was happening. She couldn't speak, but she was telling me with her eyes: Yes, yes, go ahead, for Christ's sake go ahead, Chollie!

Unfair. Unfair. But nothing is ever fair, I thought. Or else if there is justice in the universe it exists only on levels we can't perceive, in some chilly macrocosmic place where everything is evened out in the long run but the sin is not necessarily atoned by the sinner. I pushed her into the slot down next to Fazio and slammed the sled shut. And went to the dropdock's wall console and keyed in the departure signal, and watched as the sled went sliding down the track toward the exit hatch on its one-way journey to Betelgeuse. The red light of the activated repellers glared for a moment, and then the blue-green returned. I turned away, wondering if the symbiont had managed to get a piece of itself into me too at the last moment. I waited to feel that tickle in the mind. But I didn't. I guess there hadn't been time for it to get us both.

And then, finally, I dropped down on the launching track and let myself cry. And went out of there, after a while, silent, numb, purged clean, thinking of nothing at all. At the inquest six weeks later I told them I didn't have the slightest notion why Elisandra had chosen to get aboard that ship with Fazio. Was it a suicide pact, the inquest panel asked me? I shrugged. I don't know, I said. I don't have any goddamned idea what was going on in their minds that day, I said. Silent, numb, purged clean, thinking of nothing at all.

So Fazio rests at last in the blazing heart of Betelgeuse. My Elisandra is in there also. And I go on, day after day, still working the turnaround wheel here at the Station, reeling in the stargoing ships that come cruising past the fringes of the giant red sun. I still feel haunted, too. But it isn't Fazio's ghost that visits me now, or even Elisandra's—not now, not after all this time. I think the ghost that haunts me is my own.

Sunrise on Pluto

From *The Planets*, December 1985

We have waited out the night, and now at last we will go forth onto the frozen face of Pluto. One by one we take our places—Leonides, Sherrard, Gartenmeister, me—and ready ourselves to clamber down the ladder to the icy surface of the outermost of worlds.

Soon we will have an answer to the question that has obsessed us all during this long night.

Night on Pluto is 6.39 Earth-days long, and that night is blacker and colder than anything any of us has ever known. It is a true dark night of the soul, a dismal time made infinitely more terrible by our awareness of the monstrous distance separating us from all that we love. That distance imposes a burden which our spirits can scarcely carry. God knows, the dark side of Luna is a bleak and terrible place, but one never feels so wholly crushed by its bleakness as we have felt here. On Luna one need make only a brief journey to the edge and there is the lovely blue Earth hovering overhead, close, familiar, beckoning. But here stand we on forlorn Pluto, knowing that we are nearly four billion miles from home. No one has ever been so far from home before.

Now at last the fierce interminable night is ending. When we made our touchdown here the night was half spent; we used what remained of the dark hours to carry out our preliminary observations and to prepare for the extravehicular journey. Now, as we make ready to emerge, there comes the first trembling hint of a dawn. The utter and absolute and overwhelming darkness, which has been made all the more intense by the chilly glitter of the stars, is pierced by a strange pale glow. Then a sudden astonishing burst of light enters the sky—the light of a giant star whose cold radiance is hundreds of times as bright as that of the full moon seen from Earth.

It is the sun, *our* sun, the well of all warmth, the fountain of life. But how sadly its splendor is altered and diminished by those billions of miles! What reaches us here is not the throbbing golden blaze of summer but only a brilliant wintry beacon that sends glittering tracks of dazzling merciless brightness across the stark icefields of Pluto.

We move toward the hatch. No one speaks. The tension is rising and our faces show it.

We are edgy and uneasy, but not because we are about to be the first humans to set foot on this world: that is trivial, entirely unimportant to us, as I think it has always been to those who have carried the great quest outward into space. No, what concerns us is a mystery that no previous explorers of the Solar System have had to confront. Our instruments, during the long Plutonian night, have been recording apparent indications that living creatures, Plutonian life-forms, are moving about out there.

Life-forms? Here, on the coldest and most remote of worlds? It seems absurd. It *is* absurd. Nowhere in the Solar System has anyone ever found a trace of extraterrestrial life, not on any of the explored planets nor on any of their moons. Unless something unimaginable lurks deep within the impenetrable gaseous mantles of Jupiter or Saturn or Uranus, our own small planet is the sole repository of life in the System, and, for all we know, in the entire universe. But our scanners have picked up the spoor of life here: barely perceptible electromagnetic pulses that indicate something in motion. It is strictly a threshold phenomenon, the most minimal trace-output of energy, the tiniest trickle of exertion. The signal is so faint that Sherrard thinks it is nothing more than an instrumentation error, mere noise in the circuitry. And Gartenmeister *wants* it to be an error—he fears the existence of extraterrestrial life, so it seems, the way Pascal feared the eternal silence of the infinite heavens. Leonides argues that there is nothing that could produce such distinct vectors of electromagnetic activity except neural interaction, and therefore some sort of living beings must be crawling about on the icefields. "No," I say, "they could be purely mechanical, couldn't they? Robots left behind by interstellar explorers, say?"

Gartenmeister scowls at me. "Even more absurd," he says.

No, I think, not more absurd, merely more disturbing. No matter what we discover out there, it is bound to upset deeply held convictions about the unique place of Earth in the cosmos. Who would have thought it, that Pluto, of all places, would harbor life? On the other hand, perhaps Sherrard is right. Perhaps what we have imagined to be life-forms emitting minuscule flickers of electrical energy is in truth nothing more than deceptive Brownian tremors in the atoms that make up our ship's sensors. Perhaps. Soon we may have an answer.

"Let's go," Leonides says.

We swing downward and outward, into the cheerless Plutonian dawn.

The blackness of the sky is tinged with green as the distant sunlight bounces through the faint wispy swirls of methane that are Pluto's atmosphere. Visible now overhead, hovering ominously close, is the dull menacing bulk of Charon, Pluto's enormous moon, motionless and immense. Our shadows are weird things, sharp-edged and immensely long. They seem to strain forward as though trying to escape from us. Cold tendrils of sunlight glide unhurriedly toward the jagged icy cliffs in the distance.

Sunrise! Sunrise on Pluto!

How still it is, an alien sunrise. No birds sing, no insects buzz and drone. We four have seen many such sunrises—on Luna, on Mars, on Titan, on Ganymede, on Iapetus: standing with our backs to the rising sun, looking out on a harsh and silent landscape. But none so silent as this, none so harsh.

We fan out across the surface of Pluto, moving lithely, all but floating: Pluto is the lightest of worlds, its mass only a few hundredths that of Earth, and its gravitational grip is less secure than those of some of the larger moons. What do I see? Ice. A joyless methane sea far away, shining faintly by the dull light of dawn. Fangs of black rock. Despair begins to rise in me. To have come billions of miles, merely for the sake of being able to say that this world, too, has been explored—

"Here!" Leonides calls.

He is far in front of us, almost at the terminator line beyond which the sun has not yet reached. He is pointing ahead, into the darkness, stabbing at it with the beam of his light.

"Look! I can see them moving!"

We run toward him, leaping in great bounds, soaring, gliding. Then we stand beside him, following the line of his light, staring in awe and astonishment toward the darkness.

Yes. Yes. We have the answer at last to our question, and the answer is a stunning one. Pluto bears life. Small dome-shaped things are scrabbling over the ice!

They move slowly, unhurriedly, and yet one somehow feels that they are going as fast as possible, that indeed they are racing for cover, pushing their bodies to the limits. And we know what it is that they are struggling to escape; for already the ones closest to us have been overtaken by the advancing light of day, and as the rays touch them they move more slowly, and more slowly yet, and then they fall entirely still, stopping altogether between one moment and the next, like wind-up toys that have run down. Those that are in sunlight now lie stranded on the ice, and those ahead of them are being overtaken, one after another.

We hasten to them, kneel, examine them. None of us says a word. We hardly dare look at one another. The creatures are about the size of large crabs, with thick smooth waxy-textured gray shells that reveal neither eyes nor mouths. They are altogether motionless. I touch one with a trembling hand, nudge it, get no response, nudge it a bit more forcefully. It does not move. I glance at Leonides. He nods, and I tip the creature on its side, which shows us a great many small, jointed legs that seem to sprout from the shell surface itself. What a simple creature! A mere armored box!

"I don't believe it," Sherrard mutters.

"You still think it's an error in the circuitry?" Leonides asks him gently.

Sherrard shakes his head. Carefully he gathers one of the creatures into his gloved hands and brings it close to his faceplate. "It doesn't move at all," he says quietly. "It's playing possum, isn't it?"

"It may not be able to move," says Leonides. "Not with anything as warm as you so close to it. They're tremendously sensitive to heat,

I imagine. You see how they start to shut down, the moment the sun strikes them?"

"Like machines," says Sherrard. "At the wrong operating temperature they cease to function."

"*Like* machines, yes," Leonides replies. "But surely you aren't going to try to argue that they are machines, are you?"

Sherrard shrugs. "Machines can have legs. Machines can have shells." He looks toward me. "It's like you said, Tom: robots left behind by explorers from some other part of the galaxy. Why not? Why the hell not?"

There is nothing to gain by debating it out here. We return to the ship to get collection chambers and scoop three of the creatures into cryotanks, along with liquid methane and lumps of frozen-ammonia ice. The discovery is so wholly unexpected and so numbing in its implications that we can hardly speak. We had thought we were making a routine reconnaissance of an unimportant planet; instead we have made one of the most astonishing discoveries in the history of science.

We store our finds in the ship's lab at a temperature of two- or three-degrees Kelvin. Gartenmeister and Sherrard set about the job of examining them while Leonides and I continue the extravehicular exploration.

The crab-creatures are littered all over the place, dozens of them, hundreds, scattered like jetsam on a beach. They appear to be dead, but very likely Leonides' notion that they are extremely heat-sensitive tells the real story: to the native life-forms of Pluto—and how strange it is to have a phrase like that running through my mind!—the coming of day must be an inexorable signal bringing a halt to all metabolic activity. A rise of just a few degrees and they are compelled to stop in their tracks, seemingly lifeless, in fact held in suspended animation, until the slow rotation of the planet brings them back, in another 6.39 Earth-days, into the frigid darkness that they must have in order to function. Creatures of the night: creatures of the inconceivable realm at the borderland of absolute zero. But why? It makes so little sense: to move by night, to go dormant at the first touch of the life-giving sun! Why? Why?

Leonides and I explore for hours. There is so much to do: collecting mineral samples, drilling for ice-cores that may yield data on earlier epochs of Pluto's history, searching for other forms of life. We move carefully, for we are not yet used to the lightness of the gravitational field, and we prowl in a slow, systematic way, as if we are going to be the only expedition ever to land on this remote outpost of the Solar System and must take pains not to overlook anything. But I see the fallacy in that. It is true that this is the first time anyone has bothered to visit Pluto, although centuries have passed since the earliest human voyages into space. And it is true also that when we planned this expedition it was under the assumption that no one was likely to have reason to come this way again for a long time. But all that has changed. There is extraterrestrial life on this world, after all. Nowhere else is that the case. When we send back the news, it will alter the direction of virtually all scientific research, and much else besides.

The impact of our find is only just beginning to sink in.

Sherrard peers out of the ship's lab as Leonides and I come back on board. His expression is a peculiar one, a mixture of astonishment and—what?—self-satisfaction?

"We've discovered how they work," he announces. "They operate by superconductivity."

Of course. Superconductivity occurs only within a few degrees of absolute zero: a strange and miraculous thing, that resistance-free flow of current, the most efficient possible way of transmitting an electrical signal. Why *not* have it serve as the energizing principle for life-forms on a world where nighttime temperatures drop to two degrees Kelvin? It seems so obvious, now that Sherrard has said it. But at the same time it is such an unlikely thing, such an alien way for living creatures to be designed. If, that is, they are living creatures at all, and not merely some sort of cunning mechanisms. I feel the hair lifting along the back of my neck.

Gartenmeister and Sherrard have dissected one. It lies on its back, its undershell neatly cut away and its internal organs exposed to view. Its interior is lined with a series of narrow glossy green and blue tubes that cross and meet at rigid angles, with small yellow hexagonal bodies spaced at regular intervals down the center. The overall pattern is intricate, yes, but it is the intricacy of a well-designed machine. There is an almost oppressive symmetry about the arrangement. A second creature, still intact, rests unmoving and seemingly lifeless in its holding tank. The third has been placed in an adjoining tank, and it is awake and sullenly scrabbling about like a trapped turtle trying to climb the walls of its bowl.

Jerking his thumb at the one that is moving, Gartenmeister says, "We've got it at Pluto-night temperature, just a notch above absolute. The other tank's five degrees warmer. The threshold is very precise: when the temperature rises to seven degrees above absolute zero they start to go dormant. Lower the temperature and they wake up. Raise it again, they stop in their tracks again. It's like throwing a switch."

"It's exactly like throwing a switch," says Sherrard. "They're machines. Very neatly calibrated." He turns on a projector. Glittering cubical forms appear on the screen. "Here: look at the crystalline structure of one of these tubes. Silicon and cobalt, arranged in a perfect matrix. You want to tell me this is organic life? These things are nothing more than signal-processing devices designed to operate at super-cold temperatures."

"And we?" Leonides asks. "Are we not merely signal-processing devices also, designed to operate in somewhat warmer weather?"

"Merely? *Merely?*"

"We are machines of flesh and blood," says Leonides. "These are machines of another kind."

"But they have blood also," Gartenmeister says. "Of the sort that a superconductive life-form would have to have. Their blood is helium II."

How startling that is—and yet how plausible! Helium II, that weird friction-free fluid that exists only at the lowest of temperatures—capable of creeping up the side of a glass vessel in defiance of gravity, of passing through openings of incredibly small size, of doing all manner of unlikely things—and of creating an environment in which certain metals become capable of superconductive propagation of electrical signals. Helium II "blood," I realize, would indeed be an ideal carrier of nutrients through the body of a non-organic creature unable to pump a conventional fluid from one part of itself to another.

"Is that true?" Leonides asks. "Helium II? Actually?"

Gartenmeister nods. "There is no doubt of it."

"Helium II, yes," says Sherrard sullenly. "But it's just lubricating fluid. Not blood."

"Call it what you like," Gartenmeister tells him. "I use only a metaphor. I am nowhere saying yet that they are alive."

"But you imply—"

"I imply nothing!"

I remain silent, paying little attention to the argument. In awe and wonder I stare at the motionless creature, at the one that is moving about, and at the dissected one. I think of them out there on the Plutonian icefields, meandering in their unhurried way over fields of frozen methane, pausing to nibble at a hydrocarbon sundae whenever they feel the need for refreshment. But only during the night; for when their side of Pluto at last comes round to face the sun, the temperature will climb, soaring as high as 77 degrees Kelvin. They will cease motion long before that, of course—at just a few moments after dawn, as we have seen, when the day's heat rises beyond those critical few degrees at which superconductivity is possible. They slip into immobility then until night returns. And so their slow lives must go, switching from *on* to *off* for—who knows?—thousands of years, perhaps. Or perhaps forever.

How strange, I think, how alien, how wonderful they are! On temperate Earth, where animal life has taken the form of protoplasmic oxygen-breathing beings whose chemistry is based on carbon, the phenomenon of superconductivity itself is a bizarre and alien thing, sustainable only under laboratory conditions. But in the unthinkable cold of Pluto, how appropriate that the life-forms should be fashioned of silicon and cobalt, constructed in flawless lattices so that their tissues offer no resistance to electrical currents. Once generated, such a current would persist indefinitely, flowing forever without weakening—the spark of life, and eternal life at that!

They still look like grotesque crabs to me, and not the machines that Sherrard insists they must be. But even if they are animals rather than machines, they are, by comparison with any life-form known to Earth, very machine-like animals indeed.

We have spent a wearying six hours. This discovery should have been exhilarating, even exalting; instead we find ourselves bickering over whether we have found living creatures or mere ingenious mechanisms. Sherrard is adamant that they are machines; Gartenmeister seems to lean in both directions at once, though he is obviously troubled by the thought that they may be alive; Leonides is convinced that we are dealing with true life-forms. I think the dispute, now overheated and ugly, is a mere displacement symptom: we are disturbed by the deeper implications of the find, and, unwilling thus far to face them directly, we turn instead to quarreling over secondary semantic technicalities. The real question is not who created these beings—whether they are the work of what I suppose we can call the divine force, or simply of other intelligent creatures—but how we are to deal with the sudden inescapable knowledge that we are not alone in the universe.

I think we may just have settled the life-versus-machine dispute.

It is morning, ship-time. Gartenmeister calls out sharply, waking us. He has been on watch, puttering in the lab, while we sleep. We rush in and he points to the Plutonian that has been kept at superconductive temperatures.

"See there? Along the lower left-hand rim of its shell?"

I can find nothing unusual at first. Then I look more carefully, as he focuses the laser lamp to cast its beam at a steeper angle. Now I observe two fine metallic "whiskers," so delicate that they are barely visible even to my most intense scrutiny, jutting to a length of five or six millimeters from the edge of the shell.

"I saw them sprout," he says. "One came half an hour ago. The other just now. Look—here comes a third!"

We crowd in close. There can be no doubt: a third delicate whisker is beginning to protrude.

Sherrard says, "Communications devices, perhaps? It's programmed to signal for help when captured: it's setting up its antenna so that it can broadcast to the others outside."

Leonides laughs. "Do you think they get captured often? By whom?"

"Who can say?" Sherrard responds. "There may be other creatures out there that prey on—"

He stops, realizing what he has said. It is too late.

"Other *creatures?*" I ask. "Don't you mean bigger machines?"

Sherrard looks angry. "I don't know what I mean. Creatures, machines—" He shakes his head. "Even so, these might be antennae of some sort, can't they? Signaling devices that protrude automatically in time of danger? Say, when one is trapped by an ice-slide?"

"Or sensors," offers Leonides. "Like a cat's whiskers, like a snail's feelers. Probing the environment, helping it to find a way out of the tank we've got it in."

"A reproductive organ," Gartenmeister says suddenly.

We stare at him. "*What?*"

Unperturbed, he says, "Many low-phylum life-forms, when they are trapped, go automatically into reproductive mode. Even if the individual is destroyed, the species is still propagated. Let us say that these are living creatures, yes? For the sake of argument. Then they must reproduce somehow. Even though they are slow growing, virtually immortal, they must still reproduce. What if it is by budding? They take in minute quantities of silicon and cobalt, build up a surplus of nutrients, and at a certain time they put forth these filaments. Which gain in size over—who knows, a hundred years, a thousand, ten thousand?—and when they have the requisite minimum mass, they break free, take up independent life, foraging for their own food. The electrical spark of life is transferred automatically from parent to offspring and sustains itself by means of their superconductivity."

We look at him in amazement. Obviously he has been pondering deeply while we were sleeping.

"If you tell us that they metabolize—they eat, they transfer nutrients along the flow of helium II, they even reproduce," says Leonides, "then you're telling us that they're living things.

Or else you're asking us to redefine the nature of machines in such a way as to eliminate any distinction between machines and living things."

"I think," says Gartenmeister in a dark and despondent tone, "that there can be no doubt. They are alive."

Sherrard stares a long while at the three tiny filaments. Then he shrugs.

"You may be right," he says.

Leonides shakes his head. "Listen to you! Both of you! We've made the most exciting discovery in five hundred years and you sound as though you've just learned that the sun's going nova tomorrow!"

"Let them be," I tell him, touching his arm lightly. "It's not easy."

"What's not?"

"A thousand years ago everyone thought the earth was at the center of the universe, with everything else moving in orbit around it," I say. "It was a very comfortable and cozy and flattering idea, but it didn't happen to be true, as Copernicus and Kepler and Galileo were able to prove. It was such a hard thing for people to accept that Galileo was put on trial and forced to deny his own findings, wasn't he? All right. In time everyone came to admit that the earth moves around the sun, and not vice versa. And now, for centuries, we've explored space and found it absolutely lifeless—not a smidgeon of life, not a speck, no Martians, no Venusians, no Lunarians, nothing. *Nothing.* Earth the cosmic exception, the sole abode of life, the crown of creation. Until now. We have these little superconductive crabs here on Pluto. Our brothers-in-life, four billion miles away. Earth's last uniqueness is stripped away. I think that'll be harder to swallow than you may think. If we had found life right away, on the Moon back in the twentieth century, on Mars a little later on, it might have been easier. But not now, not after we've been all over the System. We developed a sort of smugness about ourselves. These little critters have just destroyed that."

"Even if they are machines," says Gartenmeister hollowly, "then we have to ask ourselves: Who built them?"

"I think I'd prefer to think they're alive," Sherrard says.

"They are alive," I tell them. "We're going to get used to that idea."

I walk to the hatch and peer outside. Small dark shapes lie huddled motionless here and there on the ice, waiting for night to return. For a long while I stare at them. My soul is flooded with awe and joy. The greatest of miracles has happened on this planet, as it had happened also long ago on Earth; and if life has been able to come into being on dismal Pluto, I know we will encounter it on a million million other worlds as we make our way in the centuries to come beyond this little Solar System into the vast galaxy. Somehow I cannot find anything to fear in that thought. Suddenly, thinking of the wonders and splendors that await us in that great beyond, I imagine that I hear the jubilant music of the spheres resounding from world to world; and when I turn and look back at the others, I realize that they also have been able to move past that first hard moment of shock and dismay which the loss of our uniqueness has brought. I see their faces transfigured, I see the doubt and turmoil gone; and it seems to me that they must be hearing that music too.

We Are for the Dark

From *Asimov's Science Fiction*, October 1988

Great warmth comes from him, golden cascades of bright, nurturing energy. The Master is often said to be like a sun, and so he is, a luminous creature, a saint, a sun indeed. But warmth is not the only thing that emanates from suns. They radiate at many frequencies of the spectrum, hissing and crackling and glaring like furnaces as they send forth the angry power that withers, the power that kills. The moment I enter the Master's presence I feel that other force, that terrible one, flowing from him. The air about him hums with it, though the warmth of him, the benevolence, is evident also. His power is frightful. And yet all he is, is a man, a very old one at that, with a smooth round hairless head and pale, mysteriously gentle eyes. Why should I fear him? My faith is strong. I love the Master. We all love him.

This is only the fifth time I have met him. The last was seven years ago, at the time of the Altair launch. We of the other House rarely have reason to come to the Sanctuary, or they to us. But he recognizes me at once, and calls me by name, and pours cool clear golden wine for me with his own hand. As I expect, he says nothing at first about his reason for summoning me. He talks instead of his recent visit to the Capital, where great swarms of ragged hungry people trotted tirelessly alongside his palanquin as he was borne in procession, begging him to send them into the Dark. "Soon, soon, my children," is what he tells me now that he told them then. "Soon we will all go to our new dwelling places in the stars." And he wept, he says, for sheer joy, feeling the intensity of their love for him, feeling their longing for the new worlds to which we alone hold the keys. It seems to me that he is quietly weeping now, telling me these things.

Behind his desk is a star-map of extraordinary vividness and detail, occupying the rear wall of his austere chamber. Indeed, it is the rear wall: a huge curving shield of some gleaming dark substance blacker than night, within which I can see our galaxy depicted, its glittering core, its spiraling arms. Many of the high-magnitude stars shine forth clearly in their actual colors. Beyond, sinking into the depths of the dark matrix in a way that makes the map seem to stretch outward to infinity, are the neighboring galaxies, resting in clouds of shimmering dust. More distant clusters and nebulae are visible still farther from the map's center. As I stare, I feel myself carried on and on to the outermost ramparts of the universe. I compliment him on the ingenuity of the map, and on its startling realism.

But that seems to be a mistake. "Realism? This map?" the Master cries, and the energies flickering around him grow fierce and sizzling once again. "This map is nothing: a crazy hodgepodge. A lunacy. Look, this star sent us its light twelve billion years ago, and that one six billion years ago, and this other one twenty-three years ago, and we're seeing them all at once. But this one didn't even exist when that one started beaming its light at us. And this one may have died five billion years ago, but we won't know it for five billion more." His voice, usually so soft, is rising now and there is a dangerous edge on it. I have never seen him this angry. "So what does this map actually show us? Not the absolute reality of the universe but only a meaningless ragbag of subjective impressions. It shows the stars as they happen to appear to us just at this minute and we pretend that that is the actual cosmos, the true configuration." His face has grown flushed. He pours more wine. His hand is trembling, suddenly, and I think he will miss the rim of the glass, but no: his control is perfect. We drink in silence. Another moment and he is calm again, benign as the Buddha, bathing me in the glow and luster of his spirit.

"Well, we must do the best we can within our limitations," he says gently. "For the closer spans the map is not so useless." He touches something on his desk and the star-map undergoes a dizzying shift, the outer clusters dropping away and the center of our own galaxy coming up until it fills the whole screen. Another flick of his finger and the inner realm of the galaxy stands out in bright highlighting: that familiar sphere, a hundred light-years in diameter, which is the domain of our Mission. A network of brilliant yellow lines cuts across the heart of it from star to star, marking the places where we have chosen to place our first receiver stations. It is a pattern I could trace from memory, and, seeing it now, I feel a sense of comfort and well-being, as though I am looking at a map of my native city.

Now, surely, he will begin to speak of Mission matters, he will start working his way round to the reason for my being here. But no, no, he wants to tell me of a garden of aloes he has lately seen by the shores of the Mediterranean, twisted spiky green rosettes topped by flaming red torches of blooms, and then of his visit to a lake in East Africa where pink flamingos massed in millions, so that all the world seemed pink, and then of a pilgrimage he has undertaken in the highest passes of the Sierra Nevada, where gnarled little pines ten thousand years old endure the worst that winter can hurl at them. As he speaks, his face grows more animated, his eyes taken on an eager sparkle. His great age drops away from him: he seems younger by thirty, forty, fifty years. I had not realized he was so keen a student of nature. "The next time you are in my country," I tell him, "perhaps you will allow me to show you the place along the southern shore where the fairy penguins come to nest in summer. In all the world I think that is the place I love the best."

He smiles. "You must tell me more about that some time." But his tone is flat, his expression has gone slack. The effort of this little talk must have exhausted him. "This Earth of ours is so beautiful," he says. "Such marvels, such splendors."

What can he mean by that? Surely he knows that only a few scattered islands of beauty remain, rare fortunate places rising above the polluted seas or sheltered from the tainted air, and that everything else is soiled, stained, damaged, corroded beyond repair by one sort of human folly or another.

"Of course," he says, "I would leave it in a moment, if duty beckoned me into the Dark. I would not hesitate. That I could never return would mean nothing to me." For a time he is silent. Then he draws a disk from a drawer of his desk and slides it toward me. "This music has given me great pleasure. Perhaps it will please you also. We'll talk again in a day or two."

The map behind him goes blank. His gaze, though it still rests on me, is blank now also.

So the audience is over, and I have learned nothing. Well, indirection has always been his method. I understand now that whatever has gone wrong with the Mission—for surely something has, why else would I be here?—is not only serious enough to warrant calling me away from my House and my work, but is so serious that the Master feels the need of more than one meeting to convey its nature to me. Of course I am calm. Calmness is inherent in the character of those who serve the Order. Yet there is a strangeness about all this that troubles me as I have never been troubled before in the forty years of my service. Outside, the night air is warm, and still humid from earlier rain.

The Master's lodge sits by itself atop a lofty stepped platform of pink granite, with the lesser buildings of the Order arrayed in a semicircle below it on the side of the great curving hill. As I walk toward the hostelry where I am staying, novitiates and even some initiates stare at me as though they would like to prostrate themselves before me. They revere me as I revere the Master. They would touch the hem of my robe, if they could. I nod and smile. Their eyes are hungry, God-haunted, star-haunted.

"Lord Magistrate," they murmur. "God be with you, your grace. God be with you." One novitiate, a gaunt boy, all cheekbones and eyebrows, dares to run to my side and ask me if the Master is well. "Very well," I tell him. A girl, quivering like a bowstring, says my name over and over as though it alone can bring her salvation. A plump monkish-looking man in a gray robe much too heavy for this hot climate looks toward me for a blessing, and I give him a quick gesture and walk swiftly onward, sealing my attention now inward and heavenward to free myself of their supplications as I stride across the terraced platform to my lodging.

There is no moon tonight, and against the blackness of the highlands sky the stars shine forth resplendently by the tens of thousands. I feel those stars in all their multitudes pressing close about me, enclosing me, enfolding me, and I know that what I feel is the presence of God. I imagine even that I see the distant nebulas, the far-off island universes. I think of our little ships, patiently sailing across the great Dark toward the remote precincts of our chosen sphere of settlement, carrying with them the receivers that will, God willing, open all His heavens to us. My throat is dry. My eyes are moist. After forty years I have lost none of my ability to feel the wonder of it.

In my spacious and lavishly appointed room in the hostelry I kneel and make my devotions, and pray, as ever, to be brought ever closer to Him. In truth I am merely the vehicle by which others are allowed to approach Him, I know: the bridge through which they cross to Him. But in my way I serve God also, and to serve Him is to grow closer to Him. My task for these many years has been to send voyagers to the far worlds of His realm. It is not for me to go that way myself: that is my sacrifice, that is my glory. I have no regret over remaining Earthbound: far from it! Earth is our great mother. Earth is the mother of us all. Troubled as she is, blighted as she now may be, dying, even, I am content to stay here, and more than content. How could I leave? I have my task, and the place of my task is here, and here I must remain.

I meditate upon these things for a time.

Afterward I oil my body for sleep and pour myself a glass of the fine brandy I have brought with me from home. I go to the wall dispenser and allow myself thirty seconds of ecstasy. Then I remember the disk the Master gave me, and decide to play it before bed. The music, if that is what it is, makes no impression on me whatever. I hear one note, and the next, and the one after that, but I am unable to put them together into any kind of rhythmic or melodic pattern. When it ends I play it again. Again I can hear only random sound, neither pleasant nor unpleasant, merely incomprehensible.

The next morning they conduct me on a grand tour of the Sanctuary complex to show me everything that has been constructed here since my last visit. The tropical sunlight is brilliant, dazzling, so strong that it bleaches the sky to a matte white, against which the colorful domes and pavilions and spires of the complex stand out in strange clarity and the lofty green bowl of surrounding hills, thick and lush with flowering trees bedecked in yellow and purple, takes on a heavy, looming quality.

Kastel, the Lord Invocator, is my chief guide, a burly, redfaced man with small, shrewd eyes and a deceptively hearty manner. With us also are a woman from the office of the Oracle and two subAdjudicators. They hurry me, though with the utmost tact, from one building to the next. All four of them treat me as though I were something extremely fragile, made of the most delicate spun glass—or, perhaps, as though I were a bomb primed to explode at the touch of a breath.

"Over here on the left," says Kastel, "is the new observatory, with the finest scanning equipment ever devised, providing continuous input from every region of the Mission. The scanner itself, I regret to say, Lord Magistrate, is out of service this morning. There, of course, is the shrine of the blessed Haakon. Here we see the computer core, and this, behind it under the opaque canopy, is the recently completed stellarium."

I see leaping fountains, marble pavements, alabaster walls, gleaming metallic facades. They are very proud of what they have constructed here. The House of the Sanctuary has evolved over the decades, and by now has come to combine in itself aspects of a pontifical capital, a major research facility, and the ultimate sybaritic resort. Everything is bright, shining, startlingly luxurious. It is at once a place of great symbolic power, a potent focus of spiritual authority as overwhelming in its grandeur as any great ceremonial center of the past—ranking with the Vatican, the Potala, the shrine at Delphi, the grand temple of the Aztecs—and an efficient command post for the systematic exploration of the universe. No one doubts that the Sanctuary is the primary House of the Order—how could it be anything else?—but the splendors of this mighty eyrie underscore that primacy beyond all question. In truth I prefer the starker, more disciplined surroundings of my own desert domain, ten thousand kilometers away. But the Sanctuary is certainly impressive in its way.

"And that one down there?" I ask, more for politeness' sake than anything else. "The long flat-roofed building near that row of palms?"

"The detention center, Lord Magistrate," replies one of the subAdjudicators.

I give him a questioning look.

"People from the towns below constantly come wandering in here," he explains. "Trespassers, I mean." His expression is cold. Plainly the intruders of which he speaks are annoyances to him; or is it my question that bothers him? "They hope they can talk us into shipping them out, you understand. Or think that the actual transmitters are somewhere on the premises and they can ship themselves out when nobody's looking. We keep them for a while, so that they'll learn that trying to break in here isn't acceptable. Not that it does much good. They keep on coming. We've caught at least twenty so far this week."

Kastel laughs. "We try to teach them a thing or two, all right! But they're too stupid to learn."

"They have no chance of getting past the perimeter screen," says the woman from the Oracle's office. "We pick them up right away. But as Joseph says, they keep on coming all the same." She shivers. "They look so dirty! And mean, and frightening. I don't think they want to be shipped out at all. I think they're just bandits who come up here to try to steal from us, and when they're caught they give us a story about wanting to be colonists. We're much too gentle with them, let me tell you. If we started dealing with them like the thieves they are, they wouldn't be so eager to come creeping around in here."

I find myself wondering just what does happen to the detainees in the detention center. I suspect that they are treated a good deal less gently than the woman from the Oracle's office thinks, or would have me believe. But I am only a guest here. It's not my place to make inquiries into their security methods.

It is like another world up here above the clouds. Below is the teeming Earth, dark and troubled, cult-ridden, doom-ridden, sweltering and stewing in its own corruption and decay; while in this airy realm far above the crumbling and sweltering cities of the plain these votaries of the Order, safe behind their perimeter screen, go quietly about their task of designing and clarifying the plan that is carrying mankind's best outward into God's starry realm. The contrast is vast and jarring: pink marble terraces and fountains here, disease and squalor and despair below.

And yet, is it any different at my own headquarters on the Australian plains? In our House we do not go in for these architectural splendors, no alabaster, no onyx, just plain green metal shacks to house our equipment and ourselves. But we keep ourselves apart from the hungry sweaty multitudes in hieratic seclusion, a privileged caste, living simply but well, undeniably well, as we perform our own task of selecting those who are to go to the stars and sending them forth on their unimaginable journeys. In our own way we are as remote from the pressures and torments of mankind as these coddled functionaries of the Sanctuary. We know nothing of the life beyond our own Order. Nothing. Nothing.

The Master says, "I was too harsh yesterday, and even blasphemous." The map behind him is aglow once again, displaying the inner sphere of the galaxy and the lines marking the network of the Mission, as it had the day before. The Master himself is glowing too, his soft skin ruddy as a baby's, his eyes agleam. How old is he? A hundred fifty? Two hundred? "The map, after all, shows us the face of God," he says. "If the map is inadequate, it simply reveals the inadequacies of our own perceptions. But should we condemn it, then? Hardly, any more than we should condemn ourselves for not being gods. We should revere it, rather, flawed though it may be, because it is the best approximation that we can ever make of the reality of the Divine."

"The face of God?"

"What is God, if not the Great Totality? And how can we expect to see and comprehend the Totality of the Totality in a single glance?" The Master smiles. These are not thoughts that he has just had for the first time, nor can his complete reversal of yesterday's outburst be a spontaneous one. He is playing with me. "God is eternal motion through infinite space. He is the cosmos as it was twelve billion years ago and as it was twelve billion years from now, all in the same instant. This map you see here is our pitiful attempt at a representation of something inherently incapable of being represented; but we are to be praised for making an attempt, however foredoomed, at doing that which cannot be done."

I nod. I stare. What could I possibly say?

"When we experience the revelation of God," the Master continues softly, "what we receive is not the communication of a formula about a static world, which enables us to be at rest, but rather a sense of the power of the Creator, which sets us in motion even as He is in motion." I think of Dante, who said, "In His will is our peace." Is there a contradiction here? How can "motion" be "peace"? Why is the Master telling me all this? Theology has never been my specialty, nor the specialty of my House in general, and he knows that. The abstruse nature of this discussion is troublesome to me. My eyes rest upon the Master, but their focus changes, so that I am looking beyond him, to red Antares and blue Rigel and fiery blue-white Vega, blazing at me from the wall.

The Master says, "Our Mission, you must surely agree, is an aspect of God's great plan. It is His way of enabling us to undertake the journey toward Him."

"Of course."

"Then whatever thwarts the design of the Mission must be counter to the will of God, is that not so?"

It is not a question. I am silent again, waiting.

He gestures toward the screen. "I would think that you know this pattern of lights and lines better than you do that of the palm of your hand."

"So I do."

"What about this one?"

The Master touches a control. The pattern suddenly changes: the bright symmetrical network linking the inner stars is sundered, and streaks of light now skid wildly out of the center toward the far reaches of the galaxy, like errant particles racing outward in a photomicrograph of an atomic reaction. The sight is a jarring one: balance overthrown, the sky untuned, discordancy triumphant. I wince and lean back from it as though he has slapped my face.

"Ah. You don't like it, eh?"

"Your pardon. It seems like a desecration."

"It is," he says. "Exactly so."

I feel chilled. I want him to restore the screen to its proper state. But he leaves the shattered image where it is.

He says, "This is only a probability projection, you understand. Based on early fragmentary reports from the farther outposts, by way of the Order's relay station on Lalande 21185. We aren't really sure what's going on out there. What we hope, naturally, is that our projections are inaccurate and that the plan is being followed after all. Harder data will be here soon."

"Some of those lines must reach out a thousand light-years!" "More than that."

"Nothing could possibly have gotten so far from Earth in just the hundred years or so that we've been—"

"These are projections. Those are vectors. But they seem to be telling us that some carrier ships have been aimed beyond the predetermined targets, and are moving through the Dark on trajectories far more vast than anything we intend."

"But the plan—the Mission—"

His voice begins to develop an edge again. "Those whom we, acting through your House, have selected to implement the plan are very far from home, Lord Magistrate. They are no longer subject to our control. If they choose to do as they please once they're fifty light-years away, what means do we have of bringing them into check?"

"I find it very hard to believe that any of the colonists we've sent forth would be capable of setting aside the ordinances of Darklaw," I say, with perhaps too much heat in my voice.

What I have done, I realize, is to contradict him. Contradicting the Master is never a good idea. I see the lightning playing about his head, though his expression remains mild and he continues to regard me benignly. Only the faintest of flushes on his ancient face betrays his anger. He makes no reply. I am getting into deep waters very quickly.

"Meaning no disrespect," I say, "but if this is, as you say, only a probability projection—"

"All that we have devoted our lives to is in jeopardy now," he says quietly. "What are we to do? What are we to do, Lord Magistrate?"

We have been building our highway to the stars for a century now and a little more, laying down one small paving-block after another. That seems like a long time to those of us who measure our spans in tens of years, and we have nibbled only a small way into the great darkness; but though we often feel that progress has been slow, in fact we have achieved miracles already, and we have all of eternity to complete our task.

In summoning us toward Him, God did not provide us with magical chariots. The inflexible jacket of the relativistic equations constrains us as we work. The speed of light remains our limiting factor while we establish our network. Although the Velde Effect allows us to deceive it and in effect to sidestep it, we must first carry the Velde receivers to the stars, and for that we can use only conventional spacegoing vehicles. They can approach the velocity of light, they may virtually attain it, but they can never exceed it: a starship making the outward journey to a star forty light-years from Earth must needs spend some forty years, and some beyond, in the doing of it. Later, when all the sky is linked by our receivers, that will not be a problem. But that is later.

The key to all that we do is the matter/antimatter relationship. When He built the universe for us, He placed all things in balance. The basic constituents of matter come in matched pairs: for each kind of particle there is an antiparticle, identical in mass but otherwise wholly opposite in all properties, mirror images in such things as electrical charge and axis of spin. Matter and antimatter annihilate one another upon contact, releasing tremendous energy. Conversely, any sufficiently strong energy field can bring about the creation of pairs of particles and antiparticles in equal quantities, though mutual annihilation will inevitably follow, converting the mass of the paired particles back into energy.

Apparently there is, and always has been since the Creation, a symmetry of matter and antimatter in the universe, equal quantities of each—a concept that has often been questioned by physicists, but which we believe now to be God's true design. Because of the incompatibility of matter and antimatter in the same vicinity, there is very little if any antimatter in our galaxy, which leads us to suppose that if symmetry is conserved, it must be through the existence of entire galaxies of antimatter, or even clusters of galaxies, at great distances from our own. Be that as it may: we will probably have no way of confirming or denying that for many thousands of years.

But the concept of symmetry is the essential thing. We base our work on Velde's Theorem, which suggests that the spontaneous conversion of matter into antimatter may occur at any time—though in fact it is an event of infinitesimal probability—but it must inescapably be accompanied by a simultaneous equal decay of antimatter into matter somewhere else, anywhere else, in the universe. About the same time that Velde offered this idea—that is, roughly a century and a half ago—Wilf demonstrated the feasibility of containment facilities capable of averting the otherwise inevitable mutual annihilation of matter and antimatter, thus making possible the controlled transformation of particles into their antiparticles. Finally came the work of Simtow, linking Wilf's technical achievements with Velde's theoretical work and giving us a device that not only achieved controlled matter/antimatter conversion but also coped with the apparent randomness of Velde symmetry-conservation.

Simtow's device tunes the Velde Effect so that conversion of matter into antimatter is accompanied by the requisite balancing transformation of antimatter into matter, not at some random site anywhere in the universe, but at a designated site. Simtow was able to induce particle decay at one pole of a closed system in such a way that a corresponding but opposite decay occurs at the other. Wilf containment fields were employed at both ends of the system to prevent annihilation of the newly converted particles by ambient particles of the opposing kind.

The way was open now, though it was some time before we realized it, for the effective instantaneous transmission of matter across great distances. That was achieved by placing the receiving pole of a Simtow transformer at the intended destination. Then an intricate three-phase cycle carried out the transmission.

In the first phase, matter is converted into antimatter at the destination end in an untuned reaction, and stored in a Wilf containment vessel. This, following Velde's conservation equations, presumably would induce spontaneous transformation of an equivalent mass of antimatter into matter in one of the unknown remote antimatter galaxies, where it would be immediately annihilated.

In the second phase, matter is converted to antimatter at the transmitting end, this time employing Simtow tuning so that the corresponding Velde-law transformation of the previously stored antimatter takes place not at some remote and random location but within the Wilf field at the designated receiving pole, which may be situated anywhere in the universe. What this amounts to, essentially, is the instantaneous particle-by-particle duplication of the transmitted matter at the receiving end.

The final step is to dispose of the unwanted antimatter that has been created at the transmission end. Since it is unstable outside the Wilf containment vessel, its continued existence in an all-matter system is pointless as well as untenable. Therefore it is annihilated under controlled circumstances, providing a significant release of energy that can be tapped to power a new cycle of the transmission process.

What is accomplished by all this? A certain quantity of matter at the transmission end of the system is destroyed; an exact duplicate of it is created, essentially simultaneously, at the receiving end. It made no difference, the early experimenters discovered, what was being put through the system: a stone, a book, a potted geranium, a frog. Whatever went in here came out there, an apparently perfect replica, indistinguishable in all respects from the original. Whether the two poles were situated at opposite ends of the same laboratory, or in different continents, or on Earth and Mars, the transmission was instant and total. What went forth alive came out alive. The geranium still bloomed and set seed; the frog still stared and leaped and gobbled insects. A mouse was sent, and thrived, and went on to live and die a full mouse-life. A pregnant cat made the journey and was delivered, three weeks later, of five healthy kittens. A dog—an ape— a man—

A man, yes. Has anyone ever made a bolder leap into the darkness than God's great servant Haakon Christiansen, the blessed Haakon whom we all celebrate and revere? He gambled everything on one toss of the dice, and won, and by his victory made himself immortal and gave us a gift beyond price.

His successful voyage opened the heavens. All we needed to do now was set up receiving stations. The Moon, Mars, the moons of Jupiter and Saturn, were only an eyeblink away. And then? Then? Why, of course, what remained but to carry our receivers to the stars?

For hours I wander the grounds of the Sanctuary, alone, undisturbed, deeply troubled. It is as if a spell of silence and solitude surrounds and protects me. No one dares approach me, neither as a supplicant of some sort nor to offer obeisance nor merely to see if I am in need of any service. I suppose many eyes are studying me warily from a distance, but in some way it must be obvious to all who observe me that I am not to be intruded upon. I must cast a forbidding aura today. In the brilliance of the tropic afternoon a darkness and a chill have settled over my soul. It seems to me that the splendid grounds are white with snow as far as I can see, snow on the hills, snow on the lawns, snow piled high along the banks of the sparkling streams, a sterile whiteness all the way to the rim of the world.

I am a dour man, but not a melancholy or tor-mented one. Others mistake my disciplined nature for something darker, seeing in me an iciness of spirit, a somberness, a harshness that masks some pervasive anguish of the heart. It is not so. If I have renounced the privilege of going to the stars, which could surely have been mine, it is not because I love the prospect of ending my days on this maimed and ravaged world of ours, but because I feel that God demands this service of me, that I remain here and help others to go forth. If I am hard and stern, it is because I can be nothing else, considering the choices I have made in shaping my course: I am a priest and a magistrate and a soldier of sorts, all in one. I have passed a dedicated and cloistered life. Yet I understand joy. There is a music in me. My senses are fully alive, all of them. From the outside I may appear unyielding and grim, but it is only because I have chosen to deny myself the pleasure of being ordinary, of being slothful, of being unproductive. There are those who misunderstand that in me, and see me as some kind of dismal monastic, narrow and fanatical, a gloomy man, a desolate man, one whom the commonplace would do well to fear and to shun. I think they are wrong. Yet this day, contemplating all that the Master has just told me and much that he has only implied, I am swept with such storms of foreboding and distress that I must radiate a frightful bleakness which warns others away. At any rate for much of this afternoon they all leave me alone to roam as I please.

The Sanctuary is a self-sufficient world. It needs nothing from outside. I stand near the summit of the great hill, looking down on children playing, gardeners setting out new plantings, novitiates sitting cross-legged at their studies on the lawn. I look toward the gardens and try to see color, but all color has leached away. The sun has passed beyond the horizon, here at this high altitude, but the sky is luminous. It is like a band of hot metal, glowing white. It devours everything: the edges of the world are slowly being engulfed by it. Whiteness is all, a universal snowy blanket.

For a long while I watch the children. They laugh, they shriek, they run in circles and fall down and rise again, still laughing. Don't they feel the sting of the snow? But the snow, I remind myself, is not there. It is illusionary snow, metaphorical snow, a trick of my troubled soul, a snowfall of the spirit. For the children there is no snow. I choose a little girl, taller and more serious than the others, standing somewhat to one side, and pretend that she is my own child. A strange idea, myself as a father, but pleasing. I could have had children. It might not have meant a very different life from the one I have had. But it was not what I chose.

Now I toy with the fantasy for a time, enjoying it. I invent a name for the girl; I picture her running to me up the grassy slope; I see us sitting quietly together, poring over a chart of the sky. I tell her the names of the stars, I show her the constellations. The vision is so compelling that I begin to descend the slope toward her. She looks up at me while I am still some distance from her. I smile. She stares, solemn, uncertain of my intentions. Other children nudge her, point, and whisper. They draw back, edging away from me. It is as if my shadow has fallen upon them and chilled them as they played. I nod and move on, releasing them from its darkness.

A path strewn with glossy green leaves takes me to an overlook point at the cliff's edge, where I can see the broad bay far below, at the foot of Sanctuary Mountain. The water gleams like a burnished shield, or perhaps it is more like a huge shimmering pool of quicksilver. I imagine myself leaping from the stone balcony where I stand and soaring outward in a sharp smooth arc, striking the water cleanly, knifing down through it, vanishing without a trace.

Returning to the main Sanctuary complex, I happen to glance downslope toward the long narrow new building that I have been told is the detention center. A portcullis at its eastern end has been hoisted and a procession of prisoners is coming out. I know they are prisoners because they are roped together and walk in a sullen, slack way, heads down, shoulders slumped.

They are dressed in rags and tatters, or less than that. Even from fairly far away I can see cuts and bruises and scabs on them, and one has his arm in a sling, and one is bandaged so that nothing shows of his face but his glinting eyes. Three guards walk alongside them, carelessly dangling neural truncheons from green lanyards. The ropes that bind the prisoners are loosely tied, a perfunctory restraint. It would be no great task for them to break free and seize the truncheons from the captors. But they seem utterly beaten down; for them to make any sort of move toward freedom is probably as unlikely as the advent of an army of winged dragons swooping across the sky.

They are an incongruous and disturbing sight, these miserable prisoners plodding across this velvet landscape. Does the Master know that they are here, and that they are so poorly kept? I start to walk toward them. The Lord Invocator Kastel, emerging suddenly from nowhere as if he had been waiting behind a bush, steps across my path and says, "God keep you, your grace. Enjoying your stroll through the grounds?"

"Those people down there—"

"They are nothing, Lord Magistrate. Only some of our thieving rabble, coming out for a little fresh air."

"Are they well? Some of them look injured."

Kastel tugs at one ruddy fleshy jowl. "They are desperate people. Now and then they try to attack their guards. Despite all precautions we can't always avoid the use of force in restraining them."

"Of course. I quite understand," I say, making no effort to hide my sarcasm. "Is the Master aware that helpless prisoners are being beaten within a thousand meters of his lodge?"

"Lord Magistrate—!"

"If we are not humane in all our acts, what are we, Lord Invocator Kastel? What example do we set for the common folk?"

"It's these common folk of yours," Kastel says sharply—I have not heard that tone from him before—"who ring this place like an army of filthy vermin, eager to steal anything they can carry away and destroy everything else. Do you realize, Lord Magistrate, that this mountain rises like a towering island of privilege above a sea of hungry people? That within a sixty-kilometer radius of these foothills there are probably thirty million empty bellies? That if our perimeter defenses were to fail, they'd sweep through here like locusts and clean the place out? And probably slaughter every last one of us, up to and including the Master."

"God forbid."

"God created them. He must love them. But if this House is going to carry out the work God intended for us, we have to keep them at bay. I tell you, Lord Magistrate, leave these grubby matters of administration to us. In a few days you'll go flying off to your secluded nest in the Outback, where your work is undisturbed by problems like these. Whereas we'll still be here, in our pretty little mountain paradise, with enemies on every side. If now and then we take some action that you might not consider entirely humane, I ask you to remember that we guard the Master here, who is the heart of the Mission." He allows me, for a moment, to see the contempt he feels for my qualms. Then he is all affability and concern again. In a completely different tone he says, "The observatory's scanning equipment will be back in operation again tonight. I want to invite you to watch the data come pouring in from every corner of space. It's an inspiring sight, Lord Magistrate."

"I would be pleased to see it."

"The progress we've made, Lord Magistrate—the way we've moved out and out, always in accordance with the divine plan—I tell you, I'm not what you'd call an emotional man, but when I see the track we're making across the Dark my eyes begin to well up, let me tell you. My eyes begin to well up."

His eyes, small and keen, study me for a reaction. Then he says, "Everything's all right for you here?"

"Of course, Lord Invocator."

"Your conversations with the Master—have they met with your expectations?"

"Entirely so. He is truly a saint." "Truly, Lord Magistrate. Truly."

"Where would the Mission be without him?"

"Where will it be," says Kastel thoughtfully, "when he is no longer here to guide us?"

"May that day be far from now."

"Indeed," Kastel says. "Though I have to tell you, in all confidence, I've started lately to fear—"

His voice trails off.

"Yes?"

"The Master," he whispers. "Didn't he seem different to you, somehow?"

"Different?"

"I know it's years since you last saw him. Perhaps you don't remember him as he was."

"He seemed lucid and powerful to me, the most commanding of men," I reply.

Kastel nods. He takes me by the arm and gently steers me toward the upper buildings of the Sanctuary complex, away from those ghastly prisoners, who are still shuffling about like walking corpses in front of their jail. Quietly he says, "Did he tell you that he thinks someone's interfering with the plan? That he has evidence that some of the receivers are being shipped far beyond the intended destinations?"

I look at him, wide-eyed.

"Do you really expect me to violate the confidential nature of the Master's audiences with me?"

"Of course not! Of course not, Lord Magistrate. But just between you and me—and we're both important men in the Order, it's essential that we level with each other at all times—I can admit to you that I'm pretty certain what the Master must have told you. Why else would he have sent for you? Why else pull you away from your House and interrupt what is now the key activity of the Mission? He's obsessed with this idea that there have been deviations from the plan. He's reading God knows what into the data. But I don't want to try to influence you. It's absurd to think that a man of your supreme rank in the second House of the Order can't analyze the situation unaided. You come tonight, you look at what the scanner says, you make up your own mind. That's all I ask. All right, Lord Magistrate? All right?"

He walks away, leaving me stunned and shocked. The Master insane? Or the Lord Invocator disloyal? Either one is unthinkable.

I will go to the observatory tonight, yes.

Kastel, by approaching me, seems to have broken the mysterious spell of privacy that has guarded me all afternoon. Now they come from all sides, crowding around me as though I am some archangel—staring, whispering, smiling hopefully at me. They gesture, they kneel. The bravest of them come right up to me and tell me their names, as though I will remember them when the time comes to send the next settlers off to the worlds of Epsilon Eridani, of Castor C, of Ross 154, of Wolf 359. I am kind with them, I am gracious, I am warm. It costs me nothing; it gives them happiness. I think of those bruised and slumpshouldered prisoners sullenly parading in front of the detention center. For them I can do nothing; for these, the maids and gardeners and acolytes and novitiates of the Sanctuary, I can at least provide a flicker of hope. And, smiling at them, reaching my hands toward them, my own mood lightens. All will be well. God will prevail, as ever. The Kastels of this world cannot dismay me.

I see the little girl at the edge of the circle, the one whom I had taken, for a strange instant, to be my daughter. Once again I smile at her. Once again she gives me a solemn stare, and edges away. There is laughter. "She means no disrespect," a woman says. "Shall I bring her to you, your grace?" I shake my head. "I must frighten her," I say. "Let her be." But the girl's stare remains to haunt me, and I see snow about me once more, thickening in the sky, covering the lush gardens of the Sanctuary, spreading to the rim of the world and beyond.

In the observatory they hand me a polarizing helmet to protect my eyes. The data flux is an overpowering sight: hot pulsing flares, like throbbing suns. I catch just a glimpse of it while still in the vestibule. The world, which has thawed for me, turns to snow yet again. It is a total whiteout, a flash of photospheric intensity that washes away all surfaces and dechromatizes the universe.

"This way, your grace. Let me assist you."

Soft voices. Solicitous proximity. To them, I suppose, I am an old man. Yet the Master was old before I was born. Does he ever come here? I hear them whispering: "The Lord Magistrate—the Lord Magistrate—" The observatory, which I have never seen before, is one huge room, an eight-sided building as big as a cathedral, very dark and shadowy within, massive walls of some smooth moist-looking greenish stone, vaulted roof of burnished red metal, actually not a roof at all but an intricate antenna of colossal size and complexity, winding round and round and round upon itself. Spidery catwalks run everywhere to link the various areas of the great room. There is no telescope. This is not that sort of observatory. This is the central gathering-point for three rings of data-collectors, one on the Moon, one somewhere beyond the orbit of Jupiter, one eight light-years away on a world of the star Lalande 21185. They scan the heavens and pump a stream of binary digits toward this building, where the data arrives in awesome convulsive actinic spurts, like thunderbolts hurled from Olympus.

There is another wall-sized map of the Mission here, the same sort of device that I saw in the Master's office, but at least five times as large. It too displays the network of the inner stars illuminated in bright yellow lines. But it is the old pattern, the familiar one, the one we have worked with since the inception of the program. This screen shows none of the wild divagations and bizarre trajectories that marked the image the Master showed me in my last audience with him.

"The system's been down for four days," a voice at my elbow murmurs: one of the astronomers, a young one, who evidently has been assigned to me. She is dark-haired, snub-nosed, bright-eyed, a pleasant faced girl. "We're just priming it now, bringing it up to realtime level. That's why the flares are so intense. There's a terrific mass of data backed up in the system and it's all trying to get in here at once."

"I see."

She smiles. "If you'll move this way, your grace—"

She guides me toward an inner balcony that hangs suspended over a well-like pit perhaps a hundred meters deep. In the dimness far below

I see metal arms weaving in slow patterns, great gleaming disks turning rapidly, mirrors blinking and flashing. My astronomer explains that this is the main focal limb, or some such thing, but the details are lost on me. The whole building is quivering and trembling here, as though it is being pounded by a giant's hand. Colors are changing: the spectrum is being tugged far off to one side. Gripping the rail of the balcony, I feel a terrible vertigo coming over me. It seems to me that the expansion of the universe has suddenly been reversed, that all the galaxies are converging on this point, that I am standing in a vortex where floods of ultraviolet light, x-rays, and gamma rays come rushing in from all points of the cosmos at once. "Do you notice it?" I hear myself asking. "The violet-shift? Everything running backwards toward the center?"

"What's that, your grace?"

I am muttering incoherently. She has not understood a word, thank God! I see her staring at me, worried, perhaps shocked. But I pull myself together, I smile, I manage to offer a few rational-sounding questions. She grows calm. Making allowances for my age, perhaps, and for my ignorance of all that goes on in this building. I have my own area of technical competence, she knows—oh, yes, she certainly knows that!—but she realizes that it is quite different from hers.

From my vantage point overlooking the main focal limb I watch with more awe than comprehension as the data pours in, is refined and clarified, is analyzed, is synthesized, is registered on the various display units arrayed on the walls of the observatory. The young woman at my side keeps up a steady whispered flow of commentary, but I am distracted by the terrifying patterns of light and shadow all about me, by sudden and unpredictable bursts of high-pitched sound, by the vibrations of the building, and I miss some of the critical steps in her explanations and rapidly find myself lost. In truth I understand almost nothing of what is taking place around me. No doubt it is significant. The place is crowded with members of the Order, and high ones at that, everyone at least an initiate, several wearing the armbands of the inner levels of the primary House, the red, the green, even a few amber. Lord Invocator Kastel is here, smiling smugly, embracing people like a politician, coming by more than once to make sure I appreciate the high drama of this great room. I nod, I smile, I assure him of my gratitude.

Indeed it is dramatic. Now that I have recovered from my vertigo I find myself looking outward rather than down, and my senses ride heavenward as though I myself am traveling to the stars.

This is the nerve-center of our Mission, this is the grand sensorium by which we keep track of our achievement.

The Alpha Centauri system was the starting-point, of course, when we first began seeding the stars with Velde receivers, and then Barnard's Star, Wolf 359, Lalande 21185, and so on outward and outward, Sirius, Ross 154, Epsilon Indi—who does not know the names?—to all the stars within a dozen light-years of Earth. Small unmanned starships, laser-powered robot drones, unfurling great lightsails and gliding starward on the urgent breath of photonic winds that we ourselves stirred up. Light was their propulsive force, and its steady pressure afforded constant acceleration, swiftly stepping up the velocity of our ships until it approached that of light.

Then, as they neared the stars that were their destinations, scanning for planets by one method or another, plotting orbital deviations or homing in on infrared radiation or measuring Doppler shifts—finding worlds, and sorting them to eliminate the unlivable ones, the gas giants, the ice-balls, the formaldehyde atmospheres—

One by one our little vessels made landfall on new Earths. Silently opened their hatches. Sent forth the robots who would set up the Velde receivers that would be our gateways. One by one, opening the heavens. And then—the second phase, the fabricating devices emerging, going to work, tiny machines seeking out carbon, silicon, nitrogen, oxygen, and the rest of the necessary building-blocks, stacking up the atoms in the predesignated patterns, assembling new starships, new laser banks, new Velde receivers. Little mechanical minds giving the orders, little mechanical arms doing the work. It would take some fifteen years for one of our ships to reach a star twelve light-years away. But it would require much less than that for our automatic replicators to construct a dozen twins of that ship at the landing point and send them in a dozen directions, each bearing its own Velde receiver to be established on some farther star, each equipped to replicate itself just as quickly and send more ships onward. Thus we built our receiver network, spreading our highway from world to world across a sphere that by His will and our choice would encompass only a hundred light-years in the beginning.

Then from our transmitters based on Earth we could begin to send—instantly, miraculously—the first colonists to the new worlds within our delimited sphere.

And so have we done. Standing here with my hands gripping the metal rail of the observatory balcony, I can in imagination send my mind forth to our colonies in the stars, to those tiny far-flung outposts peopled by the finest souls Earth can produce, men and women whom I myself have helped to choose and prepare and hurl across the gulf of night, pioneers sworn to Darklaw, bound by the highest of oaths not to repeat in the stars the errors we have made on Earth. And, thinking now of everything that our Order has achieved and all that we will yet achieve, the malaise that has afflicted my spirit since I arrived at the Sanctuary lifts, and a flood of joy engulfs me, and I throw my head back, I stare toward the maze of data-gathering circuitry far above me, I let the full splendor of the Project invade my soul.

It is a wondrous moment, but short-lived. Into my ecstasies come intrusive sounds: mutterings, gasps, the scurrying of feet. I snap to attention. All about me, there is sudden excitement, almost a chaos. Someone is sobbing. Someone else is laughing. It is a wild, disagreeable laughter that is just this side of hysteria. A furious argument has broken out across the way: the individual words are blurred by echo but the anger of their inflection is unmistakable.

"What's happening?" I ask the astronomer beside me.

"The master chart," she says. Her voice has become thick and hoarse. There is a troubled gleam in her eyes. "It's showing the update now—the new information that's just come in—"

She points. I stare at the glowing star-map. The familiar pattern of the Mission network has been disrupted, now, and what I see, what they all see, is that same crazy display of errant tracks thrusting far out beyond our designated sphere of colonization that I beheld on the Master's own screen two days before.

The most tactful thing I can do, in the difficult few days that follow, is to withdraw to my quarters and wait until the Sanctuary people have begun to regain their equilibrium. My being here among them now must be a great embarrassment for them. They are taking this apparent deviation from the Mission's basic plan as a deep humiliation and a stinging rebuke upon their House. They find it not merely profoundly disquieting and improper, as I do, but a mark of shame, a sign that God himself has found inadequate the plan of which they are the designers and custodians, and has discarded it. How much more intense their loss of face must be for all this to be coming down upon them at a time when the Lord Magistrate of the Order's other high House is among them to witness their disgrace.

It would be even more considerate of me, perhaps, to return at once to my own House's headquarters in Australia and let the Sanctuary people sort out their position without my presence to distract and reproach them. But that I cannot do. The Master wants me here. He has called me all the way from Australia to be with him at the Sanctuary in this difficult time. Here I must stay until I know why.

So I keep out of the way. I ask for my meals in my chambers instead of going to the communal hall. I spend my days and nights in prayer and meditation and reading. I sip brandy and divert myself with music. I take pleasure from the dispenser when the need comes over me. I stay out of sight and await the unfolding of events.

But my isolation is short-lived. On the third day after my retreat into solitude Kastel comes to me, pale and shaken, all his hearty condescension gone from him now.

"Tell me," he says hoarsely, "what do you make of all this? Do you think the data's genuine?"

"What reason do I have to think otherwise?"

"But suppose"—he hesitates, and his eyes do not quite meet mine—"suppose the Master has rigged things somehow so that we're getting false information?"

"Would that be possible? And why would he do such a monstrous thing in the first place?"

"I don't know."

"Do you really have so little regard for the Master's honesty? Or is it his sanity that you question?"

He turns crimson.

"God forbid, either one!" he cries. "The Master is beyond all censure. I wonder only whether he has embarked upon some strange plan beyond our comprehension, absolutely beyond our understanding, which in the execution of his unfathomable purpose requires him to deceive us about the true state of things in the heavens."

Kastel's cautious, elaborately formal syntax offends my ear. He did not speak to me in such baroque turns and curlicues when he was explaining why it was necessary to beat the prisoners in the detention center. But I try not to let him see my distaste for him. Indeed he seems more to be pitied than detested, a frightened and bewildered man.

"Why don't you ask the Master?" I say.

"Who would dare? But in any case the Master has shut himself away from us all since the other night."

"Ah. Then ask the Oracle."

"The Oracle offers only mysteries and redundancies, as usual."

"I can't offer anything better," I tell him. "Have faith in the Master. Accept the data of your own scanner until you have solid reason to doubt it. Trust God."

Kastel, seeing I can tell him nothing useful, and obviously uneasy now over having expressed these all but sacrilegious suppositions about the Master to me, asks a blessing of me, and I give it, and he goes. But others come after him, one by one—hesitantly, even fearfully, as though expecting me to turn them away in scorn. High and low, haughty and humble, they seek audiences with me. I understand now what is happening. With the Master in seclusion, the community is leaderless in this difficult moment. On him they dare not intrude under any circumstances, if he has given the sign that he is not to be approached. I am the next highest-ranking member of the hierarchy currently in residence at the Sanctuary. That I am of another House, and that between the Master and me lies an immense gulf of age and primacy, does not seem to matter to them just now. So it is to me that they come, asking for guidance, comfort, whatever. I give them what I can—platitudes, mainly—until I begin to feel hollow and cynical. Toward evening the young astronomer comes to me, she who had guided me through the observatory on the night of the great revelation. Her eyes are red and swollen, with dark rings below them. By now I have grown expert at offering these Sanctuary people the bland reassurances that are the best I can provide for them, but as I launch into what has become my standard routine I see that it is doing more harm to her than good—she begins to tremble, tears roll down her cheeks, she shakes her head and looks away, shivering—and suddenly my own facade of spiritual authority and philosophical detachment crumbles, and I am as troubled and confused as she is. I realize that she and I stand at the brink of the same black abyss. I begin to feel myself toppling forward into it. We reach for each other and embrace in a kind of wild defiance of our fears. She is half my age. Her skin is smooth, her flesh is firm. We each grasp for whatever comfort we can find. Afterward she seems stunned, numbed, dazed. She dresses in silence.

"Stay," I urge her. "Wait until morning."

"Please, your grace—no—no—"

But she manages a faint smile. Perhaps she is trying to tell me that though she is amazed by what we have done she feels no horror and perhaps not even regret. I hold the tips of her fingers in my hands for a moment, and we kiss quickly, a dry, light, chaste kiss, and she goes.

Afterward I experience a strange new clarity of mind. It is as if this unexpected coupling has burned away a thick fog of the soul and allowed me to think clearly once again.

In the night, which for me is a night of very little sleep, I contemplate the events of my stay at the House of Sanctuary and I come to terms, finally, with the obvious truth that I have tried to avoid for days. I remember the Master's casual phrase at my second audience with him, as he told me of his suspicion that certain colonists must be deviating from the tenets of Darklaw: "Those whom we, *acting through your House,* have selected ..." Am I being accused of some malfeasance? Yes. Of course. I am the one who chose the ones who have turned away from the plan. It has been decided that the guilt is to fall upon me. I should have seen it much earlier, but I have been distracted, I suppose, by troublesome emotions. Or else I have simply been unwilling to see.

I decide to fast today. When they bring me my morning meal tray they will find a note from me, instructing them not to come to me again until I notify them.

I tell myself that this is not so much an act of penitence as one of purgation. Fasting is not something that the Order asks of us. For me it is a private act, one which I feel brings me closer to God. In any case my conscience is clear; it is simply that there are times when I think better on an empty stomach, and I am eager now to maintain and deepen that lucidity of perception that came upon me late the previous evening. I have fasted before, many times, when I felt a similar need. But then, when I take my morning shower, I dial it cold. The icy water burns and stings and flays; I have to compel myself to remain under it, but I do remain, and I hold myself beneath the shower head much longer than I might ordinarily have stayed there. That can only be penitence. Well, so be it. But penitence for what? I am guilty of no fault. Do they really intend to make me the scapegoat? Do I intend to offer myself to expiate the general failure? Why should I? Why do I punish myself now?

All that will be made known to me later. If I have chosen to impose a day of austerity and discomfort upon myself, there must be a good reason for it, and I will understand in good time.

Meanwhile I wear nothing but a simple linen robe of a rough texture, and savor the roughness against my skin. My stomach, by midmorning, begins to grumble and protest, and I give it a glass of water, as though to mock its needs. A little later the vision of a fine meal assails me, succulent grilled fish on a shining porcelain plate, cool white wine in a sparkling crystal goblet. My throat goes dry, my head throbs. But instead of struggling against these tempting images I encourage them, I invite my traitor mind to do its worst: I add platters of gleaming red grapes to the imaginary feast, cheeses, loaves of bread fresh from the oven. The fish course is succeeded by roast lamb, the lamb by skewers of beef, the wine in the glass is now a fine red Coonawarra, there is rare old port to come afterward. I fantasize such gluttonies that they become absurd, and I lose my appetite altogether.

The hours go by and I begin to drift into the tranquility that for me is the first sign of the presence of God close at hand. Yet I find myself confronting a barrier. Instead of simply accepting His advent and letting Him engulf me, I trouble myself with finicky questions. Is He approaching me, I wonder? Or am I moving toward Him? I tell myself that the issue is an empty one. He is everywhere. It is the power of God which sets us in motion, yes, but He is motion incarnate. It is pointless to speak of my approaching Him, or His approaching me: those are two ways of describing the same thing. But while I contemplate such matters my mind itself holds me apart from Him.

I imagine myself in a tiny ship, drifting toward the stars. To make such a voyage is not what I desire; but it is a useful focus for my reverie. For the journey to the stars and the journey toward God are one thing and the same. It is the journey into reality.

Once, I know, these things were seen in a different light. But it was inevitable that as we began to penetrate the depths of space we would come to see the metaphysical meaning of the venture on which we had embarked. And if we had not, we could not have proceeded. The curve of secular thought had extended as far as it could reach, from the seventeenth century to the twenty-first, and had begun to crack under its own weight; just when we were beginning to believe that we were God, we rediscovered the understanding that we were not. The universe was too huge for us to face alone. That new ocean was so wide, and our boats so very small.

I urge my little craft onward. I set sail at last into the vastness of the Dark. My voyage has begun. God embraces my soul. He bids me be welcome in His kingdom. My heart is eased.

Under the Master's guidance we have all come to know that in our worldly lives we see only distortions—shadows on the cave wall. But as we penetrate the mysteries of the universe we are permitted to perceive things as they really are. The entry into the cosmos is the journey into the sublime, the literal attainment of heaven. It is a post-Christian idea: voyages must be undertaken, motion must never cease, we must seek Him always. In the seeking is the finding.

Gradually, as I reflect on these things yet again, the seeking ends for me and the finding begins, and my way becomes clear. I will resist nothing. I will accept everything. Whatever is required of me, that will I do, as always.

It is night, now. I am beyond any hunger and I feel no need for sleep. The walls of my chamber seem transparent to me and I can cast my vision outward to all the world, the heavy surging seas and the close blanket of the sky, the mountains and valleys, the rivers, the fields. I feel the nearness of billions of souls. Each human soul is a star: it glows with unique fire, and each has its counterpart in the heavens. There is one star that is the Master, and one that is Kastel, and one that is the young astronomer who shared my bed. And somewhere there is a star that is me. My spirit goes outward at last, it roves the distant blackness, it journeys on and on, to the ends of the universe. I soar above the Totality of the Totality. I look upon the face of God.

When the summons comes from the Master, shortly before dawn, I go to him at once. The rest of the House of Sanctuary sleeps. All is silent. Taking the garden path uphill, I experience a marvelous precision of sight: as though by great magnification I perceive the runnels and grooves on each blade of grass, the minute jagged teeth left by the mower as it bit it short, the glistening droplets of dew on the jade surface. Blossoms expand toward the pale new light now streaming out of the east as though they are coming awake. On the red earth of the path, strutting like dandies in a summer parade, are little shining scarletbacked beetles with delicate black legs that terminate in intricate hairy feet. A fine mist rises from the ground. Within the silence I hear a thousand tiny noises.

The Master seems to be bursting with youthful strength, vitality, a mystic energy. He sits motionless, waiting for me to speak. The starscreen behind him is darkened, an ebony void, infinitely deep. I see the fine lines about his eyes and the corners of his mouth. His skin is pink, like a baby's. He could be six weeks old, or six thousand years.

His silence is immense.

"You hold me responsible?" I say at last.

He stares for a long while. "Don't you?"

"I am the Lord Magistrate of Senders. If there has been a failure, the fault must be mine."

"Yes. The fault must be yours."

He is silent again.

It is very easy, accepting this, far easier than I would have thought only the day before.

He says after a time, "What will you do?"

"You have my resignation."

"From your magistracy?"

"From the Order," I say. "How could I remain a priest, having been a Magistrate?"

"Ah. But you must."

The pale gentle eyes are inescapable.

"Then I will be a priest on some other world," I tell him. "I could never stay here. I respectfully request release from my vow of renunciation."

He smiles. I am saying exactly the things he hoped I would say.

"Granted."

It is done. I have stripped myself of rank and power. I will leave my House and my world; I will go forth into the Dark, although long ago I had gladly given that great privilege up. The irony is not lost on me.

For all others it is heart's desire to leave Earth, for me it is merely the punishment for having failed the Mission. My penance will be my exile and my exile will be my penance. It is the defeat of all my work and the collapse of my vocation. But I must try not to see it that way. This is the beginning of the next phase of my life, nothing more. God will comfort me. Through my fall He has found a way of calling me to Him.

I wait for a gesture of dismissal, but it does not come.

"You understand," he says after a time, "that the Law of Return will hold, even for you?"

He means the prime tenet of Darklaw, the one that no one has ever violated. Those who depart from Earth may not come back to it. Ever. The journey is a one-way trip.

"Even for me," I say. "Yes. I understand."

I stand before a Velde doorway like any other, one that differs in no way from the one that just a short time before had carried me instantaneously halfway around the world, home from Sanctuary to the House of Senders. It is a cubicle of black glass, four meters high, three meters wide, three meters deep. A pair of black-light lenses face each other like owlish eyes on its inner sides. From the rear wall jut the three metal cones that are the discharge points.

How many journeys have I made by way of transmitting stations such as this one? Five hundred? A thousand? How many times have I been scanned, measured, dissected, stripped down to my component baryons, replicated: annihilated *here,* created *there,* all within the same moment? And stepped out of a receiver, intact, unchanged, at some distant point, Paris, Karachi, Istanbul, Nairobi, Dar es Salaam?

This doorway is no different from the ones through which I stepped those other times. But this journey will be unlike all those others. I have never left Earth before, not even to go to Mars, not even to the Moon. There has been no reason for it. But now I am to leap to the stars. Is it the scope of the leap that I fear? But I know better. The risks are not appreciably greater in a journey of twenty light-years than in one of twenty kilometers.

Is it the strangeness of the new worlds which I will confront that arouses this uneasiness in me? But I have devoted my life to building those worlds. What is it, then? The knowledge that once I leave this

House I will cease to be Lord Magistrate of the Senders, and become merely a wandering pilgrim?

Yes. Yes, I think that that is it. My life has been a comfortable one of power and assurance, and now I am entering the deepest unknown, leaving all that behind, leaving everything behind, giving up my House, relinquishing my magistracy, shedding all that I have been except for my essence itself, from which I can never be parted. It is a great severance. Yet why do I hesitate? I have asked so many others, after all, to submit to that severance. I have bound so many others, after all, by the unbending oaths of Darklaw. Perhaps it takes more time to prepare oneself than I have allowed. I have given myself very short notice indeed.

But the moment of uneasiness passes. All about me are friendly faces, men and women of my House, come to bid me a safe journey.

Their eyes are moist, their smiles are tender. They know they will never see me again. I feel their love and their loyalty, and it eases my soul.

Ancient words drift through my mind.

Into thy hands, O Lord, I commend my spirit.

Yes. And my body also.

Lord, thou hast been our refuge: from one generation to another. Before the mountains were brought forth, or ever the earth and the world were made: thou art God from everlasting, and world without end.

Yes. And then:

The heavens declare the glory of God: and the firmament showeth His handiwork.

There is no sensation of transition. I was there; now I am here. I might have traveled no further than from Adelaide to Melbourne, or from Brisbane to Cairns. But I am very far from home now. The sky is amber, with swirls of blue. On the horizon is a great dull warm red mass, like a gigantic glowing coal, very close by. At the zenith is a smaller and brighter star, much more distant.

This world is called Cuchulain. It is the third moon of the subluminous star Gwydion, which is the dark companion of Lalande 21185. I am eight light-years from Earth. Cuchulain is the Order's prime outpost in the stars, the home of Second Sanctuary. Here is where I have chosen to spend my years of exile. The fallen magistrate, the broken vessel.

The air is heavy and mild. Crazy whorls of thick green ropy vegetation entangle everything, like a furry kelp that has infested the land. As I step from the Velde doorway I am confronted by a short, crisp little man in dark priestly robes. He is tonsured and wears a medallion of high office, though it is an office two or three levels down from the one that had been mine.

He introduces himself as Procurator-General Guardiano. Greeting me by name, he expresses his surprise at my most unexpected arrival in his diocese. Everyone knows that those who serve at my level of the Order must renounce all hope of emigration from Earth.

"I have resigned my magistracy," I tell him. "No," I say. "Actually I've been dismissed. For cause. I've been reassigned to the ordinary priesthood."

He stares, plainly shocked and stunned.

"It is still an honor to have you here, your grace," he says softly, after a moment.

I go with him to the chapter house, not far away. The gravitational pull here is heavier than Earth's, and I find myself leaning forward as I walk and pulling my feet after me as though the ground is sticky. But such incidental strangenesses as this are subsumed, to my surprise, by a greater familiarity: this place is not as alien as I had expected. I might merely be in some foreign land, and not on another world. The full impact of my total and final separation from Earth, I know, will not hit me until later.

We sit together in the refectory, sipping glass after glass of a sweet strong liqueur. Procurator-General Guardiano seems flustered by having someone of my rank appear without warning in his domain, but he is handling it well. He tries to make me feel at home. Other priests of the higher hierarchy appear—the word of my arrival must be traveling fast—and peer into the room. He waves them away. I tell him, briefly, the reasons for my downfall. He listens gravely and says, "Yes. We know that the outer worlds are in rebellion against Darklaw."

"Only the outer worlds?"

"So far, yes. It's very difficult for us to get reliable data."

"Are you saying that they've closed the frontier to the Order?"

"Oh, no, nothing like that. There's still free transit to every colony, and chapels everywhere. But the reports from the outer worlds are growing increasingly mysterious and bizarre. What we've decided is that we're going to have to send an Emissary Plenipotentiary to some of the rebel worlds to get the real story."

"A spy, you mean?"

"A spy? No. Not a spy. A teacher. A guide. A prophet, if you will. One who can bring them back to the true path." Guardiano shakes his head. "I have to tell you that all this disturbs me profoundly, this repudiation of Darklaw, these apparent breaches of the plan. It begins to occur to me—though I know the Master would have me strung up for saying any such thing—that we may have been in error from the beginning." He gives me a conspiratorial look. I smile encouragingly. He goes on, "I mean, this whole elitist approach of ours, the Order maintaining its monopoly over the mechanism of matter transmission, the Order deciding who will go to the stars and who will not, the Order attempting to create new worlds in our own image—" He seems to be talking half to himself. "Well, apparently it hasn't worked, has it? Do I dare say it? They're living just as they please, out there. We can't control them at long range. Your own personal tragedy is testimony to that. And yet, and yet—to think that we would be in such a shambles, and that a Lord Magistrate would be compelled to resign, and go into exile—exile, yes, that's what it is!—"

"Please," I say. His ramblings are embarrassing; and painful, too, for there may be seeds of truth in them. "What's over is over. All I want now is to live out my years quietly among the people of the Order on this world. Just tell me how I can be of use. Any work at all, even the simplest—"

"A waste, your grace. An absolute shameful waste."

"Please."

He fills my glass for the fourth or fifth time. A crafty look has come into his eyes. "You would accept any assignment I give you?"

"Yes. Anything."

"Anything?" he says.

I see myself sweeping the chapel house stairs, polishing sinks and tables, working in the garden on my knees.

"Even if there is risk?" he says. "Discomfort?"

"Anything."

He says, "You will be our Plenipotentiary, then."

There are two suns in the sky here, but they are not at all like Cuchulain's two, and the frosty air has a sharp sweet sting to it that is like nothing I have ever tasted before, and everything I see is haloed by a double shadow, a rim of pale red shading into deep, mysterious azure. It is very cold in this place. I am fourteen light-years from Earth.

A woman is watching me from just a few meters away. She says something I am unable to understand.

"Can you speak Anglic?" I reply.

"Anglic. All right." She gives me a chilly, appraising look. "What are you? Some kind of priest?"

"I was Lord Magistrate of the House of Senders, yes."

"Where?"

"Earth."

"On *Earth?* Really?"

I nod. "What is the name of this world?"

"Let me ask the questions," she says. Her speech is odd, not so much a foreign accent as a foreign intonation, a curious singsong, vaguely menacing. Standing face to face just outside the Velde station, we look each other over. She is thick-shouldered, deep-chested, with a flat-featured face, close-cropped yellow hair, green eyes, a dusting of light red freckles across her heavy cheekbones. She wears a heavy blue jacket, fringed brown leggings, blue leather boots, and she is armed. Behind her I see a muddy road cut through a flat snowy field, some low rambling metal buildings with snow piled high on their roofs, and a landscape of distant jagged towering mountains whose sharp black spires are festooned with double-shadowed glaciers. An icy wind rips across the flat land. We are a long way from those two suns, the fierce blue-white one and its cooler crimson companion. Her eyes narrow and she says, "Lord Magistrate, eh? The House of Senders. Really?"

"This was my cloak of office. This medallion signified my rank in the Order."

"I don't see them."

"I'm sorry. I don't understand."

"You have no rank here. You hold no office here."

"Of course," I say. "I realize that. Except such power as Darklaw confers on me."

"Darklaw?"

I stare at her in some dismay. "Am I beyond the reach of Darklaw so soon?"

"It's not a word I hear very often. Shivering, are you? You come from a warmer place?"

"Earth," I say. "South Australia. It's warm there, yes."

"Earth. South Australia." She repeats the words as though they are mere noises to her. "We have some Earthborn here, still. Not many. They'll be glad to see you, I suppose. The name of this world is Zima."

"Zima." A good strong sound. "What does that mean?"

"Mean?"

"The name must mean something. This planet wasn't named Zima just because someone liked the way it sounded."

"Can't you see why?" she asks, gesturing toward the far-off iceshrouded mountains.

"I don't understand."

"Anglic is the only language you speak?"

"I know some Espanol and some Deutsch."

She shrugs. "Zima is Russkiye. It means Winter."

"And this is wintertime on Winter?"

"It is like this all the year round. And so we call the world Zima."

"Zima," I say. "Yes."

"We speak Russkiye here, mostly, though we know Anglic too. Everybody knows Anglic, everywhere in the Dark. It is necessary. You really speak no Russkiye?"

"Sorry."

"Ty shto, s pizdy sarvalsa?" she says, staring at me.

I shrug and am silent.

"Bros' dumat' zhopay!"

I shake my head sadly.

"Idi v zhopu!"

"No," I say. "Not a word."

She smiles, for the first time. "I believe you."

"What were you saying to me in Russkiye?"

"Very abusive things. I will not tell you what they were. If you understood, you would have become very angry. They were filthy things, mockery. At least you would have laughed, hearing such vile words. I am named Marfa Ivanovna. You must talk with the boyars. If they think you are a spy, they will kill you."

I try to hide my astonishment, but I doubt that I succeed. *Kill?* What sort of world have we built here? Have these Zimans reinvented the middle ages?

"You are frightened?" she asks.

"Surprised," I say.

"You should lie to them, if you are a spy. Tell them you come to bring the Word of God, only. Or something else that is harmless. I like you. I would not want them to kill you."

A spy? No. As Guardiano would say, I am a teacher, a guide, a prophet, if you will. Or as I myself would say, I am a pilgrim, one who seeks atonement, one who seeks forgiveness.

"I'm not a spy, Marfa Ivanovna," I say.

"Good. Good. Tell them that." She puts her fingers in her mouth and whistles piercingly, and three burly bearded men in fur jackets appear as though rising out of the snowbanks. She speaks with them a long while in Russkiye. Then she turns to me. "These are the boyars Ivan Dimitrovich, Pyotr Pyotrovich, and Ivan Pyotrovich. They will conduct you to the voivode Ilya Alexandrovich, who will examine you. You should tell the voivode the truth."

"Yes," I say. "What else is there to tell?"

Guardiano had told me before I left Cuchulain, of course, that the world I was going to had been settled by emigrants from Russia. It was one of the first to be colonized, in the early years of the Mission. One would expect our Earthly ways to begin dropping away, and something like an indigenous culture to have begun evolving, in that much time. But I am startled, all the same, by how far they have drifted. At least Marfa Ivanova—who is, I imagine, a third-generation Ziman—knows what Darklaw is. But is it observed? They have named their world Winter, at any rate, and not New Russia or New Moscow or something like that, which Darklaw would have forbidden. The new worlds in the stars must not carry such Earthly baggage with them. But whether they follow any of the other laws, I cannot say. They have reverted to their ancient language here, but they know Anglic as well, as they should. The robe of the Order means something to her, but not, it would seem, a great deal.

She speaks of spies, of killing. Here at the outset of my journey I can see already that there will be many surprises for me as I make my way through the Dark.

The voivode Ilya Alexandrovich is a small, agile-looking man, brown-faced, weatherbeaten, with penetrating blue eyes and a great shock of thick, coarse white hair. He could be any age at all, but from his vigor and seeming reserves of power I guess that he is about forty. In a harsh climate the face is quickly etched with the signs of age, but this man is probably younger than he looks.

Voivode, he tells me, means something like "mayor," or "district chief." His office, brightly lit and stark, is a large ground-floor room in an unassuming two-story aluminum shack that is, I assume, the town hall. There is no place for me to sit. I stand before him, and the three husky boyars, who do not remove their fur jackets, stand behind me, arms folded ominously across their breasts.

I see a desk, a faded wall map, a terminal. The only other thing in the room is the immense bleached skull of some alien beast on the floor beside his desk. It is an astounding sight, two meters long and a meter high, with two huge eye-sockets in the usual places and a third set high between them, and a pair of colossal yellow tusks that rise straight from the lower jaw almost to the ceiling. One tusk is chipped at the tip, perhaps six centimeters broken off. He sees me staring at it. "You ever see anything like that?" he asks, almost belligerently.

"Never. What is it?"

"We call it a bolshoi. Animal of the northern steppe, very big. You see one five kilometers away and you shit your trousers, I tell you for true." He grins. "Maybe we send one back to Earth someday to show them what we have here. Maybe."

His Anglic is much more heavily accented than Marfa Ivanovna's, and far less fluent. He seems unable to hold still very long. The district that he governs, he tells me, is the largest on Zima. It looks immense indeed on his map, a vast blue area, a territory that seems to be about the size of Brazil. But when I take a closer look I see three tiny dots clustered close together in the center of the blue zone. They are, I assume, the only villages. He follows my gaze and strides immediately across the room to tap the map. "This is Tyomni," he says. "That is this village. This one here, it is Doch. This one, Sin. In this territory we have six thousand people altogether. There are two other territories, here and here." He points to regions north and south of the blue zone. A yellow area and a pink one indicate the other settlements, each with two towns. The whole human population of this planet must be no more than ten thousand.

Turning suddenly toward me, he says, "You are big priest in the Order?"

"I was Lord Magistrate, yes. The House of Senders."

"Senders. Ah. I know Senders. The ones who choose the colonists. And who run the machinery, the transmitters."

"That's right."

"And you are the bolshoi Sender? The big man, the boss, the captain?"

"I was, yes. This robe, this medallion, those are signs of my office."

"A very big man. Only instead of sending, you are sent."

"Yes," I say.

"And you come here, why? Nobody from Earth comes here in ten, fifteen years." He no longer makes even an attempt to conceal his suspicions, or his hostility. His cold eyes flare with anger. "Being boss of Senders is not enough for you? You want to tell us how to run Zima? You want to run Zima yourself?"

"Nothing of that sort, believe me."

"Then what?"

"Do you have a map of the entire Dark?"

"The Dark," he says, as though the word is unfamiliar to him. Then he says something in Russkiye to one of the boyars. The man leaves the room and returns, a few moments later, with a wide, flat black screen that turns out to be a small version of the wall screen in the Master's office. He lights it and they all look expectantly at me.

The display is a little different from the one I am accustomed to, since it centers on Zima, not on Earth, but the glowing inner sphere that marks the location of the Mission stars is easy enough to find. I point to that sphere and I remind them, apologizing for telling them what they already know, that the great plan of the Mission calls for an orderly expansion through space from Earth in a carefully delimited zone a hundred light-years in diameter. Only when that sphere has been settled are we to go farther, not because there are any technical difficulties in sending our carrier ships a thousand light-years out, or ten thousand, but because the Master has felt from the start that we must assimilate our first immense wave of outward movement, must pause and come to an understanding of what it is like to have created a galactic empire on so vast a scale, before we attempt to go onward into the infinity that awaits us. Otherwise, I say, we risk falling victim to a megalomaniacal centrifugal dizziness from which we may never recover. And so Darklaw forbids journeys beyond the boundary.

They watch me stonily throughout my recital of these overfamiliar concepts, saying nothing.

I go on to tell them that Earth now is receiving indications that voyages far beyond the hundred-light-year limit have taken place.

Their faces are expressionless.

"What is that to us?" the voivode asks.

"One of the deviant tracks begins here," I say.

"Our Anglic is very poor. Perhaps you can say that another way."

"When the first ship brought the Velde receiver to Zima, it built replicas of itself and of the receiver, and sent them onward to other stars farther from Earth. We've traced the various trajectories that lead beyond the Mission boundaries, and one of them comes out of a world that received its Velde equipment from a world that got its equipment from here. A granddaughter world, so to speak."

"This has nothing to do with us, nothing at all," the voivode says coolly.

"Zima is only my starting point," I say. "It may be that you are in contact with these outer worlds, that I can get some clue from you about who is making these voyages, and why, and where he's setting out from."

"We have no knowledge of any of this."

I point out, trying not to do it in any overbearing way, that by the authority of Darklaw vested in me as a Plenipotentiary of the Order he is required to assist me in my inquiry. But there is no way to brandish the authority of Darklaw that is not overbearing, and I see the voivode stiffen at once, I see his face grow black, I see very clearly that he regards himself as autonomous and his world as independent of Earth. That comes as no surprise to me. We were not so naive, so innocent of historical precedent, as to think we could maintain control over the colonies. What we wanted was quite the opposite, new Earths free of our grasp—cut off, indeed, by an inflexible law forbidding all contact between mother world and colony once the colony has been established—and free, likewise, of the compulsion to replicate the tragic mistakes that the old Earth had made. But because we had felt the hand of God guiding us in every way as we led mankind forth into the Dark, we believed that God's law as we understood it would never be repudiated by those whom we had given the stars. Now, seeing evidence that His law is subordinate out here to the will of willful men, I fear for the structure that we have devoted our lives to building.

"If this is why you really have come," the voivode says, "then you have wasted your time. But perhaps I misunderstand everything you say. My Anglic is not good. We must talk again." He gestures to the boyars and says something in Russkiye that is unmistakably a dismissal. They take me away and give me a room in some sort of dreary lodging-house overlooking the plaza at the center of town. When they leave, they lock the door behind them. I am a prisoner.

It is a harsh land. In the first few days of my internment there is a snowstorm every afternoon. First the sky turns metal-gray, and then black. Then hard little pellets of snow, driven by the rising wind, strike the window. Then it comes down in heavy fluffy flakes for several hours. Afterwards machines scuttle out and clear the pathways. I have never before been in a place where they have snow. It seems quite beautiful to me, a kind of benediction, a cleansing cover.

This is a very small town, and there is wilderness all around it. On the second day and again on the third, packs of wild beasts go racing through the central plaza. They look something like huge dogs, but they have very long legs, almost like those of horses, and their tails are tipped with three pairs of ugly-looking spikes. They move through the town like a whirlwind, prowling in the trash, butting their heads against the closed doors, and everyone gets quickly out of their way.

Later on the third day there is an execution in the plaza, practically below my window. A jowly, heavily bearded man clad in furs is led forth, strapped to a post, and shot by five men in uniforms. For all I can tell, he is one of the three boyars who took me to the voivode on my first day. I have never seen anyone killed before, and the whole event has such a strange, dreamlike quality for me that the shock and horror and revulsion do not strike me until perhaps half an hour later.

It is hard for me to say which I find the most alien, the snowstorms, the packs of fierce beasts running through the town, or the execution.

My food is shoved through a slot in the door. It is rough, simple stuff, stews and soups and a kind of gritty bread. That is all right. Not until the fourth day does anyone come to see me. My first visitor is Marfa Ivanovna, who says, "They think you're a spy. I told you to tell them the truth."

"I did."

"Are you a spy?"

"You know that I'm not."

"Yes," she says. "I know. But the voivode is troubled. He thinks you mean to overthrow him."

"All I want is for him to give me some information. Then I'll be gone from here and won't ever return."

"He is a very suspicious man."

"Let him come here and pray with me, and see what my nature is like. All I am is a servant of God. Which I hope is true of the voivode as well."

"He is thinking of having you shot," Marfa Ivanovna says.

"Let him come to me and pray with me," I tell her.

The voivode comes to me, not once but three times. We do no praying—in truth, any mention of God, or Darklaw, or even the Mission, seems to make him uncomfortable—but gradually we begin to understand each other. We are not that different. He is a hard, dedicated, cautious man governing a harsh troublesome land. I have been called hard and dedicated and cautious myself. My nature is not as suspicious as his, but I have not had to contend with snowstorms and wild beasts and the other hazards of this place. Nor am I Russian. They seem to be suspicious from birth, these Russians. And they have lived apart from Earth a long while. That too is Darklaw: we would not have the new worlds contaminated with our plagues of the spirit or of the flesh, nor do we want alien plagues of either kind carried back from them to us. We have enough of our own already.

I am not going to be shot. He makes that clear. "We talked of it, yes. But it would be wrong."

"The man who was? What did he do?"

"He took that which was not his," says the voivode, and shrugs. "He was worse than a beast. He could not be allowed to live among us."

Nothing is said of when I will be released. I am left alone for two more days. The coarse dull food begins to oppress me, and the solitude. There is another snowstorm, worse than the last. From my window I see ungainly birds something like vultures, with long naked yellow necks and drooping reptilian tails, circling in the sky. Finally the voivode comes a second time, and simply stares at me as though expecting me to blurt out some confession. I look at him in puzzlement, and after long silence he laughs explosively and summons an aide, who brings in a bottle of a clear fiery liquor. Two or three quick gulps and he becomes expansive, and tells me of his childhood. His father was voivode before him, long ago, and was killed by a wild animal while out hunting. I try to imagine a world that still has dangerous animals roaming freely. To me it is like a world where the gods of primitive man are real and alive, and go disguised among mortals, striking out at them randomly and without warning.

Then he asks me about myself, wanting to know how old I was when I became a priest of the Order, and whether I was as religious as a boy as I am now. I tell him what I can, within the limits placed on me by my vows. Perhaps I go a little beyond the limits, even. I explain about my early interest in technical matters, my entering the Order at seventeen, my life of service.

The part about my religious vocation seems odd to him. He appears to think I must have undergone some sudden conversion midway through my adolescence. "There has never been a time when God has not been present at my side," I say.

"How very lucky you are," he says.

"Lucky?"

He touches his glass to mine.

"Your health," he says. We drink. Then he says, "What does your Order really want with us, anyway?"

"With you? We want nothing with you. Three generations ago we gave you your world; everything after that is up to you."

"No. You want to dictate how we shall live. You are people of the past, and we are people of the future, and you are unable to understand our souls."

"Not so," I tell him. "Why do you think we want to dictate to you? Have we interfered with you up till now?"

"You are here now, though."

"Not to interfere. Only to gain information."

"Ah. Is this so?" He laughs and drinks. "Your health," he says again. He comes a third time a couple of days later. I am restless and irritable when he enters; I have had enough of this imprisonment, these groundless suspicions, this bleak and frosty world; I am ready to be on my way. It is all I can do to keep from bluntly demanding my freedom. As it is I am uncharacteristically sharp and surly with him, answering in quick snarling monosyllables when he asks me how I have slept, whether I am well, is my room warm enough. He gives me a look of surprise, and then one of thoughtful appraisal, and then he smiles. He is in complete control, and we both know it.

"Tell me once more," he says, "why you have come to us."

I calm myself and run through the whole thing one more time. He nods. Now that he knows me better, he tells me, he begins to think that I may be sincere, that I have not come to spy, that I actually would be willing to chase across the galaxy this way in pursuit of an ideal. And so on in that vein for a time, both patronizing and genuinely friendly almost in the same breath.

Then he says, "We have decided that it is best to send you onward."

"Where?"

"The name of the world is Entrada. It is one of our daughter worlds, eleven light-years away, a very hot place. We trade our precious metals for their spices. Someone came from there not long ago and told us of a strange man named Oesterreich, who passed through Entrada and spoke of undertaking journeys to new and distant places. Perhaps he can provide you with the answers that you seek. If you can find him."

"Oesterreich?"

"That is the name, yes."

"Can you tell me any more about him than that?"

"What I have told you is all that I know."

He stares at me truculently, as if defying me to show that he is lying. But I believe him.

"Even for that much assistance, I am grateful," I say.

"Yes. Never let it be said that we have failed to offer aid to the Order." He smiles again. "But if you ever come to this world again, you understand, we will know that you were a spy after all. And we will treat you accordingly."

Marfa Ivanovna is in charge of the Velde equipment. She positions me within the transmitting doorway, moving me about this way and that to be certain that I will be squarely within the field. When she is satisfied, she says, "You know, you ought not ever come back this way."

"I understand that."

"You must be a very virtuous man. Ilya Alexandrovich came very close to putting you to death, and then he changed his mind. This I know for certain. But he remains suspicious of you. He is suspicious of everything the Order does."

"The Order has never done anything to injure him or anyone else on this planet, and never will."

"That may be so," says Marfa Ivanovna. "But still, you are lucky to be leaving here alive. You should not come back. And you should tell others of your sort to stay away from Zima too. We do not accept the Order here."

I am still pondering the implications of that astonishing statement when she does something even more astonishing. Stepping into the cubicle with me, she suddenly opens her fur-trimmed jacket, revealing full round breasts, very pale, dusted with the same light red freckles that she has on her face. She seizes me by the hair and presses my head against her breasts, and holds it there a long moment. Her skin is very warm. It seems almost feverish.

"For luck," she says, and steps back. Her eyes are sad and strange. It could almost be a loving look, or perhaps a pitying one, or both. Then she turns away from me and throws the switch.

Entrada is torrid and moist, a humid sweltering hothouse of a place so much the antithesis of Zima that my body rebels immediately against the shift from one world to the other. Coming forth into it, I feel the heat rolling toward me like an implacable wall of water. It sweeps up and over me and smashes me to my knees. I am sick and numb with displacement and dislocation. It seems impossible for me to draw a breath. The thick, shimmering, golden-green atmosphere here is almost liquid; it crams itself into my throat, it squeezes my lungs in an agonizing grip. Through blurring eyes I see a tight green web of jungle foliage rising before me, a jumbled vista of corrugated-tin shacks, a patch of sky the color of shallow seawater, and, high above, a merciless, throbbing, weirdly elongated sun shaped like no sun I have ever imagined. Then I sway and fall forward and see nothing more.

I lie suspended in delirium a long while. It is a pleasing restful time, like being in the womb. I am becalmed in a great stillness, lulled by soft voices and sweet music. But gradually consciousness begins to break through. I swim upward toward the light that glows somewhere above me, and my eyes open, and I see a serene friendly face, and a voice says, "It's nothing to worry about. Everyone who comes here the way you did has a touch of it, the first time. At your age I suppose it's worse than usual."

Dazedly I realize that I am in mid-conversation.

"A touch of what?" I ask.

The other, who is a slender, gray-eyed woman of middle years wearing a sort of Indian sari, smiles and says, "Of the Falling. It's a lambda effect. But I'm sorry. We've been talking for a while, and I thought you were awake. Evidently you weren't."

"I am now," I tell her. "But I don't think I've been for very long."

Nodding, she says, "Let's start over. You're in Traveler's Hospice. The humidity got you, and the heat, and the lightness of the gravity. You're all right now."

"Yes."

"Do you think you can stand?"

"I can try," I say.

She helps me up. I feel so giddy that I expect to float away. Carefully she guides me toward the window of my room. Outside I see a veranda and a close-cropped lawn. Just beyond, a dark curtain of dense bush closes everything off. The intense light makes everything seem very near; it is as if I could put my hand out the window and thrust it into the heart of that exuberant jungle.

"So bright—the sun—" I whisper.

In fact there are two whitish suns in the sky, so close to each other that their photospheres overlap and each is distended by the other's gravitational pull, making them nearly oval in shape. Together they seem to form a single egg-shaped mass, though even the one quick dazzled glance I can allow myself tells me that this is really a binary system, discrete bundles of energy forever locked together.

Awed and amazed, I touch my fingertips to my cheek in wonder, and feel a thick coarse beard there that I had not had before.

The woman says, "Two suns, actually. Their centers are only about a million and a half kilometers apart, and they revolve around each other every seven and a half hours. We're the fourth planet out, but we're as far from them as Neptune is from the Sun."

But I have lost interest for the moment in astronomical matters. I rub my face, exploring its strange new shagginess. The beard covers my cheeks, my jaws, much of my throat.

"How long have I been unconscious?" I ask.

"About three weeks."

"Your weeks or Earth weeks?"

"We use Earth weeks here."

"And that was just a light case? Does everybody who gets the Falling spend three weeks being delirious?"

"Sometimes much more. Sometimes they never come out of it."

I stare at her. "And it's just the heat, the humidity, the lightness of the gravity? They can knock you down the moment you step out of the transmitter and put you under for weeks? I would think it should take something like a stroke to do that."

"It is something like a stroke," she says. "Did you think that traveling between stars is like stepping across the street? You come from a low-lambda world to a high-lambda one without doing your adaptation drills and of course the change is going to knock you flat right away. What did you expect?"

High-lambda? Low-lambda?

"I don't know what you're talking about," I say.

"Didn't they tell you on Zima about the adaptation drills before they shipped you here?"

"Not a thing."

"Or about lambda differentials?"

"Nothing," I say.

Her face grows very solemn. "Pigs, that's all they are. They should have prepared you for the jump. But I guess they didn't care whether you lived or died."

I think of Marfa Ivanovna, wishing me luck as she reached for the switch. I think of that strange sad look in her eyes. I think of the voivode Ilya Alexandrovich, who might have had me shot but decided instead to offer me a free trip off his world, a one-way trip. There is much that I am only now beginning to understand, I see, about this empire that Earth is building in what we call the Dark. We are building it in the dark, yes, in more ways than one.

"No," I say. "I guess they didn't care."

They are friendlier on Entrada, no question of that. Interstellar trade is important here and visitors from other worlds are far more common than they are on wintry Zima. Apparently I am free to live at the hospice as long as I wish. The weeks of my stay have stretched now into months, and no one suggests that it is time for me to be moving along.

I had not expected to stay here so long. But gathering the information I need has been a slow business, with many a maddening detour and delay.

At least I experience no further lambda problems. Lambda, they tell me, is a planetary force that became known only when Velde jumps between solar systems began. There are high-lambda worlds and low-lambda worlds, and anyone going from one kind to the other without proper preparation is apt to undergo severe stress. It is all news to me. I wonder if the Order on Earth is aware at all of these difficulties. But perhaps they feel that matters which may arise during journeys between worlds of the Dark are of no concern to us of the mother world.

They have taken me through the adaptation drills here at the hospice somehow while I was still unconscious, and I am more or less capable now of handling Entradan conditions. The perpetual steambath heat, which no amount of air conditioning seems really to mitigate, is hard to cope with, and the odd combination of heavy atmosphere and light gravity puts me at risk of nausea with every breath, though after a time I get the knack of pulling shallow nips of air. There are allergens borne on every breeze, too, pollen of a thousand kinds and some free-floating alkaloids, against which I need daily medication. My face turns red under the force of the double sun, and the skin of my cheeks gets strangely soft, which makes my new beard an annoyance. I rid myself of it. My hair acquires an unfamiliar silver sheen, not displeasing, but unexpected. All this considered, though, I can manage here.

Entrada has a dozen major settlements and several hundred thousand people. It is a big world, metal-poor and light, on which a dozen small continents and some intricate archipelagoes float in huge warm seas. The whole planet is tropical, even at the poles: distant though it is from its suns, it would probably be inhospitable to human life if it were very much closer. The soil of Entrada has the lunatic fertility that we associate with the tropics, and agriculture is the prime occupation here. The people, drawn from many regions of Earth, are attractive and outgoing, with an appealingly easy manner.

It appears that they have not drifted as far from Darklaw here as the Zimans have.

Certainly the Order is respected. There are chapels everywhere and the people use them. Whenever I enter one there is a little stir of excitement, for it is generally known that I was Lord Magistrate of the Senders during my time on Earth, and that makes me a celebrity, or a curiosity, or both. Many of the Entradans are Earthborn themselves—emigration to this world was still going on as recently as eight or ten years ago—and the sight of my medallion inspires respect and even awe in them. I do not wear my robe of office, not in this heat. Probably I will never wear it again, no matter what climate I find myself in when I leave here. Someone else is Lord Magistrate of the House of Senders now, after all. But the medallion alone is enough to win me a distinction here that I surely never had on Zima.

I think, though, that they pick and choose among the tenets of Darklaw to their own satisfaction on Entrada, obeying those which suit them and casting aside anything that seems too constricting. I am not sure of this, but it seems likely. To discuss such matters with anyone I have come to know here is, of course, impossible. The people I have managed to get to know so far, at the hospice, at the chapel house in town, at the tavern where I have begun to take my meals, are pleasant and sociable. But they become uneasy, even evasive, whenever I speak of any aspect of Earth's migration into space. Let me mention the Order, or the Master, or anything at all concerning the Mission, and they begin to moisten their lips and look uncomfortable. Clearly things are happening out here, things never envisioned by the founders of the Order, and they are unwilling to talk about them with anyone who himself wears the high medallion.

It is a measure of the changes that have come over me since I began this journey that I am neither surprised nor dismayed by this.

Why should we have believed that we could prescribe a single code of law that would meet the needs of hundreds of widely varying worlds? Of course they would modify our teachings to fit their own evolving cultures, and some would probably depart entirely from that which we had created for them. It was only to be expected. Many things have become clear to me on this journey that I did not see before, that, indeed, I did not so much as pause to consider. But much else remains mysterious.

I am at the busy waterfront esplanade, leaning over the rail, staring out toward Volcano Isle, a dim gray peak far out to sea. It is midmorning, before the full heat of noon has descended. I have been here long enough so that I think of this as the cool time of the day.

"Your grace?" a voice calls. "Lord Magistrate?"

No one calls me those things here.

I glance down to my left. A dark-haired man in worn seaman's clothes and a braided captain's hat is looking up at me out of a rowboat just below the seawall. He is smiling and waving. I have no idea who he is, but he plainly wants to talk with me, and anything that helps me break the barrier that stands between me and real knowledge of this place is to be encouraged.

He points to the far end of the harbor, where there is a ramp leading from the little beach to the esplanade, and tells me in pantomime that he means to tie up his boat and go ashore. I wait for him at the head of the ramp, and after a few moments he comes trudging up to greet me. He is perhaps fifty years old, trim and sun-bronzed, with a lean weatherbeaten face.

"You don't remember me," he says.

"I'm afraid not."

"You personally interviewed me and approved my application to emigrate, eighteen years ago. Sandys. Lloyd Sandys." He smiles hopefully, as though his name alone will open the floodgates of my memory.

When I was Lord Magistrate I reviewed five hundred emigrant dossiers a week, and interviewed ten or fifteen applicants a day myself, and forgot each one the moment I approved or rejected them. But for this man the interview with the Lord Magistrate of the Senders was the most significant moment of his life.

"Sorry," I say. "So many names, so many faces—"

"I would have recognized you even if I hadn't already heard you were here. After all these years, you've hardly changed at all, your grace." He grins. "So now you've come to settle on Entrada yourself?"

"Only a short visit."

"Ah." He is visibly disappointed. "You ought to think of staying. It's a wonderful place, if you don't mind a little heat. I haven't regretted coming here for a minute."

He takes me to a seaside tavern where he is obviously well known, and orders lunch for both of us: skewers of small corkscrew-shaped creatures that look and taste a little like squid, and a flask of a strange but likable emerald-colored wine with a heavy, musky, spicy flavor. He tells me that he has four sturdy sons and four strapping daughters, and that he and his wife run a harbor ferry, short hops to the surrounding islands of this archipelago, which is Entrada's main population center. There still are traces of Melbourne in his accent. He seems very happy. "You'll let me take you on a tour, won't you?" he asks. "We've got some very beautiful islands out there, and you can't get to see them by Velde jumps."

I protest that I don't want to take him away from his work, but he shrugs that off. Work can always wait, he says. There's no hurry, on a world where anyone can dip his net in the sea and come up with a good meal. We have another flask of wine. He seems open, genial, trustworthy. Over cheese and fruit he asks me why I've come here.

I hesitate.

"A fact-finding mission," I say.

"Ah. Is that really so? Can I be of any help, d'ye think?

It is several more winy lunches, and a little boat-trip to some nearby islands fragrant with masses of intoxicating purple blooms, before I am willing to begin taking Sandys into my confidence. I tell him that the Order has sent me into the Dark to study and report on the ways of life that are evolving on the new worlds. He seems untroubled by that, though Ilya Alexandrovich might have had me shot for such an admission.

Later, I tell him about the apparent deviations from the planned scope of the Mission that are the immediate reason for my journey.

"You mean, going out beyond the hundred-light-year zone?"

"Yes."

"That's pretty amazing, that anyone would go there."

"We have indications that it's happening."

"Really," he says.

"And on Zima," I continue, "I picked up a story that somebody here on Entrada has been preaching ventures into the far Dark. You don't know anything about that, do you?"

His only overt reaction is a light frown, quickly erased. Perhaps he has nothing to tell me. Or else we have reached the point, perhaps, beyond which he is unwilling to speak.

But some hours later he revives the topic himself. We are on our way back to harbor, sunburned and a little tipsy from an outing to one of the prettiest of the local islands, when he suddenly says, "I remember hearing something about that preacher you mentioned before."

I wait, not saying anything.

"My wife told me about him. There was somebody going around talking about far voyages, she said." New color comes to his face, a deep red beneath the bronze. "I must have forgotten about it when we were talking before." In fact he must know that I think him disingenuous for withholding this from me all afternoon. But I make no attempt to call him on that. We are still testing each other.

I ask him if he can get more information for me, and he promises to discuss it with his wife. Then he is absent for a week, making a circuit of the outer rim of the archipelago to deliver freight. When he returns, finally, he brings with him an unusual golden brandy from one of the remote islands as a gift for me, but my cautious attempt to revive our earlier conversation runs into a familiar sort of Entradan evasiveness. It is almost as though he doesn't know what I'm referring to.

At length I say bluntly, "Have you had a chance to talk to your wife about that preacher?"

He looks troubled. "In fact, it slipped my mind."

"Ah."

"Tonight, maybe—"

"I understand that the man's name is Oesterreich," I say.

His eyes go wide.

"You know that, do you?"

"Help me, will you, Sandys? I'm the one who sent you to this place, remember? Your whole life here wouldn't exist but for me."

"That's true. That's very true."

"Who's Oesterreich?"

"I never knew him. I never had any dealings with him."

"Tell me what you know about him."

"A crazy man, he was."

"Was?"

"He's not here anymore."

I uncork the bottle of rare brandy, pour a little for myself, a more generous shot for Sandys.

"Where'd he go?" I ask.

He sips, reflectively. After a time he says, "I don't know, your grace. That's God's own truth. I haven't seen or heard of him in a couple of years. He chartered one of the other captains here, a man named Feraud, to take him to one of the islands, and that's the last I know."

"Which island?"

"I don't know."

"Do you think Feraud remembers?"

"I could ask him," Sandys says.

"Yes. Ask him. Would you do that?"

"I could ask him, yes," he says.

So it goes, slowly. Sandys confers with his friend Feraud, who hesitates and evades, or so Sandys tells me; but eventually Feraud finds it in him to recall that he had taken Oesterreich to Volcano Isle, three hours' journey to the west. Sandys admits to me, now that he is too deep in to hold back, that he himself actually heard Oesterreich speak several times, that Oesterreich claimed to be in possession of some secret way of reaching worlds immensely remote from the settled part of the Dark.

"And do you believe that?"

"I don't know. He seemed crazy to me."

"Crazy how?"

"The look in his eye. The things he said. That it's our destiny to reach the rim of the universe. That the Order holds us back out of its own timidity. That we must follow the Goddess Avatar, who beckons us onward to—"

"*Who?*"

His face flushes bright crimson. "The Goddess Avatar. I don't know what she is, your grace. Honestly. It's some cult he's running, some new religion he's made up. I told you he's crazy. I've never believed any of this."

There is a pounding in my temples, and a fierce ache behind my eyes. My throat has gone dry and not even Sandys' brandy can soothe it.

"Where do you think Oesterreich is now?"

"I don't know." His eyes are tormented. "Honestly. Honestly. I think he's gone from Entrada."

"Is there a Velde transmitter station on Volcano Isle?"

He thinks for a moment. "Yes. Yes, there is."

"Will you do me one more favor?" I ask. "One thing, and then I won't ask any more."

"Yes?"

"Take a ride over to Volcano Isle tomorrow. Talk with the people who run the Velde station there. See if you can find out where they sent Oesterreich."

"They'll never tell me anything like that."

I put five shining coins in front of him, each one worth as much as he can make in a month's ferrying.

"Use these," I say. "If you come back with the answer, there are five more for you."

"Come with me, your grace. You speak to them."

"No."

"You ought to see Volcano Isle. It's a fantastic place. The center of it blew out thousands of years ago, and people live up on the rim, around a lagoon so deep nobody's been able to find the bottom. I was meaning to take you there anyway, and—"

"You go," I say. "Just you."

After a moment he pockets the coins. In the morning I watch him go off in one of his boats, a small hydrofoil skiff. There is no word from him for two days, and then he comes to me at the hospice, looking tense and unshaven.

"It wasn't easy," he says.

"You found out where he went?"

"Yes."

"Go on," I urge, but he is silent, lips working but nothing coming out. I produce five more of the coins and lay them before him. He ignores them. This is some interior struggle.

He says, after a time, "We aren't supposed to reveal anything about anything of this. I told you what I've already told you because I owe you. You understand that?"

"Yes."

"You mustn't ever let anyone know who gave you the information."

"Don't worry," I say.

He studies me for a time. Then he says, "The name of the planet where Oesterreich went is Eden. It's a seventeen-light-year hop. You won't need lambda adjustment, coming from here. There's hardly any differential. All right, your grace? That's all I can tell you." He stares at the coins and shakes his head. Then he runs out of the room, leaving them behind.

Eden turns out to be no Eden at all. I see a spongy, marshy landscape, a gray sodden sky, a raw, half-built town. There seem to be two suns, a faint yellow-white one and a larger reddish one. A closer look reveals that the system here is like the Lalande one: the reddish one is not really a star but a glowing substellar mass about the size of Jupiter. Eden is one of its moons. What we like to speak of in the Order as the new Earths of the Dark are in fact scarcely Earthlike at all, I am coming to realize: all they have in common with the mother world is a tolerably breathable atmosphere and a manageable gravitational pull. How can we speak of a world as an Earth when its sun is not yellow but white or red or green, or there are two or three or even four suns in the sky all day and all night, or the primary source of warmth is not even a sun but a giant planet-like ball of hot gas?

"Settler?" they ask me, when I arrive on Eden.

"Traveler," I reply. "Short-term visit."

They scarcely seem to care. This is a difficult world and they have no time for bureaucratic formalities. So long as I have money, and I do—at least these strange daughter worlds of ours still honor our currency— I am, if not exactly welcome, then at least permitted.

Do they observe Darklaw here? When I arrive I am wearing neither my robe of office nor my medallion, and it seems just as well. The Order appears not to be in favor, this far out. I can find no sign of our chapels or other indications of submission to our rule. What I do find, as I wander the rough streets of this jerry-rigged town on this cool, rainswept world, is a chapel of some other kind, a white geodesic dome with a mysterious symbol—three superimposed six-pointed stars—painted in black on its door.

"Goddess save you," a woman coming out says brusquely to me, and shoulders past me in the rain.

They are not even bothering to hide things, this far out on the frontier. I go inside. The walls are white and an odd, disturbing mural is painted on one of them. It shows what seems to be a windowless ruined temple drifting in blue starry space, with all manner of objects and creatures floating near it, owls, skulls, snakes, masks, golden cups, bodiless heads. It is like a scene viewed in a dream. The temple's alabaster walls are covered with hieroglyphics. A passageway leads inward and inward and inward, and at its end I can see a tiny view of an eerie landscape like a plateau at the end of time.

There are half a dozen people in the room, each facing in a different direction, reading aloud in low murmurs. A slender dark-skinned man looks up at me and says, "Goddess save you, father. How does your journey go?"

"I'm trying to find Oesterreich. They said he's here."

A couple of the other readers look up. A woman with straw-colored hair says, "He's gone Goddessward."

"I'm sorry. I don't under—"

Another woman, whose features are tiny and delicately modeled in the center of a face vast as the map of Russia, breaks in to tell me, "He was going to stop off on Phosphor first. You may be able to catch up with him there. Goddess save you, father."

I stare at her, at the mural of the stone temple, at the other woman.

"Thank you," I say. "Goddess save you," my voice adds.

I buy passage to Phosphor. It is sixty-seven light-years from Earth. The necessary lambda adjustment costs nearly as much as the transit fee itself, and I must spend three days going through the adaptation process before I can leave.

Then, Goddess save me, I am ready to set out from Eden for whatever greater strangeness awaits me beyond.

As I wait for the Simtow reaction to annihilate me and reconstruct me in some unknown place, I think of all those who passed through my House over the years as I selected the outbound colonists—and how I and the Lord Magistrates before me had clung to the fantasy that we were shaping perfect new Earths out there in the Dark, that we were composing exquisite symphonies of human nature, filtering out all of the discordances that had marred all our history up till now. Without ever going to the new worlds ourselves to view the results of our work, of course, because to go would mean to cut ourselves off forever, by Darklaw's own constricting terms, from our House, from our task, from Earth itself. And now, catapulted into the Dark in a moment's convulsive turn, by shame and guilt and the need to try to repair that which I had evidently made breakable instead of imperishable, I am learning that I have been wrong all along, that the symphonies of human nature that I had composed were built out of the same old tunes, that people will do what they will do unconstrained by abstract regulations laid down for them a priori by others far away. The tight filter of which the House of Senders is so proud is no filter at all. We send our finest ones to the stars and they turn their backs on us at once. And, pondering these things, it seems to me that my soul is pounding at the gates of my mind, that madness is pressing close against the walls of my spirit—a thing which I have always dreaded, the thing which brought me to the cloisters of the Order in the first place.

Black light flashes in my eyes and once more I go leaping through the Dark.

"He isn't here," they tell me on Phosphor. There is a huge cool red sun here, and a hot blue one a couple of hundred solar units away, close enough to blaze like a brilliant beacon in the day sky. "He's gone on to Entropy. Goddess save you."

"Goddess save you," I say.

There are triple-triangle signs on every door front in Phosphor's single city. The city's name is Jerusalem. To name cities or worlds for places on Earth is forbidden. But I know that I have left Darklaw far behind here.

Entropy, they say, is ninety-one light-years from Earth. I am approaching the limits of the sphere of settlement.

Oesterreich has a soft, insinuating voice. He says, "You should come with me. I really would like to take a Lord Magistrate along when I go to her."

"I'm no longer a Lord Magistrate."

"You can't ever stop being a Lord Magistrate. Do you think you can take the Order off just by putting your medallion in your suitcase?"

"Who is she, this Goddess Avatar everybody talks about?"

Oesterreich laughs. "Come with me and you'll find out."

He is a small man, very lean, with broad, looming shoulders that make him appear much taller than he is when he is sitting down. Maybe he is forty years old, maybe much older. His face is paper-white, with perpetual bluish stubble, and his eyes have a black troublesome gleam that strikes me as a mark either of extraordinary intelligence or of pervasive insanity, or perhaps both at once. It was not difficult at all for me to find him, only hours after my arrival on Entropy. The planet has a single village, a thousand settlers. The air is mild here, the sun yellowgreen. Three huge moons hang just overhead in the daytime sky, as though dangling on a clothesline.

I say, "Is she real, this goddess of yours?"

"Oh, she's real, all right. As real as you or me."

"Someone we can walk up to and speak with?"

"Her name used to be Margaret Benevente. She was born in Geneva. She emigrated to a world called Three Suns about thirty years ago."

"And now she's a goddess."

"No. I never said that."

"What is she, then?"

"She's the Goddess Avatar."

"Which means what?"

He smiles. "Which means she's a holy woman in whom certain fundamental principles of the universe have been incarnated. You want to know any more than that, you come with me, eh? Your grace."

"And where is she?"

"She's on an uninhabited planet about five thousand light-years from here right now."

I am dealing with a lunatic, I tell myself. That gleam is the gleam of madness, yes.

"You don't believe that, do you?" he asks.

"How can it be possible?"

"Come with me and you'll find out."

"Five thousand light-years—" I shake my head. "No. No."

He shrugs. "So don't go, then."

There is a terrible silence in the little room. I feel impaled on it. Thunder crashes outside, finally, breaking the tension. Lightning has been playing across the sky constantly since my arrival, but there has been no rain.

"Faster-than-light travel is impossible," I say inanely. "Except by way of Velde transmission. You know that. If we've got Velde equipment five thousand light-years from here, we would have had to start shipping it out around the time the Pyramids were being built in Egypt."

"What makes you think we get there with Velde equipment?" Oesterreich asks me.

He will not explain. Follow me and you'll see, he tells me. Follow me and you'll see.

The curious thing is that I like him. He is not exactly a likable man— too intense, too tightly wound, the fanaticism carried much too close to the surface—but he has a sort of charm all the same. He travels from world to world, he tells me, bringing the new gospel of the Goddess Avatar. That is exactly how he says it, "the new gospel of the Goddess Avatar," and I feel a chill when I hear the phrase. It seems absurd and frightening both at once. Yet I suppose those who brought the Order to the world a hundred fifty years ago must have seemed just as strange and just as preposterous to those who first heard our words.

Of course, we had the Velde equipment to support our philosophies.

But these people have—what? The strength of insanity? The clear cool purposefulness that comes from having put reality completely behind them?

"You were in the Order once, weren't you?" I ask him.

"You know it, your grace."

"Which House?"

"The Mission," he says.

"I should have guessed that. And now you have a new mission, is that it?"

"An extension of the old one. Mohammed, you know, didn't see Islam as a contradiction of Judaism and Christianity. Just as the next level of revelation, incorporating the previous ones."

"So you would incorporate the Order into your new belief?"

"We would never repudiate the Order, your grace."

"And Darklaw? How widely is that observed, would you say, in the colony worlds?"

"I think we've kept much of it," Oesterreich says. "Certainly we keep the part about not trying to return to Earth. And the part about spreading the Mission outward."

"Beyond the boundaries decreed, it would seem."

"This is a new dispensation," he says.

"But not a repudiation of the original teachings?"

"Oh, no," he says, and smiles. "Not a repudiation at all, your grace."

He has that passionate confidence, that unshakable assurance, that is the mark of the real prophet and also of the true madman. There is something diabolical about him, and irresistible. In these conversations with him I have so far managed to remain outwardly calm, even genial, but the fact is that I am quaking within. I really do believe he is insane. Either that or an utter fraud, a cynical salesman of the irrational and the unreal, and though he is flippant he does not seem at all cynical. A madman, then. Is his condition infectious? As I have said, the fear of madness has been with me all my life; and so my harsh discipline, my fierce commitment, my depth of belief. He threatens all my defenses.

"When do you set out to visit your Goddess Avatar?" I ask.

"Whenever you like, your grace."

"You really think I'm going with you?"

"Of course you are. How else can you find out what you came out here to learn?"

"I've learned that the colonies have fallen away from Darklaw. Isn't that enough?"

"But you think we've all gone crazy, right?"

"When did I say that?"

"You didn't need to say it."

"If I send word to Earth of what's happened, and the Order chooses to cut off all further technical assistance and all shipments of manufactured goods—?"

"They won't do that. But even if they do—well, we're pretty much self-sufficient out here now, and getting more so every year—"

"And further emigration from Earth?"

"That would be your loss, not ours, your grace. Earth needs the colonies as a safety valve for her population surplus. We can get along without more emigrants. We know how to reproduce, out here." He grins at me. "This is foolish talk. You've come this far. Now go the rest of the way with me."

I am silent.

"Well?"

"Now, you mean?"

"Right now."

There is only one Velde station on Entropy, about three hundred meters from the house where I have been talking with Oesterreich. We go to it under a sky berserk with green lightning. He seems not even to notice.

"Don't we have to do lambda drills?" I ask.

"Not for this hop," Oesterreich says. "There's no differential between here and there." He is busy setting up coordinates.

"Get into the chamber, your grace."

"And have you send me God knows where by myself?"

"Don't be foolish. Please."

It may be the craziest thing I have ever done. But I am the servant of the Order; and the Order has asked this of me. I step into the chamber. No one else is with us. He continues to press keys, and I realize that he is setting up an automatic transfer, requiring no external operator. When he is done with that he joins me, and there is the moment of flash.

We emerge into a cool, dry world with an Earthlike sun, a sea-green sky, a barren, rocky landscape. Ahead of us stretches an empty plateau broken here and there by small granite hillocks that rise like humped islands out of the flatness.

"Where are we?" I ask.

"Fifty light-years from Entropy, and about eighty-five light-years from Earth."

"What's the name of this place?"

"It doesn't have one. Nobody lives here. Come, now we walk a little."

We start forward. The ground has the look that comes of not having felt rain for ten or twenty years, but tough little tussocks of a grayish jagged-looking grass are pushing up somehow through the hard, stony red soil. When we have gone a hundred meters or so the land begins to drop away sharply on my left, so that I can look down into a broad, flat valley about three hundred meters below us. A solitary huge beast, somewhat like an elephant in bulk and manner, is grazing quietly down there, patiently prodding at the ground with its rigid two-pronged snout.

"Here we are," Oesterreich says.

We have reached the nearest of the little granite islands. When we walk around it, I see that its face on the farther side is fissured and broken, creating a sort of cave. Oesterreich beckons and we step a short way into it.

To our right, against the wall of the cave, is a curious narrow three-sided framework, a kind of tapering doorway, with deep darkness behind it. It is made of an odd glossy metal, or perhaps a plastic, with a texture that is both sleek and porous at the same time. There are hieroglyphs inscribed on it that seem much like those I saw on the wall of the stone temple in the mural in the Goddess-chapel on Phosphor, and to either side of it, mounted in the cave wall, are the triple six-pointed stars that are the emblem of Oesterreich's cult.

"What is this here?" I say, after a time.

"It's something like a Velde transmitter."

"It isn't anything like a Velde transmitter."

"It works very much like a Velde transmitter," he says. "You'll see when we step into its field. Are you ready?"

"Wait."

He nods. "I'm waiting."

"We're going to let this thing send us somewhere?"

"That's right, your grace."

"What is it? Who built it?"

"I've already told you what it is. As for who built it, I don't have any idea. Nobody does. We think it's five or ten million years old, maybe. It could be older than that by a factor of ten. Or a factor of a hundred. We have no way of judging."

After a long silence I say, "You're telling me that it's an alien device?"

"That's right."

"We've never discovered any sign of intelligent alien life anywhere in the galaxy."

"There's one right in front of you," Oesterreich says. "It isn't the only one."

"You've found aliens?"

"We've found their matter-transmitters. A few of them, anyway. They still work. Are you ready to jump now, your grace?"

I stare blankly at the three-sided doorway.

"Where to?"

"To a planet about five hundred light-years from here, where we can catch the bus that'll take us to the Goddess Avatar."

"You're actually serious?"

"Let's go, your grace."

"What about lambda effects?"

"There aren't any. Lambda differentials are a flaw in the Velde technology, not in the universe itself. This system gets us around without any lambda problems at all. Of course, we don't know how it works. Are you ready?"

"All right," I say helplessly.

He beckons to me and together we step toward the doorway and simply walk through it, and out the other side into such astonishing beauty that I want to fall down and give praise. Great feathery trees rise higher than sequoias, and a milky waterfall comes tumbling down the flank of an ebony mountain that fills half the sky, and the air quivers with a diamond-bright haze. Before me stretches a meadow like a scarlet carpet, vanishing into the middle distance. There is a Mesozoic richness of texture to everything: it gleams, it shimmers, it trembles in splendor.

A second doorway, identical to the first, is mounted against an enormous boulder right in front of us. It too is flanked by the triple star emblem.

"Put your medallion on," Oesterreich tells me.

"My medallion?" I say, stupidly.

"Put it on. The Goddess Avatar will wonder why you're with me, and that'll tell her."

"Is she here?"

"She's on the next world. This is just a way station. We had to stop here first. I don't know why. Nobody does. Ready?"

"I'd like to stay here longer."

"You can come back some other time," he says. "She's waiting for you. Let's go."

"Yes," I say, and fumble in my pocket and find my medallion, and put it around my throat. Oesterreich winks and puts his thumb and forefinger together approvingly. He takes my hand and we step through.

She is a lean, leathery-looking woman of sixty or seventy years with hard bright blue eyes. She wears a khaki jacket, an olive-drab field hat, khaki shorts, heavy boots. Her graying hair is tucked behind her in a tight bun. Standing in front of a small tent, tapping something into a hand terminal, she looks like an aging geology professor out on a field trip in Wyoming. But next to her tent the triple emblem of the Goddess is displayed on a sandstone plaque.

This is a Mesozoic landscape too, but much less lush than the last one: great red-brown cliffs sparsely peppered with giant ferns and palms, four-winged insects the size of dragons zooming overhead, huge grotesque things that look very much like dinosaurs warily circling each other in a stony arroyo out near the horizon. I see some other tents out there too. There is a little colony here. The sun is reddish-yellow, and large.

"Well, what do we have here?" she says. "A Lord Magistrate, is it?"

"He was nosing around on Zima and Entrada, trying to find out what was going on."

"Well, now he knows." Her voice is like flint. I feel her contempt, her hostility, like something palpable. I feel her strength, too, a cold, harsh, brutal power. She says, "What was your house, Lord Magistrate?"

"Senders."

She studies me as if I were a specimen in a display case. In all my life I have known only one other person of such force and intensity, and that is the Master. But she is nothing like him.

"And now the Sender is sent?"

"Yes," I say. "There were deviations from the plan. It became necessary for me to resign my magistracy."

"We weren't supposed to come out this far, were we?" she asks. "The light of that sun up there won't get to Earth until the seventy-third century, do you know that? But here we are. Here we are!" She laughs, a crazed sort of cackle. I begin to wonder if they intend to kill me. The aura that comes from her is terrifying. The geology professor I took her for at first is gone: what I see now is something strange and fierce, a prophet, a seer. Then suddenly the fierceness vanishes too and something quite different comes from her: tenderness, pity, even love. The strength of it catches me unawares and I gasp at its power. These shifts of hers are managed without apparent means; she has spoken only a few words, and all the rest has been done with movement, with posture, with expression. I know that I am in the presence of some great charismatic. She walks over to me and with her face close to mine says, "We spoiled your plan, I know. But we too follow the divine rule. We discovered things that nobody had suspected, and everything changed for us. Everything."

"Do you need me, Lady?" Oesterreich asks.

"No. Not now." She touches the tips of her fingers to my medallion of office, rubbing it lightly as though it is a magic talisman. Softly she says, "Let me take you on a tour of the galaxy, Lord Magistrate."

One of the alien doorways is located right behind her tent. We step through it hand in hand, and emerge on a dazzling green hillside looking out over a sea of ice. Three tiny blue-white suns hang like diamonds in the sky. In the trembling air they look like the three six-pointed stars of the emblem. "One of their capital cities was here once," she says. "But it's all at the bottom of that sea now. We ran a scan on it and saw the ruins, and someday we'll try to get down there." She beckons and we step through again, and out onto a turbulent desert of iron-hard red sand, where heavily armored crabs the size of footballs go scuttling sullenly away as we appear. "We think there's another city under here," she says. Stooping, she picks up a worn shard of gray pottery and puts it in my hand. "That's an artifact millions of years old. We find them all over the place."

I stare at it as if she has handed me a small fragment of the core of a star. She touches my medallion again, just a light grazing stroke, and leads me on into the next doorway, and out onto a world of billowing white clouds and soft dewy hills, and onward from there to one where trees hang like ropes from the sky, and onward from there, and onward from there—"How did you find all this?" I ask, finally.

"I was living on Three Suns. You know where that is? We were exploring the nearby worlds, trying to see if there was anything worthwhile, and one day I stepped out of a Velde unit and found myself looking at a peculiar three-sided kind of doorway right next to it, and I got too close and found myself going through into another world entirely. That was all there was to it."

"And you kept on going through one doorway after another?"

"Fifty of them. I didn't know then how to tune for destination, so I just kept jumping, hoping I'd get back to my starting point eventually. There wasn't any reason in the world why I should. But after six months I did. The Goddess protects me."

"The Goddess," I say.

She looks at me as though awaiting a challenge. But I am silent.

"These doorways link the whole galaxy together like the Paris Metro," she says after a moment. "We can go everywhere with them. Everywhere."

"And the Goddess? Are the doorways Her work?"

"We hope to find that out some day."

"What about this emblem?" I ask, pointing to the six-pointed stars beside the gateway. "What does that signify?"

"Her presence," she says. "Come. I'll show you."

We step through once more, and emerge into night. The sky on this world is the blackest black I have ever seen, with comets and shooting stars blazing across it in almost comic profusion. There are two moons, bright as mirrors. A dozen meters to one side is the white stone temple of the chapel mural I saw on Eden, marked with the same hieroglyphs that are shown on the painting there and that are inscribed on all the alien doorways. It is made of cyclopean slabs of white stone that look as if they were carved billions of years ago. She takes my arm and guides me through its squared-off doorway into a high-vaulted inner chamber where the triple six-pointed triangle, fashioned out of the glossy doorway material, is mounted on a stone altar.

"This is the only building of theirs we've ever found," she says. Her eyes are gleaming. "It must have been a holy place. Can you doubt it? You can feel the power."

"Yes."

"Touch the emblem."

"What will happen to me if I do?"

"Touch it," she says. "Are you afraid?"

"Why should I trust you?"

"Because the Goddess has used me to bring you to this place. Go on. Touch."

I put my hand to the smooth cool alien substance, and instantly I feel the force of revelation flowing through me, the unmistakable power of the Godhead. I see the multiplicity of worlds, an infinity of them circling an infinity of suns. I see the Totality. I see the face of God clear and plain. It is what I have sought all my life and thought that I had already found; but I know at once that I am finding it for the first time. If I had fasted for a thousand years, or prayed for ten thousand, I could not have felt anything like that. It is the music out of which all things are built. It is the ocean in which all things float. I hear the voice of every god and goddess that ever had worshippers, and it is all one voice, and it goes coursing through me like a river of fire.

After a moment I take my hand away. And step back, trembling, shaking my head. This is too easy. One does not reach God by touching a strip of smooth plastic.

She says, "We mean to find them. They're still alive somewhere. How could they not be? And who could doubt that we were meant to follow them and find them? And kneel before them, for they are Whom we seek. So we'll go on and on, as far as we need to go, in search of them. To the farthest reaches, if we have to. To the rim of the universe and then beyond. With these doorways there are no limits. We've been handed the key to everywhere. We are for the Dark, all of it, on and on and on, not the little hundred-light-year sphere that your Order preaches, but the whole galaxy and even beyond. Who knows how far these doorways reach? The Magellanic Clouds? Andromeda? M33? They're waiting for us out there. As they have waited for a billion years."

So she thinks she can hunt Him down through doorway after doorway. Or Her. Whichever. But she is wrong. The One who made the universe made the makers of the doorways also.

"And the Goddess—?" I say.

"The Goddess is the Unknown. The Goddess is the Mystery toward which we journey. You don't feel Her presence?"

"I'm not sure."

"You will. If not now, then later. She'll greet us when we arrive. And embrace us, and make us all gods."

I stare a long while at the six-pointed stars. It would be simple enough to put forth my hand again and drink in the river of revelation a second time. But there is no need. That fire still courses through me. It always will, drawing me onward toward itself. Whatever it may be, there is no denying its power.

She says, "I'll show you one more thing, and then we'll leave here."

We continue through the temple and out the far side, where the wall has toppled. From a platform amid the rubble we have an unimpeded view of the heavens. An immense array of stars glitters above us, set out in utterly unfamiliar patterns. She points straight overhead, where a Milky Way in two whirling strands spills across the sky.

"That's Earth right up there," she says. "Can you see it? Going around that little yellow sun, only a hundred thousand light-years away? I wonder if they ever paid us a visit. We won't know, will we, until we turn up one of their doorways somewhere in the Himalayas, or under the Antarctic ice, or somewhere like that. I think that when we finally reach them, they'll recognize us. It's interesting to think about, isn't it." Her hand rests lightly on my wrist. "Shall we go back now, Lord Magistrate?"

So we return, in two or three hops, to the world of the dinosaurs and the giant dragonflies. There is nothing I can say. I feel storms within my skull. I feel myself spread out across half the universe.

Oesterreich waits for me now. He will take me back to Phosphor, or Entropy, or Entrada, or Zima, or Cuchulain, or anywhere else I care to go.

"You could even go back to Earth," the Goddess Avatar says. "Now that you know what's happening out here. You could go back home and tell the Master all about it."

"The Master already knows, I suspect. And there's no way I can go home. Don't you understand that?"

She laughs lightly. "Darklaw, yes. I forgot. The rule is that no one goes back. We've been catapulted out here to be cleansed of original sin, and to return to Mother Earth would be a crime against the laws of thermodynamics. Well, as you wish. You're a free man."

"It isn't Darklaw," I say. "Darklaw doesn't bind anyone anymore."

I begin to shiver. Within my mind shards and fragments are falling from the sky: the House of Senders, the House of the Sanctuary, the whole Order and all its laws, the mountains and valleys of Earth, the body and fabric of Earth. All is shattered; all is made new; I am infinitely small against the infinite greatness of the cosmos. I am dazzled by the light of an infinity of suns.

And yet, though I must shield my eyes from that fiery glow, though I am numbed and humbled by the vastness of that vastness, I see that there are no limits to what may be attained, that the edge of the universe awaits me, that I need only reach and stretch, and stretch and reach, and ultimately I will touch it.

I see that even if she has made too great a leap of faith, even if she has surrendered herself to assumptions without basis, she is on the right path. The quest is unattainable because its goal is infinite. But the way leads ever outward. There is no destination, only a journey. And she has traveled farther on that journey than anyone.

And me? I had thought I was going out into the stars to spin out the last of my days quietly and obscurely, but I realize now that my pilgrimage is nowhere near its end. Indeed it is only beginning. This is not any road that I ever thought I would take. But this is the road that I am taking, all the same, and I have no choice but to follow it, though I am not sure yet whether I am wandering deeper into exile or finding my way back at last to my true home.

What I cannot help but see now is that our Mission is ended and that a new one has begun; or, rather, that this new Mission is the continuation and culmination of ours. Our Order has taught from the first that the way to reach God is to go to the stars. So it is. And so we have done. We have been too timid, limiting ourselves to that little ball of space surrounding Earth. But we have not failed. We have made possible everything that is to follow after.

I hand her my medallion. She looks at it the way I looked at that bit of alien pottery on the desert world, and then she starts to hand it back to me, but I shake my head.

"For you," I say. "A gift. An offering. It's of no use to me now."

She is standing with her back to the great reddish-yellow sun of this place, and it seems to me that light is streaming from her as it does from the Master, that she is aglow, that she is luminous, that she is herself a sun.

"Goddess save you, Lady," I say quietly.

All the worlds of the galaxy are whirling about me. I will take this road and see where it leads, for now I know there is no other.

"Goddess save you," I say. "Goddess save you, Lady."

The Tree That Grew from the Sky

From *Science Fiction Age*, September 1996

The visitor star, which the people foolishly think of as a tree, is growing larger overhead every night. Of course it is no sort of tree at all, but simply the kind of bright wandering star that starwatchers call a comet; but to the common folk it is a tree, a tree that is descending upon us from the heavens. They fear that it means to fall upon the world and bring about the destruction of all things.

It is easy enough to see why the people believe that. Through all the weeks of its presence above us the visitor star has steadily gotten bigger and brighter; it has become amazingly bright by now, astonishingly huge above us. But I know that it will not fall on us. I have plotted its position night by night; I see that it moves constantly to the north and east in the sky all the while that it is approaching us.

Plainly it will miss us by a goodly distance and sail onward through the cold empty spaces that surround us until it plummets into the sun. Or, what is more likely, it will not enter the sun but will swing on an arc about it like a pebble on a string, as comets of the past have been known to do, until finally it is caught in the hand of Maldaz, or perhaps one of the other gods that watch over us; and the god will hurl it back across the heavens to whatever place it came from.

All this week I have wanted to speak with the Alien about the comet and its movements—soon, before the king changes his mind again and decides to have him put to death after all.

The Alien, naturally, would understand these cometary matters much more deeply than I, because he has actually sailed across those dark seas of the night where the stars have their homes, and I have only looked up into them from below and wrestled with the gods for answers to my questions. During his years among us I have had many conversations with the Alien and he has taught me a great deal, but beyond doubt there will always be much more that I could learn from him.

At the moment there is, however, the problem of gaining access to him. He has been in a foul, sour mood for weeks, now—ever since the coming of the comet, in fact—sequestering himself, allowing no guests to come to him. The maze in which he dwells not only pens him in but keeps outsiders from entering unbidden. Since the comet came to take on its full brilliance we have sometimes seen him emerge at night, pacing high up along the inner wall of his enclosure with his face turned toward the sky, as well he might, for the comet is an extraordinary sight and he has few diversions in the course of his daily life. But on those occasions he has taken no notice of us; and when my daughter Theliane went to visit him the day before yesterday, as she so often has in the past, he turned her angrily from the gate, even her, his one true friend.

These moods have come to him often during his time among us, though not often with such intensity as at the present time. He has an angry heart, our Alien does. The burning poison of incurable loneliness and homesickness has spread through his veins in these fifteen years of his captivity.

The Alien fascinates me. His mere presence among us tells me that the sky is full of worlds, and those worlds are peopled, and some of those peoples go to and fro among the stars as easily as I would go from Kevorn to Stoi, from Stoi to Shagrool, from Shagrool to Kinipoil. That is a miracle to me. We thought we were alone in the universe until the Alien came. Now we see the folly of that belief: I do, at least.

How I would love to know all the things he knows! His head must be full of ideas and concepts never even dreamed by us, and what great wonders I might accomplish if I could call upon those ideas myself! His knowledge added to mine would allow me to achieve things never before attempted.

Nevertheless, I should not be too disparaging of my gifts or my accomplishments. My own mind, on its own, is far from a trivial thing. It is able to meet most intellectual tasks with distinction. I look; I see; I think; I comprehend. And so I understand this visitor star, and therefore it does not frighten me.

But the people will believe what they will believe, and how can I make them listen to me? I have never been able to make them listen to me. They respect me, yes. They employ my services and value my skills, yes. But to *listen*, when I tell them things?

No.

They will believe what they will believe. And the visitor star frightens them. The wide plain west of the city is bright with the fires of ghazul trees that they have set alight as offerings to the gods. They burn a tree to Maldaz, and nevertheless the visitor star draws ever nearer, and so they burn a tree to Kleysz, and one to Hayna, and one to Gamiridon; and still it comes toward us.

The ghazul trees are rare and very beautiful, and their sweet oil is precious for its seventy uses. It is a pity to waste them this way.

But the people will believe, and their beliefs make them afraid. What can I do? Let them believe.

At the beginning of the month, on a night when no moons were in the sky and the visitor star blazed out against the darkness like a river of light, the king sent word to me that I was to come to him in the Citadel, the great hilltop palace overlooking the Living Sea that I built for his father long ago, and explain to him the meaning of what was happening in the sky.

It always gives me great pleasure to behold the Citadel. It is not the cleverest of my buildings—the cleverest one is the maze that I built as the Alien's habitation and prison—but it is the largest and most magnificent. Still, the Citadel's design is not without a clever- ness of its own. Outside, it is massive and grand. The great sloping walls of greenish-black stone, the enormous gray exterior columns that support the heavy, blue-tiled roof, the awesome lifelike images of gods and goddesses that I spent four years carving with my own hands in high relief on the western facade: all these testify to the power and might of the dynasty that has governed us these nine hundred years past.

But once you are within the building, all is twisting and undulating and sly, and that testifies to the subtlety and vision of Kell the Artificer, who is the only man in the world who could have conceived such things. I am divine Tulabaratha's creature, he who is the builder of palaces for his fellow gods, and he, who is by far the most skillful of all the godly ones in the making of things, the Artificer of Artificers, has shared his understanding with me in generous measure.

The king was waiting for me in the Throne-Room of the Equinox. That is the long open hall on the second story at the palace's eastern end, facing the sea. There is a day in the spring every year when the sun in its northward journey crosses the celestial equator, and a day every autumn when it crosses that equator again going in the other direction, and on both of those days the hours of light and the hours of darkness are exactly equal. I have positioned the throne in that throne-room in such a way that at the moment of the equinoctial crossing a long shaft of golden-red sunlight penetrates the room and strikes a polished bronze pommel that rises above the center of the throne.

That was an easy enough effect to calculate; but King Thalk for whom I built the Citadel was so overwhelmed by his first sight of it that he paid me a bonus of five thousand pieces of gold, and King Hai-Theklon his son seats himself on the throne a day or two prior to the moment of the light-beam's semi-annual advent, for fear it might come early some year and he would miss it. And there he sits for hour after hour every spring and every autumn, despite my having advised him that it is not necessary to do so, until Maldaz has indeed hurled his golden shaft against the consecrated sphere of bronze.

I loved old King Thalk, but I have no great fondness for King Hai-Theklon his son. He was lazy and arrogant and unintelligent when he was a boy and I was his tutor; and though he is far from lazy now that he is king, he is still arrogant and unintelligent. Since he has kept those latter two qualities into his adult years, I wish he had kept his laziness as well: he would do less harm that way.

He was standing right at the brink of the throne-room's open side when I entered, hands clasped behind his back, head hunched forward, staring upward into the sky. One good shove from behind would have sent him down into the Living Sea. But I lack the blind courage of the assassin.

"Kell?" he said, without turning.

"I hail and obey, Majesty," I said, and made the formal gesticulation of submission even though he was not looking my way. Now that he is king, he demands these formalities and I am careful not to forget that. It was once easier between him and me. For many years I called him "Choyin," which was his father's pet name for him, after his fancied resemblance to the little glassy-legged serpent of the Great Central Desert. If I dared to use that name for him now he would probably lock me up for the rest of my days in the maze where the Alien lives.

Still not deigning to glance at me, he beckoned me toward him with a flick of his hand. I came up close, and impatiently he ordered me closer yet, right to the edge. Red waves of dizziness swept through me, but I took up my place right beside him at the brink and clamped my two long anchor-toes tightly around the stone rim. My hsorn-sense is keener than most—too keen, perhaps—and therefore I have some fear of edges. To soar through the air like a bird would afford me intense delight, I like to think, but standing at the very edge of a steep drop makes me queasy. Still, I forced myself.

Just below us lay the roiling strangeness of the Living Sea. Which, to be accurate, is not exactly a sea at all, but rather an immense quivering pudding-like lake of a pale pink substance that is thicker than water but thinner than mud. It stretches eastward from this shore as far as anyone can imagine. Some say it goes halfway around the world.

I have studied it for many years: I know that it is a live creature, a single tremendous entity that has some sort of intelligent mind, though of what quality that intelligence is, not even I can say. By day and by night a flickering pink radiance rises from it, and warmth. The people believe that anyone who enters it will instantly die.

Despite the competing brightness that came from the sea, the visitor star stood out clearly and vividly against the dark moonless sky. The reason why the people spoke of it as a "tree" was obvious even to me, for the tail that splayed out behind it across much of the sky was particularly long and thick, indeed somewhat like the trunk of a tree, and terminated in a multitude of twisted curling streamers of light that could be construed as bearing some resemblance to a tree's roots. Ignorant but imaginative folk might well think that what they saw was a great tapering narrow-headed tree tumbling crown-foremost toward the world.

"This new star," said the king. "Is it a tree or is it a comet, Kell?"

"A comet that looks something like a tree, Majesty."

"A comet. You're certain of that?"

"A very bright and large comet, yes. A thing of dust and ice that comes out of the cold distant darkness trailing a white stream of light, crosses our course in the heavens, and vanishes again back into the darkness from which it came."

"'No comets are seen when a poor man dies, but the fall of kings is blazoned in the skies,'" he intoned, in that dreadful pumped-up over-theatrical way that I had never succeeded in persuading him to abandon. "You know those lines, Master Kell?"

"They are from my play *Heyolf the Bold*, Sire." He had quoted the passage with uncharacteristic accuracy.

"Yes. The wise old man Vithak speaks them. And then the young wizard Greyborn replies, 'Comets, aye! Famine and pestilence pour down from them like rain from a cloud.' The fall of kings, Kell. Famine and pestilence." He still had not looked at me so much as once. His voice was hollow, sepulchral. "If your poetry has any truth to it, Master Kell, the coming of this comet means that the realm is in great danger."

"My poetry is only poetry. My play is just a play."

"All just a fabric of lies, is it, this great masterpiece of yours which once you forced me to commit to memory down to its final word?"

"The play in its totality is a thing of wisdom and truth, Majesty. But it is the sum of its differing parts. Individual characters speak according to their individual ways of thinking, and those are not necessarily ones with which the author agrees. Old Vithak believes that comets are omens of evil, and so does the young wizard Greyborn. But the era in which they purportedly lived was long ago, when men were ignorant. It is a mistake to think that Kell the Master of Sciences, who created Vithak and Greyborn and put those words in their mouths, believes everything that they happen to believe."

"So I am mistaken, am I, Kell?"

There was an ominous tone in his voice. The king is slight of build, and I am a heavy-set man; but it would have been easy enough for him to fling me into the sea with one petulant push. I found myself wondering if I would try to take him with me if he did.

"It is not a useful policy to interpret the words of characters in a play as statements of scientific verities," I said carefully. "Poetry is poetry and science is science."

"You are both a scientist and a poet, Kell. I have always assumed that your poetry is scientific."

"That is not a safe thing to assume, Majesty."

He was silent for a time, considering that. Then he said, "Is this comet going to crash into us, do you think?"

"It will pass to the north and east, traveling toward the sun, and leave us in peace."

"Am I to take that answer as science or poetry, Kell?"

"I have made observations every night since the comet appeared in the sky. It grows larger, yes, but also it travels upward and outward. Last week it was there; tonight it is here; next week it will be *there*." I pointed far to the northeast.

"Unless it decides to smash through the roof of this Citadel instead, and kill the king, and bring famine and pestilence to the world, as your wise men say in that play of yours."

"Comets make no decisions, Majesty. They follow the inexorable laws of nature. Just as a river will not suddenly decide to flow uphill, this comet will not decide to turn from its path and descend into our midst."

"The people think it will. I've sent men out into the city to listen to what they say. They think that the comet is a great tree that Kleysz has placed in the sky, or perhaps it was Hayna who put it there, and it grows downward from the heavens all the time, getting bigger and heavier, and eventually its roots will lose their hold on the sky and it will drop upon us in a terrible catastrophe. That is what they believe."

"I know that. Believing a thing doesn't make it so."

"But what am I to do, Kell?"

"About their beliefs? Very little can be done about those, I would expect. Go before them and tell them that their fears are needless, that the visitor star cannot possibly do us any—"

"Any harm, yes," he cut in, drawling the words derisively, before I could finish the sentence. "And next you will say that time will prove me right and the people will rejoice. Fine. And if the comet falls upon us anyway, what then?"

"Why, then, we will all be dead. But it is not going to happen."

"You are the great artificer, Kell. You are Tulabaratha's own likeness come to dwell among us. Fashion something for me that will blow this thing, this tree, this comet, from the skies before it can do any injury to us. Some great projectile hurled from a mighty catapult, for example, that will shatter it into a million harmless fragments."

"That is not only unnecessary, Sire—I can show you mathematical proof that the comet will pass us by—it also happens to be impossible."

"A word you rarely use," he said, and laughed.

"But appropriate in this case."

"How am I to trust these mathematical proofs of yours? What if they mean no more than the words of the characters in that play of yours?"

"We could get the Alien out of his prison and question him about these matters. He has traveled between the stars; very likely he has seen comets journeying in their courses; he will know the law by which they must abide. And they will be exactly as I have told you they are."

"The Alien," said the king moodily. "I should take him out of that maze and have his throat cut on the high altar."

I gave him a look of horror. "Sire?"

"I've felt since I was a boy that letting him live among us is dangerous. The place he comes from is one where the gods we love are unknown. He owes them no allegiance, indeed probably denies their very existence. His coddled existence here is a mockery in their faces. For fifteen years they've waited for *us* to destroy him; and, since we don't do it, they've hurled this tree at him to do the job. The fact that the tree will smash us up too is unimportant to them, I suppose."

"A comet, Sire. Not a tree."

"Whatever. If it should collide with the world—"

"It will not. And the Alien is a poor stranded wayfarer whose life among us is a misery of loneliness. He is here through no choice of his own, but while he is here he is our guest, and guests are sacred. If you were to kill him, the gods might indeed be annoyed enough to hurl something our way. I beg you, Majesty, put all thought of sacrificing him out of your mind."

"Well—"

"And your fears as well. No harm will come to us from this comet."

"Well," he said again. "Perhaps so, Master Kell."

I backed most humbly and properly out of the royal presence then, even though the king still stood with his face turned from me, looking outward to the sky, and made my way through the splendors of the palace that I had so cunningly built for his father—through the Room of Nine Metals, and past the Pool of Nine Waters, and down the spiral staircase that I had fashioned so that it drills like an auger into the Nine Levels of the world's core, far below the Citadel itself. It may be blasphemy to say so, but the divine Tulabaratha by whose grace I have attained all my skills could not have done better. And then I passed beneath the bronze dragons with which I had bedecked the Lesser Gate and was outside in the night, and saw the comet hanging overhead, a dazzling shaft of cool white fire in the sky, bright as the sword of Gamiridon.

The king's anxieties had been allayed, for the moment, and all was well.

But with Hai-Theklon all was never well for long. He is just intelligent enough to be restless of mind, but not sufficiently intelligent to know when he is putting that restlessness to a foolish purpose. It is hard for him to hold to a steady course. Would he think once again, tomorrow, that it was a good idea to have me build a catapult with which to destroy the comet as it hovers above us? Would he begin toying again with the notion of sacrificing the Alien as an offering to the angry gods? Or sacrificing me, for that matter, if the panic among the common folk continued to grow? I am more useful to him than any ten thousand of them could ever be; but logic has never prevented kings from acting against their own best interests. They usually have the luxury of surviving their mistakes and continuing as before. I though, have only one life.

Confident though I was of my own conclusions concerning the comet, I resolved to check and recheck all my calculations to make absolutely certain that this comet, unusually big as it is, would behave like all previous ones known to history and swing past the world at a comfortable distance. A conversation on that subject with the Alien would be in order, too, I thought. I have, and never have made any secret about it, high regard for my own powers of mind; but I am wise enough to know that I am not infallible. That is one of the ways in which I am different from a king.

I was positive that the comet would not hit us. But what if it came very close, much closer than I expected it to, and swept like an avenging scimitar above the tops of our tallest buildings? The people would doubtless go berserk. In their terror they would surely burn the city and perhaps try to kill the king; and the king, as the wild mobs approached the Citadel, very likely would turn his anger on me.

So my figures had to be utterly trustworthy. If I saw any possibility of error in them, it would probably behoove me to disappear from the capital until the comet had passed by, or even, perhaps, to seek permanent service with some other king. There are many who would have me, and gladly.

I would set to work on my recalculations at once, that very night.

The quickest route from the Citadel to the compound where I have my observatory and workshop passes through the Great Plaza of the Kings. That is where the Tower of the Alien, which long ago had carried its lone passenger across the great sea of suns to our world, had made its landing on the astounding day when it came hurtling down through the sky, and that was where it had stood ever since, precisely in the center of the plaza, on the grassy lawn where King Mosa-Bodrik slew his fifty brothers in the time of the myths. The grass for a considerable distance around it was badly charred, but has long since grown back. "How I marvel at the elegant way you came down in the one open space in the midst of our city without harming a thing," I told the Alien once; to which he replied, not at all flattered, "Elegant? It was outrageous idiocy. I had no business landing in the city at all. But the ship was out of control and I was doing the best I could. It was just blind luck that I didn't kill fifty thousand people."

The Tower has never ceased to fascinate me. It summons for me a deep and shivering sense of the vastness and wondrousness of the universe; and never had I crossed the Great Plaza of the Kings without pausing a moment or two to stare at it in awe. And, sometimes, not simply to stare; on many occasions I had actually entered it, clambering up the winding staircase within it in order to study the array of mysterious devices in the cabin at its summit. No one else, to my knowledge, ever went into it. No one would dare.

They utterly baffled me, those devices. But just as one will probe with one's tongue at a sore tooth, so had I gone back again and again into the Tower to stare in bewilderment at those perplexing banks of mechanisms. I am not accustomed to bewilderment, nor to perplexity. Solutions to problems, even the hardest ones, have a way of presenting them to me, after a time. But not these. The devices in the Tower were alien mechanisms and the problems they offered were alien problems; and my mind, for all its versatility, is deeply rooted in the things of this world.

This night the Tower seemed more wondrous even than usual. Rust, over the years, has flecked its battered metal skin with a coating of brilliant colors, ochre and auburn and scarlet and emerald, but now, lit by the comet's white glare, it had taken on a whole host of unfamiliar and wonderful new hues.

As I stood then before it there leaped into my mind's eye the thought of making a painting of what I beheld at that moment, the comet splitting the sky with its light and the Tower beneath it all ablaze with the colors engendered by the reflection of that light. It would be a considerable challenge to reproduce the myriad interwoven coruscating tones of the Tower and the cool contrasting brilliance of the comet with mere pigment on canvas; but when had I ever turned away from challenge?

There was, however, no time for making paintings just now. So that night I merely walked entirely around it, briefly stopping several times to admire the eerie starlit beauty of its patina, and after a few moments of that I went on my way.

When I reached my observatory I made that night's measurements and etched them on the screen that gives me my comparative locations of the comet; and I saw that it had continued to move in the direction in which I believed it should be traveling, and at the requisite velocity. I held up to the sky the instrument that tells me the size of heavenly objects, and saw that the tail had once more extended its length. This, too, was completely in accordance with my prediction.

Then I took out the calculating machine that I had fabricated from strips of reed and slivers of copper wire, and went through all my numbers from the very first, plotting the actual course of the comet across the sky against my original predictions of them. And I confirmed, to my great satisfaction, that I had been correct at every step.

These things took me all night. Just before dawn Theliane came to me, sleepy and puzzled-looking, a candle in her hand.

"Father? I awoke and saw a light in here. Is there anything wrong?"

"Only in King Hai-Theklon's head," I answered. "He's been reading old plays of mine and something he found in one of them made him start to think the comet was going to hit us after all. So I've been rechecking my calculations. It's taken me a while. The figures are right."

Of Hai-Theklon's notion of putting the Alien to death to propitiate angry gods, I said nothing. I knew of the deep love she bore for that creature from another world. And I suspected that Hai-Theklon, like his father before him, both dreaded and to some degree revered the Alien, and would not dare to harm him, so why arouse needless apprehension in her?

"Only he would doubt that your figures are right!" she said indignantly. "But it does seem so close, all the same. And constantly getting closer. I can see why he'd be worried. The whole city's muttering, you know."

"It isn't close at all," I said. "It isn't?"

"When the comet comes into the sky each night, it's in approximately the same place as the night before, right? It's moved a little to the north, a little to the east, but you still see the same stars in the background behind it, Ligur, Izka, Semilgat, Vroz. Yes?"

"Well—yes."

"The world turns, and the comet goes out of view as morning nears, and the next night it's back again. Ligur, Izka, Semilgat, Vroz. Whereas the moons, which everybody agrees are very close to us, go whizzing across the sky from horizon to horizon. If the position of the comet against the background of the stars doesn't change very much, it must be farther away than the moons, is that not so? A good deal farther, as a matter of fact. And no one worries about the moons colliding with us. Nor should we worry about the comet. It's well out there in space, and though it's going to get closer to us before it starts going away, it's not going to hit us. I promise you that, Theliane. There are laws that all comets obey—laws not made by kings, but by the gods themselves— and this comet will behave the way all the others have."

"So it's definitely a comet, then, and not some kind of gigantic tree that's dropping down on us?"

"*Theliane!*"

"Did I say something stupid again, father? You know I'm not really stupid. But I suppose to you everybody, even someone with a reasonable amount of intelligence, must seem not much better than a moron."

"Hardly so," I told her.

And I scarcely need observe that Theliane was not stupid at all: simply not a genius. Not being a genius is no sin, though, or the priests would be busy kindling absolution-offerings all day and all night. But Theliane's mind was agile enough, as the minds of ordinary folk go, and her beauty was so remarkable that I often wondered how such a creature as she could have come from the loins of one like me.

I must concede, however, that I had assistance in the fashioning of her. In the distribution of parental traits Theliane may have received only a portion of her father's boiling intelligence, but a full measure of her mother's beauty. Better that, I suppose, than the other way around; and had she been given intellectual gifts on a par with her physical ones, the gods would have had to destroy her out of sheer envy.

She said, peering through the observatory window at the paling sky, from which the comet had vanished some hours before, "Do you know, father, I wish that it really was a tree with a great solid trunk, and that it would come close enough for me to climb up into it."

"You do? You would?"

One other trait of mine that had not been inherited by her was my overriding caution.

"Wouldn't you, father? No, perhaps you wouldn't. But I'd do it in a flash. It must be half as big as the world, wouldn't you say? And I'd climb right to the top of it. Imagine the view from up there! All the stars at once, and moons that no one can see from down here. And the other planets practically within my reach. Just stretch out my arm, like this— and touch—"

She laughed. Her eyes were bright with yearning. She was twenty years old, and still had a child's eager desire to enfold the universe in her arms.

"It's not a tree," I said. "And ninety-nine percent of what you see up there is nothing but a bright stream of gas. You'd have a hard time climbing that."

"That's too bad," she said. "If I could, I would. Maybe somehow I will."

I smiled and set about putting my instruments away, and she, perhaps already beginning to plan the scheme that would cause me so much grief, went off to bring me my morning meal. She was always solicitous in that way. None of my wives ever cared for me the way Theliane did. I have had no luck in my choice of women, not even once, except that one of them, sullen and cold though she was, gave me Theliane.

As she spread the food-bowls before me I said to her, "I need to talk with the Alien. But he's been so peculiar, lately. You said he wouldn't let even you visit him the other day."

The Alien had always regarded Theliane with great warmth, ever since she was a small child. There is no one in the world who has ever been closer to him than she. He was often surly and curt, but never with her. His skill in our language was something he owed to her, the long hours she had spent cloistered with him in his prison cell across fifteen years. Now that she was grown, she would have become his lover, I suppose, if such a thing had been physically possible between a man of his race and a woman of ours.

"It must be the sky-tree that agitates him so," she said. "The comet, I mean to say. Ever since it first came into view he's been getting edgier and edgier. What can that mean?"

I had no idea. Nor did she. But she promised to try again to get him to allow her through the gate, and to win his permission for me to enter also.

I slept from dawn to mid-morning, which is all the sleep I need. When I awakened, I heard Theliane moving about on the lower level of my chambers, singing prettily to herself as she tidied and dusted. She told me, when I went downstairs to her, that she had been to the Alien, who seemed more calm today; that he had admitted her to the maze in friendly enough fashion; that he was willing to let me speak with him that very afternoon.

I clasped her in my arms and tenderly touched my forehead to hers. "What would I do without you?" I asked her. "What would I ever do?"

The maze of the Alien, as I have said, is my most ingenious creation. Old King Thalk, may the gods ever caress him, told me to spare no expense: to make it a monument that would stand for the ages, a work of wonder that would outlast him and me both and the Alien as well, and by its unique distinction of design and elegance of artifice to announce to all the world in centuries to come that it was our city that had been singled out by the gods to be the home for this extraordinary being from the far stars.

It is a building fashioned out of spirals, a great many of them, some of which go upward and some down. They interlock and overlap in an artful way that dizzies the mind: you will be carefully following a downward-sloping spiral that seems to be a direct route inward, and, though you are diligently ignoring the temptations of dead-end side-passages and brightly lit major corridors that clearly go nowhere, it will suddenly occur to you from the effort of your movements that you have somehow ceased to descend and begun to climb a steep ramp, all the while thinking you were continuing down, and that you now are heading toward the perimeter of the maze rather than toward its center. Or you will be under the impression that you are ascending until you find out that you are not, and so forth.

There are, naturally, dozens of passages that double back in short order upon themselves and return you swiftly and mockingly to your starting point. There are some that seem agreeably straightforward until they terminate in impassable walls. There are high-vaulted galleries flanked with five or six doorways of which two or three appear to lead onward in useful directions, but none of which in fact go anywhere. And so on and so on, a delicious little city of mysteries. Though many paths will take you easily and encouragingly inward through the outer third of the maze, only a few will carry you very far into the middle third, and only one will bring you to the innermost zone.

I made the maze beautiful, too, though few in our lifetimes would have a chance to appreciate its beauty. The floors of the great galleries are decorated with a host of eerie little tapering mounds of carved white stone, much like the stalagmites one finds in caves. From certain angles they have the look of animals, or people, or gods; but then when you walk around to the other side of them they become incomprehensible lumps of shapeless rock, and you wonder how you could have recognized any sort of form in them whatever.

Then there are chambers where I built canopies and draperies all of a much finer white stone cut with a myriad little openings, so that they have the appearance of the most costly of woven fabrics; and also I constructed reflecting pools and walls that have the gleam of mirrors, and long mysterious openings in the ceilings of the lower rooms that seem to look upward into other worlds, and many another decorative feature that gives evidence of my skill as an artificer. And the entire structure is run through with ventilating pipes and concealed sources of illumination, all of the most artful inventiveness. I also designed a system of speaking-tubes by which those outside the maze can communicate with the Alien, and he with us. There is nothing like these tubes anywhere else in the world, not even at the king's own Citadel.

The apartments of the Alien are at the very center of all this, and they are comfortable enough, essentially the sort of lodging one might provide for a prince of the royal house. His spacious rooms are arranged on five levels, forming a discrete structure within the structure that rises up like a thrusting arm through the heart of the maze and culminates in a flat peak surrounded by an open circular gallery, thus giving him a lofty promenade where he can enjoy a fresh-air stroll, or look outward on the joyous light of day and the brilliance of the stars. It is possible to see him from outside the wall of the maze when he appears on his balcony, a distant, tiny figure outlined against the sky, and when he does so appear the people often gather to peer at him, though by this time he is far from a novelty here.

I used six different sub-architects to build the maze, and each one employed his own team of workmen, and no members of any team were given any knowledge of the plans that the other five groups were following. As a result, no one understands the secret of how to reach the inner apartments, except for three people. I am one and the king is another—Thalk insisted on that—and the third is the official known as the Guardian of the Alien, who is the blind eunuch Kataphrazes. I taught Kataphrazes the route myself, placing his probe-fingers on each key landmark along the way until he knew them all by touch-memory. His sense of hsorn is exceedingly powerful, very likely because of his blindness: he was amazingly quick to master the correct path and was able almost at once to make his way through the passages errorlessly and with unfaltering step.

Each morning Kataphrazes leads the servitors who bring the Alien his food to the inner barrier, never taking the same approach twice the same month, nor using the same servitors. If the Alien is to have guests, Kataphrazes will lead them inward in the same ever-varying fashion, and they are blindfolded besides, more for the theatrical pomp of the thing than as a real precaution, for nobody could ever learn the way simply by observing it just one single time.

There was a fourth who knew the route, who was Theliane. With King Thalk's permission I taught it to her when she was a child, at her urgent request, for there was little I would ever refuse Theliane.

The Alien's inner apartments are surrounded by a gated wall of sharp-tipped iron spars: the Alien alone has control over who passes through that gate. It is a little privilege that we bestowed on him to pre- serve the fiction that he is our guest, not our prisoner. When he feels gloomy and withdrawn, which is often, he denies entry to those who desire access to him, and so be it.

In any event he does not ordinarily have many visitors other than Theliane, who has been by far his most frequent guest, and myself; until his recent spell of unsociability I had gone to him every few weeks, and we had enjoyed long, far-ranging talks about the nature of the world and the cosmos. Other than us, he has had little company. The four high priests of the city pay him ceremonial calls every now and then, since he is regarded officially as an emissary from the gods. For the same reason King Thalk used to go to him every month or two; King Hai-Thelkon, though, finds him troublesome to look upon, indeed, downright hideous, and I think has entered the maze no more than twice in the five years of his reign. And sometimes high priests from other cities, when their travels bring them to us, are taken by Kataphrazes to see the Alien, by way of reminding them that his presence among us confers on us the status of a city honored above all others in the world.

It was months since I had last visited the Alien and this day, when I went to him, I was startled by the changes in his appearance. He is, obviously, not very much like us in form, other than in such superficial ways as having two legs on which he stands upright, and two arms, and a head set between his shoulders to bear his eyes and breathing-holes and mouth. I have long since grown accustomed to all the little oddities of his appearance, the flatness of his face, and the fact that his fingers are more or less all of the same size and so are his toes, and that his skin is pale and soft, and that his head is shaped the way it is and his eyes are the color and shape that they are, and so forth and so forth.

But the fur atop his head, which had changed its color from black to gray in the past few years, now seemed suddenly much more sparse than I remembered. I found that pleasing; it made him seem less like a beast of the fields. His face looked broader, as though the soft flesh of it were spreading and sagging. His flat inhuman eyes had a new look that seemed to me to speak not merely of the sadness of his soul but of a deep, inescapable weariness. Even his posture was different, his shoulders now slumping forward as if he found it an increasing effort to stand erect.

"Well, what do you expect, Kell?" he said, as I stood there gaping at him while he opened the gate that gave admission to his private apartments. There was an abruptness in his tone, a whipcrack rhythm, that I knew connoted anger. "Do you think I'm going to look the same way forever? I've spent a quarter of my entire life living in this labyrinth of yours. And now I'm starting to get old."

I had not said a thing, only stared. He often responds to unspoken statements that way, as though he can see into your mind and read your hidden thoughts.

For a long while I wondered whether the Alien might actually have that ability; since he has little or no hsorn, perhaps other senses of his are correspondingly hyper-keen. But later I realized that he merely has a highly developed capacity for interpreting facial expressions. It is, I suppose, a skill that his race cultivates and we do not, though I have given some effort to mastering it since learning from him that one can discover a great deal about the thoughts of others simply by studying their faces while they speak to you.

I told him that I knew that something had been troubling him lately which had caused him to shun my company and that of my daughter, and I asked whether it could be this, the onset of age, the distress that that was causing in him.

He merely lifted his shoulders a little way at that and turned his hands outward, the gesture he calls a "shrug," which is meant to convey indifference.

Why, he asked, did I think that growing old would be upsetting to him? To the contrary: the older he became, the closer he was to dying; and death for him meant only the end of captivity, the end of exile.

To these words I made no direct reply. They had been spoken in a flat, emotionless way that seemed to me to connote just as much anger as his earlier harshness. And I could see from his stance and a certain look about his mouth and eyes that he was speaking insincerely. A long silence prevailed between us.

"Is it the coming of the visitor star, then?" I asked, finally.

"You mean the comet?"

"Yes. I've seen you on the roof gallery, staring at it for hours."

"Well, why not? It's a colossal sight, a comet that brilliant. I've never seen one quite that grand. But what would be troublesome to me about a comet?" We had reached his sitting-room, now. In shelves on every wall were the multitude of things we had brought to him from his Tower, his books, his entertainment-cubes, the various machines with which he looks after his medical needs, and so forth. We are a civilized nation; we had tried to make his captivity as tolerable as possible. He beckoned me to my usual seat and said, "Do you people know what comets are, Kell?—You understand that they aren't actually stars, don't you?"

"We call them 'visitor stars,' but only because they are so conspicuous and move so much faster than true stars. But we know that comets are different from stars in some way, or we would not have the other word for them. For my own part, I think a comet is more like a little planet, is that not so?"

"Bravo, Kell! A little planet, yes! One that travels around and around the solar system just as the big planets do, only in a much more eccentric orbit."

"But the big planets will endure for all eternity," I said. "Comets must eventually exhaust their substance and disappear, or else falter in their orbits and tumble into the sun."

"You know that much, do you, Kell?"

"Am I not correct?" I asked him.

I knew that I was, but I was holding my breath all the same while awaiting confirmation from him. And I was leaning forward in the posture of expectation, pupil to master. Thirty years had gone by since I had last adopted that posture toward any person of my own species; but when in the company of the Alien I usually found myself taking such a stance within a matter of moments.

He said, "I've read your textbooks of astronomy. They're full of myth and fantasy."

"My ideas do not come from textbooks, but rather from direct observation of the phenomena."

"Ah, Kell, Kell, you're a special one, aren't you? Then tell me: why is it that you think comets will—what did you say?—exhaust their substance and disappear?"

"Because," I said, "they seem to be small hard balls of solid matter with a great cloak of light streaming out behind them. That cloak grows brighter and longer as the comet approaches the sun. What else can it be, but the comet's own substance, boiling forth from it in the form of gas as the sun's energy heats it? That substance can never be replaced, and so the comet must inevitably dwindle with each of its journeys around the sun, until there is nothing left of it."

I knew from the gleam of approval in his eyes that what I was saying was correct. Not that I had had any serious doubt of it.

"And as for how I know that the comets travel around the sun like planets, why, I have consulted the records. Not all of our astronomy is myth and fantasy, Alien. There are comets that have come back again and again, always at regular intervals for many centuries, and thus must be locked into permanent orbits as planets are. One comet has come every fifty years, one every sixty-two, and so on. It is in the records."

He pointed toward the ceiling. "This one, too?"

"Not this one. It has never been seen by us before."

"Causing great excitement out there, is it?"

"The people find it terrifying. They're afraid that it's going to collide with us and destroy the world. It looks like a tree to them, a huge tree that's falling from the sky, perhaps as a manifestation of the anger of the gods against us. I know that they're wrong, but when an irrational idea like that takes possession of people's minds, nothing I could say or do will lift it from them. They'll simply have to wait and see that nothing bad is going to happen."

"It's a lonely business, isn't it, Kell, to be as smart as you are."

I imitated his shrug-gesture. "I have adapted to it. I will accept the loneliness, if that's the price of the intelligence."

"And you aren't completely lonely. Apparently you've managed to find a wife, at any rate."

"I have had several wives. What I have never had is a mate."

He considered that for a moment.

"You've been blessed with a wonderful daughter, at least," he said, after a little while.

"So I have, yes. I thank the gods for her each day."

We fell into another spell of silence.

Then the Alien said, "Some comets do collide with planets, you know."

"They do?"

"It's been known to happen. For one thing, their orbits are dynamically unstable. Gravitational perturbations can make changes in a comet's path as it travels, and send it heading off on a collision course with something nearby. Do you know what I'm talking about, Kell? And even without that happening, the fact remains that the orbits of comets cross those of the planets. It's altogether possible, sooner or later, for a comet and a planet to arrive at the same place at the same time as they make their separate orbital journeys around the sun."

"This comet will not hit us," I said.

The Alien made his alien equivalent of a smile. "You say that with absolute confidence."

"I feel absolute confidence."

"Yes. It's the mark of a superior mind, isn't it? But also the mark of a completely closed and rigid one."

"I have calculated the orbit of this comet. Bright and large as it is, it will pass by us at a safe distance."

"I'd like to see those calculations," he said.

"I have brought them with me," I told him, and presented my portfolio of nightly observations.

That amused him, that I should be so well prepared for this discussion. For what seemed like a very long time he looked through my pages of notes, whistling occasionally, tapping the tips of his stubby little fingers against his teeth. I will not say that I felt serious self-doubt during this time, for I was sure that I had done my calculations properly; but I am not so foolish as to think I am a perfect being, and, as I have already said, this man's knowledge of the stars and heavens must by definition be greater than mine, because he has had direct experience of interstellar travel. So I allowed for the possibility that he would find some *qualitative* error in my assumptions, something that stemmed not from my observations and calculations (which I knew to be correct) but from some lack of understanding in me of the fundamental workings of the universe.

Then he looked up and said, "Very nice, Kell. You never cease to astonish me."

"The savage who walks on his hind legs once more demonstrates his unexpectedly capable mind, eh?"

"Don't be sarcastic. I feel great affection for you, do you know that? We're two of a kind, you and I. You're nearly as much out of place here as I am."

A curious remark. But I saw the truth in it, and I could not help but be flattered.

We talked then for a time about the nature of comets. He confirmed much that I had discovered on my own, and told me a few things I had not known, such as the existence of great swarms of comets at the outer edges of most solar systems, millions and millions of them clustering together far beyond the outermost planets. Only a few of these comets, he said, ever detach themselves from their fellows and undertake journeys past the inner worlds. Which explained to me why, since the world is at least half a million years old and perhaps very much older than that, there still are comets for us to see. The ones our remote ancestors saw have long since evaporated and vanished, but there are always new ones breaking loose from that enormous population of them out beyond the orbit of the farthest planet and coming our way.

We became silent yet again, after we had talked a while.

Then abruptly he said, "What I told you when you arrived was untrue. The thing that's been troubling me *is* the comet."

His sudden reversal mystified me. "It is? And why is that?"

"I don't mean that it's the comet itself that's troublesome to me. As I told you, it's the most spectacular one I've ever seen, an extraordinary thing, and so I've been up there looking at it most nights like everybody else. But I'm *not* like everybody else. When I look up at the comet, I also see the stars."

"Ah."

"I've tried not to think about the stars, Kell. Or the planets that go around them. Especially the one I came from."

"I see," I said.

"My native star isn't visible from this hemisphere, anyway. But, all the same, when I look toward the heavens—"

"I understand."

The terrible anguish of his solitude leaped out at me like a beacon-light shining from his flat alien eyes.

I tried, as I had tried a million times before, to imagine what his home world was like, the world he had left so long ago and never would see again. To me it seemed outlandish, fantastic, even frightening. But to him it was home.

He had described it all to me again and again, so that I sometimes could almost make myself believe I had been there myself. But I knew that that was a delusion. I had no real idea of the nature of his world. I never would. My mind stretches farther than that of anyone I have ever known; but the home world of the Alien would always be inconceivably *other* to me. All those myriads of flat-faced people; the remarkable green trees; the unthinkably bizarre animals; the vast seas of blue-green water. A host of great cities, each one made up of buildings taller than our mountains, and having more people in it than we have on our entire world; machines beyond my comprehension, machines that sent pictures instantly from continent to continent, machines that enable one to fly from one planet to another and one star to another, all manner of miraculous machines.

They were like gods, those people, if his tales of his home world had any truth to them.

He said, "This was supposed to be a three-year exploratory mission. Three of my years—that's only two of yours. Come out, look around, go home and file my report. Equipment failure wasn't part of the mission plan. Neither was shipwreck. Neither was capture and imprisonment by an alien species."

"You are not our prisoner. You are our guest."

"Spare me the sophistry, Kell. We know each other too well for that. Sweet old King Thalk was well aware that the priests would hang his skin on the balcony of his palace if he let me get away from here, because I am the messenger of the gods, and so long as I'm here, the gods will smile on your city. How that fits together with the notion that the gods are currently in the process of dropping a celestial tree on your city because I'm a resident in it is not something that needs close examination, is it?—Kell, I'm not going to live forever. I want to go home." The last few words came forth in a desperate blurt.

I ached for him. I am not a man of stone.

But I said, "You know that that's impossible."

"Is it? I thought 'impossible' is a word that isn't in your vocabulary."

"There is a difference between things that are merely difficult to accomplish and things that cannot be accomplished at all."

"Yes, I know. But this one isn't of that sort." He gave me a curious look, fierce and sharp, like winter lightning out of nowhere. In a tone of voice that was oddly constricted, as though a band had tightened about his throat, he said, "Do you ever go into my ship, Kell?"

"Sometimes, yes."

"I thought you might. What condition is it in, inside?"

I wondered at this. He rarely spoke of his ship: not at all, that I could remember, in several years. "It is as it was. We preserve it with care, as a holy monument. Grown somewhat rusty, perhaps, on the outside—"

"And the inside?"

"As it was on the day you last saw it."

"Sealed, is it, against rain, and insects, and general decay?"

"Sealed, yes."

"Is it, now?" He fixed his gaze on me as though he were pinning me to a board with a dagger. He said, speaking with great precision and clarity in that same tight tone of voice, "It often crosses my mind, Kell, that it might not be difficult to put the ship back into good working order, if it hasn't deteriorated since the time of my landing. And you lead me to think that it hasn't."

Those quiet words rocked me like an earthquake.

Hoarsely I said, "Can that be true?"

"I'm sure of it." The new intensity of his features was truly disturbing. There was a glow about him. It was as though fire streamed from his eyes. "The fundamental mechanisms were still intact when I made my landing. Certain components had broken down, others had become decalibrated, but the essential instrumentation was all right. Otherwise I couldn't ever have made my landing. If nothing in it has suffered further damage since I was imprisoned here, it ought to be fixable. You and I, working together, could put everything back together."

It is the comet, I thought, that has aroused these thoughts in him. Awakening yearnings that have long lain dormant within his soul.

"If my ship were to be repaired, I'd be able at the very least to get as far as one of the survey buoys ten or fifteen light-years from here and send a signal that would bring a rescue team to pick me up. And my ship *can* be repaired, Kell. By you. I'm certain of that."

I said nothing. I could scarcely bear to look at him.

His strange five-fingered hands reached toward me in what could only have been an imploring gesture. They were shaking in agitation. His voice grew louder. "It's not impossible. It isn't! I know what kind of skills you have, Kell. You're one of those amazing universal geniuses that come along maybe every five hundred years in a race's history. No, don't turn your head away like that—you know it's true as well as I do, and this is no moment for false modesty. You're an engineer and an architect, and you have a master artisan's technical abilities and the mind of a great physicist, and you paint and sculpt and write plays and poetry as well, and I don't know how many other things you can do, but the list probably includes just about everything.—Help me escape. Help me, Kell."

I stared at him. I begged him with my eyes not to go on.

But he was merciless. "There's no way you can refuse me. A man like you, Kell, with such a roving, questing, insatiable spirit: it surely can't be hard for you to imagine what it would be like to be locked away like this for the rest of your life!"

No. It was not hard at all. I shivered at the thought. But still I did not reply.

He took my silence for assent. The agitation that had taken hold of him subsided somewhat, and his entire posture grew more relaxed. "Well, then. Are we agreed? The two of us, Kell, working side by side, would be able in a matter of months, maybe even only weeks, to—"

"No," I said, at last, and held up my hand to stem the fervid flow of his words. "Wait. Please. No more of this. I told you it isn't possible, and I meant just that."

The light went from his face.

"What would stand in the way?" he asked.

I forced myself to speak calmly. "Alien, you have no comprehension of the realities of the situation. Do you seriously think that we could simply tell the king that you have decided that you would like to go home, whereupon the king would blithely release you from this maze and allow you to instruct me in how to make it possible for you to escape? Why would he be any more willing to do that than his father was?"

"I understand that. But certainly you of all people must know how to get me out of this place. We could go to the ship secretly by night, and—"

"Secretly. Yes. I drug the guards, let us say, and we sneak over there every night and work, and at dawn I bring you back here with no one the wiser. And finally one day the work is done and the ship is fixed and you get into your Tower and fly away to the stars, and what do you think will happen to me, when you have gone from here? Think, Alien, think! Will the king believe that you escaped from this maze by yourself, by means of some magical conjuration you knew? That you repaired your ship unaided? No, Alien, you will fly away home, and once you are gone I will die the most terrible death that any mind could invent. And that is why I say that what you ask is impossible. You want me to commit suicide for you. That is something I will not do."

Ultimately it did not greatly surprise him, I suspect, that I was unwilling to help. He knew what risks it would involve for me. But he would have had no peace if he had not asked.

And I had no peace now that he had.

I left him soon afterward. A deep and abiding melancholy had come over me and I needed to be alone. I walked through the streets of the city looking neither to the left nor the right, and responding not at all to such greetings as came my way, until I had left the paved streets behind and found myself on the earthen path that leads down to the shore of the Living Sea.

Twilight was coming on, now. Two or three of the smaller moons had risen in the eastern sky. I stood beneath the cliff on which the royal Citadel sits and its long shadow stretched far out before me into the sea.

In the changing light of the waning day the sea itself was taking on its evening colors, a deeper radiance, a stronger pink hue shot through with hints of crimson and aquamarine. The phantasmagorical giant creature that is the Living Sea is more active by night. It stirs and tosses and ripples; small spiky projections and scalloped turrets rise from its surface and are quickly reabsorbed; little bubbling mouths appear, gape two or three times, and vanish.

I stood for a long while staring intently outward as if somehow I could see across to the mythical lands on its far shore, where the ones we call the Other Folk are said to dwell, those who subsist on nothing but stone and sand, and speak in whistling tones, and sacrifice three thousand wild songbirds to their sun-god every morning. They have a third eye set in the middle of their forehead, so we are told, and dozens of fingers clustering at the ends of their arms, and blue skin pockmarked everywhere with deep circular craters. But who knows if any of these things are true? Nobody in ten thousand years has crossed the Living Sea to visit the Other Folk; and tales ten thousand years old are no more to be trusted than the books we read in our dreams.

Such a great sadness had taken hold of me after my visit to the Alien that for a time I considered giving myself up to the sea then and there. I had felt that temptation often enough before, for I had long been curious about the occult transformative powers the mysterious substance of the sea was rumored to possess, and what better way to understand those powers than to experience them directly?

But this was different. What was surging through me now was a yearning not for knowledge but for oblivion. Perhaps the sea would dissolve and consume me, as everyone believed it would consume any creature foolhardy enough to enter it; or perhaps I would simply drown the way one might drown in a lake or river of ordinary water; or maybe the current would carry me eastward, on and on, until at last I came ashore in the land of the Other Folk, who would hail me as a god. Whatever happened, I would be relieved of the feelings of shame and guilt that gripped me now.

But I knew what foolish, useless thoughts those were, and I put them from my mind.

I put, indeed, everything from my mind. I turned myself into a statue of myself, and stood empty of thought, while the sky grew dark and the long glowing tree-shaped streak of white that was the comet came out of the southwest and took up its place high above me. And I remained that way for an hour, or perhaps two, or three, or maybe it was only a couple of minutes.

I must have begun to walk along the shore, after a time, for when consciousness and volition returned to me I found myself far down at the southern end of the beach, where the Tree of Purple Flame stands in its great solitary splendor at the edge of the Living Sea.

It is a marvelous thing, that mighty tree. Its roots go deep down into the bed of the sea and its trunk is a smooth white unbranching shaft that rises nearly as high as the cliffs that border the shore. I think the tree is made of sea-stuff too, for strange ghostly purple light emanates from it, and the shadow that it casts is blue, and its great spreading crown is in constant motion, everything writhing, swarming, changing, never the same for a moment. You can see eyes in that writhing crown, faces, beating wings, long serpentine shapes that coil about each other to form intricate knots.

The tree surges and quivers with the constant transformation that is the essence of life. No one that I know of has ever dared to go close to it. Even the shadow that it casts is said to be deadly. But I have pondered that tree ever since I was a boy. To me it is a tree of magic. Now, standing nearer to it than I had ever been before, I pondered its nature yet again, for a time. There I stood, with one strange tree in front of me, another of a very different sort plunging through the dark sky overhead; and gradually my gloom and my pain went from me, and I was myself again, and I turned and went up the steep path that led from the seashore to the town.

A message from the Citadel was waiting for me at my chambers. The king had sent for me again: I was to come at once.

This time I found him not in his usual haunt, the Equinox throne-room, but rather in the Grand Council-Hall, which is the great room that occupies most of the third level of the building. That was a disturbing thing in itself, for the Grand Council-Hall is a huge and awesome place, and Hai-Theklon tends to go to it whenever some huge and awesome thought is rattling around in his mind. Which usually presages trouble for me.

He was seated at the far end of the room, which obliged me to walk its entire considerable length before I could make my gesture of obeisance. A great fire was burning in each of the fire-pits down there, so that his kingly grandeur was enhanced by the impressive and dramatic shadows of him that flickered on the blank white wall behind him.

He is fond of that effect. I spent five months painting vivid scenes from the lives of the gods all up and down the other walls of the Grand Council-Hall—I used a process I invented myself, grinding dry pigments into powder and applying them to the wall with a wet brush while the undercoating of freshly applied lime-plaster was still drying, so that the colors would set with the plaster and remain forever bright—but I deliberately left the rear wall unpainted, as though anticipating that King Thalk's successor would want to magnify his own importance with this sort of shadow-show. I wonder if Hai-Theklon realizes that.

He said right away, before I could rise from my deep genuflection, "I have thought of a way of defending ourselves against the comet, Kell."

"Did I not explain, Sire, that there is no need for—"

He waved me to silence.

"The metal tower, Master Kell, in which the Alien flew from his world to ours: is it not the case that it could be repaired, and made to fly through the heavens once again?"

That stunned me, coming so soon after my conversation on the same subject with the Alien himself.

Fumblingly I said, "Well, Majesty—it may well be that that can be done, but it is just as likely—that is—if the mechanisms that operate it—we know that they were already somewhat damaged when the Alien came, and the passage of time could well have—but—on the other hand—perhaps—"

I have never sounded like such an idiot in all my life.

The king cut serenely into my blathering babble. "No matter what the difficulties are, Kell, you can deal with them. I know that you can."

I said, making a desperate effort to recover some fragment of my poise, "I lack your assurance of that, Sire. But possibly—just possibly—" A hopeful, cajoling note came into my voice now. "Perhaps, Majesty, it could be done, yes. If the Alien were allowed to be with me in the Tower as I worked at the repairs—if he were to instruct and direct me, and even to assist me, let us say—"

"No. He must not leave the maze, not now or ever."

"But how, then, will I be able—?"

"He can tell you what must be done, and you can go there and do it, and when you are done the ship will fly again."

I closed my eyes and nodded solemnly. Then after a moment I said, very gently, "And may I ask, Sire, what connection this has with defending ourselves from the comet?"

"Why, that ought to be obvious, Kell! Don't you see, you can cause the ship to go aloft on a course that will send it crashing into the comet. Thus destroying it as it passes overhead, before it can do us any harm!"

He was serious. It was all I could manage to keep from laughing aloud at this grotesque multiplication of absurdities.

But I maintained a certain degree of gravity, and soberly told the king that I would give his plan the most careful consideration; and then

I extricated myself from his presence as quickly as I could, before I betrayed my true opinion of his splendid idea.

I hurried home and told Theliane of my conversations with the Alien and the king. She reacted with the greatest excitement and enthusiasm for the project. This, in my folly, I misinterpreted as growing entirely out of her affection for the hapless prisoner in the maze.

The next day I told the Alien also of the king's eagerness to have the ship repaired. The irony of the coincidence amused him greatly. He laughed—it has always seemed remarkable to me that the Alien's way of showing amusement should be so much like our own—and shook his head in a sidewise fashion again and again, which is his sign of bemused disbelief. Then he turned his head away from me and put his hands over his face. His shoulders moved in an odd convulsive way, and a low muffled sound came from him, out of his throat and chest, that I had never heard him make before.

"Are you all right?" I asked.

"Yes."

"What are you doing?"

He swung around to face me. There was the sheen of fresh moisture on his cheeks, as if some unusual gland had discharged a substance from his eyes.

"Expressing my happiness at the thought of going home," he said.

The comet grew even brighter in the days immediately following, so that it seemed to fill half the sky and obscured the light of the stars and the moons.

And as it waxed ever more brilliant overhead, the mood in the city, already sufficiently ugly, turned much uglier still.

Burning ghazul trees as offerings to the gods had been bad enough, I thought; but now the people began burning temples also. The gods, it now was widely declared, had withdrawn their favor from the city, and they must be informed that we were displeased by that. If they would threaten us with a comet, well, then, we would retaliate by threatening them with the loss of our love. And so there was a serious fire at the House of the Ceremonies and a lesser one, though still very destructive, at the lovely little Shrine of Kleysz. Two priests of the cult of Hayna were beaten in the streets, and one of them died. The sanctuary of Gamiridon was looted of its treasures by an angry mob. An animal was slaughtered in a sacrilegious way at the foot of the golden statue of Maldaz in Pelathas Square.

I would have told them, if anyone had been willing to listen to me, that the continuing increases in the comet's brightness and apparent size were normal and not at all dangerous. I would have explained to them that the comet had not yet reached its closest point of approach to the world and would grow brighter yet in the days ahead before it grew smaller, but that it was still embarked on a course that would take it safely past us and out into the darkness of space again.

But no one was willing to listen to me, nor in any case did I feel much desire to go forth expounding on these matters to those who do not have the capacity to understand them.

Besides, it appeared that going out among the populace would have been dangerous for me. Theliane reported that she had heard tales circulating in the streets that blamed me, not the gods, for bringing the comet—the "tree," they kept calling it, with idiotic persistence—down upon the world. It was all my fault; supposedly I had engaged in some grandiose scientific experiment that had gone awry and as a result the "tree" had been pulled toward our world from some other part of the heavens.

"They have started speaking of it as 'Kell's tree,'" Theliane told me, trembling. I had never seen her show fear before. But it was for me, not herself, that she trembled.

It was easy enough for me to keep out of sight. By day I was safe in the heart of the maze, receiving instruction from the Alien on the location and workings of his ship's controls. And by night I was in the ship itself, striving to find some way of making the vessel functional again.

The first few days there were purely exploratory ones. I made careful sketches of the panels and dials and levers that had puzzled me for so long, and took them to the Alien, who pored over them and tried to identify the role of each piece of equipment and determine whether it still might be capable of operation. Of course he had not been inside the ship for fifteen years, and much had grown unclear to him; but gradually the details started to return to his mind.

It was on the fifth day that I first felt the emotion, unusual to me, of despair. The control mechanisms of the Alien's ship had been defective to some degree in the first place, or he would never have had to make his forced landing here. They had been further damaged in that very landing, and afterward had suffered fifteen years of natural deterioration; and here was I, a man of a civilization entirely different from the one that had built this ship, trying to undo all those various kinds of damage without any knowledge of the underlying technology! It was the wildest sort of fantasy to think that I could succeed.

I have not had much experience of despair in my life. I felt it as a leaden weight within my throat, and an aching behind my eyes, and a griping of my gut that left me unable for a day or more at a time to take sustenance.

Theliane was dismayed by the darkness of my mood. "Perhaps I can help you with your work, father," she suggested.

I saw no way that she could. But she so fervently wanted to take part, and I was so reluctant to rebuff her in any way, that I began bringing her into the Tower with me. She stood at my side, she shined lights for me into the dusty crannies, she handed me tools as I requested them. Her very presence compelled me to moderate the pessimism that continued each night to mount in me. But I could not conceal from myself the reality of the situation, which was that I was making no progress.

The intensity of the comet's light was baleful now and disconcerting even to me. It illuminated the night sky almost like a second sun, though it was a sun that emitted no heat, only a cold terrible glow.

One could see, even with the naked eye, the huge rocky sphere that was its head, jagged and ominous, with thick masses of luminous smoke streaming away behind it. The color of its long tail had changed, now, from its earlier pure white to a kind of frightful yellowish-green, with a hard metallic forcefulness to it that struck the eye the way the clangor of a bell strikes the ear. That change of color troubled me. Could the comet be closer than I had calculated, so close that the stream of gaseous matter that it threw off was reacting with the gases that make up our atmosphere?

It was a terrible hour for me. Yet again I doubted my own figures; but I checked and rechecked, and came away convinced once more that I had made no error.

The king called me to him once more. This time I found him in his private quarters in the Citadel, surrounded by the sculptures and paintings and tapestries I had so lovingly made for his father long ago.

"Was it you that summoned the comet to our world, Kell?" he asked sternly.

"You give me too much credit, Majesty. I have many skills, but drawing comets down from the skies is not among them."

"The people speak of it now as 'Kell's tree.' Are you aware of that, Kell?"

I sighed. "I am, yes. The people say many things, Sire, and not all of them are founded in fact. The comet is not a tree, and it is not mine." "Finish the job of fixing the Alien's ship," he said, "and hurl it against this comet, and let us have an end to this thing. How goes the work?" "It goes very well, Majesty. I hope to have excellent news for you very soon." That was an utter lie, not the first I had told this king. It is often necessary for an ordinarily trustworthy man to provide some sort of shady response to the peremptory demands of unreasonable people.

But on that very night I made the first breakthrough toward success.

By baleful comet-light I crossed from the Citadel to the Plaza of the Kings and entered the Tower of the Alien, and ascended the spiraling metal ramp to the control cabin at the top. Theliane was not with me on this particular evening; she had gone to the maze, to the Alien.

I laid my hands against the plates and dials of the control panel, which I had inspected without avail so many times before. But this time, because of things the Alien had explained to me about functions and capacities that had suddenly begun to cohere in my mind, I began to see the pattern. I saw only its corner at first, and even that was shrouded in mist; but I am such that even if I see only the corner of a pattern, I often can in time make out the whole of it, and that was what happened now.

I drew new sketches and brought them to the Alien, and he studied them and nodded and drew some sketches of his own, and asked certain questions of me and sent me back to the Tower to find the answers. And I found them; and that led to more questions, and more answers still. And one night a few days later I began to pull broken sections free from the master panel, and to set about the task of designing and forging replacements for them.

So did the real work of repair begin, and so did it proceed. I will not claim that I understood all of what I was doing, or even a great deal of it. The mind that directed the work was the Alien's, from a distance, guiding me from his prison as though he was standing by my shoulder and whispering instructions in my ear; what I contributed were the eyes and the hands, and the metallurgy, and the intuitive skills. It was as though a god had taken hold of me and was bringing forth wonders from me as I lay in his grasp.

Theliane was of no small assistance. Her mind did not have the wide-ranging perception of mine, the ability to make sudden swooping leaps of comprehension and connection, but even so her learning and skills were far from trifling. She had helped me before; she knew why metals behave as they do, how they respond to temperature and pressure, how they are refined and annealed. She had learned more than a little of the purifying arts of melting and reducing and fusing.

She worked with me step by step, phase by phase. She asked sensible and useful questions; she made keen observations. I was proud of her.

I should have burned that Tower to the ground. Instead, with the aid of the Alien's instructions and Theliane's faithful help, and working as ever under the benevolent guidance of my patron god Tulabaratha who is the special deity of artificers, I succeeded in restoring it to working order. It was a triumphant demonstration of my skill. I never knew before that one might live to regret a triumph.

On a day when I saw beyond any doubt that success was within my reach, that the completion of the task was at hand, I began to give some thought once again to the predicament I had been creating for myself.

The king had ordered me to repair the Tower for the sake of using it to shatter the encroaching comet; but that, of course, was nonsense. What the ship would be used for was to facilitate the Alien's escape from our world.

And what would happen to me, once the Tower went roaring up into the sky with the Alien on board?

Why, very likely the king would hold me responsible for his departure. I understood the workings of Hai-Theklon's mind only too well. No matter that I had repaired the ship at the king's own direct order; no matter that I had no apparent motive for aiding the Alien to flee; someone had to be the scapegoat, and I was the one who had done the work. The king would also probably hold me to blame for the coming of the comet, as so many others already were doing. So I would die in some ghastly fashion and the king's anger would be assuaged, and sooner or later the comet would leave the vicinity of our world and Hai-Theklon would take credit for that, too. But I would still be dead.

So the thought occurred to me that it might be a sensible thing for me to be on board that ship when the Alien took off for his home.

I played with that idea as if it were some wondrous new toy that I had fashioned for myself. To rise into the heavens atop a bellowing column of flame; to soar across the darkness, looking down on our world from on high until it dwindled to the size of a grain of sand; to plunge outward into that infinity of stars of which the Alien had so often spoken—what joy that would be!

And then one day to arrive at the Alien's own world! To behold that prodigiously fantastic landscape with my own eyes!

The mere contemplation of that dizzied me. The blue-green water and the green-leafed trees; the gleaming titanic buildings rising like arrows into the cloud-flecked sky; the hordes of flat-faced people moving through the streets; the vehicles that go forward with no beasts to draw them, the air-ships that stay aloft without movement of their wings; the mountains that give forth bursts of flame and rivers of molten rock; the flakes of frozen water falling from the skies. I have traveled widely on this world of ours and I have seen many of its famous wonders, the wheel-beasts of the western plains and the phosphorescent lakes of Gemborionta and the voriagar hives of the Velk Peninsula and the trees of salt that grow in Domrin Land, and much else. I have been to the chapel of Kleysz at Galfi and the bottomless pools of Grelf, and I have seen what there is to see at Pangu and Rorm and Glay. But all those things would not be a patch on the marvels of the world of the Alien. Endless astonishments would await me there, all the days of my life.

So much to see! So much to learn! The strangenesses, the wonders, the inexplicable enigmas with which I would wrestle. Things that were utterly unfamiliar, that had only shape and color, but no meaning. Things that were fascinating because they were incomprehensible: things whose purposes were unguessable, because they filled needs that were themselves beyond the compass of my mind. What ecstasy to confront such things! What delight to find in every hour of every day the necessity to struggle to understand the simplest things of that other world! I would be like a child again, wandering breathless through a world of mysteries, finding and solving puzzle after puzzle until the larger patterns began to connect themselves and overwhelming revelations came rushing in on my ever-avid mind.

And then I thought of Theliane, and the whole fantasy collapsed into ashes.

I could never leave her. She was the joy of my life, the music of my heart. Without her I would be nothing but a strange lonely old man with an unusual mind and an empty soul.

But to bring her with me: how could I do that? To rip her away from all that was familiar to her, and carry her off to a world of unutterable alienness where every moment of every day would confront her with a bewildering jumble of insoluble riddles, and where she would grow old and die without ever having known the touch of a loving mate or heard the laughter of her own children?

No. No. It was impossible. Insane. I banished the idea from my mind. The ship was ready, though, for testing. I had no idea what to do. And while I hesitated—concealing for the moment the extent of the recent progress I had made, both from the Alien and, of course, the king—catastrophe came down upon me.

It was night. I was in my observatory, measuring the position of the comet. So concerned with my work was I that although I was aware of a curious booming sound, quite loud, and saw out of the corner of my eye an odd flash of red light passing just above the rooftops, it was thirty seconds, at least, before I reacted. By that time I could hear the first sounds of uproar in the city.

"Theliane?" I called. "What's going on out there?"

No answer came. The noises from the street grew louder and more agitated: wild shouts, hysterical outcries of fear. Out of the midst of chaotic yelling came one man's voice, loud and clear as a god's, crying over and over, "The tree is falling into the city! We all are doomed! The tree! The tree! The tree!"

The tree, yes. I knew what he meant by that. But the comet was still in its proper place in the sky, a fiercely bright yellowish-green slash across the belly of the darkness. It was not falling on us. It would not fall on us.

I looked for Theliane downstairs, running from room to room, calling her name. She was nowhere in the house. But tacked to the inside of the front door was a note in her handwriting:

Father—

I have gone up into the sky to look at the tree. I must see; I must know. You understand what I am saying.

I love you.

Gods, no! No!

A reverberating drumbeat of thunder rolled in my head. White fire flashed. I heard a loud buzzing as of ten thousand insects all at once, marching through my brain. For a moment everything grew disjointed, and I was unable to see. The faces of mocking gods whirled about me in a pulsating circle.

Then I collected myself a little and stepped outside the house, and saw throngs running through the streets, hundreds of people, thousands, perhaps, many of them wild-eyed and screaming as they ran, and everyone heading in the same direction, eastward, toward the cliffs, the shore, the Living Sea. It was a raging river of panicky humanity; and like a man caught up in some terrible nightmare I allowed myself to be engulfed by that river and borne along by it on its inexorable journey to the sea.

Long before I reached the shore I was able to see what it was that was drawing them there. From the high rim of the cliff I saw it, by pale pink sea-glow and yellow comet-light. I would gladly have screened my eyes from the sight. But there was no hiding from it, none.

Theliane's flight in the starship had been very brief. The rust-flecked Tower of the Alien was lying on its side, a short distance out in the Living Sea, jutting up at an angle with perhaps half its length above the surface. Theliane had succeeded in getting the ship aloft, which was miraculous enough, but evidently she had been unable to control it, and it had executed a wobbly, erratic flight lasting no more than a matter of moments, during which it traveled just above rooftop level across the width of the city from its starting point in the Great Plaza of the Kings, over the temple district and the residential quarter and out past the hill of the royal Citadel, and onward a short distance over the sea.

But there it had reached the end of its journey. The ship's power must have cut off when Theliane was barely beyond the edge of the shore: in my mind's eye I saw the vessel halting in mid-air, standing upright and seemingly motionless above the sea for a moment, and then toppling in a steady downward plunge.

I tell you all this by putting one word after another, in calm, dispassionate, orderly fashion. But I assure you that I was neither calm nor dispassionate nor orderly as I went running down that sloping earthen path from the top of the cliff to the shore of the sea. Nothing was in my mind but the fact that the Tower had gone aloft and that it had crashed and that my daughter was in it, out there in the unknown and threatening substance that is the Living Sea. No: not even that. My only thought was that Theliane was in danger and I must rescue her.

The crowd on the shore melted away to either side of me like mist before the piercing rays of the summer sun as I ran past. Do you know how you seem to move in a dream, as though floating, your feet not touching the ground? That was how I moved then.

I reached the edge of the sea and I did not pause at all. In that dreamlike drifting way I moved out onto the strand of steaming pink mud that forms at the border between land and not-land, and, without breaking my stride, I continued unhesitatingly on out into the body of that great unknown thing that no one had ever entered before.

What did I expect to happen to me? I expected nothing. I hoped only that I would survive the short journey out to the fallen ship, and bring Theliane forth from it alive.

The sea was warm and steaming, and very shallow even when I was fifty or sixty paces out from shore, no more than chest-deep for me. It did not seem to grow deeper at all as I proceeded outward. Its strange odor, sweet and not unpleasant, struck my nostrils. I felt its pink substance warm about me, rising past my calves, my knees.

It had a thick consistency, oddly agreeable to the touch. A quiet hissing sound came from it, a burbling, a kind of gentle squeak. Each step I took produced a soft sucking effect as I lifted my feet. Small wriggling protrusions rising from the surface of the sea danced playfully about me like little serpents standing on their tails.

Was there pain? No. Were my legs dissolving? No. Was I being transformed into something unimaginably strange? No. I was still myself, still alive, still moving forward. The sea's grasp was like a sly caress, unseen slithering tendrils sliding over my body, across my thighs, my belly, my loins. Sea-stuff was in my mouth, my eyes, my ears. A strand of it had wrapped itself around my throat.

Colors flashed everywhere. There was purple haze all around me. I saw ghosts circling in a shimmering golden aura in the air, faces that seemed almost familiar, one that might have been my father's, and one that resembled King Thalk, and one that could have been Theliane's.

I felt no fear. The sea was too warm, too welcoming, too comforting for that.

What I did feel was a strange sense of *contact*, with the sea, with the sky, with everything that existed in the world. I was immensely extended; I was infinite; I understood what it must be like to be a god.

It seemed to me that I could stretch out my arms and touch the fingertips of one hand to the cliffs behind me and those of the other to the coast of the distant unreachable eastern continent halfway around the world, where the three-eyed whistling Other Folk live. It seemed to me also that my head rose high above the clouds, so that I could stare face to face at the gleaming pockmarked visage of the comet, and it could stare at me. And I felt the roots of the planet beneath my feet, the tumbling, churning fires of the core, where the toiling god Manibal sweats eternally over the forge of creation.

I touched a myriad souls at once: the soul of the king, and the soul of the Alien, and the souls of all the people who were clustered along the beach. I made contact with everyone in the world at once. Everyone except one; the only soul I could not find was that of my daughter.

Once I glanced back toward the shore. It was surprisingly far away, a black line against the comet-riven sky. The multitude of townspeople who had gathered there now looked to me like so many insects. They stood motionless, watching, watching, watching, as Kell the lunatic artificer went striding ever farther into the Living Sea.

From the cliff, the starship had seemed only a little way from shore, but the actual distance was greater than I had thought. An endless time went by until at last I came to the ship.

It had fallen into the sea in such a way that the entry hatch was on the underside, beneath the sea's surface. I would have had to submerge myself completely in order to reach it, and that gave me pause for the first time since I had gone out from the shore; but also I realized that Theliane, intending a flight into the cold and darkness of the farther sky, would have dogged the hatch shut before taking off. I would never be able to enter it from without.

Instead I began to clamber up the side of the ship, crawling hand to hand along its ridged skin. There were handholds there, perhaps for the use of maintenance personnel on that faraway planet from which it had been launched. Bright droplets of sea-stuff fell away from my hands and arms like glistening pearls as I emerged into the air.

Near the top of the vessel is a porthole made of something like glass, though it is not glass, that provides a view for the occupant of the control cabin. In a desperate plodding way I pulled myself up the ship until I was looking in that porthole, and I looked upon the face of my daughter Theliane.

Her eyes were open, but she was dead.

I had no doubt of that, from the moment I first saw her. Her eyes, those lovely glowing eyes whose color was the delicate color of thyrla eggs, were glassy and unblinking, and filmed over with the unmistakable film of death. Her finely tapered nostril-slits were slack; her mouth drooped and sagged to one side. The posture of her body as she sat in the straps of the pilot's cradle was the posture of the dead.

The shock of the landing impact, no doubt, had killed her. I could not accept that thought, but neither could I deny it. I hammered my hands against the side of the ship until I thought my bones would break. I pressed my face against that porthole and shouted her name again and again, knowing that no sound from outside could possibly penetrate those metal walls. But in any case she could never have heard me.

Then my strength failed me and I dropped away from the ship's skin, falling free of the vessel's flank and landing in the sea. My landing was soft and easy. The sea seemed to reach up to catch me and it drew me down gently into itself. Quietly I lay just beneath the surface, unmoving, not even bothering to breathe, cushioned by the density of the strange warm fluid. I floated. I drifted. I was in the caressing arms of a vast mother.

It embraced me and enfolded me and very soon, I think, it would have begun to digest me. I imagined my skin and my flesh peeling painlessly away, and soon afterward my bones as well. The particles that had composed me would distribute themselves through the body of the sea, and I would be part of it forever.

But that did not happen. Numbly, unthinkingly, I began to paddle with my arms, and after a moment more to drop my feet to the shallow bottom and to push myself forward, and step by step I made my way toward shore.

I came to land close by the Tree of Purple Flame, far down the beach from the place where I had entered the sea. I saw the bright shaft of its smooth white trunk and the ghostly flickering of its unceasing purple radiance, and they drew me onward. The tree was singing, too, a low, gentle, soothing, wordless song of comfort and strength, and as I drew close to it I began to sing also.

Its gnarled roots rose above the surface of the sea. I seized one and clung to it and pulled myself across its smooth slippery sides until I was up out of the sea entirely. I lay there for a time, gasping, looking up into the crown of the tree, seeing the faces there, the eyes, the coiling shapes, the beating wings. Then I rose and walked down the narrow ridge of the root's upper face until I arrived at the trunk itself, and I embraced it, stretching out my arms as wide as they would go. But that was hardly enough to reach one-fiftieth of the way around that great trunk.

People had come down the beach toward me. But they would not go close to the tree; they stood back, gaping, eyes very wide, whispering among themselves.

I saw that the king himself was among them.

"Majesty," I said in a voice that was like a voice from the next world, and let go of the tree-trunk and took a few tottering steps toward him. "Majesty, I repaired the ship, and my daughter rode it into the sky without my knowledge or permission. She wanted to see the great comet at close range. And now the ship is in the Living Sea and she is dead within it."

For once there was no bluster about him and no foolishness either. His face was sad and solemn. "She had the same hunger for knowledge that burns in you, Kell."

"Yes. And a great deal more courage."

"She was very brave, yes."

I sank down on the sand before him and tried to make the gesture of obeisance, but I was trembling too much from my exertions to manage it. Hai-Theklon, bending, caught me by the elbows and lifted me to my feet. His eyes stared into mine.

"What will you do now?" he asked me.

"I will build a machine that will go out into the sea and bring the Tower back to shore," I told him. "And I'll open it up and take her from it, and carry her out of the city to the burial-place and do the things that are done there. And then—then—"

I went faltering into silence. To my great surprise a wrenching sound came from me, from deep down in my throat, a sound that was something like the sound that the Alien had made that time when his face had become moist and he told me that he was expressing his happiness at the thought of going home. It had not seemed like a sound of happiness then. It was not a sound of happiness when it came from me now.

"She was very brave," said the king again. "And very beautiful, I am told."

"Very beautiful, yes, Sire," I said. "She was that. And much more."

The next day I designed, and over the following week, under my direction, fifty artisans constructed, the machine that is to pull the Tower of the Alien from the place where it lies half submerged in the Living Sea. It is a great wooden framework on wheels, a kind of giant wagon, equipped at its front end with a large and sturdy leather hoop that can be tightened by the operation of an arrangement of cogs and wheels.

Pulleys and levers connect the machine to a large and sturdy iron band that I have caused to be set into the face of the cliff along the shore. Pressure on the levers induces the pulleys to tighten, moving the wagon-wheels and thrusting the machine outward into the sea. Reversing the action of the levers will draw the wagon back toward land. It is a cunning device. The old artificer may have been shattered by grief, but he has not yet lost his skills.

I will ride the wagon tomorrow as it goes into the sea. Despite my demonstration that it is possible for us to go into the Living Sea and return unharmed, there is still no one else who will venture close to its pink surf. But that is all right. I should be the one who brings Theliane back from the sea, and I will be the one who does it. From my seat atop the wagon, I will operate the controls that bring the hoop into place around the ship and tighten it; and then I will give the signal and the men on shore will pull the wagon and the ship up onto the land.

And what will happen after that?

"Do you think the ship can be repaired again?" I asked the Alien, the day before yesterday. I have gone to visit him every day, since Theliane's death. He is nearly as deeply moved by it as I am.

He said, "I think the ship will turn out not to be very seriously damaged, despite the crash."

"But it fell down into the sea!"

"Not because of any mechanical failure, I think, but simply because she gave it the wrong commands," the Alien said. "She must have become confused. She was speaking a foreign language, after all."

"Speaking?"

"The ship responds to spoken commands. In the language of my planet."

"How would Theliane have known the language of your planet?"

"I taught her," he said quietly. "Years ago. She asked me to. It gave me great pleasure, being able to speak again with someone in my native language. And so she knew how to tell the ship what to do. But once it was aloft she must have become confused. If you give the ship conflicting commands, or say something that makes no sense to it, it might very well tumble out of control."

"Ah," I said. There were signs of anguish plainly visible on his face again; and, I suspect, on mine. Together we had conspired to kill her, he and I, and we had not understood what we were doing at all.

He held out his hands, his odd little stubby-fingered hands, and clasped my larger ones within them, and we stood like that for a while, face to face, one mourner to another. He made a small sound deep in his throat again; and I made one also. It gives some relief from sorrow, that sound.

Then I said, "In two or three days we will pull the ship out of the sea, and after I have taken Theliane from it and sent her to her eternal rest, I will go into back it and do whatever has to be done to make sure that it is still in working order. And then, Alien, I will come for you here in the maze."

Color came into his long pallid face, and light. "Will you, then?"

"By night, yes, when the guards are sleeping or drunk. And if your official guardian Kataphrazes the eunuch happens to be here, I will take him and turn him and turn him and turn him in circles until his hsorn-sense is altogether befuddled, and I will lock him up here in your apartment and bring you forth out of this maze that long ago I built for you, and we will go to the ship, you and I, and this time it will receive the proper instructions and it will take you into the sky."

"And you, Kell? Won't the king punish you for that, as you said he would, once I've disappeared? He'll know it was you that was responsible."

"The king will have to find me, first," I said. "And I will be in the sky with you."

"*What?*"

"Yes," I said. "That is my plan."

Why not? Why not?

Nothing holds me here now. I will go with him to his world, and let whatever may happen to me there happen. It will be my turn to be the Alien, there. Let them build a maze for me to live in, if that is what they want. Will that be any worse than the way I live here among my own people? I have always been a stranger in their midst. So I will leave, and I will be an alien among the aliens of the Alien's world, and everything will be new and fresh and strange to me, and so be it.

So be it.

The comet, I noticed when I took my measurements last night, has passed its point of maximum brightness and soon will begin to fade. Day by day now it will grow ever dimmer, until at last it cannot be seen at all, and then it will be gone from our skies, perhaps for a hundred years, perhaps for a hundred thousand. And I will be gone with it, and gone forever.

So I make my farewell now to this world, and even to its gods, for they will not go with me where I am going. I had faith in them: and what sort of faith did they keep with me, to take me from my only child? Kleysz, goodbye. Goodbye to you, Gamiridon of the bright sword. Maldaz who rules the sun, Hayna, ever-toiling Manibal, goodbye. And you also, Tulabaratha, you greatest of artificers. You served me well, even as I was serving you. I will take something of you with me, wherever it is that I go now. But I say farewell even to you.

Perhaps the people, not knowing what has become of me, will tell one another gravely that the comet has carried me off to some place in the stars. I like that. Let them say it. "Kell's Tree," they always called it, in their invincible ignorance. The tree that grew from the sky. "The tree reached down to us to get him," they will say. "And he has climbed it and vanished into the sky." But no. No. Whatever they say, it was never a tree. A comet is what it is, and nothing else: my comet, Kell's Comet. And now its brightness fades. It begins to take its leave of them. And so does the Artificer Kell.

Travelers

From *Amazing Stories*, Summer 1999

Are we all ready, then?" Nikomastir asks. He has fashioned a crown of golden protopetaloids for himself and gleaming scarlet baubles dangle from his ears: the bright translucent shells of galgalids, strung on slender strands of pure gold. His long pale arms wave in the air as though he is conducting a symphony orchestra. "Our next destination is—" and he makes us wait for the announcement. And wait. And wait.

"Sidri Akrak," says Mayfly, giggling.

"How did you know?" cries Nikomastir. "Sidri Akrak! Yes! Yes! Set your coordinates, everybody! Off we go! Sidri Akrak it is!"

A faint yelp of dismay comes from Velimyle, and she shoots me a look of something that might almost have been fear, though perhaps there is a certain component of perverse delight in it also. I am not at all happy about the decision myself. Sidri Akrak is a nightmare world where gaudy monsters run screaming through the muddy streets. The people of Sidri Akrak are cold and dour and inhospitable; their idea of pleasure is to wallow in discomfort and ugliness. No one goes to Sidri Akrak if he can help it, no one.

But we must live by our rules; and this day Nikomastir holds the right of next choice. It is devilish of Mayfly to have put the idea of going to Sidri Akrak into his head. But she is like that, is Mayfly. And Nikomastir is terribly easily influenced.

Will we all perish on hideous Sidri Akrak, victims of Mayfly's casual frivolity?

I don't think so, however nasty the visit turns out to be. We often get into trouble, sometimes serious trouble, but we always get out of it. We lead charmed lives, we four travelers. Someday Mayfly will take one risk too many, I suppose, and I would like not to be there when she does. Most likely I will be, though. Mayfly is my mask-sister. Wherever she goes, I go. I must look after her: thoughtful, stolid, foolish me. I must protect her from herself as we four go traveling on and on, spinning giddily across the far—flung worlds.

Sidri Akrak, though—

The four of us have been to so many wondrous lovely places together: Elang-Lo and the floating isle of Vont, and Mikni and Chchikkikan, Heidoth and Thant, Milpar, Librot, Froidis, Smoor, Xamur and Iriarte and Nabomba Zom, and on and on and on. And now—Sidri Akrak? Sidri Akrak?

We stand in a circle in the middle of a field of grass with golden blades, making ourselves ready for our relay-sweep departure from Galgala.

I wouldn't have minded remaining here a few months longer. A lovely world indeed is Galgala the golden, where myriads of auriferous microorganisms excrete atoms of gold as metabolic waste. It is everywhere on this planet, the lustrous pretty metal. It turns the rivers and streams to streaks of yellow flame and the seas to

shimmering golden mirrors. Huge filters are deployed at the intake valve of Galgala's reservoirs to strain the silt of dissolved gold from the water supply. The plants of Galgala are turgid in every tissue, leaf and stem and root, with aureous particles. Gold dust, held in suspension in the air, transforms the clouds to golden fleece.

Therefore the once-precious stuff has grievously lost value throughout the galaxy since Galgala was discovered, and on Galgala itself a pound of gold is worth less than a pound of soap. But I understand very little about these economic matters and care even less. Only a miser could fail to rejoice in Galgala's luminous beauty. We have been here six weeks; we have awakened each morning to the tinkle of golden chimes, we have bathed in the golden rivers and come forth shining, we have wrapped our bodies round with delicate golden chains. Now, though, it is time for us to move along, and Nikomastir has decreed that our new destination is to be one of the universe's most disagreeable worlds. Unlike my companions I can see nothing amusing about going there. It strikes me as foolish and dangerous whimsy. But they are true sophisticates, untrammeled creatures made of air and light, and I am the leaden weight that dangles from their soaring souls. We will go to Sidri Akrak.

We all face Nikomastir. Smiling sweetly, he calls out the coordinate numbers for our journey, and we set our beacons accordingly and doublecheck the settings with care. We nod our readiness for departure to one another. Velimyle moves almost imperceptibly closer to me, Mayfly to Nikomastir.

I would have chosen a less flighty lover for her than Nikomastir if matters had been left to me. He is a slim elegant youth, high-spirited and shallow, a prancing fantastico with a taste for telling elaborate fanciful lies. And he is very young: only a single rebirth so far. Mayfly is on her fifth, as am I, and Velimyle claims three, which probably means four. Sembiran is Nikomastir's native world, a place of grand valleys and lofty snow-capped mountains and beautiful meadows and thriving cities, where his father is a minor aristocrat of some sort. Or so Nikomastir has said, although we have learned again and again that it is risky to take anything Nikomastir says at face value.

My incandescent mask-sister Mayfly, who is as small and fair as Nikomastir is tall and dark, encountered him while on a visit to Olej in the Lubrik system and was immediately captivated by his volatile impulsive nature, and they have traveled together ever since. Whither Mayfly goeth, thither go I: that is the pledge of the mask. So do I trudge along now from world to world with them, and therefore my winsome, sly, capricious Velimyle, whose psychosensitive paintings are sought by the connoisseurs of a hundred worlds but who belongs to me alone, has willy-nilly become the fourth member of our inseparable quartet.

Some people find relay-sweep transport unlikable and even frightening, but I have never minded it. What is most bothersome, I suppose, is that no starship is involved: you travel unprotected by any sort of tangible container, a mere plummeting parcel falling in frightful solitude through the interstices of the continuum. A journey-helmet is all that covers you, and some flimsy folds of coppery mesh. You set up your coordinates, you activate your beacon, and you stand and wait, you stand and wait, until the probing beam of some far-off sweep-station intersects your position and catches you and lifts you and carries you away. If you've done things right, your baggage will be picked up and transported at the same time. Most of the time that is so.

It is a stark and unluxurious mode of travel. The relay field wraps you in cocooning bands of force and shoots you off through one auxiliary space and another, kicking you through any convenient opening in the space-time lattice that presents itself, and while you wait to be delivered to your destination you drift like a bauble afloat in an infinite sea, helpless, utterly alone, bereft of all power to override the sweep. Your metabolic processes are suspended but the activity of your consciousness is not, so that your unsleeping mind ticks on and on in the most maddening way and there is nothing you can do to quiet its clamor. It is as though you must scratch your itching nose and your hands are tied behind your back. Eventually—you have no idea whether it has been an hour, a month, a century—you are plunked unceremoniously down into a relay station at the planet of your choice and there you are. Relay-sweep transport is ever so much more efficient than any system requiring vast vessels to plough the seas of space from world to world; but all the same it is a disquieting and somewhat degrading way to get around.

So now we depart. Mayfly is the first to be captured by the sweep-beam. Perhaps half an hour later Nikomastir disappears, and then, almost immediately after, Velimyle. My own turn does not arrive for many long hours, which leaves me fidgeting gloomily in that golden meadow, wondering when, if ever, I will be taken, and whether some disjunction in our routes will separate me forever from my three companions. There is that risk—not so much that we would fail to arrive on Sidri Akrak at all, but that we might get there many years apart. I find that a melancholy thought indeed. More than that: it is terrifying.

But finally the dazzling radiance of the sweep aura engulfs me and hurls me out into the Great Dark, and off I go, dropping freely through hundreds of light-years with nothing but an invisible sphere of force to protect me against the phantoms of the auxiliary spaces through which I fall.

I hang in total stasis in a realm of utter blackness for what feels like a thousand centuries, an infinity of empty space at my elbow, as I go my zigzag way through the wormholes of the adjacent continua.

Within that terrible passivity my hyperactive mind ponders, as it all too often does, the deep questions of life—issues of honor, duty, justice, responsibility, the meaning of existence, subjects about which I have managed to learn nothing at all, basically, either in this life or the four that preceded it. I arrive at many profound conclusions during the course of my journey, but they fly away from me as fast as I construct them.

I begin to think the trip will never end, that I will be one of those few unfortunate travelers, the one out of a billion who is caught in some shunt malfunction and is left to dangle in the middle of nowhere for all eternity, or at least for the ten or twenty thousand realtime years it will take for his metabolically suspended body to die. Has this actually ever happened to anyone? There are only rumors, unfounded reports. But there comes a time in every sweep-jump when I am convinced that it has happened to me.

Then I see a glare of crimson and violet and azure and green, and my mask-sister Mayfly's voice purrs in my ear, saying, "Welcome to Sidri Akrak, darling, welcome, welcome, welcome!"

Nikomastir stands beside her. A moment later Velimyle materializes in a haze of color. The four of us have made a nearly simultaneous arrival, across who knows how many hundreds of light-years. We definitely do lead charmed lives, we four.

Everyone knows about Sidri Akrak. The place was settled at least a thousand years ago and yet it still has the feel of a frontier world. Only the main streets of the half-dozen big cities are paved and all the rest are mere blue dirt that turn into rivers of mud during the rainy season. The houses are ramshackle slovenly things, lopsided and drafty, arrayed in higgledy-piggledy fashion as though they had been set down at random by their builders without any regard for logic or order. After all this time the planet is mostly jungle, a jungle that doesn't merely encroach on the settlements but comes right up into them. Wild animals of the most repellent sorts are permitted to rampage everywhere, wandering about as they please.

The Akrakikans simply don't care. They pretend the animals— monstrous, appalling—aren't there. The people of Sidri Akrak are a soulless bloodless bunch in the main, altogether indifferent to such things as comfort and beauty and proper sanitation. Primitive squalor is what they prefer, and if you don't care for it, well, you're quite free to visit some other world.

"Why, exactly, did we come here?" I ask.

It is a rhetorical question. I know perfectly well why: because Nikomastir, clueless about our next destination, had opened a void that Mayfly had mischievously filled with one of the most unappealing suggestions possible, just to see what Nikomastir would do with it, and Nikomastir had as usual given the matter about a thousandth of a second of careful consideration before blithely leaping headlong into the abyss, thereby taking the rest of us with him, as he has done so often before.

But Nikomastir has already rearranged the facts in what passes for his mind.

"I absolutely had to come here," he says. "It's a place I've always felt the need to see. My daddy was born on Sidri Akrak, you know. This is my ancestral world."

We know better than to challenge Nikomastir when he says things like that. What sense is there in arguing with him? He'll only defend himself by topping one whopper with another twice as wild, building such a towering edifice of spur-of-the-moment fantasy that he'll end up claiming to be the great-grandson of the Fourteenth Emperor, or perhaps the reincarnation of Julius Caesar.

Velimyle whispers at my side, "We'll just stay here two or three days and then we'll move along."

I nod. We all indulge Nikomastir in his whims, but only up to a point.

The sky of Sidri Akrak is a sort of dirty brown, broken by greasy, sullen green clouds. The sunlight is greenish too, pallid, tinged with undertones of dull gray. There is a sweet, overripe, mildly sickening flavor to the warm, clinging air, and its humidity is so intense that it is difficult to distinguish it from light rain. We have landed within some city, apparently—in a grassy open space that anywhere else might have been called a park, but which here seems merely to be a patch of land no one had bothered to use for anything, vaguely square and a couple of hundred meters across. To our left is an irregular row of bedraggled two-story wooden shacks; on our right is a dense clump of ungainly asymmetrical trees; before and behind us are ragged aggregations of un-painted buildings and scruffy unattractive shrubbery.

"Look," says Mayfly, pointing, and we have our first encounter with the famous wildlife of Sidri Akrak.

An ugly creature comes bounding toward us out of the trees: a bulky, round-bodied thing, dark and furry, that rises to a disconcerting height atop two scrawny hairless legs covered with bright yellow scales. Its face is something out of your worst dreams, bulging fiery eyes the size of saucers and dangling red wattles and jutting black fangs, and it is moving very quickly in our direction, howling ferociously.

We have weapons, of course. But it swiftly becomes apparent that the thing has no interest in us, that in fact it is fleeing an even more ghastly thing, a long bristle-covered many-legged monster built close to the ground, from whose spherical head emerge three long horn-like projections that branch and branch again, terminating in scores of writhing tendrils that are surely equipped with venomous stings. First one vile creature and then the other runs past us without seeming to notice us and they lose themselves in the shrubbery beyond. We can hear wild shrieking and hissing in there, and the sound of cracking branches.

Nikomastir is smiling benignly. All this must be delightful to him. Mayfly too looks entranced. Even Velimyle, who is closest to me in temperament, almost normal in her desires and amusements, claps her hands together in fascination. I alone seem to be troubled by the sight of such creatures running about unhindered on what is supposedly a civilized world.

But it is ever thus in our travels: I am fated always to stand a little to one side as I follow these three around the universe. Yet am I linked irrevocably to them all the same.

Mayfly was my lover once, two lives back. That was before we took the mask together. Now, of course, it would be unthinkable for anything carnal to happen between us, though I still cherish cheerful memories of her pixy breasts in my hands, her slim sleek thighs about my hips. Even if we have forsworn the sexual part of our friendship, the rest is deeper than ever, and in truth we are still profoundly a couple, Mayfly and I, despite the rich and rewarding relationship I maintain with Velimyle and the frothy, sportive one Mayfly has built with Nikomastir. Above and beyond all that, there is also the bond that links us all. The lines of attraction go this way and that. We are inseparables. They are my world;

I am a citizen only of our little group. Wherever we go, we go together. Even unto Sidri Akrak.

In a little while two immigration officers show up to check us out. Sidri Akrak is an Imperium world and therefore the local immigration scanners have been automatically alerted to our arrival.

They come riding up in a sputtering little snub-nosed vehicle, a man and a woman in baggy brown uniforms, and begin asking us questions. Nikomastir does most of the answering. His charm is irresistible even to an Akrakikan.

The questioning, brusque and hard-edged, is done in Imperial, but from time to time the immigration officers exchange comments with each other in their own dialect, which sounds like static. The woman is swarthy and squat and flat-faced and the man is even less lovely, and they are not at all obliging; they seem to regard the arrival of tourists on their planet simply as an irritating intrusion. The discussion goes on and on— do we plan to remain here long, are we financially solvent, do we intend to engage in political activity in the course of our stay? Nikomastir meets every query with glib easy reassurances. During our interrogation a slimy rain begins to fall, oily pink stuff that coats us like grease, and a massive many-humped blue-green beast that looks like an ambulatory hill with purple eyes appears and goes lolloping thunderously past us with utter unconcern for our presence, leaving an odor of decay and corruption in its wake. After a time I stop listening to the discussion. But finally they flash bright lights in our faces—passports are validated retinally on Sidri Akrak—and Nikomastir announces that we have been granted six-month visas. Lodgings are available three streets away, they tell us.

The place they have sent us to turns out to be a dismal rickety hovel and our innkeeper is no more friendly than the immigration officials, but we are grudgingly allowed to rent the entire upper floor. The rooms I am to share with Velimyle face the rear garden, a patch of uncouth tangled wilderness where some slow-moving shaggy monster is sluggishly browsing about, nibbling on the shrubbery. It lifts its head in my direction and gives me a cold glare, as though to warn me away from the plants on which it's feeding. I signal it that it has nothing to worry about and turn away from the window. As I unpack I see a procession of glassy-shelled snail-like things with huge bulbous red eyes crawling diagonally across the bedroom wall. They too stare back at me. They seem almost to be smirking at me.

But Nikomastir and Mayfly claim to be delighted to be here, and Velimyle seems to have no complaints. I feel outnumbered by them. Velimyle announces that she would like to do a painting of Nikomastir in the hotel garden. She only paints when she's in a buoyant mood. Buoyant, here? They run off together downstairs, hand in hand like happy children. I watch from above as Velimyle sets up her easel outside and goes about the task of priming the psychosensitive surface of her canvas. She and Nikomastir are as untroubled as any Akrakikan by the shambling shaggy thing that grazes noisily nearby. How quickly they have acclimated.

"Are you very miserable here, darling?" Mayfly asks, running her fingertips lightly along my cheeks.

I give her a stoic smile. "I'll be all right. We'll find things to amuse us, I'm sure. It's all for the best that Nikomastir brought us to this place."

"You don't mean that, do you? Not really."

"Not really, no."

Yet in some sense I do. I often tell myself that it's important not to live as though life is just a perpetual holiday for us, even though in fact it is. It would be too easy to lose ourselves, if we aren't careful, in the nightmare that is perfection.

This is an era when all things are possible. We have godlike existences. We have every imaginable comfort close at hand. Beauty and long life are ours for the asking; we are spared the whole dreary business of sagging flesh and spreading waistlines and blurry eyesight and graying hair and hardening arteries that afflicted our remote ancestors. And all the incredible richness of the galaxy lies open to us: key in your coordinates, snap your fingers, off you go, any world you choose to visit instantly available. Never in the history of the universe has any species lived such a life as ours.

I fear the terrible ease of this existence of ours. I think sometimes that we'll eventually be asked to pay a great price for it. That thought engulfs me in secret terror.

Mayfly, who knows me almost as well as I know myself, says, "Think of it this way, love. There's something to be learned even from ugliness. Isn't it true that what we're trying to get out of all this travel is experience that has meaning? If that's what we want, we can't just limit ourselves to the beautiful places. And maybe a horrid place like Sidri Akrak has something important to teach us."

Yes. She's right. Is she aware that she's voicing my own most private thoughts, or is she just being playful? Perhaps it's all self-delusion, but I do indeed seek for meaning as we travel, or at least think that I do. These furtive broodings in which I indulge in the hidden places of my soul are, so it seems to me, the thing that sets me apart from Nikomastir and Mayfly and Velimyle, who take life as it comes and ask no questions.

Velimyle and Nikomastir return from the garden a little while later. She puts the rolled canvas away without showing it to me. There is an uncharacteristically somber expression on Velimyle's face and even giddy Nikomastir seems troubled. Plainly something has gone awry.

I know better than to ask for details.

We eat at our hotel that night. The surly innkeeper slams the dishes down before us almost angrily: a thin greenish gruel, some sort of stewed shredded meat, a mess of overcooked vegetables. The meat tastes like cooked twine and the vegetables have a dank swampy flavor. I pretend we are back on Iriarte, where food is the highest art and every meal is a symphony. I pretend we have returned to Nabomba Zom, to that wondrous palatial hotel by the shore of the scarlet sea, the waters of which at dawn would reverberate as if struck by a hammer as the first blue rays of morning fell upon it.

But no, no, we are on Sidri Akrak. I lie sleepless through the night with Velimyle breathing gently beside me, listening to the fierce honkings and roarings and screechings of the wild beasts that roam the darkness beyond our windows. Now and again then the sounds of the lovemaking of Mayfly and Nikomastir come through the thin walls that separate our bedroom from theirs, giggles and gasps and long indrawn sighs of pleasure.

In the morning we go out exploring.

This city, we have learned, is called Periandros Andifang. It has a population of just under one hundred thousand, with not a single building of the slightest architectural distinction and a year-round climate of clamminess and drizzle. The plant life is, generally speaking, strikingly unsightly—a preponderance of gray leaves, black flowers—

and the air is full of clouds of little stinging midges with malevolent purple beaks, and of course one has to deal with the fauna, too, the fiend's gallery of grisly monstrosities, seemingly no two alike, that greet you at every turn: huge beasts with beady eyes and slavering fangs and clacking claws, things with pockmarked pustulent skins or writhing furry tentacles or clutching many-jointed arms. Almost always they appear without warning, galloping out of some clump of trees uttering banshee shrieks or ground-shaking roars. I begin to understand now the tales of unwary travelers who have total mental breakdowns within an hour of their arrival on Sidri Akrak.

It quickly becomes clear to us, though, that none of these horrendous creatures has any interest in attacking us. The only real risk we run is that of getting trampled as they go charging past. Very likely it is the case that they find human flesh unpalatable, or indigestible, or downright poisonous. But encountering them is an unnerving business, and we encounter them again and again and again.

Nikomastir finds it all fascinating. Painstakingly he searches out the ill-favored, the misshapen, the feculent, the repulsive—not that they are hard to find. He drifts ecstatically from one eyesore of a building to the next, taking an infinite number of pictures. He adores the plants' sooty foul-smelling blossoms and sticky blighted-looking leaves. The rampaging animals give him even greater pleasure; whenever some particularly immense or especially abhorrent-looking loathsomeness happens to cross our path he cries out in boyish glee.

This starts to be very irritating. His callow idiocy is making me feel old.

"Remember, sweet, he's not even seventy yet," Mayfly reminds me, seeing my brows furrowing. "Surely you were like that yourself, once upon a time."

"Was I? I'd like to think that isn't so."

"And in any case," says Velimyle, "Can't you manage to find that enthusiasm of his charming?"

No. I can't. Perhaps it's getting to be time for my next rebirth, I think. Growing old, for us, isn't a matter so much of bodily decay—that is fended off by efficient processes of automatic bioenergetic correction—as of increasing inward rigidity, a creakiness of the soul, a corrugation of the psyche, a stiffening of the spiritual synapses. One starts to feel sour and petty and crabbed. Life loses its joy and its juice. By then you begin to become aware that it is time to clamber once more into the crystal tank where an intricate spiderweb of machinery will enfold you like a loving mother, and slip off into sweet oblivion for a while, and awaken to find yourself young again and ready to start all over. Which you can do over and over again, until eventually you arrive at the annoying point, after the eleventh or twelfth rebirth, where the buildup of solar poisons in your system has at last become ineradicable under any circumstances, and that is the end of you, alas. Even gods have to die eventually, it would seem.

Nikomastir is a young god, and I am, evidently, an aging one. I try to make allowances for that. But I find myself fervently hoping, all the same, that he will tire of this awful place very soon and allow us to go onward to some happier world.

He does not tire of it, though.

He loves it. He is in the grip of what some ancient poet once called the fascination of the abomination. He has gone up and down every street of the city, peering at this building and that one in unstinting admiration of their imperfections. For several days running he makes it clear that he is searching for some building in particular, and then he finds it: a rambling old ruin of great size and formidable ugliness at the very edge of town, standing apart from everything else in a sort of private park.

"Here it is!" he cries. "The ancestral mansion! The house where my father was born!"

So Nikomastir still clings to the claim that he is of Akrakikan descent. There is no way that this can be true; the natives of this world are a chilly bloodless folk with mean pinched hard souls, if they have souls at all and not just some clicking chattering robotic mechanisms inside their skulls. Indeed I have known robots with personalities far more appealing than anyone we have met thus far on Sidri Akrak. Nikomastir, bless him, is nothing at all like that. He may be silly and frivolous and empty-headed, but he also is sweet-natured and lively and amiable and vivacious, terms that have never yet been applied to any citizen of Sidri Akrak, and never will be.

Velimyle has tried to paint him again. Again the attempt was a failure. This time she is so distressed that I dare to breach the wall of privacy behind which she keeps her art and ask her what the difficulty is.

"Look," she says.

She unrolls the second canvas. Against the familiar swirling colors of a typical Velimyle background I see the slender, angular form of Nikomastir, imprinted there by the force of Velimyle's mental rapport with the psychosensitive fabric. But the features are all wrong. Nikomaster's perpetual easy smile has given way to a dreadful scowling grimace. His lip curls backward menacingly; his teeth are the teeth of some predatory beast. And his eyes—oh, Velimyle, those harsh, glaring eyes! Where is his cheerful sparkle? These eyes are hard, narrow, fierce, and above all else sad. The Nikomastir of Velimyle's painting stares out at the universe with tragic intensity. They are the eyes of a god, perhaps, but of a dying god, one who knows he must give up his life for the redemption of his race.

"The first one was almost as bad," Velimyle says. "Why is this happening? This isn't Nikomastir at all. I've never had something like this happen."

"Has he seen either of the paintings?"

"I wouldn't let him. All I told him was that they didn't come out right, that they would depress him if I showed them to him. And of course he didn't want to see them after that."

"Something about this planet must be shading your perceptions," I say. "Burn this, Velimyle. And the other one too. And forget about painting him until we've left here."

Nikomastir wants to have a look inside the crumbling, lurching pile that he says is his family's ancestral home. But the place, ruinous though it is, happens to be occupied by Akrakikans, a whole swarm of them, and when he knocks at the front door and grandly introduces himself to the major-domo of the house as Count Nikomastir of Sembiran, who has come here on a sentimental journey to his former paternal estate, the door is closed in his face without a word. "How impolite," Nikomastir says, not seeming very surprised. "But don't worry: I'll find a way of getting in."

That project gets tabled too. Over the next few days he leads us farther and farther afield, well out into the uninhabited countryside beyond the boundaries of Periandros Andifang. The land out here is swampy and uningratiating, and of course there are the animals to contend with, and the insects, and the humidity. I can tell that Mayfly and Verimyle are growing a little weary of Nikomastir's exuberance, but they both are as tolerant of his whims as ever and follow him loyally through these soggy realms. As do I—partly, I suppose, because we agreed long ago that we would journey everywhere as a single unit, and partly because I have been stung, evidently, by various hints of Mayfly's and Velimyle's that my recent crotchetiness could mean I might be getting ready for my next rebirth.

Then he turns his attention once more to the old house that he imagines once belonged to his family. "My father once told me that there's a pool of fire behind it, a phosphorescent lake. He used to swim it when he was a boy, and he'd come up dripping with cool flame. I'm going to take a swim in it too, and then we can head off to the next planet. Whose turn is it to pick our next planet, anyway?"

"Mine," I say quickly. I have Marajo in mind—the sparkling sands, the City of Seven Pyramids. "If there's a lake behind that house, Nikomastir, I advise you very earnestly to stay away from it. The people who live there don't seem to look favorably on trespassers. Besides, can't you imagine the kind of nastinesses that would live in a lake on this world?"

"My father went swimming in that one," Nikomastir replies, and gives me a defiant glare. "It's perfectly safe, I assure you."

I doubt, of course, that any such lake exists. If it's there, though, I hope he isn't fool enough to go swimming in it. My affection for the boy is real; I don't want him to come to harm.

But I let the matter drop. I've already said too much. The surest way to prod him into trouble, I know, is oppose him in one of his capricious fancies. My hope is that Nikomastir's attention will be diverted elsewhere in the next day or two and all thought of that dismal house, and of the fiery lake that may or may not be behind it, will fly out of his mind.

It's generally a good idea, when visiting a world you know very little about, to keep out of places of unknown chemical properties. When we toured Megalo Kastro, we stood at the edge of a cliff looking down into the famous living sea, that pink custardy mass that is in fact a single living organism of gigantic size, spreading across thousands of kilometers of that world. But it did not occur to us to take a swim in that sea, for we understood that in a matter of hours it would dissolve and digest us if we did.

And when we were on Xamur we went to see the Idradin crater, as everyone who goes to Xamur does. Xamur is the most perfect of worlds, flawless and serene, a paradise, air like perfume and water like wine, every tree in the ideal place, every brook, every hill. It has only one blemish—the Idradin, a huge round pit that reaches deep into the planet's primordial heart. It is a hideous place, that crater. Concentric rings of jagged cooled lava surround it, black and eroded and bleak. Stinking gases rise out of the depths, and yellow clouds of sulfuric miasma belch forth, and wild red shafts of roaring flame, and you peer down from the edge into a roiling den of hot surging magma. Everyone who goes to Xamur must visit the Idradin, for if you did not see perfect Xamur's one terrible flaw you could never be happy on any other world. And so we stared into it from above, and shivered with the horror we were expected to feel; but we were never at all tempted to clamber down the crater's sides and dip our toes into that realm of fire below.

It seems unlikely to me that Nikomastir will do anything so stupid here. But I have to be careful not to prod him in the wrong direction. I don't mention the lake to him again.

Our exploration of Sidri Akrak proceeds. We visit new swamps, new groves of fetid-smelling malproportioned trees, new neighborhoods of misshapen and graceless buildings. One drizzly disheartening day succeeds another, and finally I am unable to bear the sight of that brown sky and greenish sun any longer. Though it is a violation of our agreements, I stay behind at the hotel one morning and let the other three go off without me.

It is a quiet time. I spend the hours reflecting on our travels of years past, all the many worlds we have seen. Icy Mulano of the two suns, one yellow, one bloody red, and billions of ghostly electric life-forms glimmering about you in the frigid air. Estrilidis, where the cats have two tails and the insects have eyes like blue diamonds. Zimbalou, the sunless nomad world, where the cities are buried deep below the frozen surface. Kalimaka, Haj Qaldun, Vietoris, Nabomba Zom—

So many places, so many sights. A lifetime of wonderful experiences; and yet what, I ask myself, has it all meant? How has it shaped me? What have I learned?

I have no answers, only to say that we will continue to go onward, ever onward. It is our life. It is what we do. We are travelers by choice, but also by nature, by destiny.

I am still lost in reverie when I hear Velimyle's voice outside my window, calling to me, telling me that I must come quickly. "Nikomastir—" she cries. "Nikomastir!"

"What about him?"

But she can only gesture and wave. Her eyes are wild. We run together through the muddy streets, paying no heed to the bulky and grotesque Akrakikan monstrosities that occasionally intersect our path. I realize after a time that Velimyle is leading me toward the tumbledown house at the edge of town that Nikomastir has claimed as his family's former home. A narrow grassy path leads around one side of it to the rear; and there, to my amazement, I see the phosphorescent lake of Nikomastir's fantasies, with Mayfly beside it, leaping up and down in agitation that verges on frenzy.

She points toward the water. "Out there—there—"

On this ugly world even a phosphorescent lake can somehow manage to be an unlovely sight. I saw one once on Darma Barma that flashed like heavenly fire in rippling waves of cobalt and amethyst, magenta and gold, aquamarine and emerald and jade. But from this lake emanates the most unradiant of radiances, a dull, prosaic, sickly gleam, dark-toned and dispiriting, except in one place off toward the farther shore where a disturbance of some sort is setting up whirlpools of glinting metallic effects, swirls of eye-jabbing bright sparkles, as though handfuls of iron filings are being thrown through a magnetic field.

The disturbance is Nikomastir. He—his body, rather—is tossing and heaving at the lake's surface, and all about him the denizens of the lake can be seen, narrow scaly jutting heads popping up by the dozens, hinged jaws snapping, sharp teeth closing on flesh. A widening pool of blood surrounds him. They, whatever they are, are ripping him to shreds.

"We have to get him out of there," Mayfly says, her voice congested with horror and fear.

"How?" I ask.

"I told him not to do it," says trembling Velimyle. "I told him, I told him, I told him. But he plunged right in, and when he was halfway across they began to break the surface, and then—then he began screaming, and—"

Mayfly plucks urgently at my sleeve. "What can we do? How can we rescue him?"

"He's beyond rescuing," I tell her hollowly.

"But if we can get his body back," she says, "there'll be a way to revive him, won't there? I know there is. Scientists can do anything nowadays." Velimyle, more tentatively, agrees. Some kind of scientific miracle, Nikomastir gathered up and repaired somehow by the regeneration of tissue—

But tissue is all that's left of him now, frayed sorry scraps, and the creatures of the lake, frantic now with bloodlust, are devouring even those in furious haste.

They want me to tell them that Nikomastir isn't really dead. But he is: really, really, really dead. Dead forever. What has been played out on this shore today was not a game. There is nothing that can be saved, no way to regenerate. I have never seen the death of a human being before. It is a dizzying thing to contemplate: the finality, the utterness. My mind is whirling; I have to fight back convulsions of shock and horror.

"Couldn't you have stopped him?" I ask angrily, when I am able to speak again.

"But he wanted so badly to do it," Mayfly replies. "We couldn't have stopped him, you know. Not even if we—"

She halts in midsentence.

"Not even if you had wanted to?" I say. "Is that it?" Neither of them can meet my furious gaze. "But you didn't want to, did you? You thought it would be fun to see Nikomastir swim across the phosphorescent lake. Fun. Am I right? Yes. I know that I am. What could you have been thinking, Mayfly? Velimyle?"

There is no sign of Nikomastir at the surface any longer. The lake is growing still again. Its phosphorescence has subsided to a somber tarnished glow.

For a long time, minutes, hours, weeks, none of us is capable of moving. Silent, pale, stunned, we stand with bowed heads by the shore of that frightful lake, scarcely even able to breathe.

We are in the presence of incontrovertible and permanent death, which to us is a novelty far greater even than the living sea of Megalo Kastro or the blue dawn of Nabomba Zom, and the immense fact of it holds us rooted to the spot. Was this truly Nikomastir's ancestral world? Was his father actually born in that great old falling-down house, and did he really once swim in this deadly lake? And if none of that was so, how did Nikomastir know that the lake was there? We will never be able to answer those questions. Whatever we do not know about Nikomastir that we have already learned, we will never come to discover now. That is the meaning of death: the finality of it, the severing of communication, the awful unanswerable power of the uncompromising curtain that descends like a wall of steel. We did not come to Sidri Akrak to learn about such things, but that is what we have learned on Sidri Akrak, and we will take it with us wherever we go henceforth, pondering it, examining it.

"Come," I say to Mayfly and Velimyle, after a time. "We need to get away from here."

So, then. Nikomastir was foolish. He was bold. He has had his swim and now he is dead. And why? Why? For what? What was he seeking, on this awful world? What were we? We know what we found, yes, but not what it was that we were looking for. I wonder if we will ever know.

He has lived his only life, has Nikomastir, and he has lost it in the pursuit of idle pleasure. There is a lesson in that, for me, for Velimilye, for Mayfly, for us all. And one day I will, I hope, understand what it is.

All I do know after having lived these hundreds of years is that the universe is very large and we are quite small. We live godlike lives these days, flitting as we do from world to world, but even so we are not gods. We die: some sooner, some later, but we do die. Only gods live forever. Nikomastir hardly lived at all.

So be it. We have learned what we have learned from Nikomastir's death, and now we must move on. We are travelers by nature and destiny, and we will go forward into our lives. Tomorrow we leave for Marajo. The shining sands, the City of Seven Pyramids. Marajo will teach us something, as Xamur once did, and Nabomba Zom, and Galgala. And also Sidri Akrak. Something. Something. Something.

The Colonel Returns
to the Stars

From *Between Worlds*, August 2004

On the day that the Colonel found himself seized by circumstances and thrust back against his will into active service he had risen early, as usual, he had bathed in the river of sparkling liquid gold that ran behind his isolated villa in a remote corner of the Aureus Highlands, he had plucked a quick handful of dagger-shaped golden leaves from the quezquez tree for the little explosive burst of energy that chewing them always provided, and he had gone for his morning stroll along the glimmering crescent dunes of fine golden powder that ran off down toward the carasar forest, where the slender trunks of the long-limbed trees swayed in the mild breeze like the elongated necks of graceful lammis-gazelles. And when the Colonel got back to the villa an hour later for his breakfast the stranger was there, and everything began to change for him in the life that he had designed to be changeless forever more.

The stranger was young—*seemed* young, anyway; one never could really tell—and compactly built, with a tightly focused look about him. His eyes had the cold intensity of a fast-flowing river of clear water; his lips were thin, with deep vertical lines at their sides; his thick, glossy black hair was swept backward against his head like the wings of a raven. The little silver badge of the Imperium was visible on the breast of his tunic.

He was standing on the open patio, arms folded, smiling a smile that was not really much of a smile. Plainly he had already been inside. There was nothing to prevent that. One did not lock one's doors here. The Colonel, looking past him, imagined that he could see the fiery track of the man's intrusive footsteps blazing up from the green flagstone floor. He had entered; he had seen; he had taken note. The Colonel kept about himself in his retirement the abundant memorabilia of a long life spent meddling in the destinies of worlds. In his sprawling house on golden Galgala he had set out on display, for his eyes alone, a vast array of things, none of them very large or very showy—bits of pottery, fossils, mineral specimens, gnarled pieces of wood, coins, quaint rusted weapons, all manner of ethnographic artifacts, and a great number of other tangible reminders of his precise and devastating interventions on those many worlds.

Most of these objects—a scrap of bone, a painted stone, a bit of tapestry, a blunted knife, a tattered banner that bore no emblem, a box of sullen-looking gray sand—had no obvious significance. They would have been baffling to any visitor to the Colonel's Galgala retreat, if ever a visitor were to come, although there had not been any in many years, until this morning. But to the Colonel each of these things had special meaning. They were talismans, touchstones that opened a century and a half of memories. From Eden, from Entrada, from Megalo Kastro, from Narajo of the Seven Pyramids, from snowy Mulano, from unhappy Tristessa, even, and Fenix and Phosphor and some two dozen others out of mankind's uncountable string of planets had they come, most of them collected by the Colonel himself but some by his pinch-faced limping father, the Old Captain, and even a few that had been brought back by his swaggering buccaneer of a grandfather, who had carved a path through the universe as though with a machete five hundred years before him.

The Colonel now was old, older than his father had lived to be and beginning to approach the remarkable longevity of his grandfather, and his days of adventure were over. Having outlived the last of his wives, he lived alone, quietly, seeking no contact with others. He did not even travel any more. For the first two decades after his retirement he had, more from habit than any other motive, gone off, strictly as a tourist, on journeys to this world and that, planets like Jacynth and Macondo and Entropy and Duud Shabeel that he had never found occasion to visit during the course of his long professional career. But then he had stopped doing even that.

In his time he had seen enough, and more than enough. He had been everywhere, more or less, and he had done everything, more or less. He had overthrown governments. He had headed governments. He had survived a dozen assassination attempts. He had carried out assassinations himself. He had ordered executions. He had refused a kingship. He had lived through two poisonings and three marriages. And then, growing old, old beyond the hope of many further rejuvenations, he had put in for retirement and walked away from it all.

When he was young, restless and full of insatiable hungers, he had dreamed of striding from world to world until he had spanned the entire universe, and he had leaped with savage eagerness into the shining maw of each new Velde doorway, impatient to step forth onto the unknown world that awaited him. And no sooner had he arrived but he was dreaming of the next. Now, though, obsessive questing of that sort seemed pointless to him. He had decided, belatedly, that travel between the stars as facilitated by the Velde doorways or by the other and greater system of interstellar transport, the Magellanic one, was too easy, that the ease of it rendered all places identical, however different from one another they might actually be. Travel should involve travail, the Colonel had come to think. But modern travel, simple, instantaneous, unbounded by distance, was too much like magic. Matters had been different for the ancient explorers of ancient Earth, setting out on their arduous voyages of discovery across the dark unfriendly seas of their little planet with almost incomprehensible courage in the face of impossible odds. Those men of so many thousands of years ago, staking their lives to cross uncharted waters in tiny wooden ships for the sake of reaching alien and probably hostile shores on the very same world, had been true heroes. But now—now, when one could go almost anywhere in the galaxy in the twinkling of an eye, without effort or risk, did going anywhere at all matter? After the first fifty worlds, why not simply stay home?

The visitor said, "Your home is fascinating, Colonel." He offered no apology for trespassing. The Colonel did not expect one. With the smallest of gestures he invited the man inside. Asked him, in a perfunctory way, if he had had a good journey. Served him tea on the terrace overlooking the river. Awaited with formal politeness the explanation for the visit, for surely there had to be some explanation, though he did not yet know that it was ultimately going to break the atoms of his body apart once again, and scatter them once more across the cosmos, or he would have shut the man out of his house without hearing another word.

The man's surname was one that the Colonel recognized, one that had long been a distinguished one in the archives of the Imperium. The Colonel had worked with men of that name many years ago. So had his father. Men of that name had pursued his buccaneering grandfather across half the galaxy.

"Do you know of a world called Hermano?" the man asked. "In the Aguila sector, well out toward the Core?"

The Colonel searched his memory and came up with nothing. "No," he said. "Should I?"

"It's two systems over from Gran Chingada. The records show that you spent some time on Gran Chingada ninety years back."

"Yes, I did. But two systems over could be a dozen light-years away," said the Colonel. "I don't know your Hermano."

The stranger described it: an ordinary-sounding world, a reasonably pleasant world-shaped world, with deserts, forests, oceans, flora, fauna, climate. One of six planets, and the only habitable one, around a standard sort of star. Apparently it had been colonized by settlers from Gran Chingada some thirty or forty years before. Its exports were medicinal herbs, precious gems, desirable furs, various useful metals. Three years ago, said the stranger, it had ejected the Imperium commissioners and proclaimed itself independent.

The Colonel, listening in silence, said nothing. But for a moment, only a moment, he reacted as he might have reacted fifty years earlier, feeling the old reflexive stab of cold anger at that clanging troublesome word, *independent*.

The stranger said, "We have, of course, invoked the usual sanctions. They have not been effective." Gran Chingada, itself not the most docile of worlds, had chosen to people its colony-world by shipping it all the hard cases, its most bellicose and refractory citizens, a rancorous and uncongenial crowd who were told upon their departure that if they ever were seen on Gran Chingada again they would be taken to the nearest Velde doorway and shipped out again to some randomly chosen destination that might not prove to be a charming place to live, or even one that was suitable for human life at all. But the Hermano colonists, surly and contentious though they were, had found their new planet very much to their liking. They had made no attempt to return to their mother world, or to go anywhere else. And, once their settlement had reached the point of economic self-sufficiency, they had blithely announced their secession from the Imperium and ceased remitting taxes to the Central Authority. They had also halted all shipments of the medicinal herbs and useful metals to their trading partners throughout the Imperium, pending a favorable adjustment in the general structure of prices and tariffs.

A familiar image had been ablaze in the Colonel's mind since the first mention of Hermano's declaration of independence: the image of a beautiful globe of brilliantly polished silver, formerly flawless, now riven by a dark hideous crack. That was how he had always seen the Imperium, as a perfect polished globe. That was how he had always seen the attempts of one world or another to separate itself from the perfection that was the Imperium, as an ugly crevasse on the pure face of beauty. It had been his life's work to restore the perfection of that flawless silvery face whenever it was marred. But he had separated himself from that work many years ago. It was as though it had been done by another self.

Now, though, a little to his own surprise, a flicker of engagement leaped up in him: he felt questions surging within him, and potential courses of action, just as if he were still on active duty. Those medicinal herbs and useful metals, the Colonel began to realize, must be of considerably more than trifling significance to interstellar commerce. And, over and beyond that, there was the basic issue of maintaining the fundamental integrity of the Imperium. But all that was only a flicker, a momentarily renewed ticking of machinery that he had long since ceased to use. The maintenance of the fundamental integrity of the Imperium was no longer his problem. The thoughts that had for that flickering moment sprung up reflexively within him subsided as quickly as they arose. He had devoted the best part of his life to the Service, and had served loyally and well, and now he was done with all that. He had put his career behind him for good.

But it was clear to him that if he wanted to keep it that way he must be prepared to defend himself against the threat that this man posed, and that it might not be easy, for obviously this man wanted something from him, something that he was not prepared to give.

The stranger said, "You know where I'm heading with this story, Colonel."

"I think I can guess, yes."

The expected words came: "There is no one better able to handle the Hermano problem than you."

The Colonel closed his eyes a moment, nodded, sighed. Yes. What other reason would this man have for coming here? Quietly he said, "And just why do you think so?"

"Because you are uniquely fitted to deal with it."

Of course. Of course. They always said things like that. The Colonel felt a prickling sensation in his fingertips. It was clear now that he was in a duel with the Devil. Smiling, he said, making the expected response, "You say this despite knowing that I've been retired from the Service for forty years." He gestured broadly: the villa, the display of souvenirs of a long career, the garden, the river, the dunes beyond. "You see the sort of life I've constructed for myself here."

"Yes. The life of a man who has gone into hiding from himself, and who lives hunkered down and waiting for death. A man who dies a little more than one day's worth every day."

That was not so expected. It was a nasty thrust, sharp, brutal, intended to wound, even to maim. But the Colonel remained calm, as ever. His inner self was not so easily breached, and surely this man, if he had been briefed at all properly, knew that.

He let the brutality of the words pass unchallenged. "I'm old, now. Hunkering down is a natural enough thing, at my age. You'll see what I mean, in a hundred years or so."

"You're not *that* old, Colonel. Not too old for one last round of service, anyway, when the Imperium summons you."

"Can you understand," the Colonel said slowly, "that a time comes in one's life when one no longer feels an obligation to serve?"

"For some, yes," said the stranger. "But not for someone like you. A time comes when one *wishes* not to serve, yes. I can understand that. But the sense of obligation—no, that never dies. Which is why I've come to you. As I said, you are uniquely fitted for this, as you will understand when I tell you that the man who has made himself the leader of the Hermano rebellion is a certain Geryon Lanista."

Lanista?

It was decades since the Colonel had last heard that name spoken aloud. It crashed into him like a spear striking his breast. If he had not already been sitting, he would have wanted now to sink limply into a seat.

He controlled himself. "How curious. I knew a Geryon Lanista once," he said, after a moment. "He's long dead, that one."

"No," said the stranger. "He isn't. I'm quite sure of that."

"Are we talking about Geryon Lanista of Ultima Thule in the San Pedro Cluster?" The Colonel was struggling for his equilibrium, and struggling not to let the struggle show. "The Geryon Lanista who was formerly a member of our Service?"

"The very one."

"Well, he's been dead for decades. He killed himself after he bungled the Tristessa job. That was probably long before your time, but you could look it all up. He and I handled the Tristessa assignment together. Because of him, we failed in a terrible way."

"Yes. I know that."

"And then he killed himself, before the inquiries were even starting. To escape from the shame of what he had done."

"No. He *didn't* kill himself." Profoundly unsettling words, spoken with quiet conviction that left the Colonel a little dizzied.

"Reliable sources told me that he did."

Calm, the Colonel ordered himself. Stay calm.

"You were misinformed," the visitor said, in that same tone of deadly assurance. "He is very much alive and well and living on Hermano under the name of Martin Bauer, and he is the head of the provisional government there. The accuracy of our identification of him is beyond any doubt. I can show him to you, if you like. Shall I do that?"

Numbly the Colonel signaled acquiescence. His visitor drew a flat metal case from a pocket of his tunic and tapped it lightly. A solido figure of a man sprang instantly into being a short distance away: a stocky, powerfully built man, apparently of middle years, deep-chested and extraordinarily wide through the shoulders, a great massive block of a man, with a blunt-tipped nose, tight-clamped downturned lips, and soft, oddly seductive brown eyes that did not seem to be congruent with the bulkiness of his body or the harshness of his features. The face was not one that the Colonel remembered having seen before, but time and a little corrective surgery would account for that. The powerful frame, though, was something that no surgery, even now when surgery could achieve almost anything, could alter. And the eyes—those strange, haunted eyes—beyond any question they were the eyes of Geryon Lanista.

"What do you think?" the visitor asked.

Grudgingly the Colonel said, "There are some resemblances, yes. But it's impossible. He's dead. I know that he is."

"No doubt you want him to be, Colonel. I can understand that, yes. But this is the man. Believe me. You are looking at your old colleague Geryon Lanista."

How could he say no to that? Surely that was Lanista, here before him. Surely. Surely. An altered Lanista, yes, but Lanista all the same. What was the use of arguing otherwise? Those eyes—those freakishly wide shoulders—that barrel of a chest—

But there was no way that Lanista could be alive.

Clinging to a stubborn certainty that he was beginning not to feel was really solid the Colonel said, "Very well: the face is his. I'll concede that much. But the image? Something out of the files of fifty years ago, tarted up with a few little tweaks here and there to make him look as though he's tried recently to disguise himself? What's here to make me believe that this is a recent image of a living man?"

"We have other images, Colonel." The visitor tapped the metal case again, and there was the stocky man on the veranda of an imposing house set within a luxurious garden. Two small children, built to the same stocky proportions as he, stood beside him, and a smiling young woman. "At his home on Hermano," said the visitor, and tapped the case again. Now the stocky man appeared in a group of other men, evidently at a political meeting; he was declaiming something about the need for Hermano to throw off the shackles of the Imperium. He tapped the case again—

"No. Stop. You can fake whatever scene you want. I know how these things are done."

"Of course you do, Colonel. But why would we bother? Why try to drag you out of retirement with a bunch of faked images? Sooner or later a man of your ability would see through them. But we *know* that this man is Geryon Lanista. We have all the necessary proof, the incontrovertible genetic data. And so we've come to you, as someone who not only has the technical skills to deal with the problem that Lanista is creating, but the personal motivation to do so."

"Incontrovertible genetic data?"

"Yes. Incontrovertible. Shall I show you the genomics? Here: look. From the Service files, sixty years back, Geryon Lanista, his entire genome. And here, this one, from the Gran Chingada immigration records, approximately twenty years old, Martin Bauer. Do you see?"

The Colonel glanced at the images, side by side in the air and identical in every respect, shook his head, looked away. The pairing was convincing, yes. And, yes, they could fake anything they liked, even a pair of gene charts. There wasn't all that much difficulty in that. But to fake so much—to go to such preposterous lengths for the sake of bamboozling one tired old man—no, no, the logic that lay at the core of his soul cried out against the likelihood of that.

His last resistance crumbled. He yielded to the inescapable reality. Despite everything he had believed all these years, this man Martin Bauer *was* Geryon Lanista. Alive and well, as this stranger had said, and conspiring against the Imperium on a planet called Hermano. And the Service wanted him to do something about that.

For an instant, contemplating this sudden and disastrous turn of events, the Colonel felt something that wasn't quite fear and not quite dismay—both of them feelings that he scarcely understood, let alone had ever experienced—but was certainly a kind of discomfort. This had been a duel with the Devil, all right, and the Devil had played with predictably diabolical skill, and the Colonel saw that here, in the very first moments of the contest, he had already lost. He had not thought to be beaten so easily. He had lived his life, he had put in his years in the Service, he had met all dangers with bravery and all difficulties with triumphant ingenuity, and here, as the end of it all approached, he had come safely to rest in the harbor of his own invulnerability on this idyllic golden world; and in a moment, with just a few quick syllables, this cold-eyed stranger had ripped him loose from all of that and had tumbled him back into the remorseless torrents of history. He ached to refuse the challenge. It was within the range of possibility for him to refuse it. It was certainly his right to refuse it, at his age, after all that he had done. But—even so—even so—

"Geryon Lanista," the Colonel said, marveling. "Yes. Yes. Well, perhaps this really is him." There was a touch of hoarseness in his tone.—"You know the whole story, Lanista and me?"

"That goes without saying. Why else would we have come to you?"

The odd prickling in the Colonel's fingertips began to give way to an infuriating trembling. "Well, then—"

He looked across the table and it seemed to him that he saw a softening of those icy eyes, even a hint of moisture in them. An upwelling of compassion, was it, for the poor old man who had been so cruelly ensnared in the sanctity of his own home? But was that in any way likely, coming from *this* particular man, who had sprung from *those* ancestors. Compassion had never been a specialty of that tribe. Perhaps they are making them softer nowadays, the Colonel thought, yet another example of the general decadence of modern times, and felt renewed pleasure in the awareness that he was no one's ancestor at all, that his line ended with him. And then he realized that he was wrong, that there was no compassion in this man at all, that those were simply the jubilant self-congratulatory tears of triumph in the other man's eyes.

"We can count on you?" the visitor asked.

"If you've been lying to me—"

"I haven't been lying," said the visitor, saying it in a flat offhanded way that conveyed more conviction than any number of passionate oaths might have done.

The Colonel nodded. "All right. I give in. You win. I'll do what I can do," he said, in a barely audible voice. He felt like a man who had been marched to the edge of a cliff and now was taking a few last breaths before jumping off. "Yes. Yes. There are, I hardly need to say, certain practical details that we need to discuss, first—"

There was something dreamlike about finding himself making ready for a new assignment after so many years. He wouldn't leave immediately, of course, nor would the journey to Hermano be anything like instantaneous. The maintenance of the villa during his absence had to be arranged for, and there was the background information of the Hermano situation to master, and certain potentially useful documents to excavate from the archives of his career, and then he would have to make the long overland journey to Elsinore, down on the coast, where the nearest Velde doorway was located. Even after that he still would have some traveling to do, because Gran Chingada and its unruly colony-world Hermano, both of them close to the central sector of the galaxy, were beyond the direct reach of Velde transmission. To complete his journey he would have to shift over to the galaxy's other and greater teleportation system, the ancient and unfathomable one that had been left behind by the people known as the Magellanics.

He had not expected ever to be jaunting across the universe again. The visit to Duud Shabeel, two decades before, had established itself in his mind as the last of all his travels. But plainly there was to be one more trip even so; and as he prepared for it, his mind went back to his first journey ever, the one his ferocious fiery-eyed grandfather had taken him on, in that inconceivably remote epoch when he was ten years old.

He had lived on Galgala even then, though not in the highlands but along the humid coast, where liquid gold came bubbling up out of the swamps. His grandfather had always had a special love for Galgala, the planet that had ruined the value of gold for the entire galaxy. Gold was everywhere there, in the leaves of the trees, in the sands of the desert, in the stones of the ground. Flecks of gold flowed in the veins of Galgala's native animals. Though it had been thousands of years since the yellow metal had passed as currency among humankind, the discovery of Galgala had finished it for all eternity as a commodity of value. But the old pirate who had engendered the Colonel's father was a medieval at heart, and he cherished Galgala for what its gold might have meant in the days when the whole of the human universe was just the little blue world that was Earth. He had made it his headquarters during his privateering career, and when he was old he had gone there to dwell until the end of his days. The Colonel's father, who in his parsimonious pinch-faced way claimed only the honorary title of Captain, was in the Service then, traveling constantly from world to world as need arose and only rarely coming to rest, and, not knowing what to do with the boy who would someday become the Colonel, had sent him to Galgala to live with his grandfather.

"It's time you learned what traveling is like," the old man said one day, when the boy who would become the Colonel was ten.

He was already tall and sturdy for his age, but he was still only ten, and his grandfather, even then centuries old—no one knew exactly how old he was, perhaps not even he himself—rose up and up beside him like a great tree, a shaggy-bearded tree with furious eyes and long black coils of piratical hair dangling to his shoulders and horrendous jutting cheekbones sharp as blades. The gaunt, bony old man had spent the many years of his life outside the law, the law that the Captain and later the Colonel would serve with such devotion, but no one in the family ever spoke openly of that. And although he had finally abandoned his marauding ways, he still affected the showy costume of his trade, the leather jerkin and the knee-high boots with the tapered tips and the broad-brimmed hat from which the eternally black coils of his long hair came tumbling superabundantly down.

They stood before the doorway, the future Colonel and his formidable grandfather, and the old man said, "When you step through it, you'll be scanned and surveyed, and then you'll be torn apart completely, down to the fragments of your atoms, altogether annihilated, and at the same moment an exact duplicate of you will be assembled at the other end, wherever that may be. How do you like that?"

The old man waited, then, searching for signs of fear or doubt on his grandson's face. But even then the boy understood that such feelings as fear or doubt ought not to be so much as felt, let alone displayed, in the presence of his grandfather.

"And where will we come out, then?" the boy who would be the Colonel asked.

"At our destination," said the old pirate, and casually shoved him toward the doorway. "You wait for me there, do you hear me, boy? I'll be coming along right behind."

The doorway on Galgala, like Velde doorways everywhere in the considerable sector of the galaxy where Velde-system terminals had been established, was a cubicle of black glass, four meters high, three meters wide, three meters deep. Along its inner walls a pair of black-light lenses stared at each other like enigmatic all-seeing eyes. On the rear wall of the cubicle were three jutting metal cones from which the Velde force emanated whenever a traveler crossed the threshold of the cubicle.

The theory of Velde transmission was something that everyone was taught when young, the way the law of gravity is taught, or the axioms of geometry; but one does not need to study Newton or Euclid very deeply in order to know how to descend a staircase or how to calculate the shortest way to get across a street, and one could make a fifty-light-year Velde hop without any real understanding of the concept that the universe is constructed of paired particles, equal masses of matter and antimatter, and that matter can decay spontaneously into antimatter at any time, but each such event must invariably be accompanied by the simultaneous conversion of an equivalent mass of antimatter into matter somewhere else—anywhere else—in the universe, so that the symmetry of matter is always conserved.

Velde's Theorem had demonstrated the truth of that, long ago, millennia ago, back in those almost unimaginable primeval days when Earth and Earth alone was mankind's home. Then Conrad Wilf, freebooting physicist, provided a practical use for Velde's equations by showing how it was possible to construct containment facilities that could prevent the normally inescapable mutual annihilation of matter and antimatter, thereby making feasible the controlled conversion of particles into their antiparticles. Matter that was held within a Wilf containment field could be transformed into antimatter and stored, without fear of instant annihilation, while at the same moment a corresponding quantity of antimatter elsewhere in the universe was converted into matter and held in a corresponding Wilf field far away.

But Wilf conversions, contained though they were, still entailed a disconcerting randomness in the conservation of symmetry: when matter was destroyed here and a balancing quantity of antimatter was created elsewhere, *elsewhere* could be at any point at all in the universe, perhaps ten thousand kilometers away, perhaps ten billion light-years; everything was open-ended, without directionality or predictability. It remained for Simtow, the third of the three great pioneers of interstellar transport, to develop a device that tuned the Velde Effect so that the balancing transactions of Wilf conversions took place not randomly but within the confines of a specific closed system with Wilf containment fields at both ends. At the destination end, antimatter was stored in a Wilf containment vessel. At the transmission end, that which was to be transmitted would undergo a Velde transformation into antimatter, a transformation that was balanced, at the designated destination end, by the simultaneous and equivalent transformation of the stored antimatter into a quantity of matter identical to that which had been converted by the transmitter. The last step was the controlled annihilation of the antimatter that had been created at the transmission end, thereby recapturing the energy that had powered the original transmission. The effect was the simultaneous particle-by-particle duplication of the transmission matter at the receiving end.

The boy who would become the Colonel comprehended all this, more or less, at least to the extent of understanding that one was demolished *here* and reassembled instantaneously *there*. He knew, also, of the ancient experiments with inanimate objects, with small animals and plants, and finally with the very much living body of the infinitely courageous pioneering voyager Haakon Christiansen, that showed that whatever went into a transmission doorway would emerge unharmed at its destination. All the same it was impossible for him to avoid a certain degree of uncertainty, even of something not very different from terror, in the moment when his grandfather's bony hand flung him toward the waiting doorway.

That uncertainty, that terror, if that is what it was, lasted only an instant's part of an instant. Then he was within the doorway and, because Velde transmission occurs in a realm where relativistic laws are irrelevant, he found himself immediately outside it again, but he was somewhere else, and it all looked so completely strange that there was no point in being frightened of it.

Where he found himself was a world with a golden-red sun that cast a hard metallic light altogether unlike the cheerful yellow light of Galgala's sun, which was the only sunlight he had ever seen. He was on a barren strip of flat sandy land with a lofty cliff at his back and what looked like a great oceanic expanse of pink mud in front of him. There were no living creatures in sight, no plants, no trees. He had never been in the presence of such utter emptiness before.

That sea of pink mud at whose border he stood stretched out as far as the horizon and, for all he knew, wrapped itself around it and kept going down the other side of the planet. It was indeed an ocean of mud: quivering, rippling mud, mud that seemed almost to be alive. Perhaps it was alive, a single living organism of colossal size. He could feel warmth radiating from it. He sensed a kind of sentience about it. Again and again some patch of its surface would begin throbbing spasmodically, and then it would send up odd projections and protuberances that slowly wriggled and writhed like questing tentacles before sinking down again into the huge sluggish mass from which it had arisen. He stared at it for a long while, fascinated by its eerie motions.

After a time he wondered where his grandfather was.

He should have followed instantly, should he not? But it didn't appear that he had. Instead the boy discovered himself alone in a way that was completely new to him, perhaps the only human being on a vast strange planet whose name he did not even know. At least twenty minutes had gone by. That was a long time to be alone in a place like this. He was supposed to wait here; but for how long? He wondered what he would do if, after another hour or two, his grandfather still had not arrived, and decided finally that he would simply step through the doorway in the hope that it would take him back to Galgala, or at least to some world where he could get help finding his way home.

Turning away from the sea, he looked backward and up, and then he understood where it was that his grandfather had sent him, for there on the edge of that towering cliff just in back of him he was able to make out the shape of a monumental stone fortress, low and long, outlined sharply against the glowering greenish sky like a crouching beast making ready to spring. Everyone in the galaxy knew what that fortress was. It was the ancient gigantic ruined building known as Megalo Kastro, from which this planet took its name—the only surviving work of some unknown extinct race that had lived here eight million years ago. There was nothing else like it in the universe.

"What do you say?" his grandfather said, stepping through the doorway with the broad self-congratulatory smile of someone arriving exactly on time. "Are you ready to climb up there and have a look around?"

It was an exhausting climb. The old man had long legs and a demon's unbounded vitality, and the boy had a ten-year-old's half-developed muscles. But he had no choice other than to follow along as closely as possible, scrambling frantically up the rough stone blocks of the staircase, too far apart for a boy's lesser stride, that had been carved in the face of the cliff. He was breathless by the time he reached the top, fifty paces to the rear of his grandfather. The old man had already entered the ruin and had begun to saunter through it with the proprietorial air of a guide leading a party of tourists.

It was too big to see in a single visit. They went on and on, and still there was no end to its vaulted chambers. "This is the Equinox Hall," his grandfather said, gesturing grandly. "You see the altar down at that end? And this—we call it the Emperor's Throne Room. And this—the Hall of Sacrifices. Our own names for them, you understand. Obviously we'll never know what they really were called." There were no orderly angles everywhere. Everything seemed unstable and oppressively strange. The walls seemed to waver and flow, and though the boy knew it was only an illusion, it was a profoundly troublesome one. His eyes ached. His stomach felt queasy. Yet his heart pounded with fierce excitement.

"Look here," said his grandfather. "The handprint of one of the builders, maybe. Or a prisoner's." They had reached the cellar level now. On the wall of one of the dungeon-like rooms was the white outline of a large hand, a hand with seven fingers and a pair of opposable thumbs, one on each side. An *alien* hand.

The boy who would become the Colonel shivered. No one knew who had built this place. Some extinct race, surely, because there was no known race of the galaxy today that could have done it except the human race—no others encountered thus far had evolved beyond the most primitive level—and mankind itself had not yet evolved when Megalo Kastro had been built. But it was not likely to have been the work of the great unknown race that humans called the Magellanics, either, because they had left their transporter doorways, immensely more efficient and useful than Velde doorways, on every world that had been part of their ancient empire, and there was no Magellanic doorway, nor any trace of one, on Megalo Kastro. So they had never been here. But someone had, some third great race that no one knew anything about, and had left this fortress behind, millions of years ago.

"Come," said his grandfather, and they descended and returned to the doorway, and went off to a world with an amber sky that had swirls of blue in it, and a dull reddish sun lying like a lump of coal along the horizon with a second star, brighter, high overhead. This was Cuchulain, said the old man, a moon of the subluminous star Gwydion, the dark companion of a star named Lalande 21185, and they were only eight light-years from Earth, which to the boy's mind seemed just a snap of the fingers away. That amazed him, to be this close to Earth, the almost legendary mother world of the whole Imperium. The air here was thick and soft, almost sticky, and everything in the vicinity of the doorway was wrapped in furry ropes of blue-green vegetation. In the distance a city of considerable size gleamed through the muzzy haze. The boy felt heavy here: Cuchulain's gravity nailed him to the ground.

"Can we go on from here to Earth?" the boy asked. "It's so near, after all!"

"Earth is forbidden," said the old man. "No one goes to Earth except when Earth does the summoning. It is the law."

"But you have always lived outside the law, haven't you?"

"Not this one," his grandfather said, and put an end to the discussion.

He was hurt by that, back then in his boyhood. It seemed unfair, a wanton shutting out of the whole universe by the planet that had set everything in motion for the human race. They should not close themselves off to their descendants this way, he told himself. But years later, looking back on that day with his grandfather, he would take a different view. They are right to keep us out, he would tell himself later. That is how it should be. Earth is long ago, Earth is far away. It should remain like that. We are the galactic people, the people born in the stars. We are the future. They are the past. They and we should not mingle. Our ways are not their ways, and any contact between them and us would be corrupting for both. For better or for worse they have turned us loose into the stars and we live a new kind of life out here in this infinite realm, nothing at all like theirs, and our path must forevermore be separate from theirs.

His grandfather had taken him to Cuchulain only because it was the contact point for a world called Moebius, where four suns danced in the sky, pearly-white triplets and a violet primary. The boy imagined that a world that had a name like Moebius would be a place of sliding dimensions and unexpected twisted vistas, but no, there was nothing unusual about it except the intricacy of the shadows cast by its quartet of suns. His grandfather had a friend on Moebius, a white-haired man as frail and worn as a length of burned rope, and they spent a day and a half visiting with him. The boy understood very little of what the two old men said: it was almost as if they were speaking some other language. Then they moved on, to a wintry world called Zima, and from there to Jackal, and from Jackal to Tycho, and from Tycho to Two Dogs, world after world, most of them worlds of the Rim where the sky was strangely empty, frighteningly black at night with only a few thousand widely spaced stars in view, not the bright, unendingly luminous curtain that eternally surrounded a Core world like Galgala, a wall of blazing light with no break in it anywhere; and then, just as the boy was starting to think that he and the old man were going to travel forever through the Imperium without ever settling down, they stepped through the doorway once more and emerged into the familiar warm sunlight and golden vegetation of Galgala.

"So now you know," his grandfather said. "Galgala is just one small world, out of many."

"How great the Imperium is!" cried the boy, dazzled by his journey. The vastness of it had stunned him, and the generosity of whatever creator it was that had made so many stars and fashioned so many beautiful worlds to whirl about them, and the farsightedness of those who had thought to organize those worlds into one Imperium, so that the citizens of that Imperium could rove freely from star to star, from world to world, without limits or bounds. For the first time in his life, but far from the last, he saw in his mind the image of that flawless silver globe, shining in his imagination like the brightest of all possible moons. His grandfather had worked hard to instill a love for anarchy in him, but the trip had had entirely the opposite effect. "How marvelous that all those different worlds should be bound together under a single government!" he cried.

He knew at once that it was the wrong thing to say. "The Imperium is the enemy, boy," said his grandfather, his voice rumbling deep down in his chest, his scowling face dark as the sky before a thunderstorm. "It strangles us. It is the chain around our throats." And went stalking away, leaving him to face his father, who had come back from a mission in the Outer Sector during his absence, and who, astonishingly, struck him across the cheek when the boy told him where he had been and what he had seen and what his grandfather had said.

"The enemy? A chain about our throats? Oh, no, boy. The Imperium is our only bulwark against chaos," his father told him. "Don't you ever forget that." And slapped him again, to reinforce the lesson. The boy hated his father in that moment as he had never hated him before. But in time the sting of the slaps was gone, and even the memory of the indignity of them had faded, and when the hour came for the boy to choose what his life would be, it was the Service that he chose, and not the buccaneering career of his demonic grandfather.

When the preparations for the start of his journey to rebellious Hermano were complete, the Colonel traveled by regular rail down to the coastal city of Elsinore, where, as he had done so many times in the distant past, he took a room in the Grand Terminus Hotel while the agents of the Imperium worked out his Velde pathway. He had not been in Elsinore for many years and had not thought ever to see it again. Nothing much had changed, he saw: wide streets, bustling traffic, cloudless skies, golden sunlight conjuring stunning brilliance out of the myriad golden flecks that bespeckled the paving stones. He realized, contemplating now a new offworld journey when he had never expected to make any again, how weary he had become of the golden sameness of lovely Galgala, how eager—yes, actually eager—he was once more to be confronting a change of scene. They gave him a room on the third floor, looking down into a courtyard planted entirely with exotic chlorophyll-based plants, stunningly green against the ubiquitous golden hue of Galgala.

Three small purple dragons from some world in the Vendameron system lay twined in a cage at the center of the garden, as always. He wondered if these were the same dragons who had been in that cage the last time, years ago. The Colonel had stayed in this very room before, he was sure. He found it difficult to accept the fact that he was staying in it again, that he was here at the Terminus waiting to make one more Velde jump, after having put his time of traveling so thoroughly behind him. But the cold-eyed emissary from the Imperium had calculated his strategy quite carefully. Whatever vestigial sense of obligation to the Imperium that might still remain in the Colonel would probably not have been enough to break him loose from his retirement in order to deal with one more obstreperous colony. The fact that Geryon Lanista, his one-time protegé, his comrade, his betrayer, was the architect of the Hermano rebellion was another matter entirely, though, one that could not be sidestepped. To allow himself to miss a chance to come face to face with Geryon Lanista after all these years would be to act as though not just his career in the Service but his life itself had come to its end.

The emissary who had come to him at his villa was gone. He had done his work and was on to his next task. Now, at the Grand Terminus Hotel, the Colonel's liaison man was one Nicanor Ternera, who had the gray-skinned, pudgy-faced look of one who has spent too much of his life in meetings and conferences, and who could not stop staring at the Colonel as though he were some statue of an ancient emperor of old Earth that had unaccountably come to life and walked out of the museum where he was on exhibit.

"These are your papers," Nicanor Ternera told him. "You'll hold formal ambassadorial accreditation as head of a trade legation that's based on Gavial, which as I think you know is a planet of the Cruzeiro system. You will not be going as a representative of the Imperium itself, but rather as a diplomat affiliated with the regional government of the Cruzeiro worlds. As you are already aware, the rebels won't at present allow officials of the Imperium to arrive on Hermano, but they're not otherwise closed to visitors from outside, even during the present period of trade embargo, which they describe as a temporary measure while they await recognition by the Imperium of their independent status."

"They'll wait a long time," said the Colonel. "Especially if they won't allow anyone from the Imperium to go in and explain the error of their ways to them." He glanced at the papers. "For the purpose of this mission my name is Petrus Haym?"

"Correct."

"Lanista will recognize me instantly for who I am. Or is this going to be the sort of mission I'll be doing in disguise?"

"You'll be disguised, to some degree, for the sake of being able to obtain entry. Once you've succeeded in getting access to Hermano as Petrus Haym of Gavial, you can decide for yourself when and how to reveal yourself to Lanista, which beyond any doubt you will at some point find necessary to do in order to bring the mission to a successful conclusion. From that point on you'll be functioning openly as an agent of the Imperium."

"And what leverage am I to have over them?" the Colonel asked.

"The ultimate," said Nicanor Ternera.

"Good," said the Colonel. He had expected no less. He would have accepted no less. Still, it was better to have it offered readily than to have to demand it.

Nicanor Ternera said, "You'll be accompanied on the trip by three genuine government people out of Gavial and another Imperium agent, a woman from Phosphor named Magda Cermak, who'll have the official rank of second secretary to the mission. She's been in the Service for a dozen years and has a good grasp of the entire situation, including your prior relationship with Geryon Lanista."

"You don't think I'd be better off handling this project entirely on my own?"

"It's altogether possible that you could. But we'd rather not take the risk. In any case it's essential to maintain the fiction of a trade delegation at least until you're safely on Hermano and have made contact with Lanista, and a properly plausible delegation involves five or six members, at least." Ternera looked to the Colonel for approval, which he reluctantly gave. "As these documents will show you, the crux of Gavial's issue is Hermano's termination of the export of a drug called cantaxion, the properties of which are beneficial to people suffering from a manganese deficiency, something that's chronic on Gavial. You'll find all the details in the attached documents. Gavial has already asked for an exception to the embargo, which you are now going to try to negotiate. Ostensibly the Hermanans are willing to discuss resumption of cantaxion exports in return for military weapons to be manufactured on Bacalhao, another of the Cruzeiro worlds."

"Which would be, of course, in complete violation of Imperium law, since the Imperium has placed an embargo of its own on doing business with Hermano. Am I supposed to conclude that Gavial is considering rebelling against the Imperium also?"

"Most definitely not. At our strong urging Gavial has indicated that it's at least open to the idea of entering into such transactions, provided they can be kept secret. That doesn't mean it actually would. How far you want to proceed with any of this once you make contact with Lanista himself is entirely up to you, naturally. I doubt that he'll find the idea that this is simply a trade mission very credible, once he realizes that it's you that he's dealing with, but of course that won't matter at that point."

"Of course," said the Colonel, who was already six moves ahead in the game that had to be played once he reached Hermano, and wished that Nicanor Ternera would hand over the rest of the briefing papers and disappear, which eventually he did, though not as swiftly as the Colonel would have preferred.

The first stop on his journey to Hermano was Entrada, where the Service's main operational center was located. Going to Entrada would be to make what could be thought of as a long jump in the wrong direction. Hermano, like Galgala, was a Core world, close to the center of the galaxy, whereas Entrada was one of what had once been called the Inner Worlds, and therefore was actually out on the Rim, because all distances had been measured from Earth in those early days. Earth itself was a Rim world, and Entrada, just a couple of dozen light-years distant from it, was off in the same obscure corner of the galaxy, far from the galactic core, as the original mother planet. But stellar distances had no significant meaning in Velde transmission and Entrada was where the Service had its most important base. Here the Colonel would undergo his transformation into Petrus Haym, diplomat from Gavial.

He had undergone so many transformations in his time that the Service had a better idea of what his baseline self looked like than he did himself. He knew that he was slightly above the median in height, that he was of mesomorphic build with longer-than-average limbs, and that the natural color of his eyes was olive-green. But his eyes had been blue and brown and violet and even scarlet on various occasions, his hair had been tinted every shade in the book and sometimes removed entirely, and his teeth and nose and ears and chin had been subjected to so much modification over the years that he no longer remembered their exact original configuration. When he had retired from the Service they had restored him, so they claimed, to baseline, but he was never entirely sure that the face he saw in the mirror each morning, the pleasant, thoughtful, agreeably nondescript face of a man who was certainly no longer young but nowhere near the end of his days, was really anything like the one that had looked back at him in the days before all the modifications had begun.

The concept of a baseline self was pretty much obsolete, anyway. Short of making fundamental rearrangements in a person's basic skeletal structure—and they were working on that one—it had, for many hundreds of years, been feasible to give anyone any appearance at all. Rebuilds were standard items for everyone, not just operatives of the Service. You could look young or old, benign or cruel, open-hearted or brooding, as you wished, and when you tired of one look you could trade it in for another, just as, up to a point, you could roll back the inroads of the aging process by fifty years or so every now and then. That sort of mutability had been available even in the Colonel's grandfather's day, and by now everyone took it for granted. It was only his sheer obstinate perversity of will that had led the Colonel's father to insist on retaining, for the last seventy years of his life, the limp that he had acquired while carrying out an assignment on one of the worlds of the Magnifico system and that he had proudly displayed forever after.

The Colonel hesitated only the tiniest part of a moment when finally he stood before the Elsinore doorway. Some fraction of him still did not want to do this, but it was, he knew, only an extremely small fraction. Then he stepped through and was annihilated instantly and just as instantly reconstituted at the corresponding doorway on Entrada.

It was close to a century since the Colonel had last been to the operations center on Entrada. Entrada was a place he had hoped never to see again. He remembered it as a tropical world, much too hot from pole to pole, humid and jungly everywhere, with two potent white suns that were set close together in the sky and went whirling around each other three or four times a day, giving the appearance of a single weird egg-shaped mass. Only Entrada's great distance from those two sizzling primaries made the planet habitable at all. The Colonel hated its steambath heat, its thick, almost liquid greenish-gold atmosphere, its lunatic profusion of vegetation, the merciless round-the-clock glare of those twin suns. And also it was a world severely afflicted by the presence of a strong lambda field, lambda being a force that had been unknown until the early days of Velde travel. In those days anyone making the transition from a low-lambda world to a high-lambda world found himself knocked flat on his back during a period of adaptation that might stretch across several months. The problem of lambda differential had been conquered over a thousand years ago, but even now some minor effects could be felt by new arrivals to a high-lambda world, a lingering malaise, a sense of spiritual heaviness, that took days or even weeks to shake off.

But the Colonel, having come once more to Entrada despite all expectation, found it easy enough to shrug off all its discomforts. This would be only a brief stop, and there would never be another, of that he was certain beyond all question. He went through it as one goes through a bad dream, waiting for the release that morning brings.

Obsequious Service officers met him at the transit station, greeting him in an almost terrified way, with a kind of heavy-handed stifling reverence, the way one might greet some frightful spectre returned from the tomb, and conveyed him to the operations center, which was ten times the size of the building the Colonel remembered. Once he was inside its windowless mass he might have been on any planet at all: Entrada and all its tropic hyperabundance had no presence within these well-insulated halls.

"Colonel, this is how you are going to look," they told him, and a full-size image of Petrus Haym sprang into view in the air before him.

They had conceived Petrus Haym as a stolid burgher, round-cheeked, complacent, with heavy-lidded sleepy eyes, full lips, a short thick neck, a fleshy body, the very model and essence of what he was supposed to be, a man who had devoted his life to issues of tariff regulation and balances of trade. Indifferently the Colonel gave his approval, offering no suggestions whatever for revisions in the Haym format, though they seemed to be expecting them. He didn't care. The format they had conceived would do. To look like an animated stereotype of a trade commissioner would make it all the simpler for the Colonel to assume the identity he was supposed to take on.

That he would be able to operate convincingly as the accredited leader of a trade delegation from a planet he knew nothing about was not anything that he doubted. He was a quick study. In his time he had assumed all kinds of roles: he had been a priest of the Goddess, an itinerant collector of zoological specimens, an organizer of disenfranchised laborers, a traveling musician, a deeply compassionate counselor to the bereaved, and many other things, whatever was required to fit the task at hand, which was always, ultimately, the engineering of consent. Preserving the integrity of the Imperium had been his constant goal. The Imperium's scope verged on the infinite; so too, then, must his.

When they had done all that they needed to do with him at the operations center, and he had done all that he needed to do as well, he went on to the next stop on his journey, Phosphor, where the rest of his team was awaiting him.

Like many of the worlds of the Imperium, Phosphor was a planet of a multiple-sun system. The Colonel had visited it once before, early in his career, but all he remembered of the visit was that he had gone there to seek out and eliminate a veteran agitator who was living there in exile from his home world and laying plans to return home to engage in a fresh round of destabilizing activities. The Colonel recalled carrying out the job successfully, but the planet itself he had forgotten. Seeing it now, he still did not remember much about his earlier stay there. He had seen so many worlds, after all. Here, a huge cool red sun, old and dying, lay like an angry blemish in the east by day, and a hot blue one that was at least a couple of hundred units away blazed out of the west, bright as a beacon in the sky. Even at night—the unnerving, intensely black night of a Rim world that the Colonel had never learned to like—stray tendrils of light from one sun or the other streamed into view at the hemisphere's darkside edge.

The people of Phosphor did not seem to go in for somatic modification. The likeness they bore toward one another indicated that they seemed to cling almost defiantly to the somatotypes of the original handful of settlers of thousands of years ago, who must predominantly have been short, sinewy, broad-based folk, swarthy-skinned, beady-eyed. Magda Cermak, who was waiting for the Colonel at the Velde station, was the perfect exemplar of her people, a dark-haired sharp-nosed woman who stood only chest-high to the Colonel but who was so solidly planted atop her thick, sturdy legs that a rolling boulder could not have knocked her down. She seemed about fifty, no more than that, and perhaps she actually was. She welcomed the Colonel in an efficient, uneffusive way, addressing him as Petrus Haym, inquiring without real curiosity about his journey, and introducing him to the three delegates from Gavial, two men and a woman, who stood diffidently to one side, a well-nigh invisible trio of pallid bureaucrats, fidgety, self-effacing, like the supernumeraries that in fact they were in the drama to come.

His point of arrival on Phosphor was its capital city, a sprawling, untidy place that bore the ancient historical name of Jerusalem. At the Imperium headquarters there, Magda Cermak provided the Colonel with an update on the activities of Geryon Lanista—Martin Bauer, as he was now—since their paths had last crossed on that ill-starred world, Tristessa, half a century before.

"The one part of the trail we don't have," Cermak said, "covers the period between his escape from Tristessa's companion planet and his arrival in the Aguila sector. The period in the immediate aftermath of the faked suicide, that is. We figure that he spent about twenty years as far out of sight as he could keep himself. Our best guess is that he may have been moving around in the Rim worlds during those years.

One informant insists that he even spent a certain amount of time on Earth itself."

"Could that be so?" asked the Colonel.

Magda Cermak shrugged. "There's no way of knowing. He's probably capable of managing it, wouldn't you say? But if he did get to Earth, Earth doesn't know anything about it, and Lanista isn't going to tell us either."

"All right. That's twenty blank years. What about the next thirty?"

"He first turns up under the name of Paul Thurm as a grape farmer on Iriarte, but he doesn't last long there. A legal problem arises, Thurm vanishes, and at that point a couple of years are gone from the record. When we pick up the trail again we find him in one of the Aguila Sector systems as Heinrich Bauer, supposedly an expert on land reclamation. He spends four years on a planet called Thraka, teaching the locals how to drain swamps, and then he moves on to Alyatta, a world of an adjacent system, where he shows the people how to irrigate a desert."

"A highly versatile man," the Colonel said.

"Very. He's on Alyatta for six or seven years, apparently marrying and having a couple of children and acquiring substantial properties. Then once again he vanishes abruptly, leaving his family behind, and shows up on Gran Chingada, where his name now is Martin Bauer. We don't know the motive for the switch. Something to do with the abandonment of his family, perhaps, although why he didn't change the surname too is hard to understand. Possibly the 'Heinrich' entry was erroneous all along. Keeping detailed track of a whole galaxy full of people is only approximately possible, you know.—You have been to Gran Chingada, I understand."

"A long time ago. It's a rough place."

"It's quieter now. They got rid of their worst malcontents thirty years back."

"Shipping them off to Hermano, two star-systems away, I'm told."

"Correct."

"Was Martin Bauer among those who was sent into exile?"

"No. He emigrated voluntarily, a dozen years ago, after the settlement on Hermano was fairly well established. Supposedly he was brought in by the plantation owners who grow the herb from which cantaxion is made, on account of his old specialty, land reclamation. He became a plantation owner himself in a major way, and involved himself very quickly in politics there, and before long he had won election to the Council of Seven, the oligarchy that was the ruling body on Hermano before its declaration of independence from the Imperium."

"An oligarchy whose members are *elected?*" said the Colonel. "Isn't that a little unusual?"

Magda Cermak smiled. "'Politics' on Hermano doesn't mean that they have universal suffrage. The richest landowners have run the place from the beginning. In the days of the Council of Seven, new members of the Council were chosen by the existing ones whenever a vacancy developed. It appears that Bauer got very rich very fast and was able to buy his way onto the Council. From what I hear, he was always an extremely persuasive man."

"Quite," the Colonel said.

"The last report of the Imperium commissioners before their expulsion indicates that he quickly made himself the dominant figure on it. He was the one, as I expect you've already guessed, who maneuvered Hermano into breaking with the Imperium."

"And what is he now, King of Hermano? Emperor of Hermano?"

"First Secretary of the Provisional Government is his title. He and four other members of the old Council of Seven make up the provisional government."

"An oligarchy of five being more manageable than an oligarchy of seven, I suppose. The next phase in the process being the replacement of the provisional government with an even more manageable one-man dictatorship."

"No doubt," said Magda Cermak.

She had more to tell him, little details of Martin Bauer's life on Hermano—he had married again, it seemed, and had had another set of children, and lived in monarchical splendor on a great estate on the southern coast of Hermano's one settled continent. The Colonel paid no more attention to what she was saying than professional courtesy required. It came as no surprise to hear that Geryon Lanista was looking after himself well. That had always been a specialty of his.

What occupied the center of the Colonel's attention was the fact of the rebellion on Hermano itself. That the person formerly known as Geryon Lanista was the instrument by which that rebellion had come about concerned him only in an incidental way now; it was a purely personal datum that had succeeded nicely in entangling him, at a time when he had thought he had completely shed his identity as a functionary of the Service, in this enterprise. If he could settle the score with Geryon Lanista after all this time, so be it. That would not be a trivial thing, but it was nevertheless a peripheral one. It was the existence of the rebellion, rather than Lanista's involvement in it, that had in these recent days brought powerful old emotions up from the center of the Colonel's being, had reawakened in him that sense of the necessity of protecting the Imperium that had been the essential driving factor of his personality through his entire adult life.

A rebellion was an act of war, nothing else. And in a galaxy of many thousands of inhabited worlds war could not be allowed to come back into existence.

There had been strife once, plenty of it, in the early years of the great galactic expansion. There had been trade wars and there had been religious wars and there had been real wars, in which whole worlds had been destroyed. The immensity of the spaces that separated one planet from another, one solar system from another, one stellar cluster from another, meant nothing at all in a civilization in which the far-flung Velde system and the even more expansive network of Magellanic gateways rendered travel over unthinkable distances a simpler and faster and safer process than a journey from one city to the next on the same continent had been in that era, many thousands of years in the past, when all of mankind had been confined to a single small world of the galaxy.

In those ancient days war between cities, and then between states when states had evolved, had been commonplace events. Schoolchildren on a million worlds still studied the history and literature of Earth as if they themselves were citizens of that little planet. They would not be able to find Earth's sun on a chart of the skies if they searched for thirty centuries, but they could recite the names of a dozen or more of Earth's famous wars, going back even into dim prehistory to the oldest war of all, the great war between the Greeks and the Trojans, when men had fought with clanging swords.

That had been a small war fought by great men. Later, millennia later, when humanity had spilled forth into all the galaxy, had come great wars fought by small men, wars not between tiny cities but between worlds, and there had been raging chaos in the stars, terrible death, terrible destruction. And then the chaos had at last burned itself out and there had come peace, fragile at first, then more certain. The galaxy-spanning institution known as the Imperium maintained that peace with iron determination.

The Imperium would not allow war. The age of chaos was over forever. That was universally understood, understood by all—or nearly all—

"Well, then, shall we start out on our way to Hermano, and get on with the job?" said the Colonel, when Magda Cermak had finished her briefing at last.

The first segments of the Velde system had been constructed at a time when Earth was all there was to the human galaxy and no one seriously expected that the multitudinous stars of the galactic center would ever come within mankind's reach. Though Velde transmission itself was non-relativistic, the setting up of the original system had had to be carried out under the constraints of the old Einsteinian rules, in which the speed of light was the limiting velocity.

And so, piece by piece, the necessary receiving equipment was put in place by conventional methods of delivery on one after another of the so-called Inner Worlds, those that orbited stars lying within a sphere a hundred light-years in diameter with Earth at its center. Even though the equipment was shipped out aboard vessels traveling close to the Einsteinian limit, unmanned starships journeying outward with great sails unfurled to the photonic winds, finding potentially habitable worlds, releasing robots that would set the Velde receivers in position, then going on to the next world and the next, extending the highway of receiving stations from one star system to another, it took centuries to get the job done. And by then the Magellanics' transit system had been discovered, impinging—just barely—on the tiny segment of the galaxy where Earth had managed to set up its little network of Velde stations.

Nobody knew how old the Magellanic system was, nor who had built it, nor even how it worked. That their builders had originated in the nearby galaxy known as the Greater Magellanic Cloud was only a guess, which somehow everyone had embraced as though it were a proven fact. They might just as readily have come from the Andromeda galaxy, or the great spiral galaxy in Eridanus, or some other stellar cluster ten or twelve billion light-years away, whose component stars and all the inhabitants of its many worlds had perished back in the ungraspable remoteness of the distant past. No one knew; no one expected to find out. The only thing that was certain was that the so-called Magellanics had traveled freely through the galaxy that one day would be mankind's, roaming it some unknowable number of years ago, using a system of matter transmission to journey from world to world, and that among the artifacts they had left behind on those worlds were their matter-transmitters, still in working order, apparently designed to function through all of eternity to come.

They operated more or less as the Velde transmitters did—you stepped through here and came out there—but whether they worked on similar principles was also something that was unknowable. There was nothing to analyze. Their doorways had no moving parts and drew on no apparent power source. Certain brave souls, stumbling upon these doorways during the early days of exploration on the outer worlds of humanity's sphere of expansion, had stepped through them and emerged on other planets even farther out, and eventually some working knowledge of the network, which doorway led to what other world, had been attained. How many lives had been lost in the course of attaining that knowledge was another thing that could never be known, for only those explorers who had survived their trips through the doorways could report on what they had done. The others—instantly transported, perhaps, to some other galaxy, or to the heart of a star, or to a world of intolerable gravitational force, or one whose doorway had been surrounded, over the millennia, by a sea of molten lava—had not been able to send back useful information about their trips.

By now, though, humankind had been making use of the Magellanic doorways for upwards of ten thousand years. The usable routes had all been tested and charted and the doorways had played a determining role in mankind's expansion across immense galactic distances that otherwise might not have been crossed until some era unimaginably far off in the future. The little sphere of planets that once had been known as the Inner Worlds was now thought of as the Rim, out there on the edge of galactic civilization; Earth, the primordial world where everything had begun, had become almost a legend, unvisited and shrouded in myth, that had very little reality for most of the Imperium's trillions of citizens; the essential life of galactic mankind long ago had moved from the Rim to the close-packed worlds of the Core. Though Velde stations still were an important means of travel within local sectors of the galaxy, and new Velde links were being constructed all the time, most long-hop travel now was carried out via the Magellanic system, which required no input of energy and maintained itself free of cost to those who used its gateways. The Colonel's journey to Hermano would involve the use of both systems.

The first jump took him via Velde transmission from Phosphor to nearby Entropy, a world that the Colonel had visited as a tourist forty years before, in the early days of his retirement. He did not remember it as a particularly interesting place. He had gone there only to gain access to the Magellanic doorway on Trewen, fifty light-years away, where he could leap across the galaxy to lovely Jacynth, his intended destination back then.

Entropy was no more interesting now: a yellow-green sun, mild weather, a few small cities, three big moons dangling in a row across the daytime sky. Magda Cermak preceded him there, and his three Gavial associates followed along behind. When the whole group was assembled they did a Velde hop to Trewen, now as before a virtually uninhabited world, cool and dry and bleak, notable only because the Magellanics had chosen to plant one of their doorways on it. Transit agents from the Service were waiting there to conduct the Colonel and his party to the doorway, which was tucked away within a deep cave on a rocky plateau a few hundred meters from the Velde station.

It seemed like only the day before yesterday that the Colonel had made his previous visit to this place. There on the right side of the cave was the sleek three-sided doorway, tapering upward to a sharp point, framing within itself a darkness so intense that it made the darkness of a Rim-world night seem almost inconsequential. Along each of its three sides was a row of gleaming hieroglyphs, an incomprehensible message out of a vanished eon. The doorway was wide enough for several to go through at a time. The Colonel beckoned the three Gavial people through first, and then stepped through himself, with Magda Cermak at his side. There was no sensation of transition: he walked through the darkness and came out of another doorway on Jacynth, one of the most beautiful of all worlds, as beautiful, almost, as lost Tristessa: a place of emerald meadows and a ruby-red sky, where great trees with feathery silver leaves and scarlet trunks sprang up all about them and a milky waterfall went cascading down the side of an ebony mountain that rose in serried pinnacles just ahead. The Colonel would have been happy to end the journey at that point and simply remain on Jacynth, where even the most troubled soul could find contentment for a while, but there was no hope of that, for more Service personnel awaited him there to lead him on to the next doorway, and by day's end the Colonel had arrived on Gavial of the Cruzeiro system, halfway across the galaxy from that morning's starting point at the Grand Terminus Hotel on Galgala.

Not even a Colonel in the Service was able to know everything about every one of the worlds of the Imperium, or even very much about very many of them. The galaxy was simply too big. Before the dark-haired intruder had enmeshed him in this undertaking the Colonel had been aware of Cruzeiro only because it was that rare thing, a solar system that had more than one world—four, in fact—that was inhabitable by human beings without extensive modification. Of Gavial itself, or its neighbor Bacalhao, or the other two worlds of the Cruzeiro system, he knew nothing at all. But now he was going to be masquerading as a native of the place, no less, and so he needed to acquire some first-hand familiarity with it. He had carried out the usual sort of research in the days before leaving home, and that had given him all the background on Gavial that he needed, though not a fully three-dimensional sense of what sort of world it was. For that you had to spend a little time there. He did know how large Gavial was, though, its climatic and geographical details, the history of its colonization, its major products, and a host of other things that he was probably not going to need to draw upon during his stay on Hermano, but which, simply by being present in some substratum of his mind, would allow him to make a convincing pretense of being Gavialese. As part of that he had learned to speak in the thick-tongued Gavialese way, spitting and sputtering his words in a fashion that accurately mimicked the manner of speech of his three Gavialese companions.

At first Magda Cermak, who spoke Galactic with the sharp-edged precision that seemed to be typical of the natives of Phosphor, could be seen smothering laughter every time the Colonel began to speak.

"Is it so comic, then?" he asked her.

"You sound like a marthresant," she said, giggling.

"Remind me of what a marthresant is," said the Colonel.

It was, she explained, one of her world's marine mammals, a huge ungainly creature with a wild tangle of bristly whiskers and long flaring tusks, which made coarse whooping snorts that could be heard half a kilometer away when it came up for air. Saying that he sounded like a marthresant did not appear to be a compliment. But he thanked her gravely for the explanation and told her that he was happy that his accent provided her with a little reminder of home.

That seemed to amuse her. But perhaps she was wondering whether she had offended him, for she made a point of telling him that she found his own accent, the accent of Galgala, extremely elegant. Which obliged the Colonel to inform her that his accent was not Galgalan at all, that he had lived on Galgala only during his boyhood and in the years since his retirement, and that in the years between he had spent so much time on so many different worlds, counterfeiting so many different accents, that he had lost whatever his original manner of speech had been. What he normally spoke now was actually a kind of all-purpose pan-Galactic, a randomly assorted mixture of mannerisms that would baffle even the most expert student of linguistics.

"And will you have some Gavialese in the mix when this is all over?" she asked.

"Perhaps nothing worse than a little snorting and whooping around the edges of the consonants," he told her, and winked.

She appeared to be startled by his sudden playfulness. But it had emerged only in response to hers, when she had begun giggling over his accent. The Colonel had been aware from the first that she felt an almost paralyzing awe for him, which she had been attempting to conceal with great effort. Nothing unusual about that: he was a legendary figure in the Service, already famous throughout the galaxy long before she was born, the hero of a hundred extravagantly risky campaigns. Everyone he had come in contact with since taking on this assignment had regarded him in that same awe-stricken way, though some had been a little better at hiding it than others. There were times, looking back at all he had done, that he almost felt a twinge of awe himself. The only one who had seemed immune to the power of his fame was the cold-eyed man who had gone to him in the first place, someone, obviously, who was so highly placed in the modern Service that he was beyond all such emotion.

All the others were overwhelmed by the accumulated grandeur of his reputation. But it would only make things more difficult all around as this project unfolded if Magda went on thinking of him as some sort of demigod who had condescended to step down from the heavens and move among mortals again this one last time. He was relieved that she was professional enough to shake some of that off.

They remained on Gavial for a week while he soaked up the atmosphere of the place, did a little further research, and endured a round of governmental banquets and tiresome speeches that were designed to help him believe that he really *was* a trade representative from this planet whose only purpose in visiting Hermano was to get the flow of a vitally needed medicine going again. By the time that week was nearing its end Magda's attitude toward him had loosened to the extent that she was able to say, "It must be strange to think that in a few days you're finally going to get a chance to come face to face with the man you hate more than anyone else in the universe."

"Lanista? I don't even know if that's really him, over there on Hermano."

"It is. There's no question that it is."

"The Service says he is, and says it has the proof, but I've had too much experience with the way the Service creates whatever evidence it needs to buy a hundred percent of anything the Service claims. But suppose that *is* Lanista on Hermano. Why do you think I would hate him? I don't even know what the word means, really."

"The man who was working against you behind your back on one of your most important projects, and who, when things were heading toward an explosion that he himself had set up, went off without giving you a word of warning that you were very likely to get killed? What do you call that, if not treachery?"

"Treachery is exactly what I would call it, indeed," said the Colonel.

"And yet you don't hate him for that?" She was floundering now.

"I told you," the Colonel said, trying to choose his words with great care, "that 'hate' isn't a word I understand very well. Hate seems so useless, anyway. My real concern here is that I could have misjudged that man so completely. I *loved* him, you know. I thought of him almost as a son. I brought him into the Service, I taught him the craft, I worked with him on a dozen jobs, I personally insisted on his taking part in the

Tristessa thing. And then—then—then he—he—"

His throat went dry. He found himself unable to continue speaking. He was swept by feelings that he could only begin to comprehend.

Magda was staring at him in something close to horror. Perhaps she feared that she had pushed into territory that she had had no right to be exploring.

But then, as though trying to repair whatever damage she had caused, she pressed desperately onward. "I didn't realize that you and Lanista were actually that—close. I thought he was just your partner on an assignment. Which would be bad enough, selling you out like that. But if in fact he was almost like—your—"

She faltered.

"My protegé," the Colonel said. "Call him my protegé." He went to the window and stood with his back to her, knotting his hands together behind him. He wished he had never let this conversation begin.

The sun, Cruzeiro, was starting to set, an unspectacular yellowish sun tinged with pale pink. A hard-edged crescent moon was edging upward in the sky. Behind it lay two sharp points of brilliant light, two neighboring worlds of this system. Bacalhao and Coracao, their names were. He thought that Bacalhao was the one on the left, but wasn't entirely sure which was which. You could usually see them both in the twilight sky here. The odd names, he supposed, were derived, as so many planetary names were, from one of the ancient languages of Earth, a world where, so it was said, they had had a hundred different languages all at once, and people from one place could scarcely understand what people from another place were saying. It was a wonder they had been able to accomplish anything, those Earthers, when they wouldn't even have been able to make themselves understood if they went as much as five hundred kilometers away from home. And yet they had managed to make the great leap out into space, somehow, and to spread their colonies over thousands of solar systems, and to leave their words behind as the names of planets, although no one remembered any more what most of those words once meant.

"My protegé," he said again, without turning to face her. "Who betrayed me, yes. That has always mystified me, that he would have done such a thing. But do I hate him for it? No."

Yes, he told himself. *Of course you do.*

Tristessa. A magical place, the Colonel had once thought. On Tristessa your eye encountered beauty wherever it came to rest. He remembered everything about it down to the finest detail: the sweet fragrance of its soft, moist atmosphere, the bright turquoise-emerald glory of its double sun, the throngs of magnificent, winged reptiles soaring overhead, the glistening smoothness of the big, round white pebbles, like the eggs of some prehistoric monster, that formed the bed of the clear rushing stream that ran past his lodging. The pungent flavor of a triangular yellow fruit that dangled in immense quantities from nearby trees. The many-legged crab-like things, glossy black carapaces crisscrossed with jagged blood-red streaks, that roamed the misty forests searching in the dark rich loam for food, and looked up from their foraging to study you like solemn philosophers with a multitude of faceted amber eyes.

Its name, someone had told him once, was derived from a word of one of the languages of ancient Earth, a word that carried a connotation of "sadness," and certainly sadness was appropriate in thinking of Tristessa now. But how could they have known, when giving such a melancholy name to such a beautiful world, what sort of destiny was awaiting it five thousand years in the future?

For the Colonel, who was in the late prime of his career as an arch-manipulator of worlds, the Tristessa affair had begun as a routine political intervention, the sort of assignment he had dealt with on more occasions than he could count. He saw no special challenge in it. He expected that Geryon Lanista, whom he had been grooming for a decade or so to be his successor in the Service, would do much of the real work; the Colonel would merely supervise, observe, confirm in his own mind that Lanista was fully qualified to take things over from him.

Tristessa, lovely, underpopulated, economically undeveloped, had a companion world, Shannakha, less than thirty million kilometers away. Shannakha had been settled first. Its climate, temperate rather than tropical, wasn't as appealing as Tristessa's, nor was its predominantly sandy, rocky landscape anywhere near as beautiful. But it offered a wider range of natural resources—pretty little Tristessa had nothing much in the way of metals or fossil fuels—and it was on Shannakha that cities had been founded and an industrial economy established. Tristessa, colonized by Shannakha a few hundred years later, became the holiday planet for its neighbor in the skies. Shannakha's powerful merchant princes set up plantations where Tristessa's abundant fruits and vegetables could be raised and shipped to eager markets on the other world, and created great estates for themselves in the midst of those plantations; Shannakha's entrepreneurs built grand resort hotels for middle-class amusement on the beautiful island archipelagoes of Tristessa's tropical seas; and thousands of less fortunate Shannakhans settled on Tristessa to provide a labor force for all those estates, plantations, and hotels. It all worked very well for hundreds of years, though of course it worked rather better for the absentee owners on Shannakha than it did for their employees on Tristessa, since the Shannakhans prohibited any kind of ownership of Tristessan real estate or other property by Tristessans, kept payrolls as low as possible, and exported all profits to Shannakha.

But, as any student of history as well informed as the Colonel was would certainly know, the unilateral exploitation of one world by another does not work well forever, any more than the unilateral exploitation of one city or state by another had worked well in that long-ago era when all the human race was confined to that one little world called Earth. At some point a malcontent will arise who will argue that the assets of a place belong to the people who dwell in that place, and should not be tapped for the exclusive benefit of a patrician class living somewhere else, far away. And, if he is sufficiently persuasive and charismatic, that malcontent can succeed in finding followers, founding a movement, launching an insurrection, liberating his people from the colonial yoke.

Just that was in the process of happening when the Colonel was called in. Tristessa's charismatic malcontent had arisen. His name was Ilion Gabell; he came from a long line of farmers who raised and grew the agreeably narcotic zembani leaf that was the source of a recreational drug vastly popular on Shannakha; and because his natural abilities of leadership were so plainly manifest, he had been entrusted by a group of the plantation owners with the management of a group of adjacent zembani tracts that stretched nearly halfway across Tristessa's primary continent. That, unfortunately for the plantation owners, gave him access to clear knowledge of how profitable the Tristessa plantations really were. And now—so reliable informants had reported—he was on the verge of launching a rebellion that would break Tristessa free of the grasp of its Shannakhan owners. It was the Colonel's assignment to keep this from happening. He had chosen Geryon Lanista to assist him.

Lanista, who was fond of exploring both sides of an issue as an intellectual exercise, said, "And why, exactly, should this be any concern of the Imperium? Is it our job to protect the economic interests of one particular group of landowners against its own colonial employees? Are we really such conservatives that we have to be the policemen of the status quo all over the universe?"

"There would be wider ramifications to a Tristessa uprising," the Colonel said. "Consider: this Ilion Gabell gives the signal, and in a single night every Shannakhan who happens to be on Tristessa is slaughtered. Such things have occurred elsewhere, as you surely know. The Imperium quite rightly deplores wholesale murder, no matter what virtuous pretext is put forth for it. Next, a revolutionary government is proclaimed and transfers title to all Shannakhan-owned property on Tristessa to itself, to be held in the name of the citizenry of the Republic of Tristessa. What happens after that? Will Shannakha, peace-loving and enlightened, simply shrug and say that inasmuch as war between planets is illegal by decree of the Imperium, it therefore has no choice but to recognize the independence of Tristessa, and invites the Tristessans to enter into normal trade relationships with their old friends on the neighboring world?"

"Maybe so," said Lanista. "And that might even work."

"But the downside—"

"The downside, I suppose, is that it would send a signal to other planets in Tristessa's position that a rebellion against the established property interests can pay off. Which will create a lot of little Tristessa-style uprisings all over the galaxy, one of which might eventually explode into actual warfare between the mother world and its colony. Therefore a great deal of new toil for the Service will be required in order to keep those uprisings from breaking out, in which case it might be better to snuff out this one before it gets going."

"It might indeed," said the Colonel. "Now, the opposite scenario—"

"Yes. Shannakha, infuriated by the expropriation of its properties on Tristessa, retaliates by sending an armed expedition to Tristessa to get things under control. Thousands of Tristessans die in the first burst of hostilities. Then a guerrilla war erupts as Gabell and his insurrectionists are driven underground, and in the course of it the plantations and resorts of Tristessa are destroyed, perhaps with unusually ugly ecological consequences, and many additional casualties besides. Shannakha wrecks its own economy to pay for the war and Tristessa is ruined for decades or centuries to come. And at the end of it all we either wind up with something that's worse than the status quo ante bellum, Shannakha still in charge of Tristessa but now perhaps unable to meet the expense of rebuilding what was there once, or else with two devastated planets, Tristessa independent but useless and Shannakha bankrupt."

"And therefore—" the Colonel said, waiting for the answer that he knew would be forthcoming.

Lanista provided it. "Therefore we try to calm Ilion Gabell down and negotiate the peaceful separation of Tristessa and Shannakha by telling Gabell that we will obtain better working conditions for his people, while at the same time leading the Shannakhans to see that it's in their own best interest to strike a deal before a revolution can break out. If we can't manage that, I'd say that the interests of Tristessa, Shannakha, and the Imperium would best be served by suppressing Ilion Gabell's little revolution out of hand, either by removing him permanently or by demonstrating to him in a sufficiently persuasive way that he stands no chance of success, and simultaneously indicating to the Shannakhans that they'd better start treating the Tristessans a little more generously or they're going to find themselves faced with the same problem again before long, whether the revolution is led by Gabell or by someone else with the same ideas. Yes?"

"Yes," said the Colonel.

So it was clear, then, what they had to try to achieve, and what they were going to do to achieve it. All scenarios but one led to a violent outcome, and violence was a spreading sore that if not checked at its source could consume an entire civilization, even a galactic one. The problems on Tristessa, which were easily enough identified, needed to be corrected peacefully before a worse kind of correction got under way. The Colonel was as skillful an operative as there was and Geryon Lanista was nearly as shrewd as he was, and he still had all the energy of youth, besides. Why, then, had it all gone so terribly wrong?

And then it was time at last to make the last jump in the sequence, the one from Gavial to Hermano, where, despite all that the Colonel had believed for the last fifty years, Geryon Lanista was very much alive and at the head of his own insurrectionist government.

Despite the general trade embargo, the Velde link between Hermano and certain worlds of the galaxy, such as Gavial, was still operational. Only the wildest of insurrectionists would take the rash step of cutting themselves completely off from interstellar transit, and Lanista was evidently not that wild. Velde connections required two sets of tuned equipment, one at each end of any link, and once a planet chose to separate itself from Velde travel it would need the cooperation of the Imperium to re-establish the linkage. Lanista hadn't cared to risk handing the Imperium a unilateral stranglehold over his planet's economy. There had been other rebellions, as he of all people would have known very well, in which the Imperium had picked a time of its own choosing to restore contact once it had been broken off by the rebels.

The Colonel was completely composed as they set out on this final hop of the long journey. He searched for anxiety within himself and found none. He realized that it must have been destined all along that before the end of his life he would once again come face to face with Geryon Lanista, so that there might be a settlement of that troublesome account at last.

And why, he asked himself, should there be any immediate cause for anxiety? For the moment he was Petrus Haym, emissary plenipotentiary from the Cruzeiro system to the provisional government of independent Hermano, and Lanista was Martin Bauer, the head of that provisional government. Whatever meeting there was to be between the two of them would be conducted, at least at first, behind those masks.

Hermano, the Colonel saw at once, was no Tristessa. Perhaps he had arrived in this hemisphere's winter: the air was cool, even sharp, with hardly any humidity at all. He detected a hint of impending snow in it. The sky had a grayish, gloomy, lowering look. There was an odd acrid flavor to the atmosphere that would require some getting used to. The gravity was a little above Standard Human, which was going to exacerbate the task of carrying the extra flesh of Petrus Haym.

Everything within immediate view had a thrown-together, improvised appearance. The area around the Velde station was one of drably utilitarian tin-roofed warehouses, with an unprepossessing medium-sized town of low, anonymous-looking buildings visible in the distance against a backdrop of bleak stony hills. Tufts of scruffy vegetation, angular and almost angry-looking, sprang up here and there out of the dry, sandy soil. There was nothing to charm the eye anywhere. The Colonel reminded himself that this planet had been settled only about forty years before by a population of exiles and outcasts. Its people probably hadn't found time yet for much in the way of architectural niceties. Perhaps they had little interest in such things.

Somber-faced port officials greeted him in no very congenial way, addressing him as Commissioner Haym, checking through his papers and those of his companions, and unsmilingly waving him and his four companions aboard a convoy of antiquated lorries that took them down a ragged, potholed highway into town. Alto Hermano, the place was called. A signpost at the edge of town identified it grandiosely as the planetary capital, though its population couldn't have been much over twenty or thirty thousand. The vehicles halted in a stark open square bordered on all four sides by identical five-story buildings with undecorated mud-colored brick facades. An official who introduced himself as Municipal Procurator Tambern Collian met them there. He was a gray-eyed unsmiling man, just as dour of affect as everyone else the Colonel had encountered thus far here. He did not offer the expectable conventional wishes that Commissioner Haym had had an easy journey to Hermano nor did he provide pleasantries of any other sort, but simply escorted the delegation from Cruzeiro into one of the buildings on the square, which turned out to be a hotel, grimly functionalist in nature, that the government maintained for the use of official visitors. It was low-ceilinged and dim, with the look of a third-class commercial hotel on a backwater world. Municipal Procurator Collian showed the Colonel to his quite modest suite without apologies, indifferently wished him a good evening, and left, saying he would call again in the morning to begin their discussions.

Magda Cermak's room was adjacent to his. She came by to visit, rolling her eyes, when the Municipal Procurator was gone. The coolness of their welcome plainly hadn't been any cause of surprise to her, but she was irritated all the same. A dining room on the ground floor of the hotel provided them with a joyless dinner, choice of three sorts of unknown meat, no wine available of any kind. Neither of them had much to say. Their hosts were all making it very clear that Hermano was a planet that had declared war on the entire universe. They were willing to allow the delegation from the Cruzeiro system to come here to try to work out some sort of trade agreement, since they appeared to see some benefit to themselves in that, but evidently they were damned if they were going to offer the visitors much in the way of a welcome.

Municipal Procurator Collian, it developed, was to be Commissioner Haym's primary liaison with the provisional government. Precisely what Collian's own role was in that government was unclear. There were times when he seemed to be just the mayor of this starkly functional little city, and others when he appeared to speak as a high functionary of the planetary government. Perhaps he was both; perhaps there was no clear definition of official roles here at the moment. This was, after all, a provisional government, one that had seized power only a few years before from a previous government that had itself been mostly an improvisation.

It was clear, at any rate, that First Secretary Bauer himself did not plan to make himself a party to the trade talks, at least not in their initial stages. The Colonel did not see that as a problem. He wanted a little time to take the measure of this place before entering into what promised to be a complex and perhaps dangerous confrontation.

Each morning, then, the Colonel, Magda, and the three Gavialese would cross the plaza to a building on the far side that was the headquarters of the Ministry of Trade. There, around a squarish conference table of the sort of inelegant dreary design that seemed especially favored by the Hermanan esthetic, they would meet with Municipal Procurator Collian and a constantly shifting but consistently unconvivial assortment of other Hermanan officials to discuss the problem of Hermano's embargo on all foreign trade, and specifically its discontinuation of pharmaceutical exports to Gavial that Gavial regarded as vital to the health of its citizens.

The factor behind the unconviviality soon became clear. The Hermanans, a prickly bunch inexperienced in galactic diplomacy, apparently were convinced that Commissioner Haym and his companions were here to accomplish some sort of trickery. But the Hermanans had no way of knowing that and had been given no reason to suspect it. And the faintly concealed animosity with which they were treating the visitors from Gavial would surely get in the way of reaching any agreement on the treaty that the Gavialese had ostensibly come here to negotiate, a treaty that would be just as beneficial to Hermano as it would to Gavial.

So it became the Colonel's immediate job—in the role of Petrus Haym, envoy from the Cruzeiro system, not as a functionary of the Imperium—to show the Hermanans that their own frosty attitude was counterproductive. For that he needed to make himself seem to be the opposite of deceitful: a good-hearted, willingly transparent man, open and friendly, a little on the innocent side, maybe, not in any way a fool but so eager to have his mission end in a mutually advantageous agreement that the Hermanans would think he might allow himself to be swayed into becoming an advocate for the primary interests of Hermano. Therefore, no matter the provocation, he was the soul of amiability. The technicians of the Service had designed him to look stout and sleepy and unthreatening, and he spoke with a comic-opera Gavialese accent, which was helpful in enabling him to play the part of an easy mark. He spoke of how much he longed to be back on Gavial with his wife and children, and he let it be perceived without explicitly saying so that for the sake of an earlier family reunion he might well be willing to entertain almost any proposal for a quick settlement of the negotiations. He made little mild jokes about the discomforts of his lodgings here and the inadequacies of the food to underscore his desire to be done with this job and on his way. When one of the authentic Gavialese betrayed some impatience with the seeming one-sidedness of the talks in their early stage, Commissioner Haym rebuked him good-naturedly in front of the Hermanans, pointing out that Hermano was a planet that had chosen an exceedingly difficult road for itself, and needed to be given the benefit of every doubt. And gradually the Hermanans began to thaw a bit.

The sticking point in the discussions was Hermano's request that the Cruzeiro worlds serve as Hermano's advocate before the Imperium in its quest for independence. What the Cruzeiro people knew, and Hermano probably knew it as well, was that the Imperium was never going to permit any world to secede. The only way that Gavial was going to get the pharmaceuticals that it wanted from Hermano, and for Hermano to get the weapons it wanted from the Cruzeiro worlds, was for the two groups to cook up a secret and completely illegal deal between them, in utter disregard not just of the wishes of the Imperium but of its laws.

Gavial had already signaled, disingenuously, that it was willing to do this—urged on by the Imperium, which had pledged that it would provide them with a continued supply of cantaxion in return for its cooperation. But Hermano, perhaps because it quite rightly was mistrustful of Gavial's willingness to enter into a secret illegal deal or perhaps because of the obstinate naivete of its leaders, was continuing to hold out for official recognition by Gavial and the other Cruzeiro worlds of Hermanan independence.

By prearrangement the Colonel and Magda Cermak took opposite positions on this issue. Magda—stolid, brusque, rigid, unsmiling—bluntly told the Hermanan negotiators the self-evident truth of the situation, which was that Gavial was not going to align itself with the Hermanan independence movement because nobody's requests for independence from the Imperium were ever going to get anywhere, that the Imperium would never countenance any kind of official recognition of any member world's independence. Such a thing would set a wholly unacceptable precedent. It was out of the question; it was scarcely worth even discussing. If Gavialese recognition of Hermanan independence was the price of reopening trade relations between Gavial and Hermano, she said coldly, then the Gavialese trade delegation might as well go home right now.

Meanwhile her associate, Commissioner Haym—genial, placid, undogmatic, a trifle lacking in backbone, maybe, and therefore readily manipulable—sadly agreed that getting the Imperium to allow a member world, no matter how obscure, to pull out of the confederation would be a very difficult matter to arrange, perhaps impossible. But he did point out that it was the belief of the rulers of Gavial that the current philosophy of the Imperium was strongly nonbelligerent, that the Central Authority was quite eager to avoid having to launch military action against unruly members. For that reason, Commissioner Haym suggested, certain highly influential officials in the government of Gavial felt that the Imperium might be willing under the right circumstances to forget about Hermano entirely and look the other way while Hermano went right on regarding itself as independent. "I am not, you realize, speaking on behalf of the Imperium," Commissioner Haym said. "How could I? I have no right to do that. But we of Gavial have been given to understand that the Imperium is inclined toward leniency in this instance." The essential thing was that Hermano would have to keep quiet about its claim to independence, though it could go on behaving as though it were independent all the same. That is, in return for that silence, Commissioner Haym indicated, the Central Authority might be willing to overlook Hermano's refusal to pay taxes to it, considering that those taxes were a pittance anyway. And Hermano would be free to strike whatever private deals with whatever Imperium worlds it liked, so long as it kept quiet about those too—such as, he said, the proposed weapons-for-drugs arrangement that would get a supply of cantaxion flowing to Gavial once again and allow Hermano to feel capable of protecting itself against possible Imperium aggression.

Commissioner Haym communicated these thoughts to Procurator Collian at a time when Magda Cermak was elsewhere. Demanding immediate independence, he reiterated, was probably going to achieve nothing. But independence for Hermano might just be achievable in stages. Accepting a kind of de facto independence now might well clear the way for full independence later on. And he offered—unofficially, of course—Gavial's cooperation in persuading the Imperium to leave Hermano alone while it went on along its present solitary way outside the confederation of worlds.

Collian looked doubtful. "Will it work? I wonder. And how can you assure me the cooperation of your planet's government when not even your own colleague Commissioner Cermak is in agreement with you on any of this?"

"Ah, Commissioner Cermak. Commissioner Cermak!" Commissioner Haym favored Procurator Collian with a conspiratorial smile. "A difficult woman, yes. But not an unreasonable one. She understands that our fundamental goal in coming here, after all, is to restore trade between Gavial and Hermano by any means possible. Which ultimately should be Hermano's goal, too." Commissioner Haym allowed a semblance of craftiness to glimmer in his heavy-lidded eyes. "This is, of course, a very ticklish business all around, because of the Imperium's involvement in our dealings. You and I understand how complicated it is, eh?" A wink, a nudge of complicity. "But I do believe that your planet and mine, working toward our mutual interests, can keep the Imperium out of our hair, and that Gavial will stand up for Hermano before the Imperium if we commissioners bring back a unanimous report. And do you know how I think I can swing her over to the position that you and I favor?" he asked. "If I could show her that we have the full backing of First Secretary

Bauer—that he sees the plan's advantages for both our worlds, that he wholeheartedly supports it—I think we can work out a deal."

Municipal Procurator Collian seemed to think that that was an interesting possibility. He proposed that Commissioner Haym quickly prepare a memorandum setting forth all that they had discussed between themselves, which he could place before the First Secretary for his consideration. Commissioner Haym, though, replied mildly that Municipal Procurator Collian did not seem to have fully understood his point. Commissioner Haym was of the opinion that he could most effectively make his thoughts clear to the First Secretary during the course of a personal meeting. Collian was a bit taken aback by that. The evasive look that flitted across his chilly features indicated that very likely one was not supposed to consume the time of the First Secretary in such low-level things as meetings with trade commissioners. But then—the Colonel watched the wheels turning within the man—Collian began, so it seemed, to appreciate the merits of letting First Secretary Bauer have a go at molding with his own hands this extremely malleable envoy from Gavial. "I'll see what I can do," he said.

Not all of Hermano was as bleak as the area around the capital city, the Colonel quickly discovered. The climate grew moister and more tropical as he headed southward, scraggy grasslands giving way to forests and forests to lush jungles in the southernmost region of the continent, the one continent that the Hermanans had managed to penetrate thus far. The view from the air revealed little sign of development in the southern zone, only widely scattered plantations, little isolated jungle domains, separated from one another by great roadless swaths of dense green vegetation. He did not see anything amounting to continuous settlement until he was nearly at the shores of the ocean that occupied the entire southern hemisphere of this world, stretching all the way to the pole. Here, along a narrow coastal strip between the jungle and the sea, the elite of Hermano had taken up residence.

First Secretary Bauer's estate was situated at the midpoint of that strip, on a headland looking out toward the green, peaceful waters of that southern sea. It was expectably grand. The only surprising thing about it was that it was undefended by walls or gates or even any visible guard force: the road from the airstrip led straight into the First Secretary's compound, and the estate house itself, a long, low stone building rising commandingly on the headland in a way that reminded the Colonel of the fortress at Megalo Kastro, seemed accessible to anyone who cared to walk up to its door.

But the Colonel was taken instead to one of the many outbuildings, a good distance down the coastal road from the First Secretary's villa itself, and there he was left in comfortable seclusion for three long days. He had a five-room cottage to himself, with a pretty garden of flowering shrubs and a pleasant view of the sea. No one kept watch over him, but even so it seemed inappropriate and perhaps unwise to wander any great distance from his lodgings. His meals were brought to him punctually by silent servants: seafood of various kinds, mainly, prepared with skill and subtlety, and accompanied by pale wines that were interestingly tangy and tart. A small library had been provided for him, mostly familiar classics, the sort of books that Geryon Lanista had favored during their years of working together. He inspected the garden, he strolled along the beach, he ventured a short way into the dense forest of scrubby little red-leaved trees with aromatic bark on the inland side of the compound. The air here was soft and had a mildly spicy flavor, not at all bitter like the air up at Alto Hermano. The water of the sea, into which he ventured ankle-deep one morning, was warm and clear, lapping gently at the pink sands. Even the strong pull of this world's gravity was less oppressive here, though the Colonel knew that that was only illusion.

On the fourth day the summons to the presence of the First Secretary came to him.

The dispassionate tranquility that had marked the Colonel's demeanor since his departure from Gavial remained with him now. He had brought himself to his goal and whatever was fated to happen next would happen; he faced all possibilities with equanimity. He was taken into the great villa, conveyed down long silent hallways floored with gleaming panels of dark polished wood, led past huge rooms whose windows looked toward the sea, and delivered, finally, into a much smaller room, simply furnished with a desk and a few chairs, at the far end of the building. A man who unquestionably was Geryon Lanista waited for him there, standing behind the desk.

He was greatly altered, of course. The Colonel was prepared for that. The face of the man who stood before him now was the one he had seen in the solido that the dark-haired visitor had shown him in his villa on Galgala, that day that now seemed so long ago: that blunt-tipped nose, those downturned lips, the flaring cheekbones, the harsh jutting jaw, all of them nothing like the features of the Geryon Lanista he once had known. This man looked only to be sixty or so, and that too was unsurprising, though actually Lanista had to be close to twice that age; but no one ever looked much more than sixty anymore, except those few who preferred to let a few signs of something approaching their true age show through to the surface. Lanista had had every reason to transform himself beyond all recognition since the debacle on Tristessa. The surprising thing, the thing that forced the Colonel for an instant to fight against allowing an uncontrolled reaction to make itself visible, was how easy it was for him to see beyond the cosmetic transformations to the real identity behind them.

Was it the hulking frame that gave him away, or the expression of the eyes? Those things had to be part of it, naturally. Very few men were built on such a massive scale as Lanista, and not even the canniest of cosmetic surgeons could have done anything about the breadth of those tremendous shoulders and that huge vault of a chest. His stance was Lanista's stance, the rock-solid stance of a man of enormous strength and physical poise: one's habitual way of holding one's body could not be unlearned, it seemed. And the eyes, though they were brown now and the Colonel remembered Lanista to have had piercingly blue ones, still had that eerie, almost feminine softness that had given such an odd cast to the old Lanista's otherwise formidably masculine face. Surely a surgeon could have done something about that. But perhaps one had tried, and even succeeded, and then the new eyes had come to reveal the innate expression of Lanista's soul even so, shining through inexorably despite everything: for there were the veritable eyes of Geryon Lanista looking out at him from this unfamiliar face.

The eyes—the stance—and something else, the Colonel thought, the mere intangible presence of the man—the inescapable, unconcealable essence of him—

While the Colonel was studying Martin Bauer and finding Geryon Lanista behind the facade, Martin Bauer was studying Commissioner Petrus Haym, giving him the sort of close scrutiny that any head of state trying to evaluate a visiting diplomat of whom he intended to make use could be expected to give. Plainly he was reading Petrus Haym's bland meaty face to assure himself that the Gavialese commissioner was just as obtuse and pliable as the advance word from Procurator Collian had indicated. The precise moment when Lanista made the intuitive leap by which he saw through the mask of Commissioner Petrus Haym to the hidden Colonel beneath was difficult for the Colonel to locate. Was it when the tiniest of muscular tremors flickered for an instant in his left cheek? When there was that barely perceptible fluttering of an eyelid? That momentary puckering at the corner of his mouth? The Colonel had had a lifetime's training in reading faces, and yet he wasn't sure. Perhaps it was all three of those little cues that signaled Lanista's sudden stunned realization that he was in the presence of the man he had looked to as his master and mentor, or perhaps it was none of them; but somewhere in the early minutes of this encounter Lanista had identified him. The Colonel was certain of that.

For a time neither man gave any overt indication of what he knew about the other. The conversation circled hazily about the ostensible theme of an exchange of arms for medicine and how that could be arranged in conjunction with Hermano's desire to break free from the political control of the Central Authority of the Imperium. The Colonel, as Haym, took pains to radiate an amiability just this side of buffoonery, while always drawing back from full surrender to the other man's wishes. Lanista, as Bauer, pressed Haym ever more strongly for a commitment to his cause, though never quite pouncing on him with a specific demand for acquiescence. Gradually it became clear to the Colonel that they were beginning to conduct these negotiations in the voices of Lanista and the Colonel, not in those of First Secretary Bauer and Commissioner Haym. Gradually, too, it became clear to him that Lanista was just as aware of this as he was.

In the end it was Lanista who was the one who decided to abandon the pretense. He had never been good at biding his time. It had been his besetting flaw in the old days that a moment would always come when he could no longer contain his impatience, and the Colonel saw now that no surgery could alter that, either. Commissioner Haym had been moving through the old circular path once more, asking the First Secretary to consider the problems that Gavial faced in weighing its need for cantaxion against the political risks involved in defying the decrees of the Central Authority, when Lanista said abruptly, in a tone of voice far more sharply focused and forceful than the woolly diplomatic one he had been using up until then, "Gavial doesn't have the slightest intention of speaking up for us before the Imperium, does it, Colonel? This whole mission has been trumped up purely for the sake of inserting you into the situation so you can carry out the Imperium's dirty work here, whatever that may be. Am I not right about that?"

"Colonel?" the Colonel said, in the Haym voice.

"Colonel, yes." Lanista was quivering, now, with the effort to maintain his composure. "I can see who you are. I saw it right away.—I thought you had retired a long time ago."

"I thought so too, but I was wrong about that. And I thought you were dead. I seem to have been wrong about that too."

For half a century the Colonel had lived, day in, day out, with the memories of his last two weeks on the paradise-world that Tristessa once had been. Like most bad memories, those recollections of the Tristessan tragedy, and his own narrow escape from destruction, had receded into the everyday background of his existence, nothing more now than the dull, quiet throbbing of a wound long healed, easily enough ignored much of the time. But in fact the wound had never healed at all. It had merely been bandaged over, sealed away by an act of sheer will. From time to time it would remind him of its existence in the most agonizing way. Now the pain of it came bursting upward once again out of that buried part of his consciousness in wave upon wave.

He was back on Tristessa again, waiting for Lanista to return from his mission to Shannakha. Lanista had gone to the companion world ten days before, intending to see the minister who had jurisdiction over Tristessan affairs and make one last effort to head off the conflict between the two planets that had begun to seem inevitable. He was carrying with him documents indicating that the Tristessa colonists were ready to launch their rebellion, and that only the promulgation by Shannakha of a radical program of economic reform could now avoid a costly and destructive struggle. Recent developments on Shannakha had given rise to hope that at least one powerful faction of the government was willing to offer some significant concessions to the Tristessan colonists. The Colonel, meanwhile, was holding talks with Ilion Gabell, the rebel leader, in an attempt to get him to hold his uprising off a little while longer while Lanista worked out the details of whatever concessions Shannakha might offer.

Gabell's headquarters were on the floating island of Petra Hodesta, five hundred hectares of grasses thick as hawsers that had woven themselves tightly together long ago and broken free of the mainland. The island, its grassy foundation covered now with an accretion of soil out of which a forest of slender blue-fronded palms had sprouted, circled in a slow current-driven migration through the sparkling topaz waters of Tristessa's Triple Sea, and Gabell's camp was a ring of bamboo huts along the island's shore. The Colonel had arrived five days earlier. He had a good working relationship with Gabell, who was a man of commanding presence and keen intelligence with a natural gift for leadership, forty or fifty years old and still in the first strength and flourish of his early manhood. The Colonel had laid out in great detail and more than customary forthrightness everything that Lanista had gone to the mother world to request; and Gabell had agreed to wait at least until he saw what portion of the things Lanista was asking for would be granted. He was not a rash or hasty man, was Gabell. But he warned that any kind of treachery on Shannakha's part would be met with immediate and terrible reprisals.

"There will be no treachery," the Colonel promised.

Petra Hodesta's wandering route now was taking it toward the northernmost of Triple Sea's three lobes, the one adjacent to Gespinord, the Tristessan capital province. Since Lanista was due back from Shannakha in a few more days, it was the Colonel's plan to go ashore on the coast of Gespinord and make his way by airtrain to the main Velde terminal, two hundred kilometers inland at the capital city, to await his return. But he was less than halfway there when the train came spiraling down to its track with the sighing, whistling sound of an emergency disconnect and someone in uniform came rushing through the cars, ordering everyone outside.

Tristessa was under attack. Without warning Shannakhan troops had come pouring through every Velde doorway on the planet. Gespinord City, the capital, had already been taken. All transit lines had been cut. The Colonel heard distant explosions, and saw a thick column of black smoke rising in the north, and another, much closer, to the east.

They were hideous blotches against the flawless emerald-green of the Tristessan sky; and there in the west the Colonel saw a different sort of blemish, the harsh dark face of stark stony Shannakha, low and swollen and menacing on the horizon. What had gone wrong up there? What—even while they were in the midst of delicate negotiations—had led the Shannakhans to break the fragile peace?

The train had halted at some provincial station bordered on both sides by rolling crimson meadows. Somehow the Colonel found a communications terminal. Reaching Lanista on Shannakha proved impossible: no outgoing contact with other worlds was being allowed. But against all probability he did manage to get a call through to the rebel headquarters on Petra Hodesta, and, what was even less probable than that, Ilion Gabell himself came to the screen. His handsome features now had taken on a wild, almost bestial look: the curling golden mane was greasy and disheveled, the luminous, meditative eyes had a frenzied glaze, his lips were drawn back in a toothy grimace. He gave the Colonel a look of searing contempt. "No treachery, you said. What do you call this? They've invaded us everywhere at once. Without warning, without any declaration of hostilities. They must have been planning it for years."

"I assure you—"

"I know what your assurance is worth," Gabell said. "Well, mine is worth more. The reprisals have already begun, Colonel. And as for you—"

A blare of visual static sliced across the screen and it went black. "Hello?" the Colonel shouted. "Hello? Hello?"

The stationmaster, bald and plump and nearly as wild-eyed as Gabell had looked, appeared from a back room. The Colonel identified himself to him. He gaped at the Colonel in amazement and blurted, "There's an order out for your arrest. You and that other Imperium agent, both. You're supposed to be seized by anyone who finds you and turned over to the nearest officers of the republic."

"What republic is that?"

"Republic of Tristessa. Proclaimed three hours ago by Ilion Gabell. All enemies of the republic are supposed to be rounded up and—"

"Enemies of the republic?" the Colonel said, astonished. He wondered if he was going to have to kill him. But the plump stationmaster clearly had no appetite for playing policeman. He let his eye wander vaguely toward the open door to his left and shrugged, and made an ostentatious show of turning his attention away from the Colonel, busying himself with important-looking papers on his desk instead. The Colonel was out through the door in a moment.

He saw no option but to make his way to the capital and find whatever was left of the diplomatic community, which no doubt was attempting to get off Tristessa as quickly as possible, and get himself off with them. Something apocalyptic was going on here. The sky was black with smoke in every direction, now, and the drumroll of explosions came without a break, and frightful tongues of flame were leaping up from a town just beyond the field on his left. Was the whole planet under Shannakhan attack? But that made no sense. This place was Shannakha's property; destroying it by way of bringing it back under control was foolishness.

Gabell had spoken of reprisals. Was he the one behind the explosions?

It took the Colonel a week and a half to cover the hundred kilometers from the train station to the capital, a week and a half of little sleep and less food while he traversed a zigzag route through the devastated beauty of Gespinord Province, dodging anyone who might be affiliated with the rebels. That could be almost anybody, and was likely to be nearly everybody. A woman who gave him shelter one night told him of what the rebels were doing, the broken dams and torched granaries and poisoned fields, a war of Tristessa against itself that would leave the planet scarred for decades and worse than useless to its Shannakhan masters. At dawn she came to him and told him to go; he saw men wearing black rebel armbands entering the house on one side as he slipped away from it on the other.

He had three more such narrow escapes in the next four days. After the last of them he stayed away from inhabited areas entirely. He hurt his leg badly, slogging across a muddy lake. He cut his hand on a sharp palm frond and it became infected. He ate some unknown succulent-looking fruit and vomited for a day and a half. Skulking northward through swamps and over fresh ash heaps still warm from the torching, he started to experience the breaking down of his innate unquenchable vitality. The eternal self-restoring capacity of his many-times-rejuvenated body was no longer in evidence. A great weariness came over him, a sense of fatigue that approached a willingness to cease all striving and lie down forever. That was a new experience for him, and one that shocked him.

He began to feel his true age and then to feel older than his true age, a thousand years older, a million. He was ragged and dirty and lame and his throat was perpetually parched and there was a pounding against the right side of his skull in back that would not stop; and as he grew weaker and weaker with the passing days he began to think that he was going to die before much longer, not from some rebel's shot but only from the rigors of this journey, the fever and the chill and the hunger. He cursed Geryon Lanista a thousand times. Whatever Lanista had been up to on Shannakha, could he not have taken a moment to send his partner on Tristessa some warning that everything was on the verge of blowing up? Evidently not.

And then, at last, he stumbled into Gespinord City, where uniformed soldiers of Shannakha patrolled every street. He identified himself to one of them as a representative of the Imperium, and was taken to a makeshift dormitory in a school gymnasium where members of the diplomatic corps were being given refuge. There were about a dozen of them from five or six worlds, consular officials, mainly, who in ordinary times looked after the interests of tourists from their sectors of the galaxy that were holidaying on Tristessa. All the tourists were long gone, and the few officials who remained had stayed behind only to supervise the final stages of the evacuation of the planet. One of them, a woman from Thanda Bandanareen, saw to it that the Colonel was washed and fed and medicated, and afterward, when he had rested awhile, explained that the Tristessan Authority, which was the name under which the invaders from Shannakha were going, had ordered all outworlders to leave Tristessa at once. "I've been shipping people out for five days straight," she said, and the Colonel perceived for the first time that she was not much farther from exhaustion than he was himself. "There's no time to set coordinates. You go to the doorway and you step through and you work things out for yourself on the other side. Are you ready to go?"

"Now?"

"The sooner I get the last few stragglers out of here, the sooner I can go myself."

She led him to the doorway and, offering a word or two of thanks for her help, he entered its Velde field, a blind leap to anywhere, and came out, to his relief, on that glorious planet, Nabomba Zom, identifiable instantly by the astounding scarlet sea before him, which was shimmering with a violet glow as the first blue rays of morning struck its surface. There, in a guest lodge of the Imperium at the base of pale green mountains soft as velvet, the Colonel learned from a fellow member of the Service what had taken place on Shannakha.

It seemed that Geryon Lanista had badly overplayed his hand. For the sake of persuading the Shannakhans to adopt a more lenient Tristessa policy, Lanista had shown them forged documents indicating that Ilion Gabell's revolutionary army would not simply launch a rebellion on Tristessa if concessions weren't granted but would invade Shannakha itself. The Shannakhans had taken this fantasy seriously, much too seriously. Lanista had meant to worry them with it, but instead he terrified them; and in a frantic preemptive overreaction they hurriedly shipped an invading army to Tristessa to bring the troublesome colonists to heel. The worst-case scenario that Lanista had foreseen as a theoretical possibility, but did not seem to believe could happen, was going to occur.

The Colonel shook his head in disbelief. That Lanista—his own protegé—would have done anything so stupid was next to impossible to accept; that he would have done so without telling him that he had any such crazy tactic in mind was an unpardonable breach of Service methodology. That he had not sent word to the fellow officer whom he had left behind in harm's way on Tristessa that events in this planetary system had begun to slide toward a ghastly cataclysm as a result of his bizarrely clumsy maneuver was unforgivable for a different reason.

It seemed Gabell had been anticipating an invasion from Shannakha and had had a plan all ready for it: a scorched-earth program by which everything on Tristessa that was of value to Shannakha would be destroyed within hours after the arrival of Shannakhan invaders. One overreaction had led to another; by the end of the first week of war Tristessa was utterly ruined. Between the furious destructiveness of the rebels and the brutal repression of the rebellion by the invaders that had followed, nothing was left of Tristessa's plantations, its great estates, its hotels, its towns and cities, but ashes.

"And Lanista?" the Colonel asked leadenly. "Where is he?"

"Dead. By his own hand, it would seem, though that isn't a hundred percent certain. Either he was trying to get away from Shannakha in a tremendous hurry and accidentally made a mess out of his Velde coordinates, or else he deliberately scrambled up the coding so that he wouldn't be reassembled alive at his destination. Whichever it was, there wasn't very much left of him when he got there."

"You really believed I was dead?" Lanista asked.

"I *hoped* you were dead. I *wanted* you to be dead. But yes, yes, I believed you were dead, too. Why wouldn't I? They said you had gone into a doorway and come out in pieces someplace far away. Considering what you had managed to achieve on Shannakha, that was a completely appropriate thing to have done. So I accepted what they told me and I went on believing it for the next fifty years, until some bastard from the Imperium showed up at my house with proof that you were still alive."

"Believe me, I thought of killing myself. I imagined fifty different ways of doing it. Fifty *thousand*. But it wasn't in me to do a thing like that."

"A great pity, that," the Colonel said. "You allowed yourself to stay alive and you lived happily ever after."

"Not happily, no," said Lanista.

He had fled from Shannakha in a desperate delirious vertigo, he told the Colonel: aware of how badly awry it all had gone, frantic with shame and grief. There had been no attempt at a feigned suicide, he insisted. Whatever evidence the Service had found of such a thing was its own misinterpretation of something that had nothing to do with him. Fearing that the truth about the supposed Tristessan invasion would emerge, that the Shannakhans would discover that he had flagrantly misled them, he had taken advantage of the confusion of the moment to escape to the nearest world that had a Magellanic doorway and in a series of virtually unprogrammed hops had taken himself into some shadowy sector of the Rim where he had hidden himself away until at last he had felt ready to emerge, first under the Heinrich Bauer name, and then, as a result of some kind of clerical error, as *Martin* Bauer.

In the feverish final hours before the Shannakhan invasion began he had, he maintained, made several attempts to contact the Colonel on Tristessa and urge him to get away. But all communications lines between Shannakha and its colony-world had already been severed, and even the Imperium's own private communications channels failed him. He asked the Colonel to believe that that was true. He *begged* the Colonel to believe it. The Colonel had never seen Geryon Lanista begging for anything, before. Something about the haggard, insistent look that came into his eyes made his plea almost believable. He himself had been unable to get any calls through to Lanista on Shannakha; perhaps the systems were blocked in the other direction too. That was not something that needed to be resolved just at this moment. The Colonel put the question aside for later consideration. For fifty years the Colonel had believed that Lanista had deliberately left him to die in the midst of the Tristessa uprising, because he could not face the anger of the Colonel's rebuke for the clumsiness of what he had done on Shannakha. Perhaps he didn't need to believe that any longer. He would prefer not to believe it any longer; but it was too soon to tell whether he was capable of that.

"Tell me this," he said, when Lanista at last had fallen silent. "What possessed you to invent that business about a Tristessan invasion of Shannakha in the first place? How could you ever have imagined it would lead to anything constructive? And above all else, why didn't you try the idea out on me before you went off to Shannakha?"

Lanista was a long while in replying. At length he said, in a flat, low, dead voice, the voice of a headstrong child who is bringing himself to confess that he has done something shameful, "I wanted to surprise you."

"What?"

"To surprise you and to impress you. I wanted to out-Colonel the Colonel with a tremendous dramatic move that would solve the whole crisis in one quick shot. I would come back to Tristessa with a treaty that would pacify the rebels and keep the Shannakhans happy too, and everything would be sweetness and light again, and you would ask me how I had done it, and I would tell you and you would tell me what a genius I was." Lanista was looking directly at the Colonel with an unwavering gaze. "That was all there was to it. An idiotic young subaltern was fishing for praise from his superior officer and came up with a brilliant idea that backfired in the most appalling way. The rest of my life has been spent in an attempt to atone for what I did on Shannakha."

"Ah," the Colonel said. "That spoils it, that last little maudlin bit at the end of the confession. 'An attempt to atone'? Come off it, Geryon. Atoning by starting up a rebellion of your own? Against the Imperium, which you once had sworn to defend with your life?"

Icy fury instantly replaced the look of intense supplication in Lanista's eyes. "We all have our own notions of atonement, Colonel. I destroyed a world, or maybe two worlds, and since then I've been trying to build them. As for the Imperium, and whatever I may have sworn to it—"

"Yes?"

"The Imperium. The Imperium. The universal foe, the great force for galactic stagnation. I don't owe the Imperium a thing." He shook his head angrily. "Let it pass. You can't begin to see what I mean— The Imperium has sent you here, I gather. For what purpose? To work your old hocus-pocus on our little independence movement and bring me to heel the way you were trying to do with Ilion Gabell on Tristessa?"

"Essentially, yes."

"And how will you do it, exactly?" Lanista's face was suddenly bright with expectation. "Come on, Colonel, you can tell me! Consider it the old pro laying out his strategy one more time for the bumptious novice. Tell me. Tell me. The plan for neutralizing the revolution and restoring order."

The Colonel nodded. It would make no real difference, after all. "I can do two things. The evidence that you are Geryon Lanista and that you were responsible for the catastrophic outcome of the Tristessa rebellion is all fully archived and can quickly be distributed to all your fellow citizens here on Hermano. They might have a different view about your capability as a master schemer once they find out what a botch you made out of the Tristessa operation."

"They might. I doubt it very much, but they might.—What's the other thing you can do to us?"

"I can cut Hermano off from the Velde system. I have that power. The ultimate sanction: you may recall the term from your own Service days. I pass through the doorway and lock the door behind me, and Hermano is forever isolated from the rest of the galaxy. Or isolated until it begs to be allowed back in, and provides the Imperium with proof that it deserves to be."

"Will that please you, to cut us off like that?"

"What would please me is irrelevant. What would have pleased me would have been never to have had to come here in the first place. But here I am.—Of course, now that I've said all this, you can always prevent me from carrying any of it out. By killing me, for example."

Lanista smiled. "Why would I want to kill you? I've already got enough sins against you on my conscience, don't I? And I know as well as you do that the Imperium could cut us off from the Velde system from the outside any time it likes, and would surely do so if its clandestine operative fails to return safely from this mission. I'd wind up in the same position but with additional guilt to burden me. No, Colonel, I wouldn't kill you. But I do have a better idea."

The Colonel waited without replying.

"Cut us off from the Imperium, all right," Lanista said. "Lock the door, throw away the key. But stay here on the inside with us. There's no reason for you to go back to the Imperium, really. You've given the Imperium more than enough of your life as it is. And for what? Has serving the Imperium done anything for you except twisting your life out of shape? Certainly it twisted mine. It's twisted everybody's, but especially those of the people of the Service. All that meddling in interstellar politics— all that cynical tinkering with other people's governments—ah, no, no, Colonel, here at the end it's time for you to give all that up. Start your life over here on Hermano."

The Colonel was staring incredulously, wonderingly, bemusedly.

Lanista went on, "Your friends from Gavial can go home, but you stay here. You live out the rest of your days on Hermano. You can have a villa just like mine, twenty kilometers down the coast. The perfect retirement home, eh? Hermano's not the worst place in the universe to live. You'll have the servants you need. The finest food and wine. And an absolute guarantee that the Imperium will never bother you again. If you don't feel like retiring, you can have a post in the government here, a very high post, in fact. You and I could share the top place. I'd gladly make room for you. Who could know better than I do what a shrewd old bird you are? You'd be a vital asset for us, and we'd reward you accordingly.— What do you say, Colonel? Think it over. It's the best offer you'll ever get, I promise you that."

It was easiest to interpret what Lanista had said as a grotesque joke, but when the Colonel tried to shrug it away Lanista repeated it, more earnestly even than before. He realized that the man was serious. But, as though aware now that this conversation had gone on too long, Lanista suggested that the Colonel return to his own lodgings and rest for a time. They could talk again of these matters later. Until then he was always free to resume the identity of Petrus Haym of the Gavialese trade mission, and to go back to his four companions and continue to hatch out whatever schemes they liked involving commerce between Gavial and the Free Republic of Hermano.

He was unable to sleep for much of that night. So many revelations, so many possibilities. He hadn't been prepared for that much. None of the usual adjustments would work; but toward dawn sleep came, though only for a little while, and then he awoke suddenly, drenched in sweat, with sunlight pouring through his windows. Lanista's words still resounded in his mind. *The Imperium has twisted your life out of shape,* Lanista had said. Was that so? He remembered his grandfather saying, hundreds of years ago—thousands, it felt like—*The Imperium is the enemy, boy. It strangles us. It is the chain around our throats.* The boy who would become the Colonel had never understood what he meant by that, and when he came to adulthood he followed his father, who had said always that the Imperium was civilization's one bulwark against chaos, into the Service.

Well, perhaps his father had been right, and his grandfather as well. He had strapped on the armor of the Service of the Imperium and he had gone forth to do battle in its name, and done his duty unquestioningly throughout a long life, a very long life. And perhaps he had done enough, and it was time to let that armor drop away from him now. What had Lanista said of the Imperium? *The universal foe, the great force for galactic stagnation.* An angry man. Angry words. But there was some truth to them. His grandfather had said almost the same thing. An absentee government, enforcing conformity on an entire galaxy—

On that strange morning the Colonel felt something within him breaking up that had been frozen in place for a long time.

"What do you say?" Lanista asked, when the Colonel had returned to the small office with the desk and the chairs. "Will you stay here with us?"

"I have a home that I love on Galgala. I've lived there ever since my retirement."

"And will they let you live in peace, when you get back there to Galgala?"

"Who?"

"The people who sent you to find me and crush me," Lanista said. "The ones who came to you and said, *Go to a place called Hermano, Colonel. Put aside your retirement and do one more job for us.* They told you that a man you hate was making problems for them here and that you were the best one to deal with him, am I not right? And so you went, thinking you could help the good old Imperium out yet again and also come to grips with a little private business of your own. And they can send you out again, wherever else they feel like sending you, whenever they think you're the best one to deal with whatever needs dealing with."

"No," the Colonel said. "I'm an old man. I can't do anything more for them, and they won't ask. After all, I've failed them here. I was supposed to destroy this rebellion, and that won't happen now."

"Won't it?"

"You know that it won't," the Colonel said. He wondered whether he had ever intended to take any sort of action against the Hermano rebels. It was clear to him now that he had come here only for the sake of seeing Lanista once again and hearing his explanation of what had happened on Shannakha. Well, now he had heard it, and had managed to persuade himself that what Lanista had done on Shannakha had been merely to commit an error of judgment, which anyone can do, rather than to have sought to contrive the death of his senior officer for the sake of covering up his own terrible blunder. And now there was that strange sensation he was beginning to feel, that something that had been frozen for fifty years, or maybe for two hundred, was breaking up within him. He said, "Proclaim your damned independence, if you like. Cut yourselves off from the Imperium. It makes no difference to me. They should have sent someone else to do this job."

"Yes. They should have.—Will you stay?"

"I don't know."

"We're no longer of the Imperium and neither are you."

Lanista spoke once again of the villa by the sea, the servants, the wines, the place beside him in the high administration of the independent world of Hermano. The Colonel was barely listening. It would be easy enough to go home, he was thinking. Lanista wouldn't interfere with that. Hop, hop, hop, and Galgala again. His lovely house beside that golden river. His collection of memorabilia. The souvenirs of a life spent in the service of the Imperium, which is a chain about our throats. Home, yes, home to Galgala, to live alone within the security of the Imperium. The Imperium is the enemy of chaos, but chaos is the force that drives evolutionary growth.

"This is all real, what you're offering me?" he asked. "The villa, the servants, the government post?"

"All real, yes. Whatever you want."

"What about Magda Cermak and the other three?"

"What do you want done with them?"

"Send them home. Tell them that the talks are broken off and they have to go back to Gavial."

"Yes. I will."

"And what will you do about the doorways?"

"I'll seal them," Lanista said. "We don't need to be part of the Imperium. There was a time, you know, when Earth was the only world in the galaxy, when there was no Imperium at all, no Velde doorways either, and somehow Earth managed to get along for a few billion years without needing anything more than itself in the universe. We can do that too. The doorways will be sealed and the Imperium will forget all about Hermano."

"And all about me, too?" the Colonel asked.

"And all about you, yes."

The Colonel laughed. Then he walked to the window and saw that night had fallen, the radiant, fiery night of the Core, with a million million stars blazing in every direction he looked. The doorways would be sealed, but the galaxy still would be out there, filling the sky, and whenever he needed to see its multitude of stars he needed only to look upward. That seemed sufficient. He had traveled far and wide and the time was at hand, was more than at hand, for him to bring an end to his journeying. Well, so be it. So be it. No one would ever come looking for him here. No one would look for him anywhere; or, if looking, would never find. At the Service's behest he had returned to the stars one last time; and now, at no one's behest but his own, he had at last lost himself among them forever.

Defenders of the Frontier

From *Warriors*, March 2010

Seeker has returned to the fort looking flushed and exhilarated. "I was right," he announces. "There is one of them hiding quite close by. I was certain of it, and now I know where he is. I can definitely feel directionality this time."

Stablemaster, skeptical as always, lifts one eyebrow. "You were wrong the last time. You're always too eager these days to find them out there."

Seeker merely shrugs. "There can be no doubt," he says.

For three weeks now Seeker has been searching for an enemy spy—or straggler, or renegade, or whatever he may be—that he believes is camped in the vicinity of the fort. He has gone up to this hilltop and that one, to this watchtower and that, making his solitary vigil, casting forth his mind's net in that mysterious way of his that none of us can begin to fathom. And each time he has come back convinced that he feels enemy emanations, but he has never achieved a strong enough sense of directionality to warrant our sending out a search party. This time he has the look of conviction about him. Seeker is a small, flimsy sort of man, as his kind often tends to be, and much of the time in recent months he has worn the slump-shouldered look of dejection and disappointment. His trade is in finding enemies for us to kill. Enemies have been few and far between of late. But now he is plainly elated. There is an aura of triumph about him, of vindication.

Captain comes into the room. Instantly he sizes up the situation. "What have we here?" he says brusquely. "Have you sniffed out something at last, Seeker?"

"Come. I'll show you."

He leads us all out onto the flat roof adjacent to our barracks. To the right and left, the huge turreted masses of the eastern and western redoubts, now unoccupied, rise above us like vast pillars, and before us lies the great central courtyard, with the massive wall of tawny brick that guards us on the north beyond it. The fort is immense, an enormous sprawling edifice designed to hold ten thousand men. I remember very clearly the gigantic effort we expended in the building of it, twenty years before. Today just eleven occupants remain, and we rattle about it like tiny pebbles in a colossal jug.

Seeker gestures outward, into the gritty yellow wasteland that stretches before us like an endless ocean on the far side of the wall. That flat plain of twisted useless shrubs marks the one gap in the line of precipitous cliffs that forms the border here between Imperial territory and the enemy lands. It has been our task these twenty years past—we were born to it; it is an obligation of our caste—to guard that gap against the eventual incursion of the enemy army. For two full decades we have inhabited these lonely lands. We have fortified that gap, we have patrolled it, we have dedicated our lives to guarding it. In the old days entire brigades of enemy troops would attempt to breach our line, appearing suddenly like clouds of angry insects out of the dusty plain, and with great loss of life on both sides we would drive them back. Now things are quieter on this frontier, very much quieter indeed, but we are still here, watching for and intercepting the occasional spies that periodically attempt to slip past our defenses.

"There," says Seeker. "Do you see those three little humps over to the northeast? He's dug in not very far behind them. I know he is. I can feel him the way you'd feel a boil on the back of your neck."

"Just one man?" Captain asks.

"One. Only one."

Weaponsmaster says, "What would one man hope to accomplish? Do you think he expects to come tiptoeing into the fort and kill us one by one?"

"There's no need for us to try to understand them," Sergeant says. "Our job is to find them and kill them. We can leave understanding them to the wiser heads back home."

"Ah," says Armorer sardonically. "Back home, yes. Wiser heads."

Captain has walked to the rim of the roof and stands there with his back to us, clutching the rail and leaning forward into the dry, crisp wind that eternally blows across our courtyard. A sphere of impenetrable chilly silence seems to surround him. Captain has always been an enigmatic man, solitary and brooding, but he has become stranger than ever since the death of Colonel, three years past, left him the ranking officer of the fort. No one knows his mind now, and no one dares to attempt any sort of intimacy with it.

"Very well," he says, after an interval that has become intolerably long. "A four-man search party: Sergeant to lead, accompanied by Seeker, Provisioner, and Surveyor. Set out in the morning. Take three days' food. Search, find, and kill."

It has been eleven weeks since the last successful search mission. That one ended in the killing of three enemies, but since then, despite Seeker's constant efforts, there have been no signs of any hostile presence in our territory. Once, six or seven weeks back, Seeker managed to convince himself that he felt emanations coming from a site along the river, a strange place for an enemy to have settled because it was well within our defense perimeter, and a five-man party led by Stablemaster hastened out to look. But they found no one there except a little band of the Fisherfolk, who swore that they had seen nothing unusual thereabouts, and the fisherfolk do not lie. Upon their return Seeker himself had to admit that he no longer felt the emanations and that he was now none too certain he had felt any in the first place.

There is substantial feeling among us that we have outlived our mission here, that few if any enemies still occupy the territory north of the gap, that quite possibly the war has long since been over. Sergeant, Quartermaster, Weaponsmaster, and Armorer are the chief proponents of this belief. They note that we have heard nothing whatsoever from the capital in years—no messengers have come, let alone reinforcements or fresh supplies—and that we have had no sign from the enemy, either, that any significant force of them is gathered anywhere nearby. Once, long ago, war seemed imminent, and indeed real battles often took place. But it has been terribly quiet here for a long time. There has been nothing like a real battle for six years, only a few infrequent skirmishes with small enemy platoons, and during the past two years we have detected just a few isolated outliers, usually no more than two or three men at a time, whom we catch relatively easily as they try to infiltrate our territory. Armorer insists that they are not spies but stragglers, the last remnants of whatever enemy force once occupied the region to our north, who have been driven by hunger or loneliness or who knows what other compulsion to take up positions close to our fort. He argues that in the twenty years we have been here, our own numbers have dwindled from ten thousand men to a mere eleven, at first by losses in battle but later by the attrition of age and ill health, and he thinks it is reasonable that the same dwindling has occurred on the other side of the border, so that we few defenders now confront an enemy that may be even fewer in number than ourselves.

I myself see much to concur with in Armorer's position. I think it might very well be the case that we are a lost platoon, that the war is over and the Empire has forgotten us, and that there is no purpose at all in our continued vigilance. But if the Empire has forgotten us, who can give the order that withdraws us from our post? That is a decision that only Captain can make, and Captain has not given us the slightest impression of where he stands on the issue. And so we remain, and may remain to the end of our days. What folly that would be, says Armorer, to languish out here forever defending this forlorn frontier country against invaders that no longer choose to invade! And I half agree with him, but only half. I would not want to spend such time as remains to me working at a fool's task; but equally I do not wish to be guilty of dereliction of duty, after having served so long and so honorably on this frontier. Thus I am of two minds on the issue.

There is, of course, the opposite theory that holds that the enemy is simply biding its time, waiting for us to abandon the fort, after which a great army will come pouring through the gap at long last and strike at the Empire from one of its most vulnerable sides. Engineer and Signalman are the most vocal proponents of this viewpoint. They think it would be an act of profound treason to withdraw, the negation of all that we have dedicated our lives to, and they become irate when the idea is merely suggested. When they propound this position I find it hard to disagree.

Seeker is the one who works hardest to keep our mission alive, constantly striving to pick up threatening emanations. That has been his life's work, after all. He knows no other vocation, that sad little man. So day by day Seeker climbs his hilltops and haunts his watchtowers and uses his one gift to detect the presence of hostile minds, and now and then he returns and sounds the alarm, and off we go on yet another search foray. More often than not they prove to be futile, nowadays: either Seeker's powers are failing or he is excessively anxious to interpret his inputs as the mental output from nearby enemies.

I confess I feel a certain excitement at being part of this latest search party. Our days are spent in such terrible empty routine, normally. We tend our little vegetable patch, we look after our animals, we fish and hunt, we do our regular maintenance jobs, we read the same few books over and again, we have the same conversations, chiefly reminiscing about the time when there were more than eleven of us here, recalling as well as we can the robust and earthy characters who once dwelled among us but are long since gone to dust. Tonight, therefore, I feel a quickening of the pulse. I pack my gear for the morning, I eat my dinner with unusual gusto, I couple passionately with my little Fisherfolk companion. Each of us, all but Seeker, who seems to know no needs of that sort, has taken a female companion from among the band of simple people who live along our one feeble river. Even Captain takes one sometimes into his bed, I understand, although unlike the rest of us he has no regular woman. Mine is called Wendrit. She is a pale and slender creature, surprisingly skillful in the arts of love. The Fisherfolk are not quite human—we and they are unable to conceive children together, for example—but they are close enough to human to serve most purposes, and they are pleasant, unassuming, uncomplaining companions. So I embrace Wendrit vigorously this night, and in the dawn the four of us gather, Sergeant, Provisioner, Seeker, and I, by the northern portcullis.

It is a bright, clear morning, the sun a hard, sharp-edged disk in the eastern sky. The sun is the only thing that comes to us from the Empire, visiting us each day after it has done its work back there, uncountable thousands of miles to the east. Probably the capital is already in darkness by now, just as we are beginning our day. The world is so large, after all, and we are so very far from home.

Once there would have been trumpeters to celebrate our departure as we rode through the portcullis, hurling a brassy fanfare for us into the quiet air. But the last of our trumpeters died years ago, and though we still have the instruments, none of us knows how to play them. I tried once, and made a harsh squeaking sound like the grinding of metal against metal, nothing more. So the only sound we hear as we ride out into the desert is the soft steady thudding of our mounts' hooves against the brittle sandy soil.

In truth this is the bleakest of places, but we are used to it. I still have memories from my childhood of the floral splendor of the capital, great trees thick with juicy leaves, and shrubs clad in clusters of flowers, red and yellow and orange and purple, and the dense green lawns of the grand boulevards. But I have grown accustomed to the desert, which has become the norm for me, and such lush abundance as I remember out of my earlier life strikes me now as discomfortingly vulgar and excessive, a wasteful riot of energy and resources. All that we have here in the plain that runs out to the north between the wall of hills is dry yellow soil sparkling with the doleful sparkle of overabundant quartz, small, gnarled shrubs and equally gnarled miniature trees, and occasional tussocks of tough, sharp-edged grass. On the south side of the fort the land is not quite so harsh, for our little river runs past us there, a weak strand of some much mightier one that must pour out of one of the big lakes in the center of the continent. Our river must be looking for the sea, as rivers do, but of course we are nowhere near the sea, and doubtless it exhausts itself in some distant reach of the desert. But as it passes our outpost it brings greenery to its flanks, and some actual trees, and enough fish to support the tribe of primitive folk who are our only companions here.

Our route lies to the northeast, toward those three rounded hillocks behind which, so Seeker staunchly asserts, we will find the campsite of our solitary enemy. The little hills had seemed close enough when we viewed them from the barracks roof, but that was only an illusion, and we ride all day without visibly diminishing the span between them and us. It is a difficult trek. The ground, which is merely pebbly close by the fort, becomes rocky and hard to traverse farther out, and our steeds pick their way with care, heedful of their fragile legs. But this is familiar territory for us. Everywhere we see traces of hoofprints or tire tracks, five years old, ten, even twenty, the scars of ancient forays, the debris of half-forgotten battles of a decade and more ago. Rain comes perhaps twice a year here at best. Make a mark on the desert floor and it remains forever.

We camp as the first lengthening of the shadows begins, gather some scrubby wood for our fire, pitch our tent. There is not much in the way of conversation. Sergeant is a crude, inarticulate man at best; Seeker is too tense and fretful to be pleasant company; Provisioner, who has grown burly and red-faced with the years, can be jovial enough after a drink or two, but he seems uncharacteristically moody and aloof tonight. So I am left to my own resources, and once we have finished our meal I walk out a short way into the night and stare, as I often do, at the glittering array of stars in this western sky of ours, wondering, as ever, whether each has its own collection of worlds, and whether those worlds are peopled, and what sort of lives the peoples of those worlds might lead. It is a perverse sort of amusement, I suppose: I who have spent half my life guarding a grim brick fort in this parched isolated outpost stare at the night sky and imagine the gleaming palaces and fragrant gardens of faraway worlds.

We rise early, make a simple breakfast, ride on through a cutting wind toward those three far-off hills. This morning, though, the perspective changes quickly: suddenly the hills are much closer, and then they are upon us, and Seeker, excited now, guides us toward the pass between the southernmost hill and its neighbor. "I feel him just beyond!" he cries. For Seeker, the sense that he calls directionality is like a compass, pointing the way toward our foes. "Come! This is the way! Hurry! Hurry!"

Nor has he led us wrongly this time. On the far side of the southernmost hill someone has built a little lean-to of twisted branches covered with a heaping of grass, no simple project in these stony ungenerous wastes. We draw our weapons and take up positions surrounding it, and Sergeant goes up to it and says, "You! Come out of there, and keep your hands in the air!"

There is a sound of stirring from within. In a moment or two a man emerges.

He has the classic enemy physiognomy: a short, stumpy body, sallow waxen skin, and heavy features with jutting cheekbones and icy blue eyes. At the sight of those eyes I feel an involuntary surge of anger, even hatred, for we of the Empire are a brown-eyed people and I have trained myself through many years to feel nothing but hostility for those whose eyes are blue.

But these are not threatening eyes. Obviously the man had been asleep, and he is still making the journey back into wakefulness as he comes forth from his shelter, blinking, shaking his head. He is trembling, too. He is one man and we are four, and we have weapons drawn and he is unarmed, and he has been taken by surprise. It is an unfortunate way to start one's day. I am amazed to find my anger giving way to something like pity.

He is given little time to comprehend the gravity of his situation. "Bastard!" Sergeant says, and takes three strides forward. Swiftly he thrusts his knife into the man's belly, withdraws it, strikes again, again.

The blue eyes go wide with shock. I am shocked myself, in a different way, and the sudden cruel attack leaves me gasping with amazement.

The stricken enemy staggers, clutches at his abdomen as though trying to hold back the torrent of blood, takes three or four tottering steps, and falls in a series of folding ripples. There is a convulsion or two, and then he is still, lying face downward.

Sergeant kicks the entrance of the shelter open and peers within. "See if there's anything useful in there," he tells us.

Still astounded, I say, "Why did you kill him so quickly?"

"We came here to kill him."

"Perhaps. But he was unarmed. He probably would have given himself up peacefully."

"We came here to kill him," Sergeant says again.

"We might have interrogated him first, at least. That's the usual procedure, isn't it? Perhaps there are others of his kind somewhere close at hand."

"If there were any more of them around here," Sergeant says scornfully, "Seeker would have told us, wouldn't he have? Wouldn't he have, Surveyor?"

There is more that I would like to say, about how it might have been useful or at any rate interesting to discover why this man had chosen to make this risky pilgrimage to the edge of our territory. But there is no point in continuing the discussion, because Sergeant is too stupid to care what I have to say, and the man is already dead, besides.

We knock the shelter apart and search it. Nothing much there: a few tools and weapons, a copper-plated religious emblem of the kind that our enemies worship, a portrait of a flat-faced blue-eyed woman who is, I suppose, the enemy's wife or mother. It does not seem like the equipment of a spy. Even to an old soldier like me it is all very sad. He was a man like us, enemy though he was, and he died far from home. Yes, it has long been our task to kill these people before they can kill us. Certainly I have killed more than a few of them myself. But dying in battle is one thing; being slaughtered like a pig while still half asleep is something else again. Especially if your only purpose had been to surrender. Why else had this solitary man, this lonely and probably desperate man, crossed this unrelenting desert, if not to give himself up to us at the fort?

I am softening with age, I suppose. Sergeant is right that it was our assignment to kill him: Captain had given us that order in the most explicit way. Bringing him back with us had never been part of the plan. We have no way of keeping prisoners at the fort. We have little enough food for ourselves, and guarding him would have posed a problem. He had had to die; his life was forfeit from the moment he ventured within the zone bordering on the fort. That he might have been lonely or desperate, that he had suffered in crossing this terrible desert and perhaps had hoped to win shelter at our fort, that he had had a wife or perhaps a mother whom he loved, all of that was irrelevant. It did not come as news to me that our enemies are human beings not all that different from us except in the color of their eyes and the texture of their skins. They are, nevertheless, our enemies. Long ago they set their hands against us in warfare, and until the day arrives when they put aside their dream of destroying what we of the Empire have built for ourselves, it is the duty of people like us to slay men like him. Sergeant had not been kind or gentle about it. But there is no kind or gentle way, really, to kill.

The days that followed were extremely quiet ones. Without so much as a discussion of what had taken place in the desert we fell back into our routines: clean and polish this and that, repair whatever needs repair and still can be repaired, take our turns working in the fields alongside the river, wade in that shallow stream in quest of water-pigs for our table, tend the vats where we store the mash that becomes our beer, and so on, so forth, day in, day out. Of course I read a good deal, also. I have ever been a man for reading.

We have nineteen books; all the others have been read to pieces, or their bindings have fallen apart in the dry air, or the volumes have simply been misplaced somewhere about the fort and never recovered. I have read all nineteen again and again, even though five of them are technical manuals covering areas that never were part of my skills and which are irrelevant now anyway. (There is no point in knowing how to repair our vehicles when the last of our fuel supply was exhausted five years ago.) One of my favorite books is The Saga of the Kings, which I have known since childhood, the familiar account, probably wholly mythical, of the Empire's early history, the great charismatic leaders who built it, their heroic deeds, their inordinately long lifespans. There is a religious text too that I value, though I have grave doubts about the existence of the gods. But for me the choice volume of our library is the one called *The Register of Strange Things Beyond the Ranges*, a thousand-year-old account of the natural wonders to be found in the outer reaches of the Empire's great expanse. Only half the book remains to us now—perhaps one of my comrades ripped pages out to use as kindling, once upon a time—but I cherish that half, and read it constantly, even though I know it virtually by heart by this time.

Wendrit likes me to read to her. How much of what she hears she is capable of understanding, I have no idea: she is a simple soul, as all her people are. But I love the way she turns her big violet-hued eyes toward me as I read, and sits in total attention.

I read to her of the Gate of Ghosts, telling her of the customs shed there that spectral phantoms guard: "Ten men go out, nine men return." I read to her of the Stones of Shao, two flat-sided slabs flanking a main highway that on a certain day every ten years would come crashing together, crushing any wayfarers who happened to be passing through just then, and of the bronze Pillars of King Mai, which hold the two stones by an incantation that forbids them ever to move again. I read to her of the Mountain of a Thousand Eyes, the granite face of which is pockmarked with glossy onyx boulders that gleam down upon passersby like stern black eyes. I tell her of the Forest of Cinnamon, and of the Grotto of Dreams, and of the Place of Galloping Clouds. Were such places real, or simply the fantasies of some ancient spinner of tall tales? How would I know, I who spent my childhood and youth at the capital, and have passed the rest of my years here at this remote desert fort, where there is nothing to be seen but sandy yellow soil, and twisted shrubs, and little scuttering scorpions that run before our feet? But the strange places described in *The Register of Strange Things Beyond the Ranges* have grown more real to me in these latter days than the capital itself, which has become in my mind a mere handful of vague and fragmentary impressions. So I read with conviction, and Wendrit listens in awe, and when I weary of the wonders of the *Register* I put it aside and take her hand and lead her to my bed, and caress her soft pale-green skin and kiss the tips of her small round breasts, and so we pass another night.

In those quiet days that followed our foray I thought often of the man Sergeant had killed. In the days when we fought battles here I killed without compunction, five, ten, twenty men at a time, not exactly taking pleasure in it but certainly feeling no guilt. But the killing in those days was done at a decent distance, with rifles or heavy guns, for we still had ammunition then and our rifles and guns were still in good repair. It was necessary now in our forays against the occasional spies who approached the fort to kill with spears or knives, and to kill at close range feels less like a deed of warfare to me and more like murder.

My mind went back easily to those battles of yesteryear: the sound of the sentry's alarm, the first view of the dark line of enemy troops on the horizon, the rush to gather our weapons and start our vehicles. And out we would race through the portcullis to repel the invaders, rushing to take up our primary defensive formation, then advancing in even ranks that filled the entire gap in the hills, so that when the enemy entered that deadly funnel we could fall upon them and slaughter them. It was the same thing every time. They came; we responded; they perished. How far they must have traveled to meet their dismal deaths in our dreary desert! None of us had any real idea how far away the country of the enemy actually was, but we knew it had to be a great distance to the north and west, just as our own country is a great distance to the south and east. The frontier that our own outpost defends lies on the midpoint between one desert and another. Behind us is the almost infinite terrain of sparse settlements that eventually culminates in the glorious cities of the Empire. Before us are equally interminable wastes that gives way, eventually, to the enemy homeland itself. For one nation to attack the other, it must send its armies far across an uncharted and unfriendly nothingness. Which our enemy was willing to do, the gods only knew why, and again and again their armies came, and again and again we destroyed them in the fine frenzy of battle. That was a long time ago. We were not much more than boys then. But finally the marching armies came no more, and the only enemies we had to deal with were those few infrequent spies or perhaps stragglers whom Seeker pinpointed for us, and whom we went out and slew at close range with our knives and spears, looking into their frosty blue eyes as we robbed them of their lives.

Seeker is in a bad way. He can go from one day to the next without saying a word. He still heads up to his watchtowers almost every morning, but he returns from his vigils in a black cloak of gloom and moves through our midst in complete silence. We know better than to approach him at such times, because, though he is a man of no great size and strength, he can break out in savage fury sometimes when his depressions are intruded upon. So we let him be; but as the days pass and his mood grows ever darker, we fear some sort of explosion.

One afternoon I saw him speaking with Captain out on the rooftop terrace. It appeared that Captain had initiated the conversation, and that Seeker was answering Captain's questions with the greatest reluctance, staring down at his boots as he spoke. But then Captain said something that caused Seeker to react with surprising animation, looking up, gesticulating. Captain shook his head. Seeker pounded his fists together. Captain made a gesture of dismissal and walked away.

What they were saying to each other was beyond all guessing. And beyond all asking, too, for if anyone is more opaque than Seeker, it is Captain, and while it is at least possible at certain times to ask Seeker what is on his mind, making such an inquiry of Captain is inconceivable.

In recent days Seeker has taken to drinking with us after dinner. That is a new thing for him. He has always disliked drinking. He says he despises the stuff we make that we call beer and wine and brandy. That is reasonable enough, because we make our beer from the niggardly sour grain of a weed that grows by the river, and we wrest our thin wine and our rough brandy from the bitter gray fruits of a different weed, and they are pitiful products indeed to anyone who remembers the foaming beers of the capital and the sweet vintages of our finest wine-producing districts. But we have long since exhausted the supplies of such things that we brought with us, and, of course, no replenishments from home ever come, and, since in this somber landscape there is comfort to be had from drinking, we drink what we can make. Not Seeker, no. Not until this week.

Now he drinks, though, showing no sign of pleasure, but often extending his glass for another round. And at last one night when he has come back with his glass more than once, he breaks his long silence.

"They are all gone," he says, in a voice like the tolling of a cracked bell.

"Who are?" Provisioner asks. "The scorpions? I saw three scorpions only yesterday." Provisioner is well along in his cups, as usual. His reddened, jowly face creases in a broad toothy smile, as if he has uttered the cleverest of witticisms.

"The enemy," says Seeker. "The one we killed—he was the last one. There's nobody left. Do you know how empty I feel, going up to the towers to listen, and hearing nothing? As if I've been hollowed out inside. Can you understand what sort of feeling that is? Can you? No, of course you can't. What would any of you know?" He stares at us in agony. "The silence . . . the silence . . ."

Nobody seems to know how quite to respond to that, so we say nothing. And Seeker helps himself to yet another jigger of brandy, and full measure at that. This is alarming. The sight of Seeker drinking like this is as strange as the sight of a torrential downpour of rain would be.

Engineer, who is probably the calmest and most reasonable of us, says, "Ah, man, can you not be a bit patient? I know you want to do your task. But more of them will come. Sooner or later, there'll be another, and another after that. Two weeks, three, six, who knows? But they'll come. You've been through spells like this before."

"No. This is different," says Seeker sullenly. "But what would you know?"

"Easy," Engineer says, laying his strong hand across the back of Seeker's frail wrist. "Go easy, man. What do you mean, 'this is different?'"

Carefully, making a visible effort at self-control, Seeker says, "All the other times when we've gone several weeks between incursions, I've always felt a low inner hum, a kind of subliminal static, a barely perceptible mental pressure, that tells me there are at least a few enemies out there somewhere, a hundred miles away, five hundred, a thousand.

It's just a kind of quiet buzz. It doesn't give me any directionality. But it's there, and sooner or later the signal becomes stronger, and then I know that a couple of them are getting close to us, and then I get directionality and I can lead us to them, and we go out and kill them. It's been that way for years, ever since the real battles stopped. But now I don't get anything. Not a thing. It's absolutely silent in my head. Which means that either I've lost my power entirely, or else there aren't any enemies left within a thousand miles or more."

"And which is it that you think is so?"

Seeker scans us all with a haggard look. "That there are no enemies out there anymore. Which means that it is pointless to remain here. We should pack up, go home, make some sort of new lives for ourselves within the Empire itself. And yet we have to stay, in case they come. I must stay, because this is the only task that I know how to perform. What sort of new life could I make for myself back there? I never had a life. This is my life. So my choice is to stay here to no purpose, performing a task that does not need to be performed any longer, or to return home to no existence. Do you see my predicament?" He is shivering. He reaches for the brandy, pours yet another drink with a trembling hand, hastily downs it, coughs, shudders, lets his head drop to the tabletop. We can hear him sobbing.

That night marks the beginning of the debate among us. Seeker's breakdown has brought into the open something that has been on my own mind for some weeks now, and which Armorer, Weaponsmaster, Quartermaster, and even dull-witted Sergeant have been pondering also, each in his own very different way.

The fact is unanswerable that the frequency of enemy incursions has lessened greatly in the past two years, and when they do come, every five or six or ten weeks apart, they no longer come in bands of a dozen or so, but in twos or threes. This last man whom Sergeant slew by the three little hills had come alone. Armorer has voiced quite openly his notion that just as our own numbers have dwindled to next to nothing over the years, the enemy confronting us in this desert must have suffered great attrition too, and, like us, has had no reinforcement from the home country, so that only a handful of our foes remain—or, perhaps, as Seeker now believes, none at all. If that is true, says Armorer, who is a wry and practical man, why do we not close up shop and seek some new occupation for ourselves in some happier region of the Empire?

Sergeant, who loves the excitement of warfare, for whom combat is not an ugly necessity but an act of passionate devotion, shares Armorer's view that we ought to move along. It is not so much that inactivity makes him restless—restlessness is not a word that really applies to a wooden block of a man like Sergeant—but that, like Seeker, he lives only to perform his military function. Seeker's function is to seek and Sergeant's function is to kill, and Seeker now feels that he will seek forever here and nevermore find, and Sergeant, in his dim way, believes that for him to stay here any longer would be a waste of his capability. He too wants to leave.

As does Weaponsmaster, who has had no weapons other than knives and spears to care for since our ammunition ran out and thus passes his days in a stupefying round of makework, and Quartermaster, who once presided over the material needs of ten thousand men and now, in his grizzled old age, lives the daily mockery of looking after the needs of just eleven. Thus we have four men—Armorer, Sergeant, Weaponsmaster, Quartermaster—fairly well committed to bringing the life of this outpost to an end, and one more, Seeker, who wants both to go and to stay. I am more or less of Seeker's persuasion here myself, aware that we are living idle and futile lives at the fort but burdened at the same time with a sense of obligation to my profession that leads me to regard an abandonment of the fort as a shameful act. So I sway back and forth. When Armorer speaks, I am inclined to join his faction. But when one of the others advocates remaining here, I drift back in that direction.

Gradually it emerges in our circular nightly discussion that the other four of us are strongly committed to staying. Engineer enjoys his life here: there are always technical challenges for him, a new canal to design, a parapet in need of repair, a harness to mend. He also is driven by a strong sense of duty and believes it is necessary to the welfare of the Empire that we remain here. Stablemaster, less concerned about duty, is fond of his beasts and similarly has no wish to leave. Provisioner, who is rarely given to doubts of any sort, would be content to remain so long as our supply of food and drink remains ample, and that appears to be the case. And Signalman still believes, Seeker's anguish to the contrary, that the desert beyond the wall is full of patient foes who will swarm through the gap and march against the capital like ravening beasts the moment we relinquish the fort.

Engineer, who is surely the most rational of us, has raised another strong point in favor of staying. We have scarcely any idea of how to get home. Twenty years ago we were brought here in a great convoy, and who among us bothered to take note of the route we traversed? Even those who might have paid attention to it then have forgotten almost every detail of the journey. But we do have a vague general idea of the challenge that confronts us. Between us and the capital lies, first of all, a great span of trackless dry wasteland and then forested districts occupied by autonomous savage tribes. Uncharted and, probably, well-nigh impenetrable tropical jungles are beyond those, and no doubt we would encounter a myriad other hazards. We have no maps of the route. We have no working communications devices. "If we leave here, we might spend the rest of our lives wandering around hopelessly lost in the wilderness," Engineer says. "At least here we have a home, women, something to eat and a place to sleep."

I raise another objection. "You all speak as though this is something we could just put to a vote. 'Raise hands, all in favor of abandoning the fort.'"

"If we did take a vote," Armorer says, "We'd have a majority in favor of getting out of here. You, me, Sergeant, Quartermaster, Weaponsmaster, Seeker—that's six out of eleven, even if Captain votes the other way."

"No. I'm not so sure I'm with you. I don't think Seeker is, either. Neither of us has really made up his mind." We all looked toward Seeker; but Seeker was asleep at the table, lost in winy stupor. "So at best we're equally divided right now, four for leaving, four for staying, and two undecided. But in any case this place isn't a democracy and how we vote doesn't matter. Whether we leave the fort is something for Captain to decide, and Captain alone. And we don't have any idea what his feelings are."

"We could ask him," Armorer suggests.

"Ask my elbow," Provisioner says, guffawing. "Who wants to ask Captain anything? The man who does will get a riding crop across the face."

There is general nodding around the table. We all have tasted Captain's unpredictable ferocity.

Quartermaster says, "If we had a majority in favor of going home, we could all go to him and tell him how we feel. He won't try to whip us all. For all we know, he might even tell us that he agrees with us."

"But you don't have a majority," Engineer points out.

Quartermaster looks toward me. "Come over to our side, Surveyor. Surely you see there's more merit in our position than in theirs. That would make it five to four for leaving."

"And Seeker?" Engineer asks. "When he sobers up, what if he votes the other way? That would make it a tie vote again."

"We could ask Captain to break the tie, and that would settle the whole thing," Armorer says.

That brings laughter from us all. Captain is very sensitive to anything that smacks of insubordination. Even the dullest of us can see that he will not react well to hearing that we are trying to determine a serious matter of policy by majority vote.

I lie awake for hours that night, replaying our discussion in my mind. There are strong points on both sides. The idea of giving up the fort and going home has great appeal. We are all getting along in years; at best each of us has ten or fifteen years left to him, and do I want to spend those years doing nothing but hunting water-pigs in the river and toiling over our scrawny crops and re-reading the same handful of books? I believe Seeker when he says that the man we killed a few weeks ago was the last of the enemy in our territory.

On the other hand there is the question of duty. What are we to say when we show up in the capital? Simply announce that by our own authority we have abandoned the outpost to which we have devoted our lives, merely because in our opinion there is no further need for us to stay on at it? Soldiers are not entitled to opinions. Soldiers who are sent to defend a frontier outpost have no option but to defend that outpost until orders to the contrary are received.

To this argument I oppose another one, which is that duty travels both ways. We might be abandoning our fort, an improper thing for soldiers to be doing, but is it not true that the Empire has long ago abandoned us? There has been no word from home for ages. Not only have we had no reinforcements or fresh supplies from the Empire, there has not been so much as an inquiry. They have forgotten we exist. What if the war ended years ago and nobody at the capital has bothered to tell us that? How much do we owe an Empire that does not remember our existence?

And, finally, there is Engineer's point that going home might be impossible anyway, for we have no maps, no vehicles, no clear idea of the route we must follow, and we know that we are an almost unimaginable distance from any civilized district of the Empire. The journey will be a terrible struggle, and we may very well perish in the course of it. For me, in the middle of the night, that is perhaps the most telling point of all.

I realize, as I lie there contemplating these things, that Wendrit is awake beside me, and that she is weeping.

"What is it?" I asked. "Why are you crying?"

She is slow to answer. I can sense the troubled gropings of her mind. But at length she says, between sobs, "You are going to leave me. I heard things. I know. You will leave and I will be alone."

"No," I tell her, before I have even considered what I am saying. "No, that isn't true. I won't leave. And if I do, I'll take you with me. I promise you that, Wendrit." And I pull her into my arms and hold her until she is no longer sobbing.

I awaken knowing that I have made my decision, and it is the decision to go home. Along with Armorer, Sergeant, Weaponsmaster, and Stablemaster, I believe now that we should assemble whatever provisions we can, choose the strongest of our beasts to draw our carts, and, taking our women with us, set out into the unknown. If the gods favor our cause we will reach the Empire eventually, request retirement from active duty, and try to form some sort of new lives for ourselves in what no doubt is a nation very much altered from the one we left behind more than twenty years ago.

That night, when we gather over our brandy, I announce my conversion to Armorer's faction. But Seeker reveals that he, too, has had an epiphany in the night, which has swung him to the other side: weak and old as he is, he fears the journey home more than he does living out the rest of his life in futility at the fort. So we still are stalemated, now five to five, and there is no point in approaching Captain, even assuming that Captain would pay the slightest attention to our wishes.

Then there is an event that changes everything. It is the day of our weekly pig-hunt, when four or five of us don our high boots and go down to the river with spears to refresh our stock of fresh meat. The water-pigs that dwell in the river are beasts about the size of cattle, big sleek purple things with great yellow tusks, very dangerous when angered but also very stupid. They tend to congregate just upriver from us, where a bend in the flow creates a broad pool thick with water-plants, on which they like to forage. Our hunting technique involves cutting one beast out of the herd with proddings of our spears and moving him downriver, well apart from the others, so that we can kill him in isolation, without fear of finding ourselves involved in a chaotic melee with seven or eight furious pigs snapping at us from all sides at once. The meat from a single pig will last the eleven of us a full week, sometimes more.

Today the hunting party is made up of Provisioner, Signalman, Weaponsmaster, Armorer, and me. We are all skilled hunters and work well together. As soon as the night's chill has left the air we go down to the river and march along its banks to the water-pig pool, choose the pig that is to be our prey, and arrange ourselves along the bank so that we will be in a semicircular formation when we enter the water. We will slip between the lone pig and the rest of his fellows and urge him away from them, and when we think it is safe to attack, we will move in for the kill.

At first everything goes smoothly. The river is hip-deep here. We form our arc, we surround our pig, we nudge him lightly with the tips of our spears. His little, red-rimmed eyes glower at us in fury and we can hear the low rumblings of his annoyance, but the half—submerged animal pulls back from the pricking without attempting to fight, and we prod him twenty, thirty, forty feet downstream, toward the killing-place. As usual, a few Fisherfolk have gathered on the bank to watch us, though there is, as ever, a paradoxical incuriosity about their bland stares.

And then, catastrophe. "Look out!" cries Armorer, and in the same moment I become aware of the water churning wildly behind me, and I see two broad purple backs breaching the surface of the river, and I realize that this time other pigs—at least a couple, maybe more, who knows?—have followed on downstream with our chosen one and intend to defend their grazing grounds against our intrusion. It is the thing we have always dreaded but never experienced, the one serious danger in these hunts. The surface of the water thrashes and boils. We see pigs leaping frenetically on all sides of us. The river is murky at best, but now, with maddened water-pigs snorting and snuffling all about us, we have no clear idea of what is happening, except that we have lost control of the situation and are in great jeopardy.

"Out of the water, everybody!" Weaponsmaster yells, but we are already scrambling for the riverbank. I clamber up, lean on my spear, catch my breath. Weaponsmaster and Armorer stand beside me. Provisioner has gone to the opposite bank. But there is no sign of Signalman, and the river suddenly is red with blood, and great, yellow-tusked pig-snouts are jutting up everywhere, and then Signalman comes floating to the surface, belly upward, his body torn open from throat to abdomen.

We carry him back borne on our shoulders, like a fallen hero. It is our first death in some years. Somehow we had come to feel, in the time that has elapsed since that one, that we eleven who still remain would go on and on together forever, but now we know that that is not so. Weaponsmaster brings the news to Captain, and reports back to us that that stony implacable man had actually seemed to show signs of real grief upon hearing of Signalman's death. Engineer and Provisioner and I dig the grave, and Captain presides over the service, and for several days there is a funereal silence around the fort.

Then, once the shock of the death has begun to ebb a little, Armorer raises the point that none of us had cared to mention openly since the event at the river. Which is, that with Signalman gone the stalemate has been broken. The factions stand now at five for setting out for home, four for remaining indefinitely at the fort. And Armorer is willing to force the issue on behalf of the majority by going to Captain and asking whether he will authorize an immediate retreat from the frontier.

For hours there is an agitated discussion, verging sometimes into bitterness and rage. We all recognize that it must be one way or another, that we cannot divide: a little group of four or five would never be able to sustain itself at the fort, nor would the other group of about the same size have any hope of success in traversing the unknown lands ahead. We must all stay together or assuredly we will all succumb; but that means that the four who would remain must yield to the five who wish to leave, regardless of their own powerful desires in the matter. And the four who would be compelled to join the trek against their wishes are fiercely resentful of the five who insist on departure.

In the end things grow calmer and we agree to leave the decision to Captain, in whose hands it belongs anyway. A delegation of four is selected to go to him: Engineer and Stablemaster representing those who would stay, and Armorer and me to speak for the other side.

Captain spends most of his days in a wing of the fort that the rest of us rarely enter. There, at a huge ornate desk in an office big enough for ten men, he studies piles of documents left by his predecessors as commanding officer, as though hoping to learn from the writings of those vanished colonels how best to carry out the responsibilities that the vagaries of time have placed upon his shoulders. He is a brawny, dour-faced man, thin-lipped and somber-eyed, with dense black eyebrows that form a single forbidding line across his forehead, and even after all these years he is a stranger to us all.

He listens to us in his usual cold silence as we set forth the various arguments: Seeker's belief that there are no more enemies for us to deal with here, Armorer's that we are absolved of our duty to the Empire by its long neglect of us, Engineer's that the journey home would be perilous to the point of foolhardiness, and Signalman's, offered on his behalf by Stablemaster, that the enemy is simply waiting for us to go and then will launch its long-awaited campaign of conquest in Imperial territory. Eventually we begin to repeat ourselves and realize that there is nothing more to say, though Captain has not broken his silence by so much as a single syllable. The last word is spoken by Armorer, who tells Captain that five of us favor leaving, four remaining, though he does not specify who holds which position.

Telling him that strikes me as a mistake. It implies—rightly—that a democratic process has gone on among us, and I expect Captain to respond angrily to the suggestion that any operational issue here can be decided, or even influenced, by a vote of the platoon. But there is no thunderstorm of wrath. He sits quietly, still saying nothing, for an almost unendurable span of time. Then he says, in a surprisingly moderate tone, "Seeker is unable to pick up any sign of enemy presence?" He addresses the question to Engineer, whom, apparently, he has correctly identified as one of the leaders of the faction favoring continued residence at the fort.

"This is so," Engineer replies.

Captain is silent once again. But finally he says, to our universal amazement, "The thinking of those who argue for withdrawal from the frontier is in line with my own. I have considered for some time now that our services in this place are no longer required by the Empire, and that if we are to be of use to the country at all, we must obtain reassignment elsewhere."

It is, I think, the last thing any of us had expected. Armorer glows with satisfaction. Engineer and Stablemaster look crestfallen. I, ambivalent even now, simply look at Captain in surprise.

Captain goes on, "Engineer, Stablemaster, make plans for our departure at the soonest possible date. I stipulate one thing, though: we go as a group, with no one to remain behind, and we must stay together as one group throughout what I know will be a long and arduous journey. Anyone who attempts to leave the group will be considered a deserter and treated accordingly. I will request that you all take an oath to that effect."

That is what we had agreed among ourselves to do anyway, so there is no difficulty about it. Nor do our four recalcitrants indicate any opposition to the departure order, though Seeker is plainly terrified of the dangers and stress of the journey. We begin at once to make our plans for leaving.

It turns out that we do have some maps of the intervening territory after all. Captain produces them from among his collection of documents, along with two volumes of a chronicle of our journey from the capital to the frontier that the first Colonel had kept. He summons me and gives me this material, ordering me to consult it and devise a plan of route for our journey.

But I discover quickly that it is all useless. The maps are frayed and cracked along their folds, and such information as they once might have held concerning the entire center of the continent has faded into invisibility. I can make out a bold star-shaped marker indicating the capital down in the lower right-hand corner, and a vague, ragged line indicating the frontier far off to the left, and just about everything between is blank. Nor is the old Colonel's chronicle in any way helpful. The first volume deals with the organization of the expeditionary force and the logistical problems involved in transporting it from the capital to the interior. The second volume that we have, which is actually the third of the original three, describes the building of the fort and the initial skirmishes with the enemy. The middle volume is missing, and that is the one, I assume, that speaks of the actual journey between the capital and the frontier.

I hesitate to tell Captain this, for he is not one who receives bad news with much equanimity. Instead I resolve that I will do my best to improvise a route for us, taking my cues from what we find as we make our way to the southeast. And so we get ourselves ready, choosing our best wagons and our sturdiest steeds and loading them with tools and weapons and with all we can carry by way of provisions: dried fruit and beans, flour, casks of water, cartons of preserved fish, parcels of the air-dried meat that Provisioner prepares each winter by laying out strips of pig-flesh in the sun. We will do as we can for fresh meat and produce on the march.

The women placidly accept the order to accompany us into the wilderness. They have already crossed over from their Fisherfolk lives to ours, anyway. There are only nine of them, for Seeker has never chosen to have one, and Captain has rarely shown more than fitful interest in them. Even so we have one extra: Sarkariet, Signalman's companion. She has remained at the fort since Signalman's death and says she has no desire to return to her village, so we take her along.

The day of our departure is fair and mild, the sun warm but not hot, the wind gentle. Perhaps that is a good omen. We leave the fort without a backward glance, going out by way of the eastern gate and descending to the river. A dozen or so of the Fisherfolk watch us in their blank-faced way as we cross the little wooden bridge upstream of their village. Once we are across, Captain halts our procession and orders us to destroy the bridge. From Engineer comes a quick grunt of shock: the bridge was one of his first projects, long ago. But Captain sees no reason to leave the enemy any easy path eastward, should the enemy still be lurking somewhere in the hinterlands. And so we ply our axes for half a morning until the bridge goes tumbling down into the riverbed.

We have never had any reason in the past twenty years to venture very far into the districts east or south of the fort, but we are not surprised to find them pretty much the same as the region north and west of the fort that we have patrolled so long. That is, we are in a dry place of pebbly yellowish soil, with low hills here and there, gnarled shrubs, tussocks of saw-bladed grass. Now and again some scrawny beast scampers quickly across our path, or we hear the hissing of a serpent from the underbrush, and solitary melancholy birds sometimes go drifting high overhead, cawing raucously, but by and large the territory is deserted. There is no sign of water all the first day, nor midway through the second, but that afternoon Seeker reports that he detects the presence of Fisherfolk somewhere nearby, and before long we reach a straggling little stream that is probably another fork of the river whose other tributary runs close below our fort. On its farther bank we see a Fisherfolk camp, much smaller than the village on the banks of our river.

Wendrit and the other women become agitated at the sight of it. I ask her what the matter is, and she tells me that these people are ancient enemies of her people, that whenever the two tribes encounter each other there is a battle. So even the passive, placid Fisherfolk wage warfare among themselves! Who would have thought it? I bring word of this to Captain, who looks untroubled. "They will not come near us," he says, and this proves to be so. The river is shallow enough to ford; and the strange Fisherfolk gather by their tents and stand in silence as we pass by. On the far side we replenish our water-casks.

Then the weather grows unfriendly. We are entering a rocky, broken land, a domain of sandstone cliffs, bright red in color and eroded into jagged, fanciful spires and ridges, and here a hard, steady wind blows out of the south through a gap in the hills into our faces, carrying a nasty freight of tiny particles of pinkish grit. The sun now is as red as new copper in that pinkish sky, as though we have a sunset all day long. To avoid the sandstorm that I assume will be coming upon us I swing the caravan around to due east, where we will be traveling along the base of the cliffs and perhaps will be sheltered from the worst of the wind. In this I am incorrect, because a cold, inexorable crosswind arises abruptly, bringing with it out of the north the very sandstorm that I had hoped to avoid, and we find ourselves pinned down for a day and a half just below the red cliffs, huddling together miserably with our faces masked by scarves. The wind howls all night; I sleep very badly. At last it dies down and we hurry through the gap in the cliffs and resume our plodding southeastward march.

Beyond, we find what is surely a dry lakebed, a broad flat expanse covered with a sparse incrustation of salt that glitters in the brutal sunlight like newly fallen snow. Nothing but the indomitable saw-grass grows here, and doubtless the lake has been dry for millennia, for there is not even a skeletal trace of whatever vegetation, shrubs and even trees, might have bordered its periphery in the days when there was water here. We are three days crossing this dead lake. Our supply of fresh water is running troublesomely low already, and we have exhausted all of our fresh meat, leaving only the dried stuff that increases our thirst. Nor is there any game to hunt here, of course.

Is this what we are going to have to face, week after week, until eventually we reach some kinder terrain? The oldest men, Seeker and Quartermaster, are showing definite signs of fatigue, and the women, who have never been far from their river for even a day, seem fretful and withdrawn. Clearly dismayed and even frightened, they whisper constantly among themselves in the Fisherfolk language that none of us has ever bothered to learn, but draw away whenever we approach. Even our pack-animals are beginning to struggle. They have had little to eat or drink since we set out and the effects are only too apparent. They snap listlessly at the tufts of sharp gray grass and look up at us with doleful eyes, as though we have betrayed them.

The journey has only just begun and already I am beginning to regret it.

One evening, when we are camped at some forlorn place near the farther end of the lake, I confess my doubts to Captain. Since he is our superior officer and I am the officer who is leading us on our route, I have come to assume some sort of equality of rank between us that will allow for confidential conversations. But I am wrong. When I tell him that I have started to believe that this enterprise may be beyond our powers of endurance, he replies that he has no patience with cowards, and turns his back on me. We do not speak again in the days that follow.

There are indications of the sites of ancient villages in the region beyond, where the river that fed that dry lake must once have flowed. There is no river here now, though my practiced eye detects the faint curves of its prehistoric route, and the fragmentary ruins of small stone settlements can be seen on the ledges above what once were its banks. But nowadays all is desert here. Why did the Empire need us to defend the frontier, when there is this gigantic buffer zone of desert between its rich, fertile territories and the homeland of the enemy?

Later we come to what must have been the capital city of this long-abandoned province, a sprawling maze of crumbled stone walls and barely comprehensible multi-roomed structures. We find some sort of temple sanctuary where devilish statues still stand, dark stone idols with a dozen heads and thirty arms, each one grasping the stump of what must have been a sword. Carved big-eyed snakes twine about the waists of these formidable forgotten gods. The scholars of our nation surely would wish to collect these things for the museums of the capital, and I make a record of our position, so that I can file a proper report for them once we have reached civilization. But by now I have arrived at serious doubt that we ever shall.

I draw Seeker aside and ask him to cast his mind forth in the old way and see if he can detect any intimation of inhabited villages somewhere ahead.

"I don't know if I can," he says. He is terribly emaciated, trembling, pale. "It takes a strength that I don't think I have anymore."

"Try. Please. I need to know."

He agrees to make the effort, and goes into his trance, and I stand by, watching, as his eyeballs roll up into his head and his breath comes in thick, hoarse bursts. He stands statue-still, utterly motionless for a very long while. Then, gradually, he returns to normal consciousness, and as he does so he begins to topple, but I catch him in time and ease him to the ground. He sits blinking for a time, drawing deep breaths, collecting his strength. I wait until he seems to have regained himself.

"Well?"

"Nothing. Silence. As empty ahead as it is behind."

"For how far?" I ask.

"How do I know? There's no one there. That's all I can say."

We are rationing water very parsimoniously and we are starting to run short of provisions, too. There is nothing for us to hunt and none of the vegetation, such as it is, seems edible. Even Sergeant, who is surely the strongest of us, now looks hollow-eyed and gaunt, and Seeker and Quartermaster seem at the verge of being unable to continue. From time to time we find a source of fresh water, brackish but at any rate drinkable, or slay some unwary wandering animal, and our spirits rise a bit, but the environment through which we pass is unremittingly hostile and I have no idea when things will grow easier for us. I make a show of studying my maps, hoping it will encourage the others to think that I know what I am doing, but the maps I have for this part of the continent are blank and I might just as well consult my wagon or the beasts that pull it as try to learn anything from those faded sheets of paper.

"This is a suicidal trek," Engineer says to me one morning as we prepare to break camp. "We should never have come. We should turn back while we still can. At least at the fort we would be able to survive."

"You got us into this," Provisioner says, scowling at me. "You and your switched vote." Burly Provisioner is burly no longer. He has become a mere shadow of his former self. "Admit it, Surveyor: we'll never make it. It was a mistake to try."

Am I supposed to defend myself against these charges? What defense can I possibly make?

A day later, with conditions no better, Captain calls the nine of us together and makes an astonishing announcement. He is sending the women back. They are too much of a burden on us. They will be given one of the wagons and some of our remaining provisions. If they travel steadily in the direction of the sunset, he says, they will sooner or later find their way back to their village below the walls of our fort.

He walks away from us before any of us can reply. We are too stunned to say anything, anyway. And how could we reply? What could we say? That we oppose this act of unthinkable cruelty and will not let him send the women to their deaths? Or that we have taken a new vote, and we are unanimous in our desire that all of us, not just the women, return to the fort? He will remind us that a military platoon is not a democracy. Or perhaps he will simply turn his back on us, as he usually does. We are bound on our path toward the inner domain of the Empire; we have sworn an oath to continue as a group; he will not release us.

"But he can't mean it!" Stablemaster says. "It's a death sentence for them!"

"Why should he care about that?" Armorer asks. "The women are just domestic animals to him. I'm surprised he doesn't just ask us to kill them right here and now, instead of going to the trouble of letting them have some food for their trip back."

It says much about how our journey has weakened us that none of us feels capable of voicing open opposition to Captain's outrageous order. He confers with Provisioner and Stablemaster to determine how much of our food we can spare for them and which wagon to give them, and the conference proceeds precisely as though it is a normal order of business.

The women are unaware of the decision Captain has made. Nor can I say anything to Wendrit when I return to our tent. I pull her close against me and hold her in a long embrace, thinking that this is probably the last time.

When I step back and look into her eyes, my own fill with tears, and she stares at me in bewilderment. But how can I explain? I am her protector. There is no way to tell her that Captain has ordered her death and that I am prepared to be acquiescent in his monstrous decision.

Can it be said that it is possible to feel love for a Fisherfolk woman? Well, yes, perhaps. Perhaps I love Wendrit. Certainly it would cause me great pain to part from her.

The women will quickly lose their way as they try to retraverse the inhospitable desert lands that we have just passed through. Beyond doubt they will die within a few days. And we ourselves, in all likelihood, will be dead ourselves in a week or two as we wander ever onward in this hopeless quest for the settled districts of the Empire. I was a madman to think that we could ever succeed in that journey simply by pointing our noses toward the capital and telling ourselves that by taking one step after another we would eventually get there.

But there is a third way that will spare Wendrit and the other women, and my friends as well, from dying lonely deaths in these lonely lands. Sergeant had shown me, that day behind the three little hillocks north of the fort, how the thing is managed.

I leave my tent. Captain has finished his conference with Provisioner and Stablemaster and is standing off by himself to one side of our camp, as though he is alone on some other planet.

"Captain?" I say.

My blade is ready as he turns toward me.

Afterward, to the shaken, astounded men, I say quietly, "I am Captain now. Is anyone opposed? Good." And I point to the northwest, back toward the place of the serpent-wrapped stone idols, and the dry lakebed beyond, and the red cliffs beyond those. "We all know we won't ever find the Empire. But the fort is still there. So come, then. Let's break camp and get started. We're going back. We're going home."

ROBERT SILVERBERG is an American author and editor, best known for writing science fiction. He is a multiple winner of both Hugo and Nebula Awards, and a member of the Science Fiction and Fantasy Hall of Fame. In 2004, the Science Fiction Writers of America gave him its Grand Master award. His many notable works include the novels *Nightwings* (1969), *Downward to the Earth* (1970), *The World Inside* (1971), *Dying Inside* (1972), and *Lord Valentine's Castle* (1980). Online at robert-silverberg.com.